DARK CAROUSEL

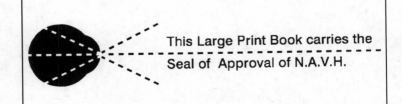

This Large Print Book carries the
Seal of Approval of N.A.V.H.

A CARPATHIAN NOVEL

DARK CAROUSEL

CHRISTINE FEEHAN

THORNDIKE PRESS
A part of Gale, Cengage Learning

GALE
CENGAGE Learning·

Farmington Hills, Mich • San Francisco • New York • Waterville, Maine
Meriden, Conn • Mason, Ohio • Chicago

GALE
CENGAGE Learning

Library of Congress Cataloging-in-Publication Data
Names: Feehan, Christine, author.
Title: Dark carousel : a Carpathian novel / by Christine Feehan.
Description: Large print edition. | Waterville, Maine : Thorndike Press, 2016. |
    Series: Thorndike Press large print romance
Identifiers: LCCN 2016025677 | ISBN 9781410489715 (hardcover) | ISBN
    141048971X (hardcover)
Subjects: LCSH: Vampires—Fiction. | Large type books. | Paranormal romance
    stories.
Classification: LCC PS3606.E36 C347 2016b | DDC 813/.6—dc23
LC record available at https://lccn.loc.gov/2016025677

Published in 2016 by arrangement with The Berkley Publishing Group, an imprint of Penguin Publishing Group, a division of Penguin Random House LLC

Printed in Mexico
1 2 3 4 5 6 7 20 19 18 17 16

For Sheila Clover English.
Thank you for always being such a good
friend. No matter if the times are good or
especially bad, you've always been there.

FOR MY READERS

Be sure to go to christinefeehan.com/ members/ to sign up for my PRIVATE book announcement list and download the FREE ebook of *Dark Desserts.* Join my community to get firsthand news, enter the book discussions, ask questions, and chat with me. Please feel free to email me at Christine@ christinefeehan.com — I would love to hear from you.

ACKNOWLEDGMENTS

With any book there are many people to thank. In this case, the usual suspects: Domini, for her research and help; my power hours group, who always make certain I'm up at the crack of dawn working; and of course Brian Feehan, who I can call anytime and brainstorm with so I don't lose a single hour. Thank you to Chris Tong for his help with the language when I can't remember what I'm doing!

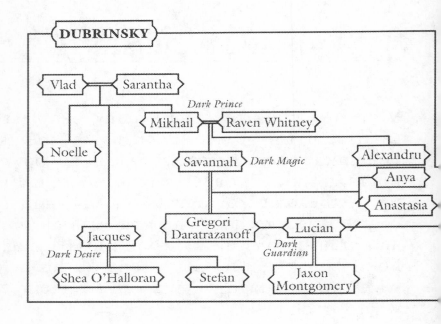

DUBRINSKY

Vlad ══ Sarantha

Noelle

Dark Prince

Mikhail ══ Raven Whitney

Savannah   *Dark Magic*

Alexandru

Anya

Anastasia

Gregori Daratrazanoff   Lucian

Jacques

Dark Desire

Shea O'Halloran   Stefan

Dark Guardian

Jaxon Montgomery

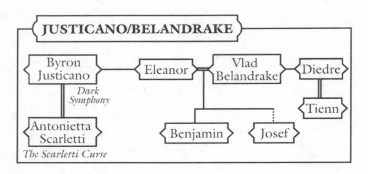

JUSTICANO/BELANDRAKE

Byron Justicano ── Eleanor ── Vlad Belandrake ── Diedre

Dark Symphony

Antonietta Scarletti

Benjamin   Josef

Tienn

The Scarletti Curse

THE CARPATHIANS

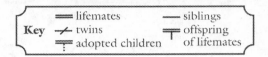

Key
— lifemates   — siblings
⧸ twins   ⊤ offspring
⚏ adopted children   of lifemates

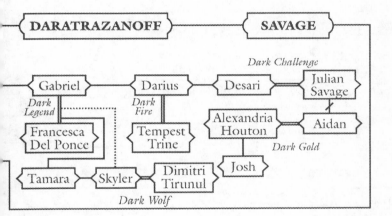

DARATRAZANOFF   **SAVAGE**

Dark Challenge

Gabriel   Darius   Desari   Julian Savage

Dark Legend   *Dark Fire*   Alexandria Houton   Aidan

Francesca Del Ponce   Tempest Trine   *Dark Gold*

Tamara   Skyler   Dimitri Tirunul   Josh

Dark Wolf

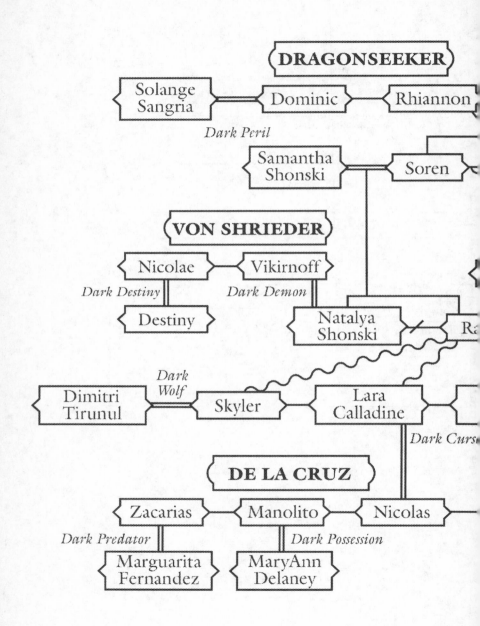

DRAGONSEEKER

Solange Sangria === Dominic — Rhiannon

Dark Peril

Samantha Shonski — Soren

VON SHRIEDER

Nicolae — Vikirnoff

Dark Destiny   *Dark Demon*

Destiny

Natalya Shonski — Ra

Dark Wolf

Dimitri Tirunul === Skyler — Lara Calladine

Dark Curse

DE LA CRUZ

Zacarias — Manolito — Nicolas

Dark Predator   *Dark Possession*

Marguarita Fernandez   MaryAnn Delaney

THE CARPATHIANS

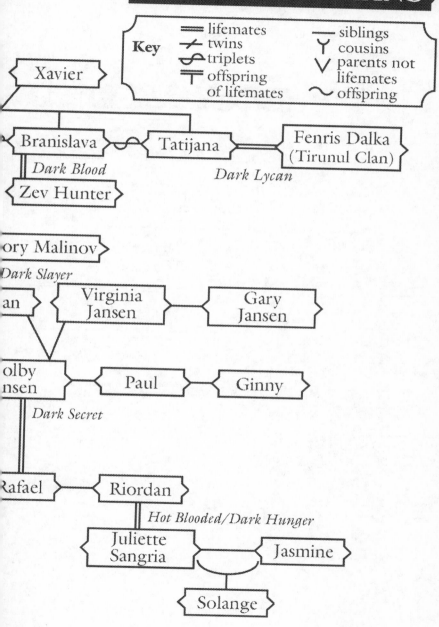

Key

≡ lifemates
⊁ twins
⨎ triplets
⊤ offspring of lifemates

— siblings
Y cousins
V parents not lifemates
∼ offspring

Xavier

Branislava — Tatijana ═ Fenris Dalka (Tirunul Clan)
Dark Blood   *Dark Lycan*
Zev Hunter

...ory Malinov
Dark Slayer

...an   Virginia Jansen — Gary Jansen

...olby ...nsen   Paul — Ginny
Dark Secret

...Rafael — Riordan
              Hot Blooded/Dark Hunger
Juliette Sangria — Jasmine

Solange

OTHER CARPATHIANS

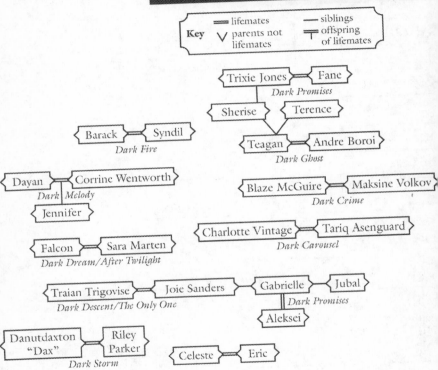

Key
— lifemates
∨ parents not lifemates
— siblings
⊤ offspring of lifemates

Trixie Jones ⟗ Fane
Dark Promises

Sherise ∨ Terence

Barack ⟗ Syndil
Dark Fire

Teagan ⟗ Andre Boroi
Dark Ghost

Dayan ∨ Corrine Wentworth
Dark Melody
Jennifer

Blaze McGuire ⟗ Maksine Volkov
Dark Crime

Charlotte Vintage ⟗ Tariq Asenguard
Dark Carousel

Falcon ⟗ Sara Marten
Dark Dream/After Twilight

Traian Trigovise ⟗ Joie Sanders ∨ Gabrielle ∨ Jubal
Dark Descent/The Only One   *Dark Promises*
Aleksei

Danutdaxton "Dax" ⟗ Riley Parker
Dark Storm

Celeste ⟗ Eric

1

Charlotte Vintage pushed the stray tendrils of dark auburn hair curling around her face back behind her shoulders and leaned toward her best friend, Genevieve Marten. Icy fingers of unease continually crept down her spine. There was no relaxing, not even with a drink in front of her and the pounding beat of the music calling.

"We know they followed us here, Genevieve," she whispered behind her hand. Whispering in the dance club with the music drumming out a wild rhythm wasn't easy, but she managed. They had accomplished what they set out to do, but now that they had drawn their three stalkers out into the open, what were they going to do?

"We must have been crazy thinking we could do this, Genevieve. Because we have no business exposing ourselves to this kind of danger." Mostly, Charlotte didn't think she should have exposed Genevieve to the danger. At least not when they were together. Not when they had a three-year-old to consider.

She took a slow perusal of the club, trying to take in every detail. The Palace was the hottest dance club in the city. Everyone who was anyone went there. In spite of the fact that it was four stories tall, every single floor was packed with bodies, as was the basement underground club. Men tried to catch her eye continually. She wasn't going to pretend she didn't know Genevieve was beautiful, or that she wasn't so hard on the eyes, either. The pair of them together drew attention everywhere they went — which was a bad thing.

"We're acting like normal women for a change," Genevieve said a little defiantly. "I'm tired of hiding. We needed to get out of the house. *You* needed to get out of the house. You work all the time. Honestly, Charlie, we're going to grow old hiding away. What good has it done us? We're not any closer to finding out who is doing this to us."

"I can't afford to be bait," Charlotte pointed out. "And I don't like you being bait, either. Certainly not both of us together when we have to look after Lourdes. She can't lose everyone in her life. It goes against everything in me to hide away, but I've got to consider what would happen to her if I was killed. They already murdered her father. She has no mother. I'm all she's got." When Genevieve sent her a look, she hastily amended,

16

"*We're* all she's got."

Charlotte wasn't the hide-from-an-enemy type any more than Genevieve was. They'd met in France, both studying art. Genevieve painted, and she was good. More than good. Already her landscapes and portraits were beginning to be noticed, sought after by collectors. Charlotte restored old paintings as well as old carvings. Her specialty and greatest passion was restoring old carousels.

Genevieve was French. She was tall, with long, glossy dark hair and large green eyes. Not just green, but deep forest green. Startling green. She had the figure of a model and in fact had had several major agencies try to convince her to sign with them. She was independently wealthy, having received inheritances from her parents and both sets of grandparents.

Genevieve's maternal grandmother had raised her. A few months earlier, that grandmother, her last living relative, had been brutally murdered. A few weeks later a man Genevieve had been dating was murdered in the same way. His blood had been drained from his body, and his throat had been torn out. Charlotte's mentor, the man she was apprenticing under, was murdered a week after that.

Twice, when they were together, the two women had become aware of someone trying to enter their house late at night. They'd locked all the windows and doors, but who-ever was after them had been persistent, rattling the glass, shaking the heavy doors, terrorizing them. The police had been called. Two officers were found dead in the courtyard, both with their blood drained and their throats torn out.

Charlotte received word a couple of weeks later that her only sibling, her brother, had been found dead, murdered in the same way. He was in California. In the United States. Far from France. Far from her. He left behind his business and his daughter, three-year-old Lourdes. Lourdes's mother had died in childbirth, leaving Charlotte's brother to raise her. Now it was up to Charlotte. Genevieve had decided to come with Charlotte to California. Whoever was after the two of them was in the States and Genevieve wanted to find them.

Genevieve laid her hand over Charlotte's. "I know Lourdes is your first priority. She's mine as well. She's a beautiful little girl and obviously traumatized by what she saw. Her nightmares wake me up and I'm not even in the same house."

Charlotte knew Genevieve wasn't exaggerating. Genevieve always knew whenever Lourdes had nightmares, even if she wasn't staying with them. At those times, she always called to make certain the child was all right. Lourdes had been present when her father was murdered. The killer had left the child alive and sitting beside her slain father. She'd been alone in the house with his body for several hours before she was found by her nanny, Grace Parducci, a woman who had gone to school with Charlotte.

"The police aren't any closer to solving the murders, Charlie. Not here and not in France. Lourdes is in danger just as much as we are. Maybe more." Genevieve leaned her chin on the heel of her hand as she hitched her chair closer to Charlotte's in order to be heard above the music. "I've been thinking a lot about this and how it all got started. What we did to draw some crazy person's attention."

Charlotte nodded. She'd been thinking about it as well. What else could she think about? Both of them had lost every family member with the exception of little Lourdes. Charlotte didn't want to lose her, and lately, in spite of taking every precaution, she hadn't felt safe. At. All. Grace had reported being followed and feeling as though someone was watching her as well.

Charlotte knew there was a part of her that had come with Genevieve to the nightclub in an effort to try to draw the murderer out. She'd certainly come prepared. She had weapons on her. Several. Most were unconventional, but she had them. She honestly didn't know if the people stalking them were

19

the same ones who had murdered her brother, but it seemed likely.

Charlotte wasn't the type of woman to run from her enemies and it upset her to think her brother's murderer was going free — that he or she was trying to terrorize them. Not trying — she was terrified for Lourdes. She had no idea why the little girl had been left alive, but she wasn't taking any chances with her. Coming to the nightclub without her was a chance to draw the killer out without endangering her.

"That stupid psychic center we went to together for testing," Charlotte murmured. "It gave me the creeps."

Genevieve nodded. "Exactly. The Morrison Center. We went for a lark, but it wasn't the least bit fun. They got interested in us way too fast and kept asking very personal questions. When we left, I thought we were followed."

Charlotte had thought so as well. The testing site had been a little hole-in-the-wall, but in a high-traffic area, so neither had thought anything of it. They both often said they were psychic, and thought it would be so much fun to go in and test it, just like having their palms read. Something fun to do. It hadn't turned out to be very fun.

Charlotte looked into Genevieve's green eyes and saw the same pain she was feeling reflected there. Who knew that something they'd done on a whim would have such horrific consequences? It was like that with them. They both thought along the same lines, knew what the other was thinking.

"Ever since going there, I feel like we're being watched," Genevieve said. "And not in a good way. When we were still in France, before *Grand-mère* was murdered, a couple of men asked me out and I got this really creepy vibe from them. When they talked I just kept having the image of the testing center crop up in my mind and I couldn't help associating them with it."

Charlotte nodded her understanding. The same thing had happened to her more than once. And then the murders happened. Since then, they'd been much more careful. No dates. No fun. No strangers in their lives. Charlotte ran her brother's cabinetmaking business, and she did a little art restoration on the side, but she hadn't really been working at her own business for months. Not since she'd returned to the United States.

"What are we going to do, Charlie?" Genevieve asked. "I can't live like this for much longer. I know I should be grateful I'm alive, that *we're* alive, and I don't want to do anything that might endanger Lourdes, but I feel like I'm suffocating."

Charlotte knew how she felt. "We've taken the first step by coming here. We weren't all that quiet about it, either, Vi. We've attracted a lot of attention. Those men, the ones who keep asking us to dance — they give off that creepy testing vibe to me. What about you? And do they look familiar to you? I swear I've seen them before. I think in France."

Genevieve followed Charlotte's gaze to the three men who had continuously asked them to dance and sent drinks to their table. They'd winked and flirted and stayed close all night. They were good dancers; they'd asked other women and Charlotte had watched them. All three men knew what they were doing on the dance floor. All three were exceptionally good-looking. They seemed like men who frequented the dance club and picked up their share of women there. Still, there was something off about them.

"Same here. The one named Vince, Vince Tidwell, touches me with one finger every time he gets close enough. He just runs it over my skin. Instead of giving me any kind of cool shiver, it gives me the creeps, and the image of the testing center is right there in my mind. I keep telling myself we tested in France, so would they really follow us here? But I'm fairly certain they did."

"So maybe we should leave and then wait for them outside and try to follow them," Charlotte suggested. "Lourdes is safe for tonight. I've called half a dozen times, and Grace assures me all is quiet on the home front. We could track them tonight and find out where they're staying and who they really are. Maybe we'll find out what they want from us."

Genevieve's vivid green eyes lit up. "Absolutely. I need to do something to make me feel like I'm not sitting on my hands, just waiting for someone to murder me. I have to do something positive to help myself."

Charlotte nodded. She knew better. She had Lourdes. Responsibilities. One *huge* responsibility. She'd always been adventuresome. She pursued her dreams with wide-open arms, rushing headlong where others were afraid to go. She hadn't stayed home with her brother. She worked hard from the time she was very young so she could finance her trip to France, where she'd always wanted to go. She learned French early and worked hard at it until she could speak like a native. She'd left behind her brother and come back only to help him when his wife died. And then she left again.

"Selfish," she murmured aloud. "I've always been selfish, doing the things I wanted to do. I want to go after them, too, Vi. I swear I do." She had to put her mouth close to Genevieve's ear to be heard over the music. She wasn't the type of woman to hide in a house with the covers over her head, but what was the right thing to do? She honestly didn't know.

"Lourdes would be a lot safer if we figured

this out, Charlie," Genevieve pointed out.

She wasn't saying anything Charlotte hadn't already told herself, but Charlotte still didn't know if she herself was making excuses to jump into action because she wanted to justify taking the fight and shoving it right down the throat of their enemy.

Charlotte made up her mind. She couldn't just keep hiding. It wasn't in her character and Genevieve was so right — Lourdes needed to settle into a normal life. They couldn't keep moving and trying to cover their tracks. "Let's do it, then, Vi. We can follow them and see if we can find out what they're up to. You can't look like you, though. You draw way too much attention."

Charlotte risked another quick glance at the three men. The one named Daniel Forester appeared to be the leader. His two friends definitely deferred to him. He was tall and good-looking and he knew it. He was staring at her even as he danced with another woman. The woman looked up at him with absolute worship, and he was ignoring her to stare at Charlie.

She raised an eyebrow at him to let him know she thought he was being rude. He grinned at her as if they shared a secret. "He is an arrogant prick," she hissed.

"So are his friends. Players. All three of them," Genevieve said. "They know they look good and they use their appearances to pick up women."

Charlotte couldn't help it; she laughed softly, breaking the stare with Daniel to regard her best friend. Genevieve was in full makeup and looked like a runway model. "Seriously? We're really getting bad here, Vi. *We* both know we look good and we came here hoping for a little fun."

"I don't know what you're talking about, Charlie," Genevieve protested haughtily. "I look like this all the time. Waking up, I look like this."

Charlotte blew her a kiss. "Truthfully, you do look like that when you wake up. It makes me sick."

"Uh-oh, here they come. They're bringing drinks. Vince and his friend Bruce at your nine o'clock. They're carrying one for their friend Daniel as well," Genevieve lowered her voice until Charlotte could barely make out what she was saying over the music.

Both women plastered on smiles as the two men toed chairs around and sat at their table without asking.

"I know you must have missed us," Bruce Van Hues said. "So we came bearing gifts." He put the drinks down in front of them, flashing them smiles as if that would convince them he was merely joking.

"Pined away," Charlotte said. "Could hardly breathe without you."

Vince laughed, nudging Genevieve playfully

with his shoulder before pulling his chair very close to hers, making a show of claiming her. Charlotte saw Genevieve's eyes darken from her normal vivid emerald green to a much deeper forest green, like moss after a rain. That was always, always a bad sign with her best friend. Genevieve had a bit of a temper. She flashed hot and wild, but it never lasted long. Charlotte, however, could hold a mean grudge. She wasn't happy about it, but if she was honest, she could. For a long time.

Charlotte knew Vince was genuinely attracted to Genevieve. Most men were. She was gorgeous. But she was fairly certain the three men had followed them to the club. They hadn't just picked them out of the crowd of women. Four stories' worth of women. Many were beautiful, and most were hungry, looking to take someone home. Genevieve and Charlotte had made it clear several times to the trio of men that they weren't there for casual hookups. That hadn't deterred them in the least.

Daniel sauntered over, pulled out the chair beside Charlotte's and dropped into it. "I think I've done my duty for the night." He picked up the drink in front of Charlotte, grinned at her and took a sip. "You haven't done yours, though, woman. You've hardly danced at all. Think of all the disappointment that's caused so many men."

Charlotte shook her head, flashing a small

smile at him. He really thought he was charming. He pushed the drink toward her and deliberately she wrapped her fingers around the glass, her fingers automatically finding the exact spots where his fingers had touched as she lifted it to her mouth and tipped some of the contents down her throat. The jolt hit her like it always did when she opened herself up to a psychic connection. Her mind tunneled and she found herself in the void, looking at the fresh memories of the men who had touched the glass before her.

The bartender first. His touch was imprinted there. He was worried about his mother and didn't like his father. He wanted a raise and was very tired of drunken women coming on to him. He wished he could come out openly and declare he preferred men, but his father had made it clear if he did so, it would ruin his family and he would be disowned. The bartender wished he had the guts to tell his father to go to hell, and just walk away from his family instead of living a lie.

Charlotte felt bad for the man and risked a quick look in the direction of the bar. There were too many bodies dancing to the music for her to see the actual bar, and she knew she was putting off the inevitable — allowing herself to read Daniel's memories. Quick flashes of horror movies pushed at her vision. A stake driven into a man's chest. Blood erupting, spraying like a fountain. The victim's eyes wide-open, revealing shock and terrible suffering. Daniel swinging a hammer to drive the stake deep. Voices urging him on. Distaste for the task but determination.

Charlotte gasped and let go of the glass, leaping up, knocking her chair over in the process as she backed away from the table. Not a horror movie. Reality. She couldn't breathe for a moment, couldn't catch a breath. There was no air in the room. He had done that. Killed a human being by driving a stake through the man's heart. Vince had been there. So had Bruce. She recognized their voices.

She was aware of the men standing, of Genevieve grasping her arm. Daniel's fingers settled around her neck, pushing her head down, afraid she would faint. His touch only made matters worse. She didn't get anything off human beings, only objects, but she imagined she was right there, watching him hammer a stake through a man's heart, torturing him while he was conscious. The idea of it made bile rise and she pushed one hand over her mouth.

"I'm going to be sick," she whispered.

Genevieve caught her around the waist and began moving her away from Daniel and the others, toward the restrooms. "What is it, Charlie?" she whispered. "What did you see?"

"He killed a man." Charlotte choked the

words out. *"Tonight.* Before they came here. He drove a stake through his heart while the man was alive. Awake. The other two were with him. And then they came here. Drinking. Dancing. *Laughing."*

Genevieve stopped right outside the ladies' room and glanced over her shoulder. "They're watching us, Charlie. Let's get inside, out of sight."

Charlotte nodded. She had to pull herself together. "It was just a shock. They killed a man and then came here to dance." She let Genevieve lead her into the ladies' room. "Or pick up women."

"Specifically us," Genevieve pointed out. "I get the vibe off of them that they're totally targeting us. Not any women. They certainly had their choice. Several women made it clear they'd be willing to go home with them tonight, but they keep coming back to us." She glanced around the crowded ladies' room and lowered her voice even more. "Do you think they could possibly be the ones who murdered your brother and my grandmother?"

Charlotte frowned and forced herself to quit leaning on Genevieve. Her stomach still churned, but she had it under control now. "I'm sorry, Vi — it was just so shocking. I let go before I could get any more. I shouldn't have, although the murder was so fresh that it probably would have covered everything

29

else." She rubbed the frown off her mouth and sent Genevieve a wry, halfhearted smile. "I panicked. I've never done that before in my life. It just goes to show what happens when you have a child. You get soft."

"What are we going to do, Charlie?"

Charlotte took a deep breath and then squared her shoulders. "We're going to get as much information as possible in as little time as possible, and then we'll leave. See if they follow us. If I can figure out the location of the body they staked, I can call in an anonymous tip to the cops and name them as the murderers."

"You want to go back to the table and sit with them?" Genevieve asked, her eyes wide with shock.

Charlotte nodded. "We can't let on that we're onto them. We have to just play it off like I was suddenly sick or something. I'll think of an explanation."

Genevieve took a breath and then slowly nodded. "Okay. I can do that if you can. But let's leave as soon as possible."

"Agreed. We'll have to get out in front of them and then find a way to watch to see if they try to follow us out. Turning the tables on them is going to be dangerous, Vi. If they're following us, then they want something. Murdering that man has to be connected."

Genevieve swallowed hard. "Did you recognize him? Was it someone we know?"

Charlotte tried to focus on the murdered man. He'd been about forty. Dark hair. His face had been twisted with pain. His eyes alive with terror and excruciating agony. She would see those eyes in her sleep. She shook her head, trying to still the shudder that ran through her body. "I don't know. He looks vaguely familiar. It's possible he was on Matt's crew. My brother had a lot of employees. When I sold the company, some of them were laid off and they were angry. I got a lot of threats." She ran her hand through her thick hair. "I just can't place him. He looked . . . terrified. In so much pain. I don't understand what they were doing to him."

"They drove a stake through his heart? You mean like they do to vampires in movies?" Genevieve asked. "Because when *Grand-mère* and your brother were murdered, the blood was drained from their bodies and their throats were torn. Someone might interpret that as being killed by a vampire."

Charlotte's eyebrows shot up. "Now we're really getting outside the realm of possibility and into complete fantasy."

"I didn't say there are vampires, only that someone nutty might think that there are." Genevieve sighed. "Okay, I'll admit, when I saw *Grand-mère,* for a moment I entertained the idea that there were such things."

Charlotte put her arm around her friend in

31

an effort to comfort her. "I'm sorry, honey. I know that was horrible for you. Anyone would have thought that after seeing her like that. Let's hope there isn't anything like a real vampire out there, because the way our luck has gone, it would be after us." She tried for a little levity, although with the bile still forming a knot in her throat, she didn't feel in the least like laughing.

Daniel, Vince and Bruce, the three handsome men who had spent the evening flirting with every woman in the place and with Genevieve and her in particular, were vicious, cold monsters. She took a step toward the door.

Genevieve caught her arm. "Wait. Wait just a minute, Charlie, and let me rethink this. I know I was the one pushing for us to get out of hiding and to try to find whoever murdered your brother and my grandmother, but maybe I was wrong to make us a target. These men clearly are murderers, and if you don't think they're the same ones who killed our families, then we shouldn't draw their attention any more than we already have."

They were staying in the restroom far too long. "We don't run. That's what we promised each other," Charlotte reminded her. "We're never going to be free if we don't find out who murdered the ones we loved. Lourdes won't ever be free. You were right, Genevieve. I was the one trying to hide. Being responsible for a child threw me, but we're strong. We've stuck together through everything so far, and we can do this."

"They aren't going to get away with it, are they?" Genevieve said, trying to pour steel into her voice. "We'll find out who took our families, and we'll do it together."

Charlotte looked up at her friend's beautiful face. There was determination there. Fear, but courage. She nodded. "Damn right we will. Let's get out there and take back control. They think they have it, but we're good at what we do."

Genevieve glanced at herself in the mirror. "Charlie?" She hesitated. Long lashes veiled her eyes. "What if there *is* such a thing as a vampire? What if these men are killing them?"

Charlotte opened her mouth and then closed it. Genevieve didn't deserve a derisive response. She needed to think about what she said carefully. Logically. "First, honey, if there were vampires, after all this time, wouldn't the world know about them? And secondly, the man they killed was no vampire. I saw his death. I saw him. I felt him. He was just as human as the two of us. Maybe they believe they're killing vampires, but I don't see how. And driving a stake through someone's heart, vampire or human, while they're alive and conscious, is just plain sadistic. We can't take any chances with these men. We have to find out what they want, and we need

33

to be very careful. If they've targeted us, we need to know why."

Genevieve took a deep breath and then nodded. She'd been the one to insist they come out of hiding and act like they were alive again, but it was Charlotte who was more the warrior woman. When it came down to facing danger, it was Charlotte who stood in front of her.

The two of them made their way back to the table, threading through the crowd. All three men waited for them, eyes examining them carefully as they approached.

"Why is there always a line for the ladies' room and not for the men's?" Charlotte asked, and threw herself into the chair beside Daniel. "Every time. It's crazy and makes me tempted to march into the men's room and do a takeover with a bunch of like-minded women."

"What happened to you?" Daniel asked. He sounded charming. Solicitous. Worried, even. But he couldn't hide the cold alertness in his eyes. The suspicion.

She had to touch that glass again without a reaction. Charlotte flashed an embarrassed smile. Deliberately she inched her fingers toward the glass from which he'd drunk. "I'm violently allergic to something they put in some of the alcohols. I should have been more careful." She wrapped her palm around the glass right where she thought his prints were and began to slowly push it away from her, making a show out of it.

Much more prepared this time, when the jolt came, she rode it out, seeking to go deeper into the tunnel to find more memories. To see if these men had murdered her brother. She caught images of Daniel following Genevieve and Grace from a store. That was how he found their home. The three men had changed places frequently while following the two women so that no one car had been close to them for any length of time, which explained how Genevieve, always so careful, hadn't spotted a tail. It also explained how they had come to follow Grace.

There, in the tunnel, Charlotte found that there were two older murders, both committed by driving a stake through a man's heart. All three men were present. She didn't feel anything but a grim hatred emanating from them. Her brother wasn't one of the victims. Still, one of the murders took place in France. She recognized the gardens where Daniel had staked his victim.

The three men were serial killers. The bodies couldn't have been found, or the murders would have been splashed across every news station imaginable. She knew she couldn't keep her hand around the glass much longer and maintain her embarrassed smile. Genevieve looked so anxious, her face pale, her gaze studiously avoiding the three men but centering on Charlotte as if her life depended on it.

As if she knew the men would see her desperate fear, Genevieve leaned toward Charlotte. "Are you certain we shouldn't leave? The last time you drank anything that affected you so adversely, I had to take you to the hospital."

Charlotte was very proud of her. Genevieve might by terrified, but she was thinking all the time. She'd said the perfect thing to reinforce Charlotte's explanation. Slowly, she let go of the glass, having pushed it halfway across the table.

"I'm all right, Vi. I just took a little sip and knew instantly something was wrong." She shrugged. "I should have spit it out, but I didn't want Daniel to think I was spitting all over him."

The men laughed, although she could tell it was forced. She wasn't certain they were buying her little charade. She leaned back in her seat. It was time to change the subject and do a little digging. "Vi and I met in France and have been best friends ever since. Where did the three of you meet? You obviously have been friends for a long time."

"School," Vince answered immediately, turning his attention to Genevieve. He ran his finger from her bare shoulder to her wrist. "Grammar school. I love that sexy little French accent you have."

Bruce nodded and leaned toward Genevieve. "How long have you been in the States?"

Charlotte was grateful for Genevieve's French accent. It always managed to be a conversation changer. As a distraction, it worked very well.

"We met while working on art projects in Paris," Genevieve supplied, deliberately taking the attention away from Charlotte. "Charlie was interning, learning art restoration from some of the greatest in the world, and I was painting. We became great friends."

Charlotte casually reached for the napkin in front of Daniel, the one he'd been resting his hand on. She crumpled it up slowly, finger by finger, dragging it into her palm as if doing so absently, smiling and nodding to indicate the introduction in France was a good moment for them both.

It was difficult to keep her smile in place and she welcomed the opportunity to shift her attention from Daniel to Genevieve, because even with the object being new and fresh rather than older, as her talent preferred, she was getting enough images to know that Daniel and his friends had been stalking Genevieve and her for a long while. And they'd definitely been in France.

Her heart pounded hard. She saw flashes of the building where she'd gone to test her psychic abilities. Genevieve and she had gone

37

in laughing, determined to have fun. It never occurred to either of them that they might be in danger or that the danger would follow them and possibly hurt others they loved.

Daniel and Vince had followed them back to the little studio they were renting together. She didn't see them anywhere near where Genevieve's grandmother lived, nor were there even the faintest memories of standing over the body after or during the time of the murder. She didn't see them near her brother or his home, either.

Taking a deep breath she let go of the napkin. The three men had been in France, followed them from the Morrison Center, where Genevieve and Charlotte had done the psychic testing, and now had followed the two women to the United States. They were Americans, but from where, she wasn't certain. She was frustrated with the fact that she didn't get clear, detailed information like she did on older objects.

Vince continued his conversation with Genevieve, all about her painting and what she liked to paint, volunteering to be her next male model if she was looking for one. Daniel and Bruce seemed to be concentrating on her, and Charlotte was afraid for a moment that they might have asked her something while she was trying to gather information.

"You restore art?" Daniel asked, hitching closer to her, extending his arm along the back of her chair, fingers gliding along her bare skin, tracing the spaghetti straps on her blouse.

She forced herself not to pull away, instead flashing him a small smile. "Yes. I specialize in restoring very old carousel horses, the wooden chariots and entire carousels. I can restore American carousels, but the ones I'm most interested in are from Europe. There isn't a lot of call for that sort of thing outside of museums or private collections, and there's even less here in the States, but it's my first love."

Daniel looked puzzled, as most people did. She couldn't explain to them why she liked touching the old wood and feeling every groove in it, every carving. She loved knowing everything there was to know about the carver, long gone from the world, but so familiar to her once she'd touched the carver's art piece.

She laughed softly at his expression. "I can see you don't get it. The horses are unique, each one carved differently, some more than three hundred years ago. How cool is that? I was able to work on one that was carved during medieval times. For young knights to prepare for the jousting competitions, a rotating platform was used with legless wooden horses so they could practice their skills." She couldn't help the enthusiasm pouring into her voice in spite of the situation. She loved the fact that the carousel could be traced back all the way to the twelfth century, when the Arabs and Turks played a game on horseback with a scented ball. Italians and Spanish had observed the competition and referred to the game as "little war": *carosella*, or *garosello.*

"Keep talking," Daniel said gruffly. "I thought it was kind of silly, but it's actually interesting."

"Right?" She nodded her head, which helped her to avoid looking straight at him. She didn't want to see the image of him driving a stake through a man's heart. "A Frenchman got the idea to build a device with chariots and carved horses suspended by chains from arms attached to a center pole. It was used to train noblemen in the art of ring spearing. Ladies and children loved the device as much as or more than the noblemen." She glanced at Genevieve. The strain was beginning to show on her friend's face. Charlotte gave a little exaggerated sigh. "We should be going. We have to get up early tomorrow."

She stood up before the three men could protest. She needed to get Genevieve out of there as quickly as possible before she gave away the fact that she was terrified. Charlotte was afraid of them as well, but she was determined to find out what was going on. The fact that the three men had followed them from France, found where they were staying and followed them to the club meant that Lourdes wasn't safe anyway. They had to change tactics. They needed to quit burying their heads in the sand and find out what threatened them and why.

"Thanks for the drinks. We'll see you around sometime," Genevieve said, flashing her million-dollar smile. She stood up as well, taking a step back as Vince climbed to his feet. Genevieve was tall, but he still towered over her.

"Give me your cell. Let me program my number in," he said, all charm.

Genevieve's gaze shifted to Charlotte's, and Charlotte's nod was nearly imperceptible. The last thing she wanted was for sharp-eyed Daniel to realize they were onto them. They'd been discouraging at first because they weren't looking to pick up men, so they had that going in their favor. The three men were very good-looking and clearly used to easy conquests. Twice Charlotte had indicated to Daniel she wasn't looking to hook up with anyone and he should move on to a sure thing. She had hoped, in the beginning, that he was interested in her only because she presented a challenge. Now she knew better.

Genevieve reluctantly took out her phone, but instead of handing it over, she programed Vince's number in herself. Charlotte caught her arm as she passed her, already on her way out the door. She lifted a hand at the three men as Daniel protested, pulling out his phone.

"Seriously?" Charlotte smiled at him and waved. "You have an entire smorgasbord of hot women fawning all over you." They had to move and they had to move fast. She knew the men would follow them, and that meant disappearing before they got outside. They'd have to get to their car, get out of the parking garage and find a place to hide, then wait for the men to come out.

"I didn't spend all evening sitting with them," Daniel protested.

"Maybe we'll see you next time," Charlotte said and deliberately hurried into the crowd, heading for the door. "Come on, Genevieve. We have to get the car and fast. We don't have much time."

Genevieve nodded, already fishing for her keys in her purse.

2

There were all kinds of ways to hunt for his quarry. Tariq Asenguard stared down from the balcony at the masses of people below. He and his partner, Maksim Volkov, had long ago converted the palatial theater into a dance club to bring in the crowds. He could stand up above them and look down all the way through four stories at the gyrating bodies below him.

Tariq had drawn up the plans for the renovations himself, making certain that the center was open, so one could see each dance floor and bar when looking over the railings to the floors below. The arrangement was unique, and customers loved it and returned as often as possible. The only place he couldn't see was the basement, which he'd renovated for use as an underground club for the goth, grunge and vampire lovers that came out at night to live their lives the way they chose, accepted by others like them.

Every floor had a different type of music

and drew in a large variety of people. The more diverse, the better for him. The better his hunting. He could hear their heartbeats and the blood pounding in their veins, calling to him. It was easy to hunt in the confines of the building with so many bodies packed in close.

He could use the eager men or women for sustenance when he was in need. It was easy enough to portray the image of the city's resident playboy with a woman on either arm. He was slowly building a reputation. A rich, eligible bachelor, co-owner of one of the hottest nightclubs in the city. Women flocked to him. That was exactly the result he'd wanted when he'd come up with the idea. He had four other clubs in various cities, and each had a different partner, one who watched over the club while he was at his main residence.

The design with the opening in the center of the dance floors was even more important now that he knew his greatest enemies had invaded his city. Vampires had gone underground. These weren't the undead of old. They were thinking, technology-using, planning-a-war vampires. Sophisticated and organized. Tariq could scan minds for news of bizarre killings signaling the possibility of a vampire close, one taking over the humans in the area in order to create an army aboveground.

"Anything new?" Maksim came up behind him. He gripped the balcony and leaned down to observe the mass of bodies dancing on each floor below them.

"No. That worries me more than if I'd discovered someone tainted." Tariq inhaled sharply. Frowned. "There is a scent . . ." He trailed off.

"Sweat," Maksim said with a wry smile.

Tariq had no sense of humor. For him, there was no riot of color as he looked down on the men and women dancing. He saw only a dull gray. He felt . . . nothing. He lived to hunt. To kill. Even in the doing of that, he felt . . . nothing. He inhaled again, and once more, it was there. That scent. Calling to him. Making his heart pound. Pumping hot blood through his veins. He leaned out farther over the rail.

"It's elusive. Faint. Barely there."

The smile faded from Maksim's rugged face. "What scent, Tariq? Vampire? There's been no hint of activity since we discovered the underground lair. We've been patrolling . . ."

Tariq shook his head. "No. Orange blossoms and vanilla and something else. It is faint but it is there. You can't smell that? Somewhere . . ." He broke off again, searching each individual floor for the source of that extraordinary fragrance. He inhaled again and caught the elusive scent, drawing it into his lungs. Instantly his body reacted of its own accord, something that had *never* happened. A stirring. His blood hot. Thick. Beginning to pool low and wicked.

He stilled as only a predator could, letting the wonder of feeling wash over him. Absorbing the shock of it. He didn't feel. He couldn't. He was ancient and long ago had lost all ability to feel anything. His body didn't react to a scent. To anything at all. And yet . . .

Maksim inhaled deeply. He nodded slowly. "I can't tell which floor she's on. A woman." He narrowed his eyes, his gaze sharp on his partner. "Interesting that the scent intrigues you when there are so many. Why focus on just that one?"

Tariq knew the answer, but he was afraid to voice it aloud after hunting for hundreds of years. His lifemate. *The* woman. His personal miracle. The fragrance wouldn't leave him alone. He had exceptional hunting skills, well proven over the centuries, yet the woman, a human, time and time again managed to escape him. More than once in these last few weeks, he'd felt her close, a ripple in the universe, the ground moving beneath his feet, or the air around him suddenly coming alive with electricity, yet she had managed to slip away. *Not this time, woman. I have you now.*

He inhaled again . . . and knew for certain. That scent . . . Orange blossoms and vanilla continued to slip past his guard, until his blood thundered in his ears and rushed hotly through his veins. Until he felt obsessed with finding its owner. He didn't feel emotions like obsession. He didn't feel. It was impossible for an ancient Carpathian male to experience emotion unless he found his lifemate. Until he heard her voice.

"She's here. In this club. Right now. I know she is. My lifemate." He whispered it aloud. In awe. Knowing it was the truth. She was there, in the building somewhere. There was no other explanation. He had to be hearing a whisper of her voice. A thread among all the others. She was there. That close. The one woman he'd searched centuries for. The one woman who would restore color to his life, ending his gray world. She would return his lost emotions after his centuries of feeling nothing. He had searched the long, endless years, every continent, but she had remained elusive. At last he was close to her, feeling her, his soul, his lifemate, his other half.

His fingers gripped the thick, hand-carved banister, the enormous pressure leaving indentations in the hard wood. He leaned down to survey the dancers pressed so closely together on the various floors. His patience was growing thin. She was defying him. He knew she felt his calls. How could she not? He whispered to her night after night, soft words to draw her to him. He allowed the beat of the music to pulse into the air, sending a web of notes to lead her back to him, yet she eluded his every net.

"She has to be close, Tariq," Maksim said, joining him at the railing. He gripped the wood as well, leaning down to listen, as if he could find her in the mass of bodies as they danced, drank and had numerous conversations.

There was the clink of glasses. The sound of laughter. Of arguments. Of flirtations. The whisper of lovers coming together in the dark. Both men tried to hear that one voice. The voice that would restore color and emotion back into Tariq's life. He'd waited centuries for her, and still she eluded him.

She could be on any floor and they would hear that whisper. She could be in the underground "cave" club. They could hear the conversations from there as well. They'd designed the club to make the occupants feel safe. Secure. The underground club had separate entrances and exits. The music loud, the place dark with deep blues and purples shadowing the dungeon-like décor.

Tariq would never stop until he had her in his hands. She didn't understand that about him. He was as relentless and as merciless as the raging sea. There was no stopping him once he had his prey in sight. He was Carpathian, hunter of the vampire, and he had survived when most of his kind had long ago succumbed to the lure of power. He had done his duty to his prince and people, keeping his assigned regions clean and safe from the stench of evil.

After all the long centuries, he knew she was close, yet she remained elusive, just out of his reach. He had turned his hunting instincts, honed by centuries of strategy, to finding her. He turned away from the blaring music and the scent of so much blood running hot in veins calling to him. It was a heady temptation he fought continually. Irritated at his inability to find her when she was so close, he wanted to roar his frustration to the night sky. He needed air, needed to go outside and breathe.

Tariq cursed softly in his own language, moving back from the railing into deeper shadows. Just the fact that he could feel frustration meant she was very, very close, and he could hear her voice, although he couldn't recognize it among all the other voices. He knew she was somewhere in the building, just out of reach, by the way his emotions, long ago gone, slipped in unexpectedly to disrupt his calm, logical thinking. She had to have a strong mind to thwart his many scans of the city in search of her. She was very strong to be able to defy his commands.

He was a powerful being, one very used to getting his way with a minimal amount of effort. He had survived centuries of battles, centuries of no emotions, no color. Always the insidious whispers of the call to evil, to power tempted him, yet he had endured for one reason. A woman. The one woman. His lifemate. Other half to his soul. Only she could restore his world, his life as it was meant to be. He had long ago resigned himself to his fate, endurance in a bleak, harsh world until the temptation of power was too strong. Yet now, when he was so near the end, he sensed her presence, that ripple of hope in a world of emptiness.

"Mataias tracked Vadim Malinov to the harbor," Maksim reported. "Vadim was always intelligent, even in his younger years. Now, as a master vampire with the splinter from Xavier, one of the most powerful mages ever born, in him, Vadim is proving to be a dangerous adversary. I do not like that he went to the harbor."

"That would suggest he went out to sea?" Tariq made it a question. His mind should have been on the hunt for the master vampire. Vadim was, without doubt, the greatest threat to the Carpathian and human world since Xavier, the mage. Tariq was too distracted by that fragrance. Now that he'd caught the scent, he knew he had to turn his attention to finding the owner. "She has to be somewhere in the building."

It was a big building. Enormous. Five stories plus the basement, four of them used for the various clubs and the fifth floor for his personal space. The basement was the underground club, so really, five clubs. Four bars on each of the club floors. Four dance floors on each floor with tables surrounding the inner balconies. Each floor was packed nearly to capacity. Still, he was Carpathian. He could cover a lot of ground fast.

"Go," Maksim said. "You're not going to be any good to me until you find that woman. Lojos and Mataias are patrolling tonight and if there is any indication that Vadim's army is working in our hometown, they'll find the evidence. It's been very quiet these last couple of weeks."

Vadim Malinov, a unique and gifted master vampire, was putting together an army of vampires. He was using the latest technology and even managing to recruit humans to do his bidding. It was unprecedented to do what Vadim had done. He'd fled the Carpathian Mountains, away from the prince of the Carpathian people and the ancient hunters there, to travel to the United States, where he clearly was amassing an army against both Carpathians and humans. He had to be stopped.

Tariq didn't wait for further conversation. He cloaked himself and floated down from his personal space to the fourth-floor club. Salsa music pounded through the air. Hard-hitting. A driving beat. This club catered to

Latin dancing and the atmosphere reflected that. It was upscale, trendy and extremely popular. Bodies ground against one another. The dance floors were always filled with every level of dancer, from beginner to competition expert.

He wound his way through the tables and then the dancers, inhaling. Searching. Being meticulous. It occurred to him that if his woman were on this floor she would be dancing hip to hip with another male. Why would the predator in him become more pronounced at the idea of his lifemate's body rubbing against another man's body if she weren't close? If he hadn't heard her voice — that magical voice that would change his world? She had to be there, the sound drifting to him through all the conversations registering as noise he tuned out on a nightly basis.

Because she has to be here, Maksim agreed, using the general Carpathian telepathic link.

Where are you? He whispered it, sending the inquiry out into the night.

When there was no answer, frustration edged with the need for violence. When his inquiry was met with silence. The fact that he could feel frustration only proved to Tariq that he'd heard his lifemate's voice. He had to have crossed paths with her and heard the sound of her voice in order to begin to feel emotions. They were negative emotions and

52

very faint, but at least he was recognizing that she was close enough to be affecting him. Changing him. Not for the better.

He had to have heard her voice blending with all the other noises, the pounding beats of the various bands as well as all the conversations on each of the floors. Now he had her scent, that wonderful elusive fragrance that had to be unique to her. He moved on from the fourth floor to the third, trying to follow the scent. Trying to listen for the sound of her voice that would fully restore his emotions and bring color back to his existence.

He sorted through the cacophony of sounds, listening to hundreds of threads of conversations, hundreds of voices, as he moved quickly through the third floor. He was certain she was heading away from him, almost as if she knew she was being pursued. He was an ancient Carpathian, his emotions long gone from him, yet he felt a kernel of excitement. A frisson of anticipation moved down his spine like the caress of fingers. Light. Barely there. The touch exquisite.

"Charlie restores old carousel horses," a male voice said. "We know she has a strong psychic talent because her testing was off the charts, but her gift seemed to be for older things. Antiques. She couldn't possibly have read anything from touching one of us or any object we'd handled." There was doubt in the voice. "Could she?"

Tariq had no idea why he'd zeroed in on that voice, but the need to hear the conversation was almost as strong as the compulsion to move through his club to find his woman. Could "Charlie" be that woman? The man said she had a psychic gift.

"Why would anyone want to restore old broken carousel horses, Daniel? Isn't that stuff manufactured every day?" another male sneered, as if he felt total contempt for anything old.

Tariq was old. Ancient in fact. He came from centuries earlier, and the thought that this man speaking wanted to throw away part of history bothered him. A first. To be bothered by an opinion of a human. A stranger of no consequence. Yet not only did the subject matter intrigue him, but now he understood why this conversation, among all the others, caught at his attention.

He dropped over the railing of the third floor and floated toward the ground floor, where he knew the conversation was taking place.

"Seriously, Bruce? What the hell are you going on about? We have to get out of here, follow them and figure out whether she knows. Stop bringing up bullshit and finish your drink fast or take it with you because they're on the move."

"You just want to fuck her, Daniel," the one called Bruce sneered. "Hell, you were all over her all night. That's what spooked her. And we can't be too obvious following them. We have to give them time. It isn't like we don't know where they live."

Tariq's world stopped. The ground rolled beneath his feet. Something dark and ugly rose up to consume him. A man dared to try to encroach on what belonged to him. He'd searched *centuries*. He'd kept Carpathians and humans alike safe by holding on to his honor by a thread. He'd endured centuries of relentless loneliness. Of nothingness. Of a gray void that was endless.

His fangs lengthened. The need for violence hit him like a blow. Emotions were difficult to control when they hit all at once. Overwhelming. Centuries of discipline saved the man called Daniel. Tariq was able to take a deep breath and force himself under control.

In the blinding lights of the bar, he had to keep his eyes narrowed to slits while he worked at toning down the color so he could see properly. His woman's scent was fading even as he dropped fast to the ground floor and began to streak his way through the dense crowd to try to reach her.

"Damn straight I want to fuck her. Don't you? She's gorgeous," Daniel said.

Tariq could tell by the way this voice blended with the music and other conversations that he was on the move. Heading toward the exit.

"Like you don't want the same thing, Bruce," Daniel continued, laughter in his voice. "You were touching her at every opportunity. Just so you know, you aren't going to get her."

"We always share," Bruce muttered, clearly annoyed.

"Yeah, well, not her. She's special, and I'm going to recruit her. Get her to join us. You want a woman, share her friend with Vince," Daniel declared.

"No way," Vince snapped. "I told both of you the moment we laid eyes on them in Paris that Genevieve was mine and mine alone. I haven't changed my mind."

Tariq felt the edge of his teeth against his tongue. The blood ran hot in his veins, yet the predator was as cold as ice. They were talking about *his* woman with no respect in their voices.

Tariq was almost on them now. He had passed the table where three men and two women had been sitting together in the bar of the West Coast Swing room. Tariq paused, his heart beginning to pound in time with the rhythm of the music. His mouth went dry. He inhaled deeply. She'd been there. Orange blossom and vanilla. He followed the unique fragrance, weaving his way through the tables, putting on speed and yanking open the door to follow the three men into the night. He came up behind them. Her scent

56

wasn't on any of the three men and that saved their lives.

She'd been in his club, probably all evening. With them. Only a short distance away from him. Dancing with them. Drinking with them. The fire in his blood increased until he could hear the roar in his ears and feel it thundering in his veins. These men had laid their hands on her. He took a step toward them, coming up behind them in utter silence. A wind. No more. A dark swirl in the air that could suck the life out of them without their even knowing before they dropped to the ground dead.

Tariq. Maksim again used the telepathic link between them. He was already on the lower floor, but away from Tariq, down toward the doors leading outside. *I feel a blank space. A foul stench is drifting in from outside each time the doors open. The undead is close. He's hunting.*

Tariq raised his head alertly. He'd been so locked onto his prey he hadn't scanned before stepping outside. Mistakes like that could cost his life. Not only his, but those of humans and Carpathians he had vowed to protect. Feelings were not an asset to a hunter. His lifemate was out in the open parking lot with a vampire close and three men stalking her. Of course she would draw a vampire to her. She had to be psychically gifted in order to be his lifemate. No vampire could resist that lure.

You stay and protect those inside. I will go after the undead. I am already outside.

Tariq whispered a command to the three men he'd been stalking, coming up behind them so closely he could have driven his teeth into their jugulars. Instead, he ordered them to go to their homes immediately. He would deal with them later if he ran across them, but he had to ensure his lifemate and her friend Genevieve were safe.

He took to the air, streaking above the large parking lot toward the parking garage. It was four stories high. His lifemate and her friend had traveled in that direction. Orange blossom and vanilla left a faint trail and he followed it. Even as he did so, he was aware of the three men getting into their car, obeying his command.

Then he was inside and moving fast toward the second story. He got his first glimpse of the two women. The shorter one caught the arm of the taller one and stepped close to her. "Wait," she hissed softly.

His entire world changed in the blink of an eye. In that one instant. It was so fast, so dramatic, he barely could comprehend, let alone adjust. The ground shifted beneath his feet. The air around him vibrated and quaked, nearly throwing him out into the open. Colors blinded him. Shook him. Made his stomach lurch and his eyes burn. He'd never believed colors could be so vivid.

There in the garage, in the dead of night with only dim lighting, he could see the tall woman had long, glossy dark hair the color of rich chestnuts. Her hair fell like a waterfall down her back. She wore dark blue jeans, a shirt with colors bleeding into one another and dark blue sandals with four-inch heels. The other woman — *his* woman — was small and curvy, with dark auburn hair that curled every which way, wild and thick; it looked silky soft and all he could think about was burying his hands in it. That was his woman. His lifemate. The miracle he'd searched long centuries for.

She wore soft blue jeans, so faded they were nearly white, and a shimmering coral top that clung to her generous curves. He stepped closer to her to inhale that elusive scent of orange blossoms and vanilla, taking the fragrance deep into his lungs. His world tilted for a moment as emotion poured in. Strong. Shaking him. His first instinct was to grab her and take to the sky to get her out of harm's way. She was in danger. Very real, mortal danger.

A man stood lounging against the hood of a car. Tall. Broad-shouldered. Wearing jeans and a white collared shirt with a sports jacket. His ankles were crossed, and he watched the women approaching the car, not taking his

59

eyes from them. His hair was combed back and short, spiked, with the latest *GQ* look. His attention was on the women and he failed to notice the small brush of wind disturbing debris on the floor.

"Ladies." The voice was cultured. The man smiled, revealing white teeth, the merest hint of sharp points, just a little like fangs, flashing. He beckoned to the women with a curl of his fingers.

Tariq's heart jerked hard in his chest before he took a deep calming breath and forced all feeling away so that only ice ran in his veins. He emerged from the shadows just as the dark-haired woman stepped toward the car.

The shorter woman, Charlie — *his* Charlie — caught her friend's arm. "Wait, Genevieve," she ordered softly and took a step to put herself in front of the other woman. It was subtle. It was protective, but there was no doubt what she was doing, and in spite of the fact that he couldn't afford any emotion, he felt pride in her. He could feel her fear, but she still put herself in front of someone she obviously cared about.

"That's our car," she said, halting a short distance from the man.

She thought she was safe. Out of reach. Tariq knew better. He knew the monster she faced. The man looked just that, a man, but he wasn't human. He was one of the most evasive vampires Tariq had chased through the centuries. He was cunning and fast and he ran with the Malinov brothers, twisted, highly intelligent siblings who very early on decided to give up their souls, turn vampire and seek to destroy the prince and all Carpathian hunters.

Tariq was surprised to see his old childhood friend, now an elusive foe. He had taken the name Fridrick Astor, although Tariq had no way of knowing if he was still using the name. Names meant little to the Carpathian people or those who had chosen to give up their souls for the rush killing while feeding gave them — becoming the undead. Fridrick had to know Tariq and Maksim resided there, and it was highly unusual to have a vampire hunt when Carpathian males were so openly living in the area.

The vampire straightened casually and widened his smile. "Ladies. So sorry." His German accent was perfect, although he'd been born and raised in the Carpathian Mountains. He raised an eyebrow. "You're looking beautiful tonight."

His voice held a compulsion. It rang compelling and soft. Persuasive. He was wholly focused on the two women. Tariq knew Fridrick had utter confidence in his ability to destroy any human who might come to the rescue of the two women. In the distance, Tariq could hear the sound of various voices as people left the dance club and returned to their cars to go home. He knew Fridrick had to hear them as well, although the vampire didn't take his gaze from the women.

Charlie stepped backward, forcing Genevieve to step back as well. She kept her body firmly placed between her friend and the stranger. "I've seen you before." She made it a statement. "In Paris. You were in Paris."

Tariq could hear her heart accelerating. He moved slowly, not wanting to draw Fridrick's attention. The air was still in the garage and it wasn't easy to allow himself to drift between Charlie and the vampire. For the first time in his entire existence that he could remember he tasted fear. Actually tasted it. It was on his tongue. Crawling down his throat to settle in tight knots in his belly. Fear permeated his skin, sank deep into his pores and into his bones. He knew he would always remember this moment. The way the parking garage smelled of oil and gas, and the scent of orange blossoms and vanilla mixing with the odor of his fear for his lifemate.

For a moment he was paralyzed, terrified that he might move too fast and give his presence away to the undead. Doubts flooded in. Would he be too slow to stop Fridrick before the vampire could kill her? He'd always had complete confidence in himself as a hunter, a renowned fighter, but this time, it wasn't his life at stake — it was hers. His miracle. The woman born with the other half of his soul.

He had no choice but to close himself off to all emotion. He dimmed the vibrancy of the colors around him and allowed himself to find that center without feeling that allowed him to function.

Fridrick smirked at Charlie. The vampire heard her heart rate rising fast as well. "Paris was beautiful and very . . . productive." He beckoned with his fingers again, his voice dropping another octave. "Come here to me." There was sure power in his voice now, a compulsion not to be denied.

Genevieve slammed her hands over her ears and shook her head. Charlie regarded the vampire with trepidation, but she didn't move toward him, as he'd commanded; instead she moved another step back, her body colliding with that of her friend, forcing Genevieve to step backward as well.

Tariq drifted closer, nothing but molecules. The air around them was very still and he didn't dare tip the vampire off to his presence.

"You were the one trying to get into our home. I saw you for a moment. And then again, right outside the museum where I was working." Charlie's voice was very soft. It trembled just a little bit, but she disregarded the compulsion in Fridrick's voice. More, it was almost as though she was immune to it.

Genevieve knew the compulsion was there, and she combated it by trying to drown it out. Charlie didn't even blink or shake her head to clear it. Instead, there was a belligerent note added to her accusation.

"That is true. You proved to be very resistant. Your friend was . . . so easy. Unlike you, he didn't put up much resistance."

"You killed Ricard Beaudet." She stated it as a fact.

"Ah yes, your mentor. He was such a little whiner. And that ridiculous little mustache he was so proud of. Weren't you just a little tired of his arrogance? He thought so much of himself."

Tariq recognized the name, Ricard Beaudet. It should have shocked him to know that he'd written to the man and that at that time his lifemate was working for Beaudet. Ricard Beaudet was considered the foremost master of restoring carousel horses in the world, and Tariq collected them. Somehow he wasn't surprised that Charlotte had already been connected to him. Their souls called to each other's.

Charlie's face paled as she watched Fridrick closely, drawing in a deep breath. "Did you kill my brother, too?" When he nodded slowly, still smiling, she went very still. "Why? You were in Paris. Why would you come all the way to the States and kill my brother? What did I do to you that you would want to kill everyone I care about?"

"Not everyone, my dear." Fridrick shook

his head. "I left you the child. I knew you would come here to protect the child."

"You killed my brother so we would come to the States?" Clearly his admission was the last thing she expected.

Genevieve caught at the loop in Charlie's jeans and pulled her a step back when it looked as if Tariq's woman might launch herself at Fridrick. Just the way she leaned toward Fridrick instead of away from him told Tariq much about his lifemate. She had a temper. She had courage. She would be a fighter, not one to flee.

"What do you want with us?" Genevieve asked.

Fridrick straightened from the lazy pose he had, shifting his weight to the balls of his feet, his handsome, easygoing demeanor changing subtly.

Instantly Tariq solidified, as if he'd come out of the shadows, angling his body so that he was between the women, but slightly facing them as well as Fridrick. He flashed a smile at all of them. "Good evening. How is everyone doing tonight?" He kept his voice friendly and open, the owner of the nightclub greeting his patrons. "Ladies." He bowed slightly toward them, an old-world, courtly gesture, before turning his attention on the undead. "Fridrick. How . . . *unexpected* to see you here." His tone said the vampire wasn't welcome and had made a very big mistake.

Fridrick smirked, seemingly not in the least bit intimidated. Tariq immediately scanned his surroundings. Fridrick would never, under any circumstances, willingly go into battle with him unless he had no other choice — or the odds were on his side.

"Mr. Asenguard," Charlotte murmured.

Of course she knew his name; everyone did. He was in magazines and, as owner of the club, was often photographed for charity events, but still — Tariq liked that she knew who he was. She put a hand on his arm. Lightly. He felt her touch burning right through the material of his jacket and shirt. Through skin and sinew straight to his bone. Her fingers curled. Exerted subtle pressure. She urged him away from Fridrick. At first he was unsure what she was trying to do, and then it occurred to him that she was trying to protect him.

"Not so unexpected seeing you, Tariq," Fridrick responded, confirming Tariq's fears that Fridrick believed he was in a position to win in an actual battle.

Fridrick had known Tariq was close and it hadn't fazed him a bit. Tariq needed to figure out what he was missing very fast. Making a mistake could be the difference between life and death for his lifemate.

He used the telepathic path he'd forged with his partner. *Something is not right here,*

Maksim. My lifemate and her friend, another potential lifemate, are being threatened. Send out the call for anyone close to come quickly. I do not want to tip him off I have reinforcements in the area. Fridrick is a master vampire and I am certain he has brought others to aid him. Unlike with the undead, there was never ego with hunters. Destroying the vampire was merely a job, something they did in any way possible.

Fridrick's smile faltered as his gaze dropped to Charlie's fingers curled around Tariq's forearm. "It will do you no good to cling to Tariq as if he is your savior, Charlotte. Yes, I know your name." His gaze traveled over Genevieve, his stare insolent. "You are for someone else, so touch the soft little playboy all you want, but, Charlotte, you need to let go of him and come here to me."

"Fridrick, you would not be threatening either of these women, would you?" Tariq kept his tone mild. Even amused. All the while he reached with all his senses to find the true threat. It wasn't Fridrick. In a fair fight, the odds would be somewhat even, a scenario Fridrick would never accept. "Ladies, Fridrick sometimes forgets himself. He likes to think he is capable of far more than he really is."

Charlie's fingers started to slip from his arm. She looked very alarmed. In that mo-

67

ment he realized she would choose to save him and her friend by obeying Fridrick's command. He turned his hand to catch her wrist, slid his palm down until he could thread his fingers through hers. The need to comfort her was a compulsion he couldn't possibly ignore. He drew her closer to him. Fit her under his shoulder. He needed room to fight, but she needed care first.

He arched one eyebrow at Fridrick, allowing a slight smile of amusement to curve his lips. It was important to send the right message. Fridrick got what he was silently saying because his cocky smirk faltered for just a moment and his gaze shifted first right and then left as if to assure himself he wasn't alone. Of course he wasn't alone. Fridrick was a master vampire. He'd been around for centuries and was skilled in battle, but he would never face a hunter of Tariq's skill without aid.

Tariq caught Charlie's arm and brought it around his waist. To his astonishment, she didn't stiffen or fight him. Her attention was on Fridrick. She didn't seem to notice that she was clinging to Tariq, and he didn't mind in the least. Nothing in his life had ever felt as right as the way her small body tucked so tightly against his did. Her skin burned through his clothes, sank through his pores to scorch her right onto his bones. He'd never felt better in his life or more alive. Perhaps that was the last thing he needed when going into battle with multiple vampires, but he allowed himself that brief moment to feel. To take it in.

3

Charlotte's stomach did a slow somersault. She knew Tariq Asenguard by sight. How could she not? He was considered one of the most eligible bachelors in town. His picture was in magazines and there were numerous articles written about him. He was gorgeous. Rugged, all muscle, wide shoulders, elegant even with his long hair tied back in a ponytail at the nape of his neck. It curled in a long tube of rich, thick chestnut down his back. He wore black trousers and a matching jacket over a blue shirt. His eyes were a vibrant blue, right now so dark they looked nearly black, and his lashes were long.

She knew she shouldn't be noticing the owner of the club when danger was right in front of him — she should be warning him. But what was she supposed to say without looking like a lunatic? The man they faced had ripped out throats and drunk blood? That he'd killed Genevieve's grandmother and boyfriend in Paris? That he'd killed her own mentor there as well? Then he'd drawn them to the States by murdering her brother? She couldn't imagine that the suave, sophisticated owner of the nightclub would believe her. He looked far too elegant to have a clue about serial killers.

She also recognized his name from the letter Ricard Beaudet had read aloud to her. This man collected carousel horses. Maybe that was why she'd chosen to go to his club. She'd subconsciously picked it, not because it was the hottest spot in the city, but because she'd hoped to run into him and maneuver a look at the coveted painted horses. Now she'd endangered him. And she knew he was in real danger. Fridrick was utterly focused on him — not on either of the two women.

Fridrick's features changed subtly — and not for the better. His eyes looked red, bloodshot, even. His teeth didn't seem so white, and there was the faintest hint of sharpness when he stretched his mouth obscenely in a smile. His skin looked different, much paler, and even his fingernails looked longer.

"Vi," she whispered softly, "back out of here." At least she could get Genevieve out alive. She was going to stay and do her best to help Tariq Asenguard survive — although she had no idea how. She'd gone to Asenguard's club and she'd drawn the serial killer to her. This was her responsibility, not Tariq's.

She wanted to run from Fridrick, telling herself she had Lourdes, but something compelled her to protect Tariq. She *needed* to protect him.

"No, Genevieve," Tariq said unexpectedly, but his voice was a command. "You stay close to me."

Genevieve halted her backward movement instantly.

"Such a good idea, little pet," Fridrick sneered. "Learn to obey a master, although Tariq is hardly that. Both of you come away from him. You really do not have a choice."

Tariq inhaled and knew he'd been right all along. Fridrick was not alone. Even as the master vampire spoke, the others emerged from the shadows. Seven of them. Three of the seven were clearly vampire and not underlings, not pawns to be sacrificed. He recognized all three of them. One was Fridrick's brother Georg. The other two were cousins of the Malinov brothers, Dorin and Cornel Malinov. Each vampire had the reputation of being extremely cruel.

The other four were a mystery to Tariq. They appeared human to him — but more. Enhanced somehow, yet not puppets. He knew Vadim had recruited humans — dregs of society that preyed on others. Humans willing to take money, knowing they were feeding the vampires and killing their enemies for them. These men were different. Human

— yet not. He needed to find out exactly what they were and what use they had for Vadim. More, he needed to know why he hadn't been able to detect a shadow of the vampires on them.

Experiments had been conducted beneath the city. There had been an entire labyrinth, another city below the one aboveground where Vadim and his brother, Sergey, plotted to gain power. Carpathian hunters had run them off, but they hadn't had time to examine all the sophisticated equipment left behind. They'd been concerned with following the two master vampires in an effort to destroy them, but now, he realized, whatever experiments had been taking place below the city had yielded results. The four men facing him were an altogether new experience. He didn't like having an unknown element in the mix when the lives of two women — one his lifemate — were in the battle zone.

He straightened to his full height, rolling his shoulders slightly, calm settling over him. It was war then. Right here. Right now. Already his brain was planning, working out what to do first. Fridrick was the most dangerous, but he wouldn't commit to the battle. He wouldn't want a scratch on him. He'd go after the women, but if he'd wanted them dead, he would have killed them long before Tariq had come on the scene.

"Stay behind me," Tariq cautioned Charlotte in a low voice. He was well aware Fridrick could hear. All four vampires would have heard his soft command, but no one would move until Fridrick gave the order. He wanted Charlie away from him, where Fridrick could hopefully keep her from the others. In the heat of battle, he couldn't imagine that one or more of the undead would lose control and their need to kill, for that ultimate high would override all orders from their master.

Charlotte took a step behind him, but both women immediately opened their small clutches and pulled something out. Weapons? He couldn't see.

"Mr. Asenguard."

Charlotte's voice was perfectly calm. A shock to him. He hadn't expected her to remain so cool when she had to realize they were in trouble, even if she had no idea what Fridrick was. Just the way her hand dropped to his arm and applied pressure — a warning — he knew she was aware.

"You may not remember, but you sent a letter to the man I trained under in Paris. Ricard Beaudet was a master at restoring art, particularly the oldest carousel horses found in Europe."

Her tone was purely conversational and it did exactly what she hoped — she'd thrown Fridrick off-balance. *Good girl,* he whispered in his mind. Stalling was good. Maksim would come, as would others. He had sent out a call for available hunters to come to San Diego when he and Maksim had discovered Vadim's lair. Those nearby would be on their way and coming fast. Tariq just needed a little more time. His woman was cool under fire and maybe, just maybe, she would provide that time.

"Of course I remember Beaudet. I asked him to come to the States and restore some horses I recently acquired." He played along, keeping his tone conversational, low, so that Fridrick and the others had to really listen to hear. "We corresponded back and forth and I sent him pictures of my collection and eventually an airplane ticket, but he never arrived."

Charlotte's gaze shifted from Tariq to Fridrick and then back again. "Ricard died, in Paris. Was murdered. The police have no idea who did it. There was a serial killer on the loose. He would drain the bodies of most of the blood and tear out the throats of his victims."

Tariq heard affection for the man in her voice. Sorrow for his death. Knowledge that Fridrick was responsible. His instinct was to hold her. Comfort her. He couldn't do either, because he needed to step farther away from her to give himself fighting room as well as to keep her out of the battle line when the others attacked.

The air grew heavy with tension. Fridrick straightened subtly, an almost imperceptible motion, but Tariq saw it and glided a few steps toward him, more to put distance between Charlotte and himself than to begin the battle. Charlie moved with him, mirroring his steps, staying close to him.

He hissed a warning at her, his gaze sliding over her briefly before returning to Fridrick. The woman was going to get herself hurt if she kept it up.

"Get away from him, Charlotte," Fridrick commanded. The compulsion in his voice was so strong, Genevieve clapped both hands over her ears, yet still took a step back from Tariq. *"Now."*

Charlotte laughed softly. "Fridrick. All these months you've had time to study me. You certainly stalked me long enough to know I am not the kind of woman to respond well to orders, especially not from a man I suspect of killing my brother. Why in the world would you think I would do a single thing you ordered me to do? Your voice? I don't hear it the way Genevieve hears it. To me it sounds grating, not in the least compelling. If you wanted me to come with you, perhaps you shouldn't have been bragging about Paris and what you did there, or about how you killed my brother and left my niece alive so I would return to the States."

Vampires were pale creatures, yet Fridrick

flushed. *As if he had feelings.* As if Charlotte's soft declaration not only angered him but embarrassed him. Tariq tried to understand how that could happen. Why it could happen. Something much more than any Carpathian had ever considered was going on, and he knew he and the other hunters had to figure it out quickly if their species was going to survive. Clearly they were under a well-thought-out and brilliantly planned attack. He had to get into the tunnels and discover exactly what Vadim, his brother, Sergey, and Fridrick had been up to.

"Fridrick." Tariq said his name softly, drawing the vampire's attention away from Charlotte. She didn't realize she was poking a stick at a hornet's nest.

Out of the corner of his eye, he could see that Fridrick's small army had become restless, eager to get on with it. That gave Tariq insight into Fridrick's mind. Fridrick didn't have nearly as much control over his men as he thought he did. And that told Tariq that Fridrick's attention was centered on Charlotte, and not on the battle.

"Did you actually admit to committing murder?"

Fridrick scowled and once more searched the large parking garage as if that would give him a clue to whatever trap Tariq might be leading him into. His gaze shifted back to Charlotte, his appearance still as handsome, but his complexion was flushed and he looked agitated instead of coolly in control. He waved a hand, dismissing the subject.

"Charlie, I am offering you one last chance to cooperate with me. If you don't, you will regret your decision." Fridrick's voice was no longer beguiling. It was hard and angry, betraying the tension boiling beneath the vampire's cool demeanor.

Before Charlotte could reply, Maksim arrived. On his heels were all three of the triplets, Mataias and his brothers Lojos and Tomas. Tariq raised his eyebrow when he saw Tomas, and quickly scanned him for wounds. He had been injured in the last battle and had been put in the earth to heal. Just two weeks had passed, and that wasn't enough time given the severity of the injuries to the Carpathian hunter.

Tomas sent him a cocky grin, the four hunters spreading out behind him, facing Fridrick's men. Another hunter emerged from the shadows. Tariq hadn't seen Dragomir Kozul since they had battled together in Russia. The centuries hadn't been so kind to him. Few Carpathians scarred, but Dragomir looked like a road map of scars. His face and neck bore tattoos that had been carved into his skin, rather than inked. His eyes were pure gold. Unusual, almost antiqued gold. A giant of a man, taller and more muscular than most Carpathian males, he looked fit, yet each natural line was carved deep, as if he was so world-weary, he had forgotten how to express any emotion, even when among humans.

Two more hunters moved into position on either side of them. One Tariq recognized as Afanasiv Balan, a hunter who, like Maksim, had been a good friend to Tariq over the years. Siv was extremely dangerous, a powerful man with unusual eyes that looked as if they swirled blue and green, both colors vibrant. His hair, rather than black, as most Carpathians' was, was long and thick and very blond. It was a rarity in the Carpathian world and it set him apart. Like Dragomir, he rarely spoke, but he was quick to take action. Tariq was grateful he was there.

The other hunter was one Tariq had very little knowledge of. He had been born a few years before Tariq had left with his father and mother, when he was still in his thirties, to go into the Russian territories. They'd shared a childhood, but Tariq only knew him by reputation now. He looked worn and grim, his eyes gray, his hair black and woven with long leather cords into a thick braid. He had one scar that was curved right over his left temple to the corner of his left eye. He was slender in comparison to hunters such as Dragomir or Siv, without an ounce of fat. His muscles were sleek and powerful, and he moved with the fluid glide of a predator. His name was Nicu Dalca. He moved like light-

79

ning, so fast when he fought that one could see only a blur of movement.

Tariq nodded to him, welcoming him to the coming battle. He hoped there wouldn't be a fight right there, not with his lifemate and her friend so close, but now, the odds were stacked in their favor.

Fridrick hissed, his sharp teeth showing as he scowled at Charlotte, focusing his attention on her. "You should have come to me while I gave you the chance," he snarled, his voice low. "You will rue this night. You will learn to feel what being alone is truly like before I am finished with you. You will learn what it is to suffer . . ."

"Enough," Tariq snapped, his tone commanding. Still, beside him, Charlie had stiffened in alarm. She had a niece. He remembered that from the earlier conversation. Fridrick had killed her brother but left the niece alive to lure Charlie back to the States.

Charlotte took a step toward Fridrick, the color leeching from her face. Tariq caught her arm and actually had to shackle her wrist to keep her from moving toward the vampire. Fridrick had found her weakness. The vampire smiled, looking truly evil as he waved his hand at his companions. All of them faded into the shadows. Several of the hunters glided after them, silent and deadly with purpose no one could possibly mistake.

"Your niece." Tariq pulled Charlotte in front of him, needing to touch her, but also to distract her so she wouldn't pay attention to the hunters following their prey. Mostly he needed to get the information immediately because Fridrick was going to retaliate. For the first time, Tariq noted the disparity in their heights. She stood so straight that he hadn't really noticed how short she was. "I need to know where she is right now."

Charlie hesitated, and he couldn't blame her. She didn't know him. He gave her a little shake. "Look at me. Right now. Look at me."

Her gaze jumped to his. Clung there. He refused to relinquish control once he had her trapped. "You know who I am. You know my reputation." And it wasn't that good. Most people thought he was either a playboy or connected to organized crime. "I can keep you safe from him, but he is going after your niece. My people have to get there first. Where is she?" She hadn't been susceptible to Fridrick's compulsion, so he doubted if he could take her memories without a fight, and he wanted her to trust him.

Her eyes searched his for what seemed an eternity. He was aware of every passing second. Her every heartbeat. The two men behind him were waiting patiently, still as statues. She had the letter to her mentor in Paris to cling to as proof that he was a businessman and he'd made it more than clear that Fridrick and he were enemies.

He knew the exact moment when she decided to trust him. "Lorell Lane. On the ranch there. It's a dirt road and it only leads to one property. She's with a friend, Grace Parducci, her nanny. Grace isn't going to let anyone take her unless they say, 'The carousel spins in a continuous circle.' Lame, but that was all we could come up with. Her name is Lourdes, and she's only three."

Maksim, Dragomir and Siv had remained with Tariq when the others drifted out, after Fridrick and his crew. Fridrick knew the hunters wouldn't attack them as long as they remained in the vicinity of the club — there were too many witnesses. He had ordered the four human puppets and one vampire master to remain behind, showing themselves, keeping the hunters busy safeguarding the humans in the club. With the hunters watching those near the humans, Fridrick and one of the Malinov cousins could hunt for Charlie's niece.

Maksim moved fast, disappearing into the shadows before taking to the air, streaking toward the ranch in the form of molecules, a fast-moving comet determined to outrace Fridrick. Dragomir followed him, a silent, terrible, brutal specter, more savage than man. He was a throwback to the ancient Carpathians, the ones never touching society, humans or civilization. They existed to hunt.

Most were long gone from the world; some had isolated themselves in a monastery high up in the Carpathian Mountains. It was impossible to tell if Dragomir was one of the monks, but if so, he was every bit as dangerous as he looked — and then some.

Siv followed, silent and deadly as he usually was, as determined as the other two hunters to keep Grace and Lourdes safe from Fridrick. In doing so, they were helping to save Tariq's lifemate, a sacred duty held by all Carpathian males.

"They'll get your niece," Tariq told Charlie with absolute confidence. Reluctantly he let go of her arm. She was warm and soft and it was amazing to touch her skin. He'd allowed the feeling to sink deep before he was even aware of it. "How did you get involved with Fridrick? He is a very dangerous man."

"I'm well aware of it. He admitted killing my brother."

"Let me take you and your friend to my home. I have several houses on my property, and you are welcome to stay there until the danger has passed." Still playing the role of a human nightclub owner, Tariq had to make the offer. "You can call the police and talk to them, tell them what Fridrick admitted to you. I have security at my home as well. There are a few families living on the property. Children for your niece to play with." Then he added the sweetener. "While you're there, perhaps you'd be willing to take a look at my carousel collection. If you're interested, you could work on it. In his letter, Monsieur Beaudet mentioned a Charlotte Vintage as his leading protégé. He actually said you had surpassed the master."

Charlie stared up at him in shock. "He said that?"

"I have the letter sitting on my desk. I kept telling myself I would ring him to find out what the delay was, but my work kept me so busy I continually put it off." He knew his explanation sounded plausible, because it was the truth. "Come home with me, at least for the remainder of the night, until both of you feel safe and you know your little niece and other friend are as well."

He stepped back, giving her room, letting her make up her mind. It was difficult to refrain from using a compulsion when normally it would be so easy, but he didn't want to risk making her uncomfortable. She was already leaning toward accepting his invitation.

"I think it's a great idea," Genevieve said. "Charlie, he has security. You saw his men. They totally intimidated that psycho. I haven't felt safe in months. And since we've been here, between those creepy men following us and Fridrick the murderer, I could use at least one night of really good sleep."

Tariq spun around. "What creepy men following you? Fridrick's men?" Daniel Forester, Vince Tidwell and Bruce Van Hues had been conspiring in his club, but he had to pretend he didn't know.

Genevieve shook her head. "No. As if it wasn't bad enough to have a serial killer on the loose — he admitted to being in Paris and killing Ricard Beaudet — and I'm certain he not only killed him but *Grand-mère* and Eugene Beaumont as well. I was dating Eugene and he died in the same way as Monsieur Beaudet, *Grand-mère* and Charlie's brother."

"What men are following you?" Tariq stared down into Charlie's eyes, forcing her to look at him. She had to tell him everything so it would appear as if he'd gotten all information from her and Genevieve.

Charlotte sighed and swept back stray tendrils of hair. He noted her hand was shaking. Just a little, but it was there. "Three men. They were in Paris as well, but I don't think they had anything to do with Fridrick. We went to a psychic testing center for fun. Just kind of a lark — you know, like getting our palms read."

Faint color swept up her neck into her face and her gaze shifted from his. Tariq realized she was afraid he would think she was crazy for believing in psychic abilities, and she was making excuses. He nodded, his expression somber to show her that he took her seriously. "Keep going."

"We both supposedly tested very high, and they asked us to take more of their tests. We agreed at first, but they were so pushy, asking us very personal questions about private things neither of us wanted to disclose. Then they wanted to separate us. We were in a little room at that point and both of us had the feeling we were being watched and recorded. We decided to leave. For a few minutes there, it didn't seem as though they'd let us go. We actually had to push past a couple of men and be very belligerent about it."

Genevieve nodded. "They kept saying we were making a mistake and that we needed to finish the testing with them. We just grabbed on to each other and made a run for it. We felt a little foolish once we were on the street with people around us, but even before we got home, we knew we were being followed."

"You saw these three men?" Tariq prompted.

Charlotte shook her head. "Not right away. We saw them there, at the psychic testing center, but off in the distance. We didn't even recognize them when we first saw them again in your club."

"These men following you were in my club?" Feigning shock, he took a step away from them as if he might go into the nightclub and drag the three men out. "Did they approach you?"

"Tonight they did," Genevieve said. "They flirted and danced with a lot of women, but they kept coming back to our table, even though we made it plain we weren't in the market for a hookup."

"And you're certain these men are the same men you saw in Paris?"

Charlie nodded. "Absolutely positive."

"What time of day did you go in for testing? Was it dark?"

"Midday," Genevieve said. "What does that have to do with anything?"

"Fridrick likes to come out at night. He thinks the cover of darkness will keep everyone from ever seeing his crimes." Tariq glanced at his watch. "Will you come back to my house with me? That's where they'll bring your friend Grace and your young niece."

Charlie glanced back at Genevieve, who nodded. "We'll stay the night," she agreed. "And thank you for the invitation. We can talk about the rest of it tomorrow when things are more settled."

Tariq didn't want to leave her, not even for a moment. He didn't feel any of the vampires close. The hunters were on the heels of the vampires and four humans Fridrick had left behind. Being pursued by Carpathian hunters would keep them from the two women, but he would have to leave his car behind because he wasn't taking any chances with his lifemate's safety.

"Maksim brought me." He murmured the lie, uncomfortable with telling an untruth to his lifemate. It wasn't done, but he knew it was necessary. She had every reason to be leery of strangers, and for all intents and purposes, he was that to her. She didn't have the same reaction to him that he had to her. She was already his world. There was no going back for him. He had searched through centuries to find her, and she was everything and more than he could have ever expected. He wasn't losing her.

Charlie took a deep breath, her green eyes moving over him slowly. "Then I guess you'll have to ride with us."

She knew he was lying. His heart jerked in his chest. Pride in her abilities shook him. Who would have thought a human woman would be able to read him so easily? He sent her a quick grin.

"I guess I will. Let me just give my car keys to the valet and tell him to make certain my car that I didn't bring with me is safe here in the parking garage."

Charlotte smiled at him, a genuine smile for the first time. She pulled her cell phone out. "I have to call Grace really quick and tell her to expect your friends. I want her to pack a couple of things for us as well."

Genevieve pushed closer to Charlie, adding her list of items for Grace to pack for her.

"And the men coming for you are really hot," the two women assured their friend.

Tariq frowned. "You find my friends hot?" His eyes were on Charlie. Assessing. Something moved inside of him, something not good. His belly tightened into several hard knots.

Charlie shrugged. "They're good-looking, Mr. Asenguard, of course we noticed. That will make Grace happier — to have her rescuers be hot guys."

"Call me Tariq. And it would please me immensely if you would not find my friends 'hot.' I would be okay with you having that assessment of me, but not of them."

Genevieve laughed.

Charlie's eyebrow shot up. "So I have your permission to find you attractive?"

He nodded solemnly, staying in step with her while they covered the short distance to her car. "More than attractive. More than hot. Is there such a thing as more?" He scanned continually to make certain no vampire was close to them. The four humans were hanging out inside his club. He thought it was a good thing that Dragomir and Siv had gone with Maksim to keep Fridrick from Charlotte's niece. He couldn't imagine either of them in a nightclub, nor did he altogether trust them with all the pounding heartbeats. They were both far, far too close to the end. Those in the monastery could no longer even hear the whisper of temptation to feel. Not even that. Putting Dragomir in the nightclub would be like putting a fox in a chicken coop.

Charlie laughed, the sound sliding inside of him, restoring his good mood. She sounded a little flirty. He liked that. "If there is something that's hotter than hot, you're it, Tariq," she assured. "But then you already know that. You have a bit of a reputation as a playboy."

Uh-oh. Not so good. "I do? Really? Because of a few publicity photos and charity events I attended? I assure you, Charlotte, I live quietly."

She slid into the driver's seat and Genevieve slipped into the backseat, leaving the passenger front for Tariq.

"You live quietly?" Charlie echoed. Her tone was quite frankly disbelieving.

She waited to start the car until he'd put on his seat belt, something he was reluctant to do because he needed to move fast if there was trouble. Still, it was expected of him and he'd lived in the world of humans a long time and had learned to fit in.

"Yes, quietly," he assured, snapping the belt around him.

She gave a little sniff that sounded very suspiciously as if she didn't believe him. "You own a nightclub."

He frowned, genuinely puzzled. "I own several of them."

"Women dress up in sexy, very skimpy club

clothes looking for someone to hook up with for the night. You're hot. You're wealthy. You can carry on a conversation. The women are going to be throwing themselves at you every night. No way are you living quietly."

He caught the underlying tone she had. She was striving for conversational and matter-of-fact, but he heard the little bite to her voice. She was far more interested than she was letting on. "Go left, out to the lake district."

Maksim. Dragomir. Siv. Tell me you have the child safe. They were taking too long to secure the little girl. Charlotte's little girl. If Fridrick managed to get his hands on the child, Charlie would be frantic. She would do anything to get her back, including handing herself over to the vampire without hesitation.

Not yet. Engaged at the moment. Maksim's reply was clipped.

Tariq turned his head away from Charlie to look out the window. He'd hoped the three hunters would get there before Fridrick. Had Maksim gone alone, he would have run up against two master vampires, but Dragomir and Siv were with him. To engage all three ancient hunters, Fridrick had to be desperate. What had he said? Genevieve was for someone else. Charlotte was for Fridrick.

He went very still. Vadim Malinov had lured two women down into the tunnels beneath the city. One of those women, Blaze, was

Maksim's lifemate. The other was her best friend, Emeline. It had been Emeline Vadim was after, but they'd also tried to acquire Blaze. When the hunters had gone through the tunnels, they'd discovered that all kinds of experiments had been conducted. They'd also discovered the gruesome remains of several women in various stages of pregnancy. Was it possible this all centered around the vampires taking women for their own? Trying to produce families? The idea seemed so far-fetched, so completely impossible Tariq could barely fathom it.

Vampire blood was acidic. It burned in one's body, *through* one's body. No baby would be able to stand that kind of pain. The Malinov brothers weren't like any other vampires. They were brilliant men who had conceived a plan to overthrow the prince of the Carpathian people and then very deliberately turned undead. All five of them. Quickly they became master vampires, and their reputations for cruelty and cunning were legendary.

From the evidence in the tunnels below, trying to have children was *exactly* what Vadim was doing. So if Emeline was for Vadim and Blaze had been for Vadim's brother Sergey, but they had rescued the women, that meant the undead would need two more women to take their places.

"Fridrick said Genevieve was taken, but

that you were for him, didn't he?" he murmured, turning back to Charlotte.

She nodded. "Yes. He implied that Genevieve was spoken for." A little shudder went through her. "He was going to kidnap us, wasn't he? And take Vi to someone equally as horrible as he is."

"But Fridrick said you were for him," he reiterated, trying to wrap his head around the fact that if Fridrick was involved, the vampires should need three women, not two. So who was the third woman? They'd rescued both Blaze and Emeline.

"What is it?" Charlie asked. "You're worried. Grace hasn't texted me that they're out safely yet. Tell me what's wrong."

How could he explain? He couldn't blurt out there were vampires in the city, not unless he wanted her to run screaming into the night. She would think he was insane, and by the time the truth came to light, it would be too late. There was no doubt in his mind that Fridrick would make another play for her.

"Fridrick runs with a couple of other really nasty men." He didn't know how else to explain it, and he didn't want to tell her any more lies. She'd caught him out anyway. "If he was looking to acquire you with the idea that you would belong to them, there should have been a third woman targeted. As nasty and powerful as Fridrick is — and he is — the other two are far worse. Fridrick wouldn't be in a position to call you his unless they had a woman for the other two first."

There was silence in the car. Charlie drummed her fingers on the steering wheel. "So you think they already have a woman? Is that what you're saying? They've kidnapped someone and they're holding her someplace?"

He rubbed the bridge of his nose. "That's possible, but . . ." He trailed off. Vadim was on the run. Mataias had trailed him to the harbor. He was gone, and there hadn't been time to kidnap another woman. There was no evidence showing they'd managed to get out with anyone else. He had taken Emeline and nearly gotten away with her. They'd been lucky that Val Zhestokly had been held prisoner and tortured. When Blaze had released him, he had managed to rush after Emeline, staying on the heels of Vadim so the vampire never had the chance to keep her. In order to save his own life, Vadim had to leave Emeline behind.

" 'Possible' but what?" Charlie prompted.

He sat up very straight, his heart slamming hard in his chest. He tasted fear in his mouth, and this time it wasn't fear for his lifemate, but fear for a young woman who had already been through so much — too much. They'd brought Emeline out of the tunnels, bloody and eerily silent, in shock. Vadim hadn't had much time with her, but he'd had time. He'd sent a small army to slow all of them down, delaying them precious minutes so that he could be alone with her. That he *was* alone with her.

"There is a young woman staying on my property. One of Fridrick's friends had her briefly, but we managed to get her back," he said, the disturbing insanity of his thoughts pushing everything else out of his mind. "If she counts as his woman, then it all makes sense." It made sense, but it was horrifying.

None of them had talked to Emeline. She'd retreated into her little house and she'd refused to allow anyone to aid her — not even Blaze. Blaze went to see her daily, but she said that Emeline wouldn't talk about what happened. She kept the rooms dark and quiet and didn't want to talk even to a counselor. It had only been two weeks, so they all stepped back to give her time to come to terms with whatever Vadim had done to her.

They all knew that Vadim had exchanged blood with Emeline. That had been horrifying enough. It would allow Vadim to find her anywhere she was. He could whisper to her, command her, see through her eyes at any time. As long as she stayed on Tariq's property, under the combined safeguards of all the hunters, Vadim couldn't get to her, or steal her mind from her, but if she were to leave . . .

He shook his head, not wanting to entertain the idea that Emeline's fate could be worse than that. She was a beautiful young woman, courageous and sweet. She'd gone in the tunnels to save children — strangers to her — all the while knowing what would happen to her. She'd seen her fate in dreams and yet she'd still gone, determined to keep the children out of the hands of an extremely cruel vampire.

"Tariq," Charlie said softly. "You've gone a long way away. What's wrong? You helped us out, let us help you."

He looked around. The road leading to his estate was just up ahead of them. "On your left. That leads to my property. Maksim's property borders mine." *Do you have the child?* He didn't know what he'd say to Charlie if Maksim, Siv and Dragomir weren't able to rescue Lourdes and Grace.

She's safe. They both are. Siv has Lourdes, and I am with the woman while she packs. She did not like the separation but she had no choice. Siv is not one for conversation. He walked in behind me while I was giving her the code, took the little girl right out of her bed and was gone before Grace could say a single word. He does not have a civilized bone in his body. Dragomir has gone after Fridrick and his brother.

Tariq wanted to smile at that. Siv had never been civilized. After centuries of battles, he was probably even less so. Val was more than

96

likely the same way. Like Val, Siv and Dragomir had been tortured over a long period of time, not by Vadim, but in other, even worse circumstances. Tariq had been spared that fate.

"Lourdes is safe," he announced in a low tone.

"How do you know?" Charlie snatched up her cell phone. "Genevieve, contact Grace. Make certain they're both safe."

"You could say I have a couple of psychic abilities myself," Tariq said, giving them both a small grin. The relief of knowing the child was safe was tremendous coming on the heels of what he feared the vampires were doing. His smile faded. He needed to talk to Emeline. More, they all needed to protect her, make certain she didn't leave the property and the protection of the safeguards.

"They're out," Genevieve confirmed, "but Grace isn't happy that they're separated. She's driving her truck and coming here with Maksim. She says Maksim's friend is a first-class jerk."

"Thank God," Charlie said. "Not about your friend who helped us being a jerk, but that Lourdes and Grace are safe." She stole another look at him. "You're still worried."

"It is just strange that both of you were in Paris and so was Emeline, the woman Vadim took prisoner down in the tunnels. Emeline went for psychic testing here in the States with Blaze, Maksim's girlfriend, and her father. You two did the same thing in Paris. Emeline must have been there at the same time. She recently returned when Blaze's father was murdered."

Charlie drove right up to the tall double gates and shifted in her seat so she could look over her shoulder at Genevieve. "Emeline is an unusual name. We met a girl named Emeline. She wasn't going by that, but someone called that name out and she turned. It was clear that was her name. She confessed to us that she had a stalker and was hiding out, using another name. We hung out with her for several days, and then one morning she was gone. I think this is all becoming one giant coincidence — far too much of one."

Tariq thought so as well. Was Paris the connection between the three women and Vadim? The psychic center? He knew that under the Malinov reign, the psychic center's computers had been hacked and all the data on psychic women had been stolen.

The double gates opened inward toward the property. Charlie put the car in drive and rolled through slowly.

"I think you're right," Tariq agreed, "but I have no idea what it all means. Did you meet Emeline before or after the psychic testing?"

"After," Genevieve said. "About three days after. It was before *Grand-mère* was murdered. Our lives went crazy after that. We could barely leave our homes between the creepy guys following us around and a serial killer going after people we loved. I honestly forgot about Emeline, and I shouldn't have because she was in trouble. Do you think this is the same Emeline?"

"If I were a betting man," Tariq said, "I'd be willing to place a very large amount on that as fact."

4

A subtle breeze came off the lake and stroked over her face, touching her with cool fingers and rifling her hair. Charlotte held herself very still, her arms wrapped around her middle, afraid her legs would give out on her. Now that the danger had passed for the moment, her body went into a kind of shock. She didn't want Tariq to notice, so she kept her face averted as she studied her surroundings.

The moment Tariq had told her and then Grace had confirmed that Lourdes was safe, she'd gone limp with relief. She hadn't realized how much she'd been holding herself together, terrified for the child and knowing she could never get to her fast enough. Tariq stood close to her, close enough that she felt his body heat, close enough that she worried she would slump to the ground at his feet. She'd never fainted in her life, but she suddenly felt terribly weak, her arms and legs like lead.

Charlotte glanced at Genevieve, and saw she was still seated in the car. The passenger door was open and she stared out at the lake, but she looked pale and just as weak as Charlotte.

Tariq's arm circled her waist, pulling her body into his, tucking her to his side. "Forgive me, Charlotte, but you look as if you might end up on the ground. You have been through a lot tonight, and you still need to talk to the police. I do not want you to fall and injure yourself."

She shouldn't cling. She really shouldn't. She told herself over and over to be strong, that she *was* strong, but confronting her brother's killer — that sophisticated, smiling murderer — she hadn't realized just how afraid she'd really been. Fridrick set her teeth on edge. There at the end, she could almost believe in vampires. His smiling *oily* good looks had suddenly disappeared. He'd looked so different, his eyes almost glowing and his teeth . . . She shook her head trying to clear her thoughts. *Vampires.* She was overtired and scared to even be considering such a thing.

Then there was Tariq Asenguard. It was definitely the wrong time to be attracted to a man, but for the first time in her life she had a real interest in someone — she was attracted both physically and intellectually. Tariq had put his life on the line for Gene-

101

vieve and her. He was courageous, and the last thing she wanted to do was appear weak in front of him.

"I'm not going to fall down," she denied, but she wasn't certain if it was a lie or not. She couldn't stop the body tremors.

"No, you're not," he agreed in his soft, way-too-mesmerizing voice. "Because I've got my arm around you. See over there, by the lake? The little house?" He waited for her to nod her head before continuing. "It used to be the boathouse, but I have a very nice couple living there. Donald and Mary Walton. Good people. You will like them. I met them one evening coming out of the club. I had taken a walk after the club closed because I couldn't sleep. They had been sleeping in their car and woke when a couple of thieves, bent on robbing them at gunpoint, trying to take what little they had, pounded on the roof of the car. I heard the noise and went to their assistance. They were a very nice couple, just down on their luck."

She stared up at his face, a little shocked that the very elegant Mr. Asenguard, owner of several nightclubs, could talk about saving a couple so casually, as if it hadn't mattered at all, just that they were a delightful couple. "And you invited them to live on your property?" She couldn't keep the astonishment from her voice. Why would he do that? She didn't know a single person who would do

102

something like that.

"Yes. They needed a home. They are good people, Charlie."

She wasn't certain if there was a hint of censure in his voice, as if he didn't get that her astonishment was because people just didn't do that kind of thing as a rule — take in complete strangers. He acted as if anyone would do it.

"Donald has a job now. He's a damned good accountant, but his old firm got rid of him because he was getting older and has a few health issues. He helps with my books and has been a huge help to my accountant but doesn't have to work full-time and can take off when his illness flares up. Now he earns enough for them to pay for a few extras, and they help look after the children."

"Children?" she echoed faintly.

His property was beautiful and very, very expensive. Every detail was perfect. The landscaping, the mansion rising three stories into the air with gables and balconies. It was Victorian architecture at its most stunning. The house had wings and bays running in various directions as well as generous amounts of gingerbread. A large octagonal tower with a steep, pointed roof rose up from the third story, forming one corner of the ornate house. A large wraparound covered porch with ornamental brackets and spindles provided a tremendous view of the lake. The other homes were some distance from the main house, but all were smaller replicas of the larger mansion.

"I have four orphans living on the property." Tariq turned to indicate the house that would have been the guardhouse. Or a home for bodyguards or servants. "A boy and three girls. They were living on the streets as well."

"*Children?*" Genevieve repeated, sliding out of the car to stand beside them. "Shouldn't they be in some form of government care? Why would they be living here?"

"I am their official guardian, or will be in a few days when the paperwork goes through. They have someone very dangerous after them. The men Fridrick runs with killed their parents, although there is not any proof of that. Vadim and Fridrick kidnapped the girls. By the time we were able to rescue them, one of the girls had been severely injured and the baby was traumatized. Thankfully I have enough money to provide the best care possible for them. I also can keep them safe."

This time there was no mistake. Tariq's voice did hold more than a note of censure, as if he thought perhaps the two of them were criticizing him for taking in children and a homeless couple.

"I think that's wonderful of you," Charlotte said immediately, because it was the strict truth — she did think he was wonderful. Almost too good to be true. Were there still men in the world who looked out for others, were gorgeous, courtly and courageous? She couldn't believe how attracted she was to the man. It was so unlike her, but everything about him appealed to her.

Tariq looked puzzled, as if she wasn't making sense. "They are children. All of them are traumatized, although Danny would never admit that he is. He is fifteen and already thinks of himself as a man. I have to go carefully with him so as not to step on that protective trait of his or his pride. Amelia is fourteen, Liv is ten and Bella is three. She is the right age to hopefully become friends with your little Lourdes."

More and more she was prepared to accept his offer of staying and working on his carousel horses. She couldn't protect Lourdes indefinitely, not from Fridrick. And there was still the puzzle of the three men who were following them. She gasped, pressing her fingers to her mouth, biting down on the pad of her index finger as she thought of the memories she'd pulled from Daniel Forester's mind.

"What is it, *sielamet*?" He shackled her wrist with deceptive gentleness, tugging until she let him remove her fingers from her lips. He pulled her hand to his chest, resting her palm over his heart, covering her hand with his own and pressing it there. "You thought of something disturbing."

Charlotte had no idea what he'd called her, but the *way* he said it, soft and low, his voice a caress, had her stomach doing a slow roll in spite of her agitation.

"The three men following us. I know this sounds crazy, but they're killers as well. Genevieve and I were going to try to find out more about them. We went to the club with the idea of luring them out into the open."

"You did what?"

He interrupted her, and the air was suddenly thick with heat. Oppressive heat. *Uh-oh.* Her gorgeous man had a temper after all. His eyes, a deep blue, had gone turbulent, a sea storm out of control. He suddenly looked much larger. Although he retained that sophisticated air, it looked more a veneer when he was very predatory.

Charlotte moistened her lips with the tip of her tongue. His gaze dropped to that small, nervous gesture, and she wished that she'd been more careful. She'd parked the car a distance from the house because she'd wanted to get out and see his property. The high fence had scared her a little and she hadn't wanted to jump into any commitment, but she definitely needed a safe haven for Lourdes. For the first time, she was really uneasy.

"We needed to draw them out into the open," Charlotte said.

"We're sick of being afraid all the time,"

Genevieve added, her voice trembling.

That told Charlotte that Genevieve saw the predator in Tariq as well. She tried to step back, to put distance between them, but Tariq pulled her closer to him, bending his head until his eyes stared directly into hers. The irises were dark, wide, and she could see flames burning there. Up that close, he was still gorgeous, maybe even more so, but he was also mesmerizing, a strong, angry male, trapping her in his stormy, turbulent gaze.

She drew in her breath sharply. Moistened her dry lips with the tip of her tongue. Tried to find her voice, even though her throat seemed to be closed. "Tariq." His name. Not his last name. Just his name. An intimacy she hadn't expected or wanted, but she'd put it out there in a low, trembling voice she hadn't meant to use.

"*Sielamet.*"

Just that. Another language, one she didn't understand, but the way he said it, so softly, so intimately, she felt the name like a caress moving over her skin.

"Why are you angry?" She had to understand. That was important. Extremely important. She rarely thought it was prudent to run, but his anger was a tangible, living entity, so oppressive, the air around them thickened.

"You put yourself in danger." An accusation. Plain. Stark. Raw.

She glanced at Genevieve, because she needed to look away from that unblinking, focused stare. He reminded her of a large wolf watching prey. Waiting for an opportunity to leap. But he was right. She *had* put herself in danger. She'd put Genevieve in danger as well. They hadn't known whether the three men following them were involved in the murders of their friends and family, but they'd known what they were doing was dangerous.

She nodded. "Yes. That's true. I did that, but we weren't safe. Lourdes wasn't safe. We had to know what we were dealing with, and we didn't know about Fridrick. We hadn't realized there were two threats, not one. So good came out of it."

His fingers tightened around her wrist and he pressed her hand tighter against his chest. So tightly she felt the steady beat of his heart. Strangely, her heart reacted, slowly picking up the same rhythm so that she thought the two hearts drummed one beat at a time together. It was such a strange phenomenon that she paused, her brain still scrambling for a defense, when her mind and body was totally tuned to him.

"Good came out of it?" he repeated slowly, each word enunciated tersely. "Fridrick could have taken both of you. Do you realize how dangerous he is? You wouldn't have been able to stop him or his men from taking you and believe me, life would have become a living hell for you."

She didn't doubt that for a moment. She knew he had saved them. He hadn't put it in so many words, but she knew without a shadow of a doubt in her mind that if Tariq and his intimidating friends hadn't come along, she and Genevieve, and most likely Lourdes, would have been in deep trouble. On that thought came another much more disturbing one.

Charlotte pressed her fingertips against Tariq's broad chest, feeling the muscles beneath his immaculate shirt ripple in response to her touch. "How did he know where Lourdes was?" She tipped her head up so she could meet Tariq's eyes again. The jolt was hard to take. It felt as if their souls connected and he could see right into her. "How could he have known?"

"She is safe and will be here soon," Tariq reminded, very gentle again. He stroked a caress along the back of her hand. "Breathe, *sielamet;* you have forgotten to take a breath. If you do not, I will have to do it for you."

His gaze dropped to her mouth, and her entire body wanted to convulse with heat. How did he do that? She didn't respond to men, not with a terrible, almost brutal need that seemed to sweep through her with just his voice or the smallest of touches. It was crazy to be so completely attracted to a man when danger surrounded her and every move she made could be putting her niece and friend in even more peril. Deliberately she took a breath, feeling the rise and fall of his chest beneath the palm of her hand. Her breath followed his in the same way her heartbeat followed his.

"Thank you. If I didn't say that before, I'm saying it now, with tremendous gratitude. I was already terrified of that hideous man and afraid we might not be able to get away from him, but I had no clue he wasn't alone. He was afraid of you." She made the last a statement, wanting an explanation. If Fridrick was a serial killer, able to tear out throats and drain bodies of blood — which was too theatrical for words — and he was afraid of Tariq, what did that make Tariq Asenguard?

"We knew each other a long time ago. I've hunted him before. He's cunning and cruel and willing to sacrifice his friends in order to save his own hide. He respects me, but fear? I do not know if Fridrick is capable of feeling true fear. He wants to live, and he will retreat if he believes the odds are not in his favor. I had enough of my friends near, and when they showed up that tipped the scales against him. He wasn't willing to accept those odds or there might have been a bloodbath."

Fridrick had been afraid of Tariq no matter what spin Tariq put on it. That meant . . . Tariq was extremely dangerous, as every instinct she had screamed at her. She wasn't certain whether that was because he was dangerous to her heart, maybe even to her soul, certainly to her body — he could own her. She was certain if she ever gave in to the craving she was feeling for him, he would own her body and soul.

Charlotte looked around her at the high fence and the several houses. "Emeline is here?" Somehow knowing the woman she'd met in Paris was living on the property as well as the couple and children he'd taken in made her feel safer.

"Yes. She's staying in that little house over there." He indicated a two-story Victorian that looked beautiful even in the night. There were no lights on, but then it was three in the morning.

"You do not have to stay, Charlie," he said softly. "I am not holding you hostage, only offering you sanctuary until this is over. There is another house for Genevieve, you and Lourdes if you wish to take it. Tonight, the three of you are welcome to stay in the main house . . ." He turned and gestured toward the mansion. "As you can see there is plenty of room. In the morning, you can decide if you wish to stay longer and I can show you the other house. Maksim's property borders mine, and he guards as well. My friends are close and they will help to look after the safety of all the children as well as the two of you and Emeline."

He dropped her hand and stepped back, giving her space. Instantly she felt cold. Alone. Her body trembled as fear swept through her. He'd been holding all that at bay. She glanced at Genevieve, one eyebrow arched in inquiry. "What do you think, Vi?"

"I want to stay, Charlie," Genevieve admitted. "I'm so sick of being afraid all the time. It's beautiful here, and if we stay, I can't imagine Fridrick or those other three getting their hands on Lourdes or us."

Charlotte turned back to Tariq. "Then we thank you once again for this. We'd love to accept your offer of a place to stay." She wasn't going to commit to working for him, but she had to admit, the carousel horses were part of the draw. Mostly, it was Tariq. Still, staying close to him would be a danger in itself.

"It's settled then. Come with me, ladies. I'll show you the house, you can pick your rooms and then I can ask the police to come if you wish to speak to them tonight. I know a detective and I trust him. He would come immediately if I called." He stepped back to allow them to precede him.

"I should tell you those other three men may have followed us here, and they're just as dangerous as Fridrick. They've killed, too. I saw them drive a stake through the heart of a man and he was alive." Charlotte felt compelled to confess. "You have to know that if you allow us to stay here, those men might go after you. I don't know what they want or why they followed us from Paris, but I know they did."

Tariq's face was devoid of all expression. Lines were etched deep. He looked rugged and tough, but still as sophisticated as ever. Charlotte had to wonder how that was even possible. God, but he was gorgeous.

"Tell me about them."

"One is named Daniel Forester. When you called that young boy Danny, it reminded me. Mostly because Daniel made a big production about his name and how he didn't want anyone calling him Danny. His friends tweaked him a bit about that. He had two friends, Vince Tidwell and Bruce Van Hues, with him. I saw them as well at the murder scene."

"Where was this?"

She couldn't tell by his stony features, his cool eyes or his matter-of-fact voice if he even believed her. She wouldn't have believed anyone telling her such a thing without proof, especially after what she'd told him about Fridrick killing so many people. Thankfully, he knew Fridrick and had "hunted" him. What did that mean? She should have asked when she'd had the chance. It was such a strange word to use, especially for the owner of a nightclub.

She remained silent as they made their way along the stone walkway to the steps leading to the wraparound porch. There was no explaining that she "saw" Daniel Forester kill another human being by driving a stake through his heart while she held a cocktail glass in her hand. Tariq and the police would think she was the crazy one.

"I don't know where the murder took place, but it wasn't the only one." That made it worse. If Fridrick was a serial killer, then she was telling Tariq that there were two separate serial killers. She almost didn't believe herself.

"You do not know where the murder took place, but you know there was one. I take it you weren't there when it actually happened. Did someone tell you about it?"

"Of course not," Genevieve snapped, answering for her. Defending her. Getting her into even more trouble. "Sometimes Charlie 'sees' things. It's a gift. That's one of the reasons we went in for psychic testing. It may have been on a whim, but both of us have a couple of very real gifts." Now she just sounded defiant. She glared at Tariq, daring him to dispute the possibility.

"So you do not have anything concrete to tell the police about these three men."

Tariq sounded as if he was talking to himself, not them. He didn't object or scoff at anything they said, and that was a relief to

114

Charlotte. She hadn't realized until that moment that she *really* didn't want Tariq Asenguard to think she was crazy. He seemed to be taking them seriously. He'd admitted to having a gift or two of his own, so maybe that contributed to his believing them.

"No, not really. Not even with Fridrick. He admitted killing in Paris and again, here, with Charlie's brother," Genevieve answered, "but there's no proof. The best we can do is maybe point the cops in the right direction." She yawned and quickly tried to cover it. "I'm sorry. This is all very exhausting."

"Let me show you to a room. Enter of your own free will." Tariq held the door open for them courteously, using his old-world charm to let them pass first.

Charlotte glanced at him sharply, hesitating as Genevieve walked right in, even reaching for her as if to stop her. Genevieve was far too fast, moving quickly into the entryway and peering around her. Charlotte stood just outside the door, feeling the pull, the longing to go inside. A sanctuary of sorts, and somewhere, on this property, was her dream job of restoring very, very old wooden carousel horses. She'd seen the pictures, and she had longed to go with Ricard Beaudet to help restore them. She yearned to get her hands on them, to feel the life in them, the treasure trove of memories locked in the wood.

"Can I look around?" Genevieve asked.

"Of course. My home is yours. You are welcome to choose any room on the ground floor."

"Thanks. If I find one I like, I'm going straight to bed. I can barely stay awake. If I get up before you, Charlie, I'll take care of Lourdes."

"Thanks, Vi." They'd been trading off getting up with the little girl, and Lourdes already loved Genevieve, so Charlotte was grateful for the help.

Tariq smiled at Genevieve as she moved deeper into the dimly lit foyer. "She's a good friend."

"Yes, she is." Charlotte still hesitated just outside the door. "What does that mean? 'Enter of your own free will'?" She couldn't make her feet move, although no harm had come to Genevieve.

"It is an ancient invitation handed down through the generations in my family. I come from the Carpathian Mountains, and family and friends use the more ancient ways. Does it bother you?" He gave her a small courtly bow.

Charlotte felt a little silly objecting to walking into his house when he'd practically saved their lives. Still, there was reluctance counterbalancing the need to enter. Maybe it was the need itself. "Can you ask your friend when Lourdes will be here? And Grace?"

"Ah, yes, Grace. I had forgotten your other

116

friend. Is she gifted? In the way you and Genevieve are?"

He continued to hold the door open, not showing any impatience whatsoever. Charlotte could no longer see Genevieve. She'd disappeared into the interior of the house and could be heard oohing and aahing. "You aren't answering me about Lourdes," she persisted, refusing to be distracted. She was beginning to be afraid all over again, but she didn't know why.

"Lourdes has already arrived, and Grace is following with Maksim. My friend Siv has brought your niece safe and sound and she is in bed inside the house. Let me take you to her."

She wanted to see for herself and she nearly stepped inside, but the moment she put one foot over the threshold, she felt a curious wrenching sensation in her body. The floor moved beneath her, a ripple, just like the beginnings of an earthquake. She stopped, her heart pounding. Again, Tariq didn't seem impatient, nor did he try to get close to her. If anything, he kept more distance than he ever had. It made her feel alone — bereft.

Her emotions were all over the place, careening out of control. It had to be from sheer fear. From the grief she felt losing her brother. She'd barely buried him when they became aware they were being followed and watched again here in the United States. At night, twice, there had been the bizarre noises at the windows and doors, just like in Paris. Charlotte had called 911, but what was there to say? She was scared. There were noises. She thought someone was outside their house. The patrol officers came and didn't find a thing either time.

"*Sielamet,* what is it?"

God. His voice. It melted her insides. Turned her stomach into a roller coaster and sent darts of fire straight to her sex. It soothed and incited. Caressed and stroked. That word he used made his accent heavier.

"What does that mean? The name you call me?"

His smile took her breath, and it hadn't even really lit his eyes. "It is an ancient endearment, hard to explain outside my native language. My people come from a remote region in the mountains, and we keep to the ancient ways."

That hadn't answered her question exactly. He had a way of doing that. Telling her absolutely nothing. She forced herself to take the last step inside. The moment her left foot followed her right one and touched the hardwood floor she felt that same shifting beneath her feet, as if her world had changed for all time.

She stayed still until the sensation passed, afraid if she said anything he would think she was crazier than she already appeared.

"Which way to Lourdes? And is your friend Siv still around?" She glanced behind her, through the open door. There was no vehicle parked next to her car.

Tariq pulled the door closed firmly, yet quietly, cutting off her view to the outside. There was intricate stained glass woven into the door, but there was no seeing through it. In the muted light from the sconces on the wall, she could see Tariq's expression. This time the blank look was gone. His face could have been carved from stone, but his eyes, that deep, dark blue, portrayed emotion. She could feel a heavy heat vibrating through the air.

"Why do you ask after Siv?" Again his voice was clipped, terse, intense and scary.

She moistened her lips with the tip of her tongue again, stalling for time, turning everything over and over in her head but not coming up with an answer why her question would upset him. And he was upset.

"I asked out of politeness. He rescued my niece and I wanted to thank him."

The tension drained out of him instantly. "Siv isn't . . . civilized. He spends most of his time alone, and he doesn't talk much to anyone, not even those of us who are his friends. He made certain Lourdes was safe and asleep and then he slipped out." He shrugged. "That is his way and we all respect it."

She wasn't about to complain. Being around Tariq was enough. She had noted that all his friends were good-looking in spite of the fact that a couple of them carried some rather vicious-looking scars. She had eyes only for Tariq. She found she inhaled him into her lungs. As much as she tried not to look at him, she couldn't help herself. She was looking now, and she couldn't help but note the satisfaction on his face. In his eyes. He didn't look smug, but he definitely was more than pleased that she'd entered his home.

She stopped abruptly because that wrenching inside her body didn't go away. It increased, and she realized it had become a compulsion to touch him. To be close to him. He was only a step behind her and she was acutely aware of him. Of his every breath. Of his masculine scent. The way his muscles rippled beneath that thin silk shirt. She had the odd desire to take the single step that separated them and run her hand under his shirt to feel those muscles on her palm. Strangely, she could hear his heartbeat. Hers matched the rhythm of his exactly. That had happened before, but now she was more aware of it than ever.

Tariq took the step, coming right up behind her, and pressed his chest to her back. She should have moved, put more space between them, but she couldn't. Her feet refused to cooperate with her brain. She melted inside. Melted into him. A part of her screamed that she wasn't in the least acting professional, and he had women throwing themselves at him all the time. She was one among hundreds — maybe thousands.

His hands came down on her shoulders. Big hands. Strong. She felt his palms and fingers like a brand pressed into her bones. He bent his head so his mouth was against her ear. Close. So close that when he spoke his lips brushed her skin.

"You haven't taken a breath in over a minute. Why is that, *sielamet*? Why do I have to remind you that you still need air?"

Oh God. She was in *such* trouble. Terrible trouble. She couldn't stop herself from leaning back into him. From turning her head, giving him access to her neck. Electrical impulses sang along her skin while every cell in her body *craved* him. Like a drug. The need was so strong she found herself trembling. Her pulse pounded in her neck, and seemed even stronger in her clit. She felt her blood thicken. Turn molten.

He murmured something in her ear and she closed her eyes. The language was ancient. He'd said so. It sounded so different. A single phrase. *Joŋesz éntölem, fél ku kuuluaak sívam belsö.* She knew French, but his language was so completely different she had no idea what he said to her. She only knew that

121

when he uttered that phrase with his accent and his low, sensual voice, she wanted more. Her world narrowed until there was only him. Only Tariq Asenguard. Genevieve had gone to bed, and there was no one to save her from herself and her reckless impulses.

His hand swept her hair over her left shoulder, leaving the right side bare. She felt his breath as his arms closed around her waist and he moved her deeper into the shadows. She could barely think with her need. His body was hot. Strong. All masculine, making her aware of the differences in them and just how fragile she was in comparison. That should have frightened her, but instead, a thrill shot through her.

He whispered again, this time in a mixture of his language and English. *"Fél ku kuuluaak sívam belső,* I have waited so long for you. I cannot wait one more minute. Tell me I do not have to. Give this to me, *sielamet."*

She would give him anything when he used that voice. She found she couldn't speak, lost in a dream world. His fist was suddenly in her hair, pulling her head back a little roughly, the spike of pain searing through her body straight to her sex so that she clenched and spasmed, was damp and needy. His hand in her hair kept her head back and to one side so that his lips skimmed down her neck. Scorching her. Setting her body on fire. Melting any thought of resistance.

His mouth settled over the pulse pounding in her neck. His teeth scraped back and forth in a sexy temptation. She wanted him to kiss her there. She wanted him to bite her. Just the thought of his mouth on her skin, leaving his mark on her, heightened the growing need coiling deep inside.

"*Te avio päläfertiilam. Éntölam kuulua, avio päläfertiilam.* You are my lifemate. I claim you as my lifemate."

He spoke firmly as if taking a vow, yet his voice was mesmerizing, just as his mouth moving over her pulse was. She didn't know what his words meant, but she liked them. She knew they meant something to him, and all she needed, all she wanted was to keep his mouth moving on her. Each time his teeth scraped over her pounding pulse her sex clenched harder and wept with need.

"*Ted kuuluak, kacad, kojed. Élidamet andam. Pesämet andam. Uskolfertiilamet andam.* I belong to you. I offer my life for you. I give you my protection. I give you my allegiance."

Her eyelids felt so heavy, but she forced them open to look at his face. His eyes blazed down into hers, little flames leaping inside the pupils. So dark. So mysterious. Beckoning her. She wanted him. It was that simple. His words seemed to draw her even closer to him, as if by uttering them, he had woven tiny threads between them, unbreakable and sacred.

Staring down into her eyes, holding her captive with that hand in her hair and his mouth on her pulse, he continued. "*Sívamet andam. Sielamet andam. Ainamet andam. Sívamet kuuluak kaik että a ted. Ainaak olenszal sívambin.* I give you my heart."

Her heart jerked in her chest at that declaration. She wanted his heart. For a moment, the sane part of her objected to the terrible need building inside her, but he continued translating for her, and his low, mesmerizing voice, so darkly sensual, robbed her of her ability to think clearly. She could only want. Only need. Only feel his breath and his mouth and those terrible, wonderful teeth scraping against her skin, each time sending shock waves straight to her sex.

"I give you my heart. I give you my soul. I give you my body."

Sielamet. She recognized that word. *My soul.* He called her that numerous times. She wanted his heart and his body.

"I take into my keeping the same that is yours. Your life will be cherished by me for all my time."

That was so beautiful. Incredibly beautiful. So much so that tears blurred her vision. And then he sank his teeth into her neck. Right into her pounding pulse. Pain seared her. Heat lashed like a whip through her bloodstream, straight to her core. The tight tension

124

in her body increased, coiling and building until she was rocking her hips helplessly in need.

His palm cupped her breast and she felt his touch on bare skin. That didn't make sense because she wore clothes . . . didn't she? She couldn't think. Only feel. Her body was a living flame of terrible brutal need.

"Please." She whispered her plea, never wanting him to stop. Needing more. Needing him. She felt empty without him. Desperate for him. Still in a dream. A hazy, wonderful, beautiful dreamworld. In it, she could do anything, including have this beautiful man for herself.

The connection between them was real. Strong. Compelling. Her body was on fire, his fingers finding her nipples, first one, then the other, tugging and rolling, pinching hard and then stroking gently, keeping her off-balance so that need only climbed higher. The flames burned out of control. A firestorm of sheer desperation.

Then his tongue swept over his brand on her, a soothing stroke to counter the erotic pain of his bite. He turned her into him, guiding her with the back of her head in his palm. His chest, that amazing, defined muscled chest was bare to her touch. To her lips. He pressed her close while one hand came up between them. His finger stroked a line above his heart and for a moment her breath caught in her throat. She could see little ruby beads there.

"For you. Dare to be with me; dare to enter my world and stay with me. I have waited so long for you, *sielamet.*"

His soul. She loved that. She let him press her face to his chest. She nuzzled all that hot skin. Felt his strength. Tasted a ruby drop. It tasted like ambrosia. Nectar. A spicy, heady potion made just for her. Once her tongue had taken that single drop into her mouth, it set up a craving. His hand pressed her head closer and she took the invitation, her mouth feeding at those drops. Her hands moving over his chest, dropping lower to find his heavy, thick cock so perfectly erect. So ready for her. Her fingers closed around him, thumb sliding through the droplets there, smearing so she could begin a lazy slide with her fist while her mouth took more of his offering.

He groaned. So sexy. Her body clenched with need. His voice whispered to her, not aloud, but in her mind, more intimate than ever. "*Te élidet ainaak pide minan. Te avio päläfertiilam. Ainaak sívamet jutta oleny. Ainaak terád vigyázak.* Your life will be placed above my own for all time. You are my lifemate. You are bound to me for all eternity. You are always in my care."

5

Charlotte cried out when Tariq's fingers stroked low and sinful, building her need beyond anything she had ever known. One hand gently inserted itself between her mouth and his chest; the other pulled at her hair, forcing her head up. He swept his finger across the line on his defined muscles and the ruby drops disappeared. Her head was held in position so that she stared into his blazing eyes. He appeared pure predator. Pure male. His hands cupped the bare cheeks of her bottom and he lifted her easily, his gaze holding her captive, refusing to allow her to look away from him.

God. *God.* Those eyes. So incredible. The color was like gemstones, that bright and pure. And then they would blaze with power, or like now, with lust. With possession. She *loved* that look. No man had ever looked at her as if she were the only woman on earth. The one woman who was his beginning and end. She could barely breathe watching that expression in his eyes deepen. He focused solely on her — as if she *were* the world. She wanted to stare into his eyes for an eternity. Lost. Cared for.

"Wrap your legs around my waist and lock your ankles."

Tariq issued the order in his low, commanding voice. The one she couldn't resist. Velvet soft. A little rough, but sexy rough. His voice made her shiver, sent her stomach rolling in a series of somersaults. Deep inside she was wet, needy. Totally desperate, and in that moment she would have done anything he asked.

She did as she was told, her hands at his shoulders, fingers biting deep. His hands moved to her hips, and he backed her against a table. She wasn't certain where she was. Not the hall. Hadn't she just been in a hallway with him? For one moment, she tried to look around her. What was she doing? Where was she? Where was everyone else?

"Charlotte."

He whispered her name, low, commanding, and her gaze jumped back to his. She had the sensation of falling into his eyes. He mesmerized her with that look. A dark sorcerer holding her captive with his spell, and she didn't ever want to escape. She felt the cool wood on her heated skin as he laid her back on the narrow table, her hips controlled entirely by him, and everything went out of her head again. Every sane thought until there was only Tariq and his incredible eyes, his voice and that perfect, gorgeous body.

"I cannot be gentle, *sielamet,* not this time, but I will make it good for you."

She didn't care. Couldn't care. She needed. *Craved.* Was burning up without him. He had to hurry. And she told him. Whispering. Pleading. "Hurry. You have to be inside me." There was no other place for him to be. He belonged with her. *Inside* her. That rough, sexy voice he used only pushed her need higher. Added an edge to the terrible hunger consuming her.

"Say my name," he ordered. His voice whispered over her skin, causing goose bumps to rise. "Know who your lifemate is."

She had no idea what a lifemate was, but she wanted to be that for him. She wanted to be anything he wanted. Her nipples were twin tight peaks, her breasts aching and swollen with need. Deep inside tension coiled tighter and tighter.

"I'm your man. Say it, Charlotte Vintage. Say you belong to me and that I belong to you." His rough voice had dropped an octave until it was almost harsh, yet it still carried that sexy, velvet sound that triggered something deep inside her — a need, a hunger — to be with him. To do anything for him. To be whatever he needed.

She would have said anything to get him inside her, so claiming him wasn't in the least difficult. She wanted that. Wanted him to be hers. "Please hurry, Tariq. I belong to Tariq Asenguard, and he *definitely* belongs to me." He did belong to her. She felt the truth of that with every ragged breath she took.

He took her hard. Brutally. One desperate stroke filling her, pushing ruthlessly through tight, scorching-hot muscles, tearing through the thin barrier to fill her with his thick, hard cock. Filling her completely. Stretching her. Burning. A blazing hot stroke of pure erotic pain and pleasure.

She heard herself scream and it was a mixture of shock, pain, and so much pleasure she hadn't known a woman could feel such a thing. Every nerve ending sizzled with pure fire. And then he was planted in her. Deep. Pulsing. She could feel his heartbeat through his cock, on the walls of her vagina as he waited, taking a breath, giving her time to adjust.

She couldn't look away from his face, those lines etched deep, the planes and angles carved into a handsome, purely masculine face. His hair was messy, wild even, long and glossy dark. His eyes blazed down into hers and she saw an absolute predator staring down at her. Focused. Brutal. Dominant. Possessive. It should have frightened her, but there was something else in his eyes, something that made her feel absolutely safe with him.

He'd branded her as his, and she knew he meant it. She could see that in his eyes. She felt it in his touch. So possessive. She'd never done anything like this in her life. Never. But she knew she belonged to him, and she needed him desperately to move. If he didn't move, she was going to go up in flames like a phoenix. Turn to ashes. Nothing left.

Tariq, watching her face, withdrew and slammed deep, all the while holding her gaze captive with his, judging her reaction to his hard, brutal stroke, and then held still again to give her body time to adjust to his invasion.

"More." She whispered it to him. "Please, Tariq. More." Even as she pleaded with him, she knew that he would take her without mercy, and God help her, that was what she wanted — even needed — from him.

He gave her more and then some. Pounding into her. Taking her thoroughly. His hands hard on her hips, holding her in place while he surged into her, again and again, jolting her body with each brutal thrust. Her breasts rocked in invitation with every hard jackhammer surge. Lightning seemed to lash through her veins. The tension inside her coiled tighter and tighter. She needed . . . something.

"Tariq." She said his name. Low. Calling out to him when she didn't know what to do to ease the terrible burn that built and built.

It was building so high fear skittered down her spine.

"I have you, *sielamet,*" he assured, his eyes scorching a brand through her.

She felt that brand with his every finger digging into her hips. With every stroke, he burned his name into her, deep inside her body, until she felt owned by him. Taken by him. Thoroughly his.

"Eyes to mine, Charlotte," he commanded, his voice sexily low and gravelly, the voice that turned her inside out. "Let me see into your soul."

She loved the way he said that. As if he meant every word. More, when she looked into his eyes, she felt anchored. Safe. Her world narrowed until there was only him. She breathed him in with every breath she took. He was inside her body, filling and stretching her until the burn was so scorching hot she was afraid she'd lose her mind. She clung to his arms, her fingernails like tiny daggers, scoring his shoulders and arms, trying to find a purchase when every brutal stroke sent waves of pleasure crashing through her. Yet, for all that, the horrible coiling inside her refused to release — just continued to build and build until she thought she might go insane.

"Tariq." She whispered his name, hips bucking to meet his, head tossing back and forth even as she stared helplessly into his eyes. "I need . . ." She didn't know. Something. He had to do something. Right. Now.

"I know, *sielamet*. I've got you."

He shifted her hips, dragged her body up just a few inches, changing the angle, and then he thrust into her, over and over, hitting the exact spot until she thought the world was exploding around her.

"Now, Charlotte. Come for me now."

Her body tumbled over the edge of a deep precipice, fragmenting, soaring. The ripples didn't stop — refused to leave her, her body not her own, out of her control — and still he didn't stop, a relentless, pistoning machine. Velvet over steel. Scorching hot. Beautiful. Perfect. Frightening. Thrilling.

"Again, *sielamet.*" It was sheer demand. A command. His face was set in implacable lines. His eyes blazed fire. He was beautiful and terrifying at the same time.

How could she possibly go again without pleasure consuming her, taking her over? She shook her head, but she knew she would give him anything he wanted. Whatever he demanded of her. She couldn't stop herself. He would always be her one weakness. Always.

She let go, this time her orgasm even more powerful, ripping through her with tremendous force, radiating out from her core down to her thighs and up to her belly, spreading out and moving to her breasts like an earthquake of mammoth proportions. She heard her thin wail, her soft cries of his name, his groan as her body took his with it. She felt the hot splash of jet after jet of his seed pulsing into her triggering yet another strong quake.

For what seemed an eternity, he stood over her, her legs wrapped around him, ankles locked in the small of his back, his cock buried deep in her, his gaze holding hers, telling her without words, just the way his body had told her, that she belonged to him. She was already having trouble catching her breath and that look just made it more difficult.

He leaned over her, breathing hard, planting a kiss on her belly button. The movement triggered another ripple, this one less forceful but no less pleasurable. His mouth swept up her rib cage to the undersides of her breasts, caressing with his tongue, suckling first one breast and then the other. His teeth on her left nipple sent yet another strong quake through her.

His mouth continued upward to take possession of her throat. Her chin. Finally, finally, her lips. He took her mouth as ruthlessly as he had her body. Claiming her. She lost herself in his kisses. One after another. Deep. Hard. Wet. Perfect. All the while his cock stayed inside her, not relaxing, not slipping away, but stretching her. Pulsing. His heart beating there. Beating in his chest against her breasts. Beating in her core, while she pulsed and her heart beat around his cock. She was acutely aware of every cell in her body. Every nerve ending. Of every inch of her. And all of her belonged to Tariq Asenguard.

"Hold on, *sielamet*. Keep your ankles locked and put your arms around my neck. Keep your face tight against my shoulder and close your eyes for me."

There was no way to resist his voice. She would always want to please him, to give him anything he desired. With his eyes staring into hers, she melted into his body, her breasts imprinting onto his chest as she slid her arms around his neck and locked her fingers at his nape. She buried her face against his shoulder and closed her eyes, actually feeling the sweep of her lashes against his skin.

She had the sensation of moving. Floating. She drifted, feeling every movement of his body through their connection — his cock stretching her, growing even thicker and harder as he carried her. He had to be incredibly strong to do that and she wanted to see where they were going, but once she closed her eyes, she couldn't seem to open them. She was exhausted. Worn-out from her constant vigilance, trying to keep Lourdes safe . . .

"Lourdes." She murmured her niece's name and tried to surface. She hadn't checked on her. Hadn't seen that her greatest treasure, the gift her brother left behind for her, was safe.

"Open your eyes, *sielamet,* and see her."

Her lashes felt as if they weighed a ton. Still wrapped tightly around Tariq's body, she opened her eyes and saw her niece through a window, as if she were outside the bedroom looking in. Lourdes slept peacefully, the covers pulled over her light little body. Charlotte's lashes drifted down, and then the lovers were moving again. The cool air didn't do a thing to cool her hot body. She began to move, helpless not to, grinding down over his cock. Needing him all over again.

He didn't seem to mind in the least. His hands cupped her bottom and he lifted her, showing her how to ride him as he continued moving. She kept her face buried against him and didn't bother to try to open her eyes — she just took her pleasure, sliding up and down that thick, velvet-covered shaft that seemed to radiate heat hotter than a furnace.

Then she was on her knees, bent over a bed, and he gripped her from behind, one arm around her waist, the other hand tugging on her nipples, first one then the other, his mouth on the nape of her neck while he pounded into her from behind. His body held her captive, and she loved the feeling of his weight on her, his mouth sucking on her neck. His teeth scraping. His bite. Sharp

136

teeth. Such an erotic pain.

She threw her head back and to the side to encourage him to bite the other side of her neck. He'd had her right side, her throat, the back of her neck, and she wanted every single part of her claimed by him. He obliged, his hips all the while thrusting hard, a relentless machine, over and over, a heady, wild ride she never wanted to end.

Even as he leaned over her, his body strong and hard, pinning her against the mattress, his hair sweeping her bare skin and his teeth biting down, she heard the murmur of his voice stroking caresses in her head. Soft. Gentle. A counterpart to the savage way his body moved into hers.

En évsatzak piwtääk tet. I have searched through centuries for you.

She didn't know how that could be the truth, but she loved that he said it, and by the look on his face, he meant it. For him, waiting for her had seemed centuries. It was the same for her. She'd looked the world over for something she desperately needed and hadn't found it until now.

His body was hard and hot, his cock sinking deep, pushing through sensitive tissues to claim her. To brand her. It was so beautiful she felt tears welling up.

Kuz̃õ, ainaak évsatzak otti jelä että íla en wäkeva ködaba. Long, endless centuries to find the light that would shine through the unrelent-

ing darkness.

With fire streaking through her body, and his hand curved around the nape of her neck, holding her in place, she could barely hear the words. They weren't so much in her ears as in her mind. For a moment she nearly surfaced, anxiety close in spite of the molten honey moving through her veins.

Ašša moo pél. There is no need for fear.

His other hand found her breast, fingers pinching her nipple hard, tugging, rolling, sending lightning sizzling through her body until she was gasping for air, crying out with need, knowing she didn't have anything to be afraid of. She trusted him with her body, and he was doing things to her she'd never imagined.

Én olenam teval it. I am with you now.

Tears spilled onto her lashes. She'd felt so alone, even when she was with her best friend. Even when she was with her brother. She loved them and knew they loved her, but there was something missing — until now. Until Tariq.

Pesäsz engemal. Stay with me.

Was he feeling the same way? That terrible need, as brutal and as beautiful as the hard strokes as he buried himself deep inside her. Did he need her to fill him the way he filled her? Her heart? Her soul? Her body?

Olensz engemal. Be with me.

She cried out as his hands shifted, moved

over her body possessively while he drove himself into her like a man possessed. She felt that coiling deep inside, a burn that became a wildfire out of control. She wanted to be with him. Always. Forever.

Ainaakä kaδasz engem jälleen. Never go away again.

His voice felt like velvet stroking against her skin. Each word murmured in his language, that ancient tongue that was totally mesmerizing, hypnotic, a voice she could listen to for far more than one lifetime.

She closed her eyes and absorbed each separate sensation. His mouth on her neck. His teeth scraping against her skin. The voice whispering in her head. His fingers tugging and rolling her nipples, pinching to send streaks of fire straight to her clit. His arm, a bar at her waist, his hand curling around her waist possessively. The way his body felt against hers. Barbaric. Savage. Claiming. The power in his hips thrusting against her. His cock, weighted. Heavy. Thick. Stretching her. The burn only added to the fiery, scorching hot blaze deep inside her.

Her body coiled tighter and tighter. Stringing her out. Sending her higher. Too high. That delicious frisson of fear skittered down her spine, filling her with trepidation, but she didn't want him to stop. She needed . . .

"Tariq." She whispered his name, but it came out like a plea. He had to do something to stop the climb before she lost herself.

"*Pesäsz engemal.* Stay with me," he repeated in English. "*Hiszasz engem vigyáz tet.* Trust me to take care of you. *Kojasz engem pita temet džinõt t'śuva vni palj3.* Let me have you a little longer."

He wasn't asking. She knew that. He was telling her, but she wanted him to have everything. Anything. She needed to give him that. His voice when he spoke his own language swept away everything but the need to give to him. To please him. Even if she was a little afraid. She found the fear only added to the wildness of the ride. It built that tension gathering so strongly in her deepest core.

"I have to let go," she whispered, not wanting to, but she truly didn't think she could stop it and she wanted to warn him.

"*Aš. Ašša bur ször. Andsz éntölam palj3 t'śuva vni teval. Várasz. No.* Not yet. Give me more time with you. You *will* wait." An order. A command. There was no plea in his voice, only that quiet, low, implacable decree.

Charlotte closed her eyes and curled her fingers into the satin sheets, making a fist, holding on with everything she had as he took complete control of her body. His hands went to her hips, pinning her, holding her still as he drove into her with hard, brutal strokes, rocking her body, stretching her until she felt as if the fire had built beyond all control and

140

would take her over, destroy her completely until there was no Charlotte without Tariq. She was so close. Each drag of his hard cock over her acutely sensitive bundle of nerves had her gasping, crying out, the sensation so extreme she knew it would throw her over the edge any second. But she held on. Tried. For him.

He murmured more in his language. "*Sivamet. Sielamet. Minden m8akam.* My everything."

His heart. His soul. His everything. She wanted that to be true, because in that moment — since the first time he had whispered to her in his language and his teeth had bitten down in that sinfully erotic bite — he had been her heart. Her soul. Her everything. There would never be a single moment when she would deny him. Deny this. Deny him — her.

"Please." She was nearly sobbing now. The pleasure too much. She was climbing too high. But she wouldn't let go. Wouldn't fail him. He wanted, and she could do this — for him.

"No, *sielamet,*" he whispered in her ear. "For us. I do this for us."

She took a breath. He slammed deep, angling her hips back into him while she sobbed out another ragged breath.

"Now, Charlotte. Give that miracle to me now."

She didn't know whether it was his giving her permission, the way his cock dragged over her clit, how the broad head stroked that sweet spot deep inside, or whether she just couldn't hold on one second longer, but her body came apart. The orgasm roared through her. Took her completely. She heard herself scream. Long. A wail of pure eroticism. The ripples became quakes and her body seemed to fragment. Come apart until she wasn't certain she could ever be put back together, but she didn't care. Didn't want to be. She was flung out into the universe. Soaring in space. Floating. Drifting.

She felt his mouth on her ear. Her neck. The side of her face. Soft kisses. He turned her over. She was aware of that on some level. The mattress firm against her back. His body stretched out beside hers. One leg flung over her thighs, pinning her down as if even then he wanted to hold her to him. One arm possessively around her rib cage, palm cupping her breast. With her every breath he was there, in her lungs.

Still she drifted. Floated. The ripples decreased in strength, but the bliss didn't diminish in the least. She nuzzled him. His lips immediately found hers.

"*Odamasz it. Džinõt t'śuva vnirt. Tsak odamasz.* Sleep now. For a short while. Just go to sleep."

There was no denying him. Not before

when his body was in hers and not now when she was exhausted and needed sleep. She let her lashes fall and snuggled closer against him.

Tariq held his lifemate as tightly as possible to him without disturbing her. He wanted to know what she dreamt. He wanted to be inside her body as well as her mind. He wanted to know every single detail about her. He'd been careful to be respectful and not attempt to read what wasn't offered, not while she was awake. She had some kind of barrier, a shield that had allowed her to resist Fridrick's compulsion. She'd known Fridrick was trying to force her obedience. He didn't want her to equate him with the undead.

He touched her mind as she slowly drifted down from the high of their union. She was floating in subspace. Happy. The sensations in her body still occupied her mind . . . along with thoughts of him. Of making him happy. Of being his woman. He loved that she wanted that. He wanted to make her happy. To be her man. To please her.

She had a strange reaction to his language as if just the sound alone resonated with her. He knew she couldn't understand meanings, but each time he spoke in his language she had complied immediately with everything he'd asked for. He'd bound her to him, and that meant even if she attempted to flee, she wouldn't get far. She would need him every bit as much as he needed her. He had exchanged blood with her. He could talk to her mind to mind, an intimate connection between just the two of them, far different from the common pathway most Carpathians used.

It would take three blood exchanges to bring her fully into his world, and he was tempted to complete that exchange in one heady night. She tasted like . . . paradise. Her body *was* paradise. A miracle he hadn't expected. He had come up with the idea of the nightclubs in order to entice women to come to him, in an effort to find his lifemate, yet he had given up any real hope of finding her. His search had gone on far too long. The temptation to have her immediately by his side for eternity was strong, but he wanted more from her than simple obedience. He wanted her to choose him.

In some way, she already had. He hadn't fogged her mind completely. Not once. Not even during the blood exchange. When he'd first taken her into his arms, she had gone to him willingly. He'd created a slight haze to make that first exchange easier for her, but he hadn't taken her will. She had complied without a hint of reluctance. She'd felt the pull between them nearly as strongly as he had.

Tariq stroked back the thick mass of hair. It was soft. Glossy. Shiny. Very wavy, like water rippling over rocks in a river. She was beautiful. Her curves were enticing and he couldn't stop stroking caresses over her body. He had to touch her. Everything about her appealed to him. Her scent. Her shape. The sound of her voice. The way her mind centered on him and stayed there. Her eagerness to please him.

He kissed the shell of her ear. Traced it with the tip of his tongue. In her sleep she shivered and moved closer to him, turning her head slightly to offer him better access.

"Do you need me?" she asked softly, moving her body against his.

His breath caught in his throat. She was exhausted. Most likely sore, feeling his brand deep inside of her, yet she was offering herself to him — if he needed her. He would always need her. Always want her. So generous a woman. His heart jerked in his chest.

"*Odamasz engem.* Dream of me," he whispered, his lips on her ear. "*Kutnisz engem teval minden ku että jutasz.* Take me with you wherever you go."

She had already set up a craving for her. For her blood. For her body. His cock had developed a mind of its own, already full, thick and ready. Almost painful. He loved the feeling of needing her physically. Of hungering for her blood alone. The sign of a Carpathian, a hunter. As predatory as he was, he no longer was in danger of becoming the undead, forever seeking the rush of the kill. That

145

temptation was gone, replaced by the exclusive hunger for his lifemate.

He listened to her breathe. Soft. Gentle. Like her voice. That melodic voice seemed to sink right into his bones to claim him. He loved her courage. He really loved that they shared a passion for old things. Especially wooden carved carousel horses. They had begun his emergence into the world of humans. Once he had done so, he'd never abandoned them. He liked living among them. He liked many of them and had formed odd, interesting friendships — he could pretend to feel by using the human emotions surrounding him. And then as more time passed, he couldn't even do that, feel through memories, his own or those of the humans around him. He felt nothing — a void where his heart and soul should have been.

Once more he pressed little kisses from her temple to the corner of her mouth, tracing every detail with the tip of his tongue. Tasting her. Savoring her. She didn't turn away, but instead lifted her head just a little toward him. An offering. The sensation sweeping through his body shook him. The way his heart jerked in his chest at that small gesture she made shocked him. She'd already taken him over, just that fast. She *owned* him. Tariq. A Carpathian hunter. She *owned* him.

He wanted to go in to see the child. He liked children. He had always been drawn to their innocence and wonder. Lourdes would be his, just as she was Charlotte's. Already the four children he'd rescued were "his." He knew they all had psychic gifts, even young Danny, the teenage boy, so brave that he knowingly challenged vampires in an effort to get his sisters to safety. They were his. He hoped Charlotte would come to think of them as hers as well.

He pressed more kisses along her chin and then nibbled. She murmured and ducked her chin down, her mouth moving against his. His belly did a slow roll and his cock jerked hard.

"Tariq." She murmured his name softly. "Can't you sleep?" She didn't open her eyes, but her lips caressed his.

"I'm savoring every moment with you. Committing it to memory. The start of us. The beginning. I do not want to miss one single second with you."

Her lips, against his, curved into a smile. Her tongue teased along the seam of his. "Silly man. If it's the beginning of us, then we have a long time ahead to savor. Go to sleep. Morning is coming and Lourdes will wake up and need me. You'll be too sleepy and worn-out to get up to meet her."

She is exhausted as well. She will sleep in. He answered her mind to mind. Intimately. His voice caressed the walls of her mind. Stroking. Conveying more than words. She would feel his hunger for her. Hunger in all forms. He wanted that. Wanted to share with her just how much his need of her was. Just how much his passion for her was. The lust rising in him. The craving for her blood. She had to know when she woke up and the fog was gone, he would never move on or abandon her. He wanted to give her that knowledge. *I belong to you. I was born just for you.*

He took her mouth, one hand cupping her jaw, holding her still for his invasion. He loved the taste of her and could never get enough. He kissed her over and over. So many times, and yet that wasn't enough. When he lifted his head, she pressed one hand to his chest, pushing him down to the satin sheets while she rose up above him.

He felt the impact of her vividly colored eyes. Her gaze roamed over his face, and he was more than pleased to see it held a hint of possession and more than a little lust.

"You need someone to watch over you, Tariq."

That simple statement shook him. *He* watched over everyone. She'd done this before. With Fridrick in the garage. She'd tried to protect him. He couldn't remember that ever happening. He'd lost most memories of his family. They hadn't been with him long enough to leave many. Mostly the Carpathian community had raised him. The raising had consisted mainly of training him. His

148

most treasured memory had been watching his father carve wood into beautiful things for his mother. He used his hands, not his mind, to make things. Although he'd been ridiculed by some of his peers, Tariq had chosen to do the same thing.

Charlotte kissed his jaw and then his throat. He wasn't certain his heart could take the way she moved her body over his. She straddled him, pressing her hot core into his flesh, branding him with scorching heat as she kissed his chest. Her tongue licked over the spot where he'd drawn the line, opening his veins for her.

Do you want more, sielamet? I belong to you. If you hunger, I provide. He couldn't stop himself; he slid one hand between her lips and his chest, his fingernail lengthening, sharpening, so that he could give her his very essence.

The little beads welled up. Tempting. Enticing her with his scent. She had to feel his hunger — it was there in his mind when he spoke to her. His need of her. His want. He craved her, and he wanted her to sip from him. To take enough for an exchange.

She licked at the ruby drops, her eyes on his, and his body reacted. She was the epitome of a beautiful, sensuous creature. She licked again and then deliberately latched onto him with her mouth. Sucking. Trying to draw out more. All the while her gaze stayed

149

on his. He knew the true meaning of sexy just watching her. Her hips moved on him, a slide of heat and fire that threatened his control, but when he caught her hips to settle her over the straining weight of his cock, she refused to allow it. She reprimanded him with her eyes, and he immediately forced his hands to stop, to just curl into her hips and wait to see what she wanted. When she'd taken enough from him for a second exchange, he slipped his hand between her mouth and his chest, closing the laceration as he did so.

She licked over the line several times and then kissed him there. Her mouth settled over his nipple, teeth tugging gently. He felt that fire shoot an arrow straight to his cock. He reached down to settle his fist around the thick spike. His need for her was brutal now, but he refused to take the control away from her. He wanted to see what she would do, what she had in mind.

Her kisses followed the path of each muscle in his abdomen as she slid down his body, right past where he wanted her to settle. Instead, she wedged her body between his legs, her mouth finding his belly button and then nipping at the skin just below it.

His breath left his lungs in a rush when her breath was on the head of his cock. Warm. Heated. Such a sensation he couldn't have ever imagined. She licked as he held himself tight in his fist. Licked at the drops leaking there, licked all around the top of the sensitive crown. Licked under it, hitting a spot that nearly took the top of his head off the pleasure was so great.

"Relax, Tariq. Let me take care of you for a change. You're so tense." The admonishment was whispered against his cock, her tongue and lips sliding over and around the large, velvety head.

One finger tugged at his hand and he instantly got the hint. She didn't want his help. He let go and her fingers curled around his shaft, low, toward the very base. At the same time, her mouth engulfed him. He nearly came off the bed. Hot. Tight. She drew him deep, her tongue lashing and curling around him. Stroking. Caressing. Massaging. Her other hand cupped his sac, rolling gently, and then her tongue was there.

She never took her gaze from his. Watching her added to his pleasure. She loved what she was doing. He knew it was a gift. He felt that in his mind, the way she relished giving him pleasure, taking care of him, taking the tension from him. Her mouth went back to working his cock and he found himself laboring just to breathe.

He'd studied sex. He'd had centuries to research the subject, every possible position and way to pleasure a partner or have her pleasure him. He'd gotten into the mind of men and women just to experience the sensation, but over the centuries, he'd forgotten the memory of the actual feeling. Now he knew this was a thousand times more potent. Already his balls were drawing up tight, his seed boiling and ready to erupt like the most violent of volcanoes. He loved what she was doing, but he wanted to be inside of her.

"Enough," he said softly. "Crawl up my body. I want you right now."

He watched her eyes as he gave the order. The softness there. The way she reluctantly slid her mouth one more time over him, taking him deep, holding him there while her tongue did amazing things to him, and then slid back off. She kissed the broad head and slowly crawled up his body, a sensual, sinful creature, craving, hungering just as deeply for him as he did for her.

He caught her hips and lifted them. "Fist my cock."

She obeyed him, just as he knew she would. She liked pleasing him, and she wanted him in her as much as he wanted to be there. Slowly, he slid her body down over his, so that he filled her sheath. She was so tight. So hot. Going slow was an exquisite torture because her inner muscles gave way reluctantly to his invasion, making him feel as if he might not actually make it inside her.

All the while he watched her face, needing to see her expression. The absolute pleasure, the curve of her mouth, the way the tip of her tongue teased at her lower lip. Her breasts swayed, drawing his attention, and all at once, along with the craving for a slow burn, he wanted her blood. He *needed* it.

"Ride me slow, Charlotte. Move up and down like you were on a carousel horse. Slowly. Very slowly."

He caught a handful of her hair and drew her down toward him. His mouth settled on her breast, suckling hard, teeth and mouth leaving marks. His marks. His brand. She did as he ordered, lifting her body to the very head of his cock and then slowly beginning the descent. Each time she did it, he felt that same exquisite torture of tightness, her silky sheath strangling him, the friction incredible.

His mouth wandered back up to the swell of her breast and he kissed along that tempting curve. Very deliberately, his eyes holding hers, he let his teeth lengthen and opened his mouth, just enough to reveal the twin, sharp daggers. He bit down hard and she climaxed, her body instantly clamping down on his, milking him with such strength there was no resisting her.

He took her blood, using the rhythm of the pulsing of their bodies while she cradled his head to her. Over and over, their orgasms raged, refusing to let up while he took her blood for the second exchange. It was hot. It was sexy. It was the most sinful, wonderful, perfect moment he had experienced.

When he finally forced himself to stop, she slumped down over him, her body still rippling around his. The strong quakes began to ease and he soothed her with his hands, stroking her back and her firm bottom. Holding her in his arms. Murmuring to her in his language. Exhausted, she fell asleep on him, just like that, his cock still buried deep, her legs straddling his hips, and her head on his shoulder. He loved that just as much.

6

Charlotte opened her eyes reluctantly. The bed was moving just enough to make her a little anxious. This was California and there were earthquakes. She turned her head to find Lourdes pushing back the covers and tugging on her arm.

"Auntie, I have to go to the bathroom."

Charlotte groaned. Lourdes was very self-sufficient when it came to the bathroom. She went all by herself until it came to the wiping part. She needed a little help with that and washing her hands. "All right, honey. Give me a minute." Usually, there wasn't a minute to be had, but she needed to orient herself.

Before anything else, she did the most important thing. She grabbed Lourdes, swung her back down and pressed kisses all over her face. Lourdes hadn't even protested waking up in a new environment — a testimony to how many times they'd moved to stay ahead of danger.

Lourdes wrapped her arms around Charlotte's neck and kissed her back, making growling noises and acting menacing. "I'm going to eat your face, Auntie. I'm a snow monster." She proceeded to kiss Charlotte all over her chin and eyes and cheeks until both of them were laughing. Lourdes pulled away first to jump on the bed, clearly wanting her aunt to move.

Forcing herself into a sitting position, Charlotte groaned again as her body protested the slightest movement. She looked around the room. It was large, with a wide bed, a dresser and an armoire rather than a closet. Heavy drapes at the window blocked any semblance of daylight. Someone had thoughtfully put in a night-light for Lourdes and it hadn't been her. She hadn't thought of anything but going to bed . . .

Her eyes went wide and she threw back the covers and looked down at herself. Thankfully she was fully clothed. Well, they weren't her clothes, but she was dressed in a long white Victorian-type nightgown. It was beautiful and looked hand stitched. Thank God, her dream was just that, a dream. She'd never had a dream so detailed. Or sexual. Or graphic.

"Auntie," Lourdes insisted. "Hurry."

That meant they had to move. Charlotte didn't know where the bathroom was, but she was fairly certain Lourdes wouldn't have been put in the bedroom if it hadn't been

156

close to a bathroom. She stood up and felt soreness in muscles she hadn't known existed. Too much soreness. Real. Every step she took there was a stretch and burn deep inside. Along her thighs. Her breasts were a little sore.

Charlotte pulled open the door, took Lourdes's hand and walked down the hall to the nearest room. Pushing open the door, she was relieved to find a good-sized bathroom with golden faucets and a deep claw-foot tub. Lourdes raced across the tiled floor to hop on the toilet while Charlie forced each foot forward, a woman going to the gallows, until she stood in front of the ornate gold-framed full-length mirror and stared at herself.

To her absolute horror, there were three rather large strawberries, one on each side of her neck and one low at the base of her throat. She closed her eyes briefly on a groan of despair. She looked like a teenager. She had circles under her eyes, but her skin was glowing. Her hair, always thick, looked shiny and, even to her, beautiful, with waves that fell down her back. She was acutely aware of smells. The scent of roses permeated the room, and she turned away from the mirror to find the source. On the long sink was a dish with beads in it and the scent was coming from there. The dish was hand painted and looked like an antique.

She turned back to the mirror, glanced at

Lourdes, who wasn't paying her any attention, and pressed the neckline of her gown down to the swell of her breasts. Sure enough she had marks there as well. There was even the hint of teeth marks along with finger smudges and more strawberries. She covered her face, feeling color sweeping up her neck to infuse her face with pure embarrassment.

"I need help, Auntie."

She took a deep breath and went over to her niece to help her. Lourdes chattered on the way back to her room and was happy when her clothes were all there, in the dresser as well as in the armoire. There were clothes for Charlotte in the armoire as well, and that *wouldn't* make her happy unless Grace had packed some things for her, but the clothes didn't look like anything she owned. Too expensive. Similar to her things, but not brands she'd ever worn before.

She pressed her hand to trembling lips. She was in way over her head. Men like Tariq Asenguard had women falling at their feet. He was handsome. Mysterious. Wealthy. Sophisticated. Men like him didn't look at girls like her. She had nothing to offer him. She'd had wild sex with him. She remembered the way he made her feel. Just thinking about it sent a spasm through her very core. Thinking about him made her damp. Needy.

Charlotte took a deep breath. She couldn't undo what had happened. It happened. Her hand went to the curve of her breast where she felt achy. Where his mark was. She had to get control and come up with a plan. At least they were all safe for the moment. She didn't understand why her sense of smell was so acute, but she found herself purposefully trying to ferret out the scent of other women who might have come before her. She was certain she was just one of many and he probably wouldn't even remember her name.

"Auntie, I'm hungry." Lourdes tugged on the lacy nightgown.

"I'll bet you are, sweetheart," Charlotte said. "Let's go find the kitchen and get you something to eat." She wasn't going to put on any of those clothes until she had a bath and eased the soreness between her legs.

Genevieve was already in the kitchen drinking a cup of coffee. She looked beautiful. Serene. So Genevieve. She looked up from the glossy magazine she was reading when Charlotte entered with Lourdes. Her smile froze when her gaze centered on Charlotte's neck.

"Oh. My. God." Jumping up, she rounded the table to sweep aside Charlotte's hair. "You are *such* a slut. You have a collar around your neck. Girl, you did the dirty with Tariq Asenguard, didn't you? The most sought-after bachelor in the city."

"You have no idea," Charlotte whispered, trying to motivate Genevieve to do the same.

She rolled her eyes toward Lourdes and hissed her response in a very low tone. "I totally *am* a slut. I couldn't help myself. He's, like, off-the-charts good, and I'm not even exaggerating." The aroma of coffee, usually something she loved, made her slightly nauseous. She pressed a hand to her stomach to quiet its churning.

"What's a slut?" Lourdes asked, clearly paying close attention.

"Your auntie," Genevieve answered. "Her picture is beside the word in the dictionary."

"Vi! Stop. Lourdes, that isn't a good word and we shouldn't have been using it. We're joking, but it isn't appropriate." Charlotte made a face at her best friend, widening her eyes to signal she needed to behave herself.

"Tell me everything, or this child is going to get an education," Genevieve warned, pulling a pan down from where it was hanging over the center aisle. "Get the bacon and eggs out of the refrigerator."

Charlotte did so, wrinkling her nose at the smell of the bacon. She'd never noticed that it was so strong even uncooked. "I don't know how it happened, Vi. Seriously. One moment I walked through the door and the next I was kissing him."

Genevieve mouthed the word *slut*. Charlotte nodded. "With him, totally. I can barely walk this morning and was hoping you'd watch Lourdes while I took a bath." More

160

than anything she needed to inspect the rest of her body for his marks.

"You can barely walk?" Genevieve echoed. "I'm *so* jealous." She expertly broke the shells of the eggs and whipped the mixture as she talked. The smile faded from her face as she really looked at Charlotte. "All kidding aside, are you all right?"

Charlotte touched the tip of her tongue to her bottom lip. She could still feel him there. Taste him in her mouth. The bacon and coffee were seriously making her feel sick. If she didn't escape soon, she might really throw up. Everything in her went still.

"Oh. My. God. Genevieve." She slammed her palm over her mouth as if that could keep her thoughts at bay. Her eyes went wide with shock and she knew she looked stricken. She stepped closer to her friend and lowered her voice even more. "I had unprotected sex. What was wrong with me?"

"What was wrong with him?" Genevieve countered. "Girl, face it, you held out forever, too busy for men and dating, and the first time you decide to indulge had to be crazy wild. But he knows better."

"*I* know better." Charlotte refused to shift the responsibility. "I wasn't thinking. And that bacon is going to make me throw up. I'm not kidding. Will you watch Lourdes just until I can pull myself together?"

"Of course. No problem. We'll eat breakfast

and then go exploring."

"Keep her away from the lake."

"Will do. And Charlie, no one gets pregnant their first time."

Charlotte wished that were the truth. She pressed her hand to her heaving, protesting stomach again and began to back out of the room.

"Wait, hon, I made coffee and he has *great* coffee, a soft brew. The best. Let me get you a cup."

Charlotte shook her head and turned and fled before she vomited all over the floor. What was wrong with her that she hadn't shown one ounce of good sense or discipline? She'd practically thrown herself at the man from the first moment that he'd touched her. Granted, he knew what he was doing. No one got to that level of skill without a *lot* of experience, but still, she had her rules. She wasn't a one-night stand kind of woman.

She locked the bathroom door and turned on the golden faucets. In the small, white, antique cupboard she found bath salts and dumped them liberally into the hot water. What kind of bachelor had scented bath salts in his guest bathroom? One who entertained all the time — that was for certain. She was grateful the fragrance didn't worsen the churning in her stomach; in fact, it seemed to make it a little better.

Waiting for the claw-foot tub to fill, she

162

pulled off her long gown and walked slowly over to the full-length mirror to stare at her body. She felt different. Not just a little different but *very* different. Her body was the same yet not. She had marks and smudges all over her. Little bites and bigger ones. A shiver went through her as she remembered how each of those brands had been placed so deliberately. She'd gloried in that last night. All night. She'd wanted him to mark her. She touched one smudge along her thigh, and instantly her feminine sheath clenched with need. For him. Tariq.

Charlotte cupped her breast, her thumb sliding across her nipple, and instantly she had a vision of his mouth over her soft mound. Sensation followed, the stroking of his fingers, the heat of his mouth, the erotic bite of his teeth. She touched the exact spot where his teeth scraped and bit, sending a streak of lightning straight to her clit. The impression was so real that damp heat collected and her body felt empty and needy all over again.

She wanted him for her lover. For her man. She wanted him to belong to her exclusively. Did men like Tariq Asenguard commit to one woman when they had several clubs and thousands of women to choose from? That was highly unlikely.

She touched the dark strawberry on the swell of her breast. Two tiny puncture wounds from his teeth were there, and once again sensations swamped her. That bite of pain resonated deep inside of her. She gasped as she felt the burn. The need settled into a continuous torture. She would never be free of her hunger for him.

The fragrance of the bath salts helped to soothe her when a part of her wanted to cry. She would never be the same, but did she even want to be? Did she wish she'd never met him — spent a long, beautiful, perfect night with him? Sinking down into the steaming water, she had to admit, she wouldn't have traded the experience for anything. Not. Ever.

She'd felt loved and protected. Safe with him. She'd trusted him with her body. Not just her body, she realized, but with her soul and maybe even her heart. It was impossible to fall for a man she barely knew, but they'd shared such intimacy she felt connected to him in ways she'd never connected to another human being.

The water soothed her body and she closed her eyes to savor the feeling. She was very sore, but every movement was a delicious reminder of his possession. She pulled her legs up and rested her head against the tops of her knees.

She was still tired, almost in a fog, but she couldn't allow herself to take advantage of Genevieve by letting her take charge of

Lourdes's first day at the Asenguard compound. She just needed a few minutes to get herself under control. What was she going to do? You didn't sleep with the boss. Essentially, if she took the job of restoring his carousels — and she wanted the job very, very much; it was her dream job — she couldn't make the mistake of sleeping with the boss.

Of course she hadn't actually accepted the job yet. But she would if she hadn't already blown it. If he had the wooden horses Ricard Beaudet had shown her in the photographs, she *had* to take the job. Ricard had been so excited, believing them to be some of the oldest carousel horses in existence. Where a collector in the United States had gotten such treasures, Ricard didn't know, but he was certain they were authentic. If they were, Charlotte wanted to be the one to restore their splendor to the world, but . . . Her boss. She'd thrown herself at Tariq, and she still wanted him . . . desperately.

"*Almost* desperately," she corrected herself, not believing it, whispering against her knees. He'd kissed her knees. He'd woken her twice more, worshiping her body. There was no other word for it. He'd worshiped her. Slowly. Making her unravel. That had been just as good as the wild — and there had been a *lot* of the wild.

Her body shuddered, remembering the pleasure his mouth and hands brought her,

165

the way his body stretched hers, filling her full, flinging her into a world of pure feeling, over and over again. The kisses. He'd kissed her like he was a starving man, so hungry for her. So worshipping of her. He'd made her feel as if she were the only woman on earth. The only woman for him. Could he do that and walk away from her the next evening?

She needed to know. She had to believe she wasn't just a one-night stand for him. If he could act that well, make her become something she had never imagined, a purely sexual creature, when she knew she wasn't, then he was the greatest actor on the face of the earth.

Charlotte sighed. She couldn't hide forever in the bathtub. The water felt wonderful on her tired, sore body, and the fog was beginning to lift. She glanced toward the window. It was covered with filmy Victorian lace and looked out over the lake. Shrubbery was everywhere, beautifully cared for, but left a little wild. Everything seemed to be a little wild on the property. She'd noted that even when she'd driven in so late and it had been dark. That should have given her a warning.

Sielamet, are you doubting me? Are you sorry you gave yourself to me last night? All night? You swore you were mine. I believed you and woke up happy. Did you?

His voice moved through her mind. Soft. Intimate. Compelling. Was there a note of hurt? Her heart clenched in her chest so hard

166

she pressed her fist to her breast. She would never hurt him, not ever. Not for anything.

I woke up confused and a little scared. She tried thinking the words in her mind. Tried projecting them to him. Instantly she felt the connection between them grow stronger, as if she'd tapped into stored energy — or his mind was just that powerful.

Scared? Of Fridrick? Those men stalking you? They cannot get to you here. Safeguards are in place. The children living here as well as Emeline need to be guarded day and night. They choose to be here because we can protect them. Your friends — Grace, Genevieve — and you as well as little Lourdes are welcome to the same protection, although I am told Grace has refused.

Charlotte hadn't known that. She hadn't checked her phone and Grace was certain to have texted her as to why she didn't want to stay. She had no family and tended to stick with Charlotte and Genevieve. She was younger than them and had taken the job of nanny to Lourdes almost from the time Charlotte's brother had lost his wife. She'd only been nineteen years old.

Charlotte knew she could easily take the out that she was afraid of those pursuing her. It was the truth, but it wasn't the reason she'd woken afraid. She detested lying to him. Twice she started to let him believe that she was concerned for her safety, but the words just wouldn't come.

I didn't want to be a one-night stand. She had no idea how she could talk telepathically to Tariq, but it felt easy. Right. *I've never in my life done anything like that and I don't want you to think . . .*

Do you think that I do not know that? I was with you last night. In your mind. Deep in your body. I know you belong only to me as I belong only to you.

Her eyes went wide with shock. What was he saying? He couldn't be whispering into her mind so intimately what the impression in his own mind was saying. She moistened her lips with the tip of her tongue, her heart pounding fast. An impossibility given the fact that he was so confident, so clearly experienced. She'd seen his picture in tabloids, in magazines. He'd been written up in the society pages of the newspapers. She was misreading what he was saying to her.

There is only you. There has never been another nor will there be. There is only you.

His voice wrapped her up like a gift, soft and caressing, holding her close. Intimately. She felt the brush of his mind in hers. So gentle. She wanted to believe she would be his only, that everything he said to her meant something. She really wasn't a woman who could hook up with a man and go unscathed.

She knew that about herself even in high school. When all her other friends were enjoying one another and relationships, she had felt an aversion to letting men touch her. She thought it was a trust issue, but she'd all but flung herself at Tariq and hadn't even been careful. Or smart. She'd gone against her very own code.

I'm not on birth control, Tariq. I swear I wasn't trying to get pregnant and trap you. I just didn't think about it, but that's no excuse. I want you to know, if something happens, I won't hold you accountable.

Of course I am accountable; it would be my child, too. Do not worry so much over this. I would have known if you could get pregnant.

What does that mean? How could you know something like that?

You are getting cold. Get out of the tub and dry off. I want to show you the carousel horses you will be working on if you take the job.

She realized she *was* getting cold, so much so that she was shivering and the water was uncomfortable. If she could feel his emotions, she knew he could feel hers, but she couldn't feel him physically, so how could he feel her? A hand reached past her, and she had to muffle a small scream as Tariq reached into the rapidly cooling water and pulled the plug.

"I'm naked," she announced, making it a scandalized accusation. She felt breathless, not as shocked as she should have been, nor should she have been so glad to see him. She covered her breasts with her hands and turned to look up at him over her shoulder. That was a *huge* mistake. She was barely able to talk herself out of wanting him when he was away from her and she'd had a little time to think about how crazy she'd acted, but up close, the moment she saw him, the moment his scent filled her lungs, hunger, sharp and terrible, became a brutal need.

Her sex clenched. Went hot. The blood in her veins coursed through her in a rush of heat. Her breasts felt swollen and achy, the need for his mouth, his touch, hitting so fast and hard, tears swam in her eyes. "What did you do to me?" She murmured the question, dazed by her lack of control and the unfamiliar hunger beating at her.

Her hunger or his? She couldn't tell, she was so far under his spell. She could hear his heart beating. The sound was in her head. Thundering in her ears. Her heart followed that steady, rhythmic beat, and then to her horror, the pulse began strong and insistent between her legs. She wanted to put her hand there. Press her fingers deep to feel the beat. To assuage the need that threatened to overwhelm her. "What did you do to me?" she whispered again.

He crouched beside the tub, his fingers under her chin, lifting her face to his. The

170

pad of his thumb slid over her skin, tracing her jaw and sending shivers down her spine with every stroke. "What is it, *sielamet*? Tell me why you have tears in your eyes and I feel your distress beating at me."

He drew her up out of the water, lifting her right over the edge of the tub so that she was standing naked and dripping in the circle of his arms. He seemed uncaring that she was up against his immaculate suit. The one that had to have cost thousands of dollars. Before she could move or protest, he took her arms and wrapped them around his waist, pressing her head against his chest at the same time, her ear right over his heart.

The moment his arms enclosed her, she felt safe and sheltered. She felt secure and a part of him. She closed her eyes on the burn of tears and let him make her feel safe when she hadn't for what seemed a very long time.

"I know, for you, this has happened fast between us, Charlotte," he said, his hand moving through her hair, fingers sliding through the wet silk, spreading the strands out and combing them as he did so. "That does not make it any less real."

It was too real. Too good to be true.

"Have you ever felt this way for anyone else? Because I haven't, Charlotte. Just you. The moment I saw you, I felt different. I saw the world differently. I have searched for you, hoping you were out there somewhere, but not believing I would find you. You're the reason I own the clubs."

She tilted her head to look up at him. He felt solid and very warm. Strangely, she felt warm, no longer covered in water drops from her bath. Even the shivering had stopped. He was magic. The way he made her feel was magic. "Kiss me again, Tariq. I want to know if I dreamt about you kissing me or if it was real."

He didn't hesitate. He bent his head to hers, his lips skimming hers in a barely there caress, but she felt that touch all the way to her toes. Her heart clenched and then her sex did. Her fists bunched in his perfect suit jacket. Held him tighter. Held him closer. Tried to become part of him. That close.

His mouth moved again over hers. Gentle. Coaxing. Not at all like his possessive kisses of the night before, but even so, he owned her with them. Just with his mouth, without all the rest of him, or what or who he was, and that was terrifying beyond anything she'd ever known, even the dangers of Fridrick and the three men stalking her. This was a threat to her heart. To her soul. If she lost him, if it wasn't real, she'd never get over him. Never. She knew that. She also knew it was already too late.

"What did you do to me?" she asked him a third time. He had stolen some part of her, and he'd managed to wind himself around her heart and steal into her soul so she couldn't tell what part of it was hers and what now belonged to him.

His coaxing kiss went from gentle to pure heat in the space of one heartbeat. Her mouth opened automatically under his when his tongue ran along the seam of her lips demanding entry. She gave it to him instantly, just like she'd given him everything else. Instantly. Without thought. There was no thinking when she was melting into him. When his hands slid down her back, taking in the curve of her bottom and going lower until he cupped both bare cheeks and brought her up on her toes so that her mound was pressed tightly against the thick hard bulge his trousers covered.

His kiss turned to pure fire pouring down her throat like lava, melting her insides, wrapping her heart in . . . him. She knew she was giving herself to him and he was claiming her. His kiss said that. It was hard and possessive and even demanding. She gave . . . everything. Everything she was and would ever be. Everything he demanded and even more.

He lifted his head, his eyes dark with desire. With passion. Lust was etched in the lines carved deep, but there was gentleness there and it turned her heart over as nothing else could have.

"You ask me what I have done to you, and

I ask you what you have done to me. I can't think about anything but you."

She liked that. No, she *loved* hearing that. His voice was a smooth silken web she was trapped in. He wrapped her up in all that beautiful silk and velvet, his arms strong and his body hard. He was safety. Heat. Paradise. He could give her everything. She knew that just by kissing him. Her body remembered his and craved him. She had a taste in her mouth, an aphrodisiac that set up a hunger she didn't understand.

He kissed his way down her throat and over the swell of her breast. She felt his breath on that spot, on the mark he'd left on her like a brand. Her sex clenched again, a need so deep she could barely breathe with wanting him. Her hands slid up around his neck, drawing him closer while her own breath hitched in her throat.

His hair was thick. Soft. Her fingers sifted through it and then clenched into fists as she cradled his head while he bit down and the pain lashed through her like a silken whip, striking every nerve ending, sending her crashing into the world of pure feeling.

Her lashes drifted down and she held him to her while his mouth pulled at that spot, tongue moving soothingly while he suckled. His tongue slid over the throbbing pulse as he kissed his way down to her bare breast, drawing her aching, demanding flesh deep into his mouth, his tongue lashing down, pressing, flicking, a weapon of destruction — destroying her. Her body fragmented, came apart, and she could only cling to him as the orgasm took her hard.

His hands pulled at her legs so that she wrapped them around him, locking her ankles at the small of his back. She had the sensation of floating. When she was with him, she couldn't quite orient herself, and even when she tried to lift her lashes, it didn't work. She fought for one moment to be strong, to at least look and see where they were going. He couldn't take her down the hall absolutely naked. And if he took her back to Lourdes's room and the child came in . . .

"See me, *sielamet.*" Tariq whispered the words in her ear even as his body drove hard into hers. The hands on her hips slammed her down over him, and she sheathed him, her tight muscles reluctantly giving way for his invasion.

The air left her lungs in a rush of shock. He was big, pushing through soft folds, a steel intruder that dragged over the bundle of nerves and set every part of her body on fire. Charlotte lifted her lashes instantly, as if by his command; her body suddenly responded when all it really wanted to do was feel. His eyes blazed down into hers. So much heat. So much passion. She would burn forever in his passion, and yet eternity wouldn't be long enough.

Her gaze went from his to the familiar room. It was the room she'd been in with him before. She recognized it, although there were more sconces lit, allowing her to see more detail.

"See *me, sielamet,*" he insisted.

Once again her gaze jumped to his face as he planted one knee on the bed, easily lowering her with one arm, proving his strength. He was as naked as she was, his suit gone and his body hard and powerful, all rippling muscle and driving cock. He never stopped moving and each brutal thrust jolted her body, setting her breasts swaying and lightning radiating from her very core to every single nerve cell in her body, inflaming them.

Her mouth moved over his chest, while her nails scored down his back as he pushed her higher and the wild tension coiled tighter and tighter. She needed . . . so much. That taste in her mouth refused to leave, making her crave him, like some terrible addiction. She nuzzled at the heavy muscles, licked at the spot where she'd left her mark. His hands tightened on her and he groaned softly.

She had the sudden urge to bite him, to leave her mark on him in the way he had her. Before she could, his hand was suddenly in her hair, jerking her head back, and his gaze blazed down into hers.

"You feel this? What we have?" He didn't stop moving, thrusting hard, burying his cock in her over and over, deeply and roughly, as if he wanted to stay inside her for all time. "Charlotte, *sielamet,* you *have* to feel this. You have to know this is real between us. The start of us."

She took a breath. There was no looking away from his eyes, so dark with lust and passion. His desire raw and possessive, but so much more. The *more* caught at her, robbed her of what little air she'd managed to draw in. He looked at her as if she were the only woman in the world. No òne had ever looked at her that way and the thing was — she believed him.

It was incredibly naïve and silly to believe a sophisticated, very wealthy, *gorgeous* man who was photographed with countless women on his arm, but she did.

"Charlotte." He tugged at her hair, a reminder to answer him. All the while his cock slammed home hard, jarring her, sending fire streaking through her and building that volcano inside her so high she thought she might implode. "Do you feel it?"

"Yes." She hissed the word, her need audible.

"Yes what?"

"Yes I feel it," she admitted softly, because it was the stark truth. "The beginning of you and me."

Satisfaction etched into the handsome face, and gentled the blaze in his eyes.

She couldn't lean in to kiss him, because he still had a fistful of her hair. The sharp bite in her scalp drove her a little mad for him. "You are so beautiful." She gave him that because she had to. She had to tell him. It wasn't just his physical looks — and truthfully, he'd been gifted far beyond the normal — it was what she found in his mind.

He had a protective streak a mile wide. Maybe more. The children on his property, the older couple, Emeline, even his partner and his partner's woman, all were family to him. He had added to that growing list Genevieve and Lourdes, and especially her. She was his number-one priority, but he would never let the others down. She couldn't see beyond that, but that trait, that unswerving loyalty and protective instinct appealed to her as nothing else could.

Then she couldn't think. Couldn't talk. He changed the angle of his hips and the friction was exquisite. Perfect.

"With me," he ordered softly.

She did exactly as he demanded and she wasn't certain she had anything to do with the decision. It was his voice. The buildup until the tension was unbearable. Wanting to please him. Wanting him to give her that much pleasure. At the sound of his low command, her body came apart, taking his with it. The burn was fierce and unrelenting. She keened his name as the firestorm swept through her, her gaze held captive by his. She saw and felt the pleasure sweeping through him, pure bliss, throwing them both into a place they drifted together, a kind of paradise she found there in his eyes.

They remained locked together for some time until reality began to encroach. She heard the sound of a child's laughter. Little Lourdes. Charlotte loved her laugh. The murmur of Genevieve's voice, soft, teasing, imploring her to finish eating or she'd make the child do the dishes. More laughter. Lourdes didn't buy it. But hearing them meant they were close to the kitchen, and she was stark naked. More, she'd had unprotected sex again.

"Don't." It was an order. His fist tightened in her hair. "I told you, you will *not* get pregnant. I'm clean and so, obviously, are you. We're together. A new beginning. I'm not going anywhere, so let yourself enjoy what we have when we manage to have it. Lourdes is already asking for you in spite of your friend trying to distract her."

"Oh, no. I've got to get up." She pushed at his chest to move him, but it was like trying to move a heavy oak tree. He didn't budge. She tried to look away, but he shook his head.

"You're doing it again, trying to put distance between us so you can talk yourself out of what happened. Not this time. We're together. We. Are. *Together.* You realize you have to get over panicking every time I touch you like this."

"I know. I do. It's just that I don't think when you're around. My brain doesn't work. I felt you carrying me, but we went through the house with me naked. Anyone could have seen us. Lourdes could have . . ."

"I don't share. Not. Ever. We're on the top floor and no one saw me carry you here — I made certain of that. I will always protect you, Charlotte. In every way. I have clothes here you can get into, but first I need the truth about how sore you are."

She blushed at that. Of course she was sore. He was still inside her, stretching her even though he was only half hard, but it would be embarrassing telling him that.

"Not embarrassing. Talk to me. I don't want to take from you what you aren't willing to give me, but in matters of safety and health, I have no choice."

She didn't understand that, but he was right. If a relationship between them was going to work out, she had to be able to communicate with him about every subject — especially sex. "I'm sore. Definitely. But I like knowing why." That was truthful and still a little embarrassing, but she managed to keep her gaze on his.

"I can take the sting away."

180

Reluctantly he opened his fist and allowed her hair to fall loose down her back. She hadn't remembered him taking the topknot out, but then she didn't remember him carrying her up to the third floor. She'd been that far gone. He slid out of her and then pressed his palm to her mound. For a moment there was intense heat. She swore she felt him moving in her. Not him. He was right there, solid and real, but when she looked at his eyes, he seemed to have "checked out." And then she blinked and he was back.

"Still as sore?"

She wasn't. "Oh. My. God. You have the gift of healing. Not only are you telepathic, but you actually can heal."

"A little," he admitted. "I have a couple of gifts. I'm not as good at healing as a couple of others I know, but it gets me by." He eased off of her and stood, pulling her up with him. "The bathroom is through that door if you want to clean up, and I put clothes right there on the chair for you. You can get dressed up here."

"Where did these clothes come from, Tariq? Because I didn't buy them." She touched the striped royal blue bra and the matching lace panties. She could never afford anything like the lingerie he gave her. The jeans were soft and fit like a glove when she drew them up over her hips. The thin camisole was formfitting, a little tighter than she was used to wearing, and emphasized her curves while drawing attention to her narrow rib cage and smaller waist. She didn't want to point out that, although beautiful, the camisole fit in a way she was certain drew attention to her hips and butt.

"A friend owns a boutique. I called her with your sizes last night. I was worried about you going back to your house in order to get more clothes so I had some delivered in your size, Genevieve's and Lourdes's. That way, your three stalkers as well as Fridrick won't have the chance of trailing you back here. They aren't going to think to look for you here. Without you going in and out often, that minimizes the danger to everyone else."

She hadn't thought of that — bringing danger to the others who lived there. She didn't like the very real possibility nor did she like that she hadn't thought of it herself. She actually felt the color drain from her face. "Maybe I should . . ."

"Don't say it," he chastised, slipping his arm around her waist. "Fridrick and Vadim are after the children and Emeline. By being here, you haven't increased the danger. And no, I'm not reading your mind, but your expression is transparent. You aren't paying for the clothes, either. It was my decision to purchase them. I didn't consult with you, so that's on me."

He nuzzled her neck, and truthfully, every

protest died just like that, with his lips on her. He took her hand once she was dressed. Strangely, she hadn't seen him dress, but he was back in his immaculate suit as they went downstairs together.

7

Bella was a beautiful little girl, just as short as Lourdes, who had the Vintage disadvantage of being in the lowest percentile for height, but not so much for weight. The two little girls were instant best friends and right now they were each clinging tightly to one of Tariq Asenguard's hands and chattering a mile a minute about hunting for trolls or zombies down by the lake in very excited voices. Charlotte *loved* that for Lourdes. The child had lost her father and had been placed with her aunt and then moved over and over before they could set down roots anywhere.

The property couldn't have been any prettier. To a child of three, the trees, shrubbery and flowers along with the gleaming blue lake and fairytale outbuildings had to be a wonderland. There was a covered patio with an outdoor kitchen and comfortable chairs, but it was the old-fashioned carousel that caught her eye. This one was an early Herschell-Spillman Company carousel made in the

United States, and it was amazing. Completely restored. Clearly it worked, and she longed to rush over and take a good look at it, but to her shock, she found watching Tariq with two three-year-olds took priority.

"Oh. My. God. You are so far gone it isn't funny," Genevieve said. The teasing note in her voice disappeared. "Seriously honey, I'm happy for you. I am. But you have to be careful. He's . . . *experienced,* and you're not. You don't let people in. Especially men. I've gotten to know you very well, and you're the type of woman who will give her heart completely to one man and if he breaks it, it will stay broken. You haven't known him more than one night. You didn't take the time, and you're falling too fast. Way too fast. You've already broken every single one of your rules. You don't sleep with a man casually, and you've already slept with him."

Charlotte ducked her head. Genevieve wasn't telling her anything she didn't already know. She even nodded a couple of times to indicate to her friend that she heard and agreed. "I know," she admitted, and risked a quick glance at Tariq again.

He had his head turned, looking back at them as if he knew what Genevieve was saying to her. The expression on his face made him look dangerous.

It is the beginning of us.

She took a breath and pressed her hand to

her suddenly churning stomach. It was a declaration inside her head. A decree. A red flag in the mind of a modern woman who would define him as a textbook dominant stalker type. His voice was implacable. He had flicked a glance at Genevieve that frankly chilled Charlotte.

Bella said something and he instantly turned his attention to the child, crouching down to her level, circling her with one strong arm and nodding his head at something she said. "Of course I can take you out in the boat, but not tonight, my little Bellarina."

His name for her sent Bella into laughter, which made Lourdes laugh. Charlotte had wanted this for the child. She was naturally upbeat and happy, but the events of the last few months had taken a toll on her.

"Stop looking at him as if he's the greatest thing in the entire world and start listening to me," Genevieve insisted. She put a hand on Charlotte's arm. "You're getting in over your head. We met the man last night under extreme circumstances. He was heroic and gallant standing up for us. He offered a place to stay and I have to say the accommodations are perfect, and the security seems tight, but still, Charlie, *we just met him.* I don't know what happened after I went to bed, but it happened fast and that means he's a very smooth operator with the emphasis on *very.*"

Why do you allow her to go on and on? You

know we are good. I am not the man she claims
I am. Send her away.

Charlotte risked another glance at him. He wasn't looking at her this time. He had taken the girls to the small playground on the property and was pushing them on swings. His home had everything they could possibly need — or want. Although his jaw was set and he looked dangerous, his voice was gentle as he answered each child when she shouted orders to him. There was even a note of laughter in his voice as the girls continued to yell for him to push them higher.

She sighed. She was going to have to answer him and that meant speaking intimately, on that strange pathway that he'd evidently forged between them. She knew every time she used it she was bound closer to him. She didn't understand it and when she was apart from him, it didn't make sense to her, but the connection between them was stronger — and better — than anything she'd ever shared with anyone. When he was touching her, holding her, it all made sense, but then logic and reasoning crept in when he wasn't right there.

Tariq, what can I say? Everything she says to me is the truth. She's my friend and she's trying to look out for me. As my friend, she should point these things out to me. That's what true friends do. They try to keep you from fall-

187

ing too hard.

Do you believe I would hurt you? Break your heart? Sielamet, you are everything to me. I would never harm you. It is impossible for me to do so. I know this happened far too fast for you to believe strongly in it or in me, but you promised to give me a chance.

She was in his mind and there was something there, a hint of danger, of warning she couldn't quite catch, as if she was missing a very important piece of a puzzle, but it was so small it seemed inconsequential. Whatever it was made her uneasy.

I'm giving us a chance. I'm still here. If I didn't plan to give us a chance, I would have already packed up Lourdes and we'd be gone.

She had nowhere to take her niece that was safe. Nowhere. They had enemies, and they had no idea why. A serial killer and three stalkers who went around staking their victims, so they were serial killers as well.

They believe in vampires.

"Are you paying attention, Charlie? Because we have to discuss this," Genevieve persisted.

Carrying on two conversations was a bit disorienting, but what Tariq said made sense. The three men from the club staked their victims while they were alive, as if that was the only method of killing them. She shuddered and wrapped her arms around her middle. She should introduce them to Frid-

188

rick. He had admitted he'd killed Genevieve's grandmother and the others in Paris in a bizarre blood-taking fashion and then gone to the United States to kill Charlotte's brother. *What is going on?* How could she remove Lourdes from Tariq's home when it was the only place she'd been so far where she felt safe at all?

"Charlie," Genevieve snapped. "I'm telling you, he's a player. That's straight. I didn't want to say it like this but you won't listen. He's going to find another woman tonight, or some other night, and bring her home and make her feel like she's the only one. You can't invest in him like this."

He hadn't brought another woman into his home. Her sense of smell was heightened, very acute. There was no way he could have removed a woman's presence completely — especially her scent. He had said he had never brought a woman there and she believed him absolutely. Still . . . Genevieve was not wrong that she was investing too much in him too soon.

"I'm listening to you, Vi, I am," Charlotte said. "But it's already too late. I'm so far gone on him there's no turning back. My heart is already involved. I don't know why or how this happened so fast, but I'm going to ride it out and see what happens. I would like to have you close for support no matter which way it goes."

Genevieve sighed and then looked up to watch Tariq, now helping the girls on the slide. "He is gorgeous, Charlie, I'll give you that. If you're going to be slutty and sleep with someone within a couple of hours of meeting them, he's definitely the one to do it with. He's sort of . . . delicious."

Charlotte burst out laughing. "You can't go to extremes. Don't be drooling over my man."

"He's definitely drool-worthy. I could do a lot of perving on him."

"Well don't." Charlotte faked a stern look. "You'll have to find someone else for your pervy ways."

It wouldn't be difficult for Genevieve. She was a man magnet. It had surprised her that Tariq hadn't even glanced at her friend when every other man focused on Genevieve first. Always. Until last night and Tariq. That pleased her when she realized it, because it only made Tariq's attention more real. From the very beginning, he had looked at Charlotte with the look a man gives to a woman who appeals to him.

Sielamet.

His voice. Gentle. Male amusement. A caress. He could do so many things with that one word spoken in his language.

There is no other woman. There will be no other woman. It is you. Only you. Always you. You are in my care and under my protection. I will cherish you for all time.

190

Charlotte frowned. She'd heard those words before. Whispered to her, first in his language and then in hers. The memory was hazy, but beautiful. She felt the slide of his hair against her bare skin. Felt his mouth moving over her. Kissing her. Following the curve of her breast. She touched the mark he'd left behind, only the thin camisole covering her skin. The brand pulsed there. Throbbed. Needed. Suddenly the taste of him was in her mouth and she craved him.

When she looked up, he was watching her with hooded eyes. His handsome face was very serious. He seemed wholly focused on her.

What is it, Charlotte?

I can't remember everything about last night. Just pieces of it. Pieces of perfection. His body moving in hers. The feel of his mouth on her skin. Between her legs. His taste. The memories sent heat spiraling through her.

You were exhausted, sielamet. I should have taken greater care, but I couldn't seem to resist you.

I didn't want you to resist me. That was the truth and maybe it wasn't such a good idea to give him that, but she couldn't help herself.

Lourdes turned around and looked at her. She tugged at her hand until Tariq let her go and then she flung her arms wide and ran to Charlotte. "Auntie, I *love* it here. And I love Bella. She's my best friend."

191

Charlotte couldn't help but marvel at how perfectly Lourdes enunciated each word. There was no baby talk. Her father had called Charlotte constantly with anecdotes about how verbal and precocious Lourdes was. Charlotte found it to be true. It hadn't been her brother's wishful thinking; Lourdes really was extremely verbal and her comprehension blew Charlotte away.

She caught the little girl and swung her around. "I love it here, too, baby. And Bella is the best." What could she say? It was all true.

"Can we stay? I want to stay."

She glanced at Genevieve, who had gone very still, and then at Tariq, who was striding toward them, Bella on his shoulders. He was tall and powerful although he wore his suit like a model. Perfection. She had committed to him. It felt like that, as if she was totally bonded to him. Connected.

You gave me your word that you would try us. That we had a beginning.

She nodded. She wanted that beginning with him. She hoped for a future with him. Right here, on this amazing piece of property. Genevieve's face told her it was too soon. Too fast. But that she'd support Charlotte's decision.

"Yes, honey, I think we're going to stay for a while."

"Bella has a cool house and a brother and

192

two sisters. When am I going to get a brother or sister?"

"That may take a little time," Charlotte hedged, blushing for no reason. If she was going to continue to burn in paradise with Tariq, she needed to be responsible and get on birth control. Not that she would mind having his baby. A child with his hair and eyes. She could go for that. Just not now. Not when their beginning was so new.

But a child would be with her long after he left her, a little voice whispered to her. She knew she would have him for a while. Maybe even a long while, but eventually, he would leave her and find another woman. One that suited him better. A woman like Genevieve. Tall. Model thin. Glossy straight hair. A face that any photographer would fall to his knees and worship.

I prefer short with lots of soft curves. I love long, wild hair that goes on forever and shows me just how wild my woman can be. I love every single thing about you, although we need to work a little on your confidence. You are my woman. My choice. I am your man. Your choice. You never have to worry that I will leave you. At this point, I don't have that same assurance. Your fear that you may be making a mistake actually makes me feel off-balance and vulnerable. Both emotions I have never felt.

He stood in front of her, Bella on his

shoulders, the child waving and shouting at Lourdes, her face lit up and happy. Tariq smiled at Lourdes. "I thank you for being a good friend to Bella. She was very sad for a while and now you have made her happy again. See . . ." He gestured toward the gatehouse where Bella's brother, Danny, and her two sisters, Amelia and Liv, had come out and were working their way toward them. "Her brother and sisters cannot believe she is once again laughing. We thought, for a short time, we had lost that."

Lourdes frowned, trying to process what he said. "Bella likes to laugh. So do I."

"We like to hear you laugh," he assured her.

Lourdes, Genevieve and Charlotte had slept all day. Charlotte had put it down to the fact that they'd been up all night, but the three older children approaching them looked as if they'd just gotten up and showered. Maybe because Tariq was so charismatic those on his property kept his hours.

Tariq reached for her hand as the three siblings arrived. "I'd like you to meet Charlotte and Genevieve, Charlotte's good friend. You've already met Lourdes this evening. Danny, did you eat? I sent dinner for the four of you, but Bella said she didn't eat." Tariq's voice was man-to-man.

Clearly Tariq regarded Danny as the head of his family. The boy was fifteen years old, the girls younger, so Charlotte was going to give Tariq that for the moment, but why were they living in a house by themselves? Why weren't they in the main house with Tariq? They were too young to be without supervision. She was going to address that as soon as possible. It wasn't even legal.

"It's been difficult to get Bella to eat anything at all, Tariq," Danny said, rubbing his thumb across his forehead in a gesture of distress. "She's been so quiet, and she's still having very bad dreams."

"Not as many," Amelia added hastily when Tariq frowned. She was fourteen. "But it's only been a couple of weeks. I'm surprised with everything she went through that she's not having more."

Tariq turned to Liv. The child was ten, and she was deathly pale. Her eyes were sunken in and she had both arms as well as part of her torso swathed in gauze. She looked terrified. Tariq reached down and slowly extended his hand toward her face. Her eyes widened and her body shuddered.

"I'm just going to touch you, *csecsemő,* just your face. You will feel better. Remember my touch, Liv? It makes you feel better and chases the nightmares away."

She nodded but didn't take her eyes from him, her entire body shuddering, much like a wild animal cornered and ready to fight — or flee. Charlotte wanted to gather her into her arms and hold her close. Clearly the child

195

had been terribly traumatized. Charlotte looked at Danny. The look in his eyes was far too old for a boy his age. He wasn't jumping around with pent-up energy, or cracking jokes; he was watching his younger sister with an expression close to tears.

She turned her attention to Amelia. She also was not an ordinary young teen. She was very subdued and far too much the mother, hovering close to her younger sister while keeping an eye on Bella, who was still on Tariq's shoulder.

Fascinated, Charlotte watched Tariq's hand cup the side of Liv's face, featherlight. A gentle caress. At the same time, he closed his eyes and went very still. She could almost feel the heat emanating from him, moving through his body and into Liv's. She visibly relaxed. Some of the terrible tension drained out of her face. Her body stopped shuddering and stood still beneath his touch. Clearly Tariq's gift was far greater than he'd made it out to be. He had a way of bringing peace and healing to those needing it, and these children clearly did.

Charlotte found it telling that the children, even Bella, made no sound while Tariq's hand was on Liv. Even Lourdes fell silent, something that rarely happened. Genevieve watched from a short distance away, not moving or speaking. It was as if Tariq had them all under his spell — and it was spellbinding to watch him work his healing magic.

She fell harder for him in that moment. It was the way he was so gentle when he touched the children or spoke to them. It was the way he crouched down in front of Bella and Lourdes when he talked to them. The way he showed patience for and interest in everything the two little girls had to say. She admired the way he spoke to Danny, making him feel as if he was on the same level. Watching over the family together.

"Better, *csitri*?"

Liv nodded. "It doesn't burn as much."

"Are you sleeping at all?"

Charlotte loved the complete focus he gave the child, and more, she loved that the other children clearly were happy with her getting his complete attention. There didn't seem to be jealousy or any vying for Tariq's attention.

"A little. I read. Thank you for the iPad. It helps when I can't sleep. I read the books you put on there for me."

"Good girl. I do want you to sleep, though, so we're going to have another healing session. I am going to bring in a counselor, someone for you to talk to . . ."

Liv gasped and shook her head, stepping back. "No. No, Tariq. I don't want to talk to anyone else. Just you. Only you. I can't talk about it unless you're there to make it all go away."

Charlotte's heart turned over. Clearly the

trauma was very, very bad. The child needed help, but she didn't think pressuring her was the way to go. *She's terrified, Tariq. Don't make her go yet. She needs you to be her rock until she can get some relief.*

She won't get relief without talking to a professional.

What happened to her?

Fridrick and his friends happened to her. They had Amelia, Liv and Bella. They were holding them underground and experimenting, torturing them. They weren't the only ones. One of my friends had been taken prisoner as well. I cannot begin to describe the horror they've been through.

Instinctively she knew that was why the children were with him and not in other foster homes. Most likely they would have been separated, and no one else was going to understand what they'd gone through.

How can I help?

"Liv, this is Lourdes's aunt Charlotte. Like you, she has had a brush with a killer. He took her brother, Lourdes's father, and a friend. Genevieve" — he indicated Charlotte's friend — "lost her grandmother and a boyfriend. It isn't the same, but they know how bad it can be. Charlotte, Genevieve and Lourdes will be staying with us."

Liv was silent for what seemed a very long moment and then her lashes lifted and she looked Charlotte directly in the eyes. "It's safe here. *He* makes it safe." She stepped closer to Tariq and wrapped her arm around his leg. He can help you sleep, and he'll help Lourdes. Bella's nightmares aren't as bad."

As Liv circled Tariq's leg with her arm, Danny and Amelia gasped.

It is the first time she has voluntarily touched me herself. It is a good sign.

Poor baby. You are going to have to tell me exactly what happened to her. My friend Grace actually has studied to be a child psychologist. She chose not to stay, but it's possible she would come back if I asked.

"But she isn't eating," Charlotte said gently, keeping the attention on Liv. She was instantly worried about her. Something in her eyes made Charlotte afraid for her. She was only ten, but she looked as if she'd seen too much and didn't want to see anything else ever again. "Are you?" Charlotte hadn't eaten that evening, either, and the thought of food made her stomach churn. She pressed her hand in deep and breathed away the nausea.

Liv looked up at Tariq and then down to the ground, shaking her head. "I can't. It makes me sick to eat."

Charlotte's gaze jumped to Tariq's. *She isn't going to make it if something isn't done soon, Tariq. I think she's contemplating . . .*

Throwing herself in the lake. I know. I can

read minds, remember?

What are you going to do? Something had to be done to save the child. *A hospital? A good doctor might help.*

Not for this. When we're alone, I'll tell you what happened to her and how I intend to help her. For now, I'm just giving her little boosts. But I need her to eat. She needs to get her strength up. They all do, all four of them. None of them are really eating. I tried to distance them from the memory of what happened, but they're all resistant, especially Liv.

"Sometimes I feel sick when I think about food, too," Charlotte admitted. "Still, I have to eat in order to be strong and take care of Lourdes. Bella, Amelia and Danny need you to be strong."

Liv shook her head. "Danny and Amelia can take care of Bella."

"Not without you," Amelia said, panic in her voice.

They all knew. Charlotte glanced up at Tariq. These children had a psychic connection. She had gifts. Genevieve did. Tariq did as well. She remembered Emeline telling her about going for testing at a psychic center in the United States with her "sister" Blaze. She was obviously gifted as well.

Tariq nodded, encouraging her to connect the dots.

Is everyone living on this property gifted in

200

some way? Even the older couple? The Waltons?

He nodded again, his eyes cool, watching her. All the while he stroked Liv's hair, murmuring softly to her. The little girl clung tighter and Bella screeched and tried to get him to take her for a "horsey" ride.

Charlotte looked around again. The property was beautiful, rolling and green, an oasis surrounded by a very high fence. It wasn't the fence that kept danger out, she was certain of that. At first glance that's what it appeared, but she was learning to see with more than her eyes. She felt a ripple of power anytime she came close to the fence. She glanced at Tariq again, raising her eyebrow in question.

Safeguards. I've placed them all along the lakefront as well so that if Liv or any of the children get too close without someone watching them — and we want eyes on them at all times — then the safeguards come into play and warn them off.

She didn't altogether understand how that would work. *An alarm?*

Anyone trying to penetrate the safeguards will run into a shield and yes, we will be alerted.

Around her, Genevieve and Lourdes talked with Danny and Amelia. Liv didn't look at anyone other than Tariq, with the exception of the occasional quick look at Charlotte. The

201

little girl took a deep breath. "Are you Tariq's girlfriend?"

Instantly everyone went silent and stared at her. She opened her mouth to answer in the negative. She didn't really know what she was to him. His lover? What would she call herself?

"In my country, with my people, Charlotte would be called *avio päläfertiilam,* which means my lifemate. She is more than a girlfriend to me. Much more." Tariq caught Bella in both hands and swung her expertly to the ground. It was clear he'd done that maneuver more than once.

"Does that mean you like her . . . a lot?" Liv persisted.

"Yes," Tariq answered.

"If she doesn't like us, do we have to leave?" That was from Danny, who studiously avoided looking at her.

Charlotte's breath caught in her throat. They were all worried about losing their home and Tariq, their safety net. Because of her. She shook her head. "First, I like all of you already. Bella has made my Lourdes laugh and be happy again, something I couldn't do for her. I would never want you to lose your home, nor can I imagine Tariq turning his back on you for a woman. If a woman asked him to do that, she wouldn't be worth anything to him and I would hope he'd dump her immediately. More, if Tariq

202

told you that you were part of his family and he has given you a place to live under his protection, he would never be anything but loyal to you."

She knew with every cell in her body that was the truth about the man. She felt things now, especially anything to do with Tariq, as though they were connected; she knew him inside and out. He was a man of his word and he was extremely loyal. She wanted the children to know that much about him because it was clear they needed stability. She intended to ask Tariq a lot of questions.

"Really, Tariq?" Amelia asked for confirmation.

The children still looked as if they were holding their collective breath. Their fear beat at her. Tariq slipped his arm around her waist, still touching Liv, consoling her with one hand stroking caresses in her hair, a soothing action meant to keep her from bolting. He tugged at Charlotte until she was beneath his shoulder, her front tight against his side. Without warning, they were all connected. Tariq to Liv, Tariq to Charlotte, Tariq the conduit between them.

Images arose, so terrible, so disturbing, at first Charlotte didn't believe they could be real. They were images from a really bad horror film. A monster of a creature crouched over Liv in a small room. There were cages in that room, cages where children were kept, a cage where a man was kept, a man bloody and tortured. Liv lay on the floor, and the thing with blazing red eyes and sharp, serrated teeth tore at her little body, ripping chunks of flesh from her, trying to devour her alive.

It couldn't have happened. Not for real. Not to that beautiful child with the pale face and bandages everywhere. She hadn't screamed. Hadn't cried out. Her older sister was locked in a cage in the other room and if the monster didn't get Liv, he would go after Amelia. Bella was in another cage close by, but not close enough for the girls to touch. Liv was terrified, and she knew she would be eaten alive, but she refused to scream. She didn't want the baby to know monsters ate little girls.

The monster's face was distorted. His skin on one side appeared to have melted and his flesh just sloughed off. One eye hung half in and half out of the socket. What was left of his hair fell in long, dank dreads. He had Liv's blood smeared all over his mouth and chin. Up this close she could see flesh in his teeth.

Charlotte's stomach lurched. This was too real. It had to have happened. There were too many details. *How did she get away?* Tariq had shown her what had happened, shown her the terrible damage that had been done to this child both physically and psychologically. How could she possibly recover? How could any of the children? She could barely believe what she'd seen. She didn't want to believe it.

Maksim's lifemate, Blaze, and Emeline went in after them. We were still a distance away and trying to get to them fast. Danny had the courage to take Blaze and Emeline down into the tunnels after them. Blaze fought the puppet and Liv got herself out, running when Blaze ordered her to. It was very hard on Liv. She was terrified and hurt. She'd lost a great deal of blood. The blood of a puppet is foul, and at first she wouldn't allow me to help her. She got an infection and I had no choice. I tried to build a relationship first, but in matters of safety or health, I had to just do what was necessary.

Charlotte's fist bunched in his shirt. He was a good man. He'd taken on a lot when he'd given the children a home. The responsibility was enormous.

They still need parents, Tariq. Someone to watch over them.

They have parents. Me. And eventually, you.

She gasped and then jammed her fist into her mouth to keep from shouting at him. *Are you crazy? I've only had Lourdes a few weeks, and I don't know what to do with her. I have no idea what I'm doing. I don't know the first thing about children.*

You will be able to read their minds.

He sounded calm and confident, as if it were normal to expect your lover to take on four traumatized children.

You'll know what they need.

Unlike you, I can't read minds. This is so far out of my wheelhouse I don't even know what to say to you right now.

"You don't want us?" Liv asked aloud.

Charlotte went very still. Genevieve had once again engaged the children in conversation, as if she knew something was going on between Charlotte and Tariq. At Liv's question, all voices ceased speaking.

"Of course I want you," Charlotte assured, feeling trapped. She did want the children, but these children needed far more help than she could ever give them. "I'm not qualified . . ."

"Yes you are," Liv said in a voice far too old for her age. "With Tariq connecting us, I see into your mind, and you can help us if you want to do it."

Charlotte had no idea what that meant. She hadn't been able to help Lourdes or Genevieve or even herself. How could she possibly help traumatized children recover from such a nightmare? She rested her cheek against Tariq's rib cage. He seemed so sure of himself, so certain he had a way to help the children. If he did, he needed to let her in on it, because she was feeling overwhelmed.

"Liv," Tariq said gently. "I'm going to take

Charlotte into the basement, where the carousel horses that need restoration are. Everything is going to be all right. Can you get through another evening?"

Liv nodded. "I want to visit Emeline. She helps."

"She's dark inside," Amelia protested. "That doesn't help you, Liv."

"I'm dark inside," Liv said. "Not the same as Emme, but she understands. No one else feels this inside me."

"I do," Tariq said, intervening between the siblings. "I feel it. I know it's there, crouching close, trying to swallow you. I know you're fighting as hard as you can. Amelia, if Emeline helps her get through a night, you need to let her go visit."

Amelia shook her head and took a step toward her younger sister. Instantly Liv transferred her hold from Tariq to Amelia.

"Come with me, then. Emeline can use company," Liv invited.

"I have to watch Bella," Amelia said.

"I can do that," Genevieve volunteered. "I'm taking Lourdes back to the play yard while Tariq talks jobs with Charlotte. Bella can come with us if she wants."

"Danny?" Amelia asked.

Danny nodded slowly. "Go with her, Amelia. Let's just get her through each night any way we can. I'll help Genevieve with Bella and Lourdes."

207

"Liv," Tariq said in his soft, persuasive, spellbinding voice. "You have to eat. I've given you help, but you need to actually try. It won't taste good and you'll feel sick, but it will stay down. In order for me to help you, you have to be strong enough. You understand? You know what I'm saying to you. Don't think you can take the easy way out. Together we'll get through this. All of us."

Tears swam in the child's eyes but she blinked them away and nodded slowly. "I'll eat. Just not meat, Tariq. I can get the broth down."

"Broth it is," he said. "Emeline will have some at her house. Amelia will see to it that you eat this evening." He held the child's eyes until she nodded a second time, clearly capitulating, falling under his spell just like Charlotte did.

Tariq took her hand and tugged, taking her away from the little group. "That's my family. The children."

"Tariq, what in the world are you going to do with them?"

"Give them time to process what happened to them and build them up as much as I can before I bring them fully into my world."

"I don't understand." And she didn't. His world? Weren't they already in it?

"The children are still in danger, as are you and Lourdes and your friend Genevieve. They know that, and they also know it's safer here than anywhere else." He led her back in the direction of the house.

"I don't understand any of this, Tariq. What's happening between us, the children, why those awful men are stalking us, Fridrick." He wasn't really answering her questions.

"It's happening to you because you're gifted. Genevieve's gifted. Lourdes is or Fridrick would have killed her."

"He said she was bait."

"You would have come home for your brother's funeral regardless. He knew that. Lourdes has some sort of psychic ability or she wouldn't be alive. Danny, Amelia, Liv and Bella do as well. Whatever his reasons, Fridrick and the others he works with want to acquire those gifts through you."

"Emeline?"

For the first time Tariq hesitated. "Emeline is complicated," he said finally. "She's got a strong psychic gift, and more than any other, she is in trouble. It is necessary for her to stay here to be safe. She will welcome friends. She needs them." His hand stroked a caress through her hair. "I guess we all need you, Charlotte."

She liked the feeling of his fingers in her hair, but it didn't ease her fears. She had no idea how to help any of these traumatized people, not even Lourdes. Not even herself.

8

Charlotte stared in total awe at the collection of carousel horses in the basement. Tariq Asenguard was a serious collector. Most were European, but like the carousel on his patio, there were two other American ones.

"Museums don't have such beautiful works," she whispered reverently. "Tariq, where did you get these? Ricard went his entire life looking for just one of the original carved horses used for training noblemen in the art of ring spearing during tournaments, and you have four of them."

"I have always been interested in carousel horses, the origins and how they evolved. The first carousels were necessarily different from the ones today, but no less intriguing and fun, maybe even more so."

Tariq sounded far away, as if he were back in time with the French some three hundred years earlier. Charlotte turned to look at his face. Clearly he had thought a lot about what had transpired. He looked as if he was remembering rather than thinking about what it would have been like.

"In the early eleven hundreds, the Turks and Arabs played a game, although they weren't really messing around. They were deadly serious about their game. The Italians and Spaniards referred to the game as 'little war' and that's where the term *carosella* came from. The carousel was born right there, but no one had a clue how it would evolve, or even that women and children would find great enjoyment on it. I love that the carousel came about with the idea of training men for warfare and ended up being something special for everyone to enjoy and relax around," Tariq said.

Charlotte had always loved that fact as well. She'd been drawn to the history of the carousel just as Tariq was. They had that in common. She loved the individual artwork on the carved wooden horses. The detail, as if the artist had taken such care to make each piece something special even knowing the nobleman training on it might not ever notice. The carvers were the artists, men exposing small bits of their souls while they worked.

"I love that you know that," Charlotte admitted. "They didn't have the tools to work with back then that we do now, but still, they were meticulous in their work. Ricard had a theory that the earliest horses were carved by

211

a single man. Two at the most. The horses were different, but the technique, the care and attention to detail, was so perfect that he doubted more than one man would have that ability."

"I would have liked to have met Ricard Beaudet. I always looked forward to our correspondence. I don't care to talk on the phone, so he obliged me by writing. I felt as if we had a lot in common." He looked down at her. "He told me about you. He was very proud of you and the work you did. He said the pupil had exceeded the master in skill."

Charlotte shook her head. "Ricard was very modest, but he was the best in the world. If you wanted your carousel restored right, to the absolute glory it once had, you asked for him."

"Which is exactly why I did. His reputation was impeccable."

Charlotte stepped down into the sunken room. The basement extended throughout the length of the house. Although it was one large room, there were several half walls that made the space appear to be a giant maze. Carousel horses of every era dominated the room, but the half walls separated them by age. There was a work space with all kinds of tools and paints. Carving tools. Old paints made from leaves and flowers. Everything anyone loving carousels could possibly want or use.

Charlotte looked over her shoulder at Tariq. "You carve."

He shrugged. "I find it satisfies something in me I can't define. There's a kind of peace in carving. The wood shavings curling, the block of wood taking shape, the detail. I feel as though I can take an inanimate piece of wood and bring it to life. I like it." He sent her a self-deprecating grin. "I can't say I'm all that good at it, so don't examine mine too closely. But I like carving."

Charlotte loved the expression on his face. He was so handsome with his long, thick, very dark hair and his gemlike blue eyes. Gorgeous. All man. Sophisticated. Yet he would sit down in his basement, using his hands to create something beautiful. He really loved the carousels just as she did; she could hear it in his voice. She liked being able to breathe life back into them, and clearly he liked creating the life in them.

"I name them," he blurted out, admitting something he clearly thought was crazy. "The older ones. I like to name them."

"Because they seem real," she murmured. "That's beautiful."

"It's insane. I don't let the children down here," he said, suddenly all business.

She was fairly certain he was embarrassed by his admission, but it endeared him to her even more.

"There are too many ways they could hurt

themselves. My tools, the horses themselves. The oldest are still wrapped." He indicated the section closest to his workstation. "I bought those from a collector's estate recently. They're the ones I wrote to Ricard about. The collector, Paul Emery, had pictures of them, and some of the wood has deteriorated as well as the original paint. Paul bought the horses and chariots for his daughter. He apparently hung the four horses up on his porch for her and her friends to use. His wife died in a car accident right after his little girl was born, and he claimed he spoiled his daughter as much as possible."

Charlotte could see the four bundles wrapped carefully in Bubble Wrap. Just behind them were four larger ones she was certain were the chariots. She couldn't wait to open the Bubble Wrap to see them. The pictures indicated they were some of the oldest carousel horses in existence.

"His little girl became ill shortly after he bought the horses for her and eventually she died. The doctors couldn't figure out what was wrong. Emery was dying when I spoke to him about the horses. He had insisted any potential buyer speak to him before the transaction was complete. He believed there was some kind of curse on the horses. He explained that over the last few centuries, anyone owning the horses and using them eventually succumbed to some unknown disease. He wanted to make me aware of the curse before I purchased them. He had been given the warning and it went unheeded as, apparently, it had for all the collectors before him."

She turned and faced him, fascinated. "He died?"

"Yes, of the same illness as his daughter. As had the collectors before him and their families. Apparently anyone who has owned those horses died of an unknown withering disease, or . . ." He paused, watching her face. "Or the owner was murdered in the same manner as your brother and Ricard Beaudet."

She felt the color drain from her face. "Tariq. Is that the truth?" A chill went down her spine and goose bumps rose on her arms. She could see by his expression that he was dead serious. "Tariq." She whispered his name. "That's horrible. How many collectors or owners over the years have been murdered? You can discount an illness, because everyone gets exposed to germs, but murdered with throats torn out and drained of blood? Does it make you afraid to own the horses?"

"Does it make you afraid to work on them?" he countered.

She inhaled deeply, drawing the masculine scent of him into her lungs. He smelled of forest and spice. A heady combination, but there was a single ingredient that smelled like danger. No matter how sophisticated and suave Tariq appeared, he could suddenly look very predatory. When that particular look crept into his vivid blue eyes, it made her all too aware she was alone with him and she didn't really know him very well.

"No," she whispered, even more horrified at herself than she was at the disclosure. "It makes me want to work on them more than ever." She needed to touch them. To feel the wood under her palm. Under the pads of her fingers. She would know everything, see everything. She would know why people became ill. Understand why some people were murdered and how. Then she would know why Fridrick had chosen to kill her brother and Genevieve's grandmother in a like manner.

Tariq stepped from the main entrance toward the back section to the four large objects covered with Bubble Wrap. "These are the four horses used, and the bundles behind them are the four chariots. On this particular carousel a horse goes between each chariot. The carousel has a center pole with arms radiating from it to hold the chains that hung the horses and chariots. Of course there is no platform. That wasn't done until much later."

"Wait." She caught his arm, excitement moving through her. "Do you have all the pieces for this carousel? Every single one of

216

them?" It couldn't be true.

"I haven't tried assembling it. It arrived a few weeks ago, shipped in separate pieces. I did inventory on everything that came in and checked all the parts off. I didn't want to make any mistakes with the thing. The pictures I sent to Ricard were the ones taken by Paul Emery and sent out to all private collectors. I wanted to purchase it and wanted to know if there was a chance he would come to do the restoration."

"He wanted to," Charlotte conceded. "Why didn't Paul Emery come out and admit he had such a rare thing? Why wouldn't he disclose that information to the world? The carousel, depending on its condition, could be worth a fortune. More specifically, it definitely belongs in a museum on display for everyone to see. It's that important of a piece. This could be the find of the century."

Tariq shook his head. "It is part of the agreement that every owner has made with the one purchasing the carousel. The new owner must swear they will not allow it on display to the public until the curse has been broken. I intend to figure out what is going wrong, if it truly is, and do something about it, but I need help. I thought Ricard would be the one to do that, but now it falls to you. I hope you meant it when you said you'd stay."

"They believe in the curse so much that

they don't want to take chances with the public," she mused. "It's an inanimate object. It can't be responsible for illness or murder."

"Unless it harbors some pathogen on the surface of it."

The tip of her tongue moistened her lips as she thought about that. "I suppose it could happen, but unlikely, right? Do you believe in this curse? Really believe in it?"

"Something has gone wrong for certain. Every single owner has had family members die, and most succumbed to the curse. I did my research before the purchase and everything Emery told me was true. Every owner and his family has met with a strange, unknown illness or murder. I wanted the chance to solve the puzzle."

She noticed he was noncommittal as to whether he believed in a curse, but that didn't matter to her. She *had* to touch those wooden carvings. She would know the history of them, see into the lives of those who had ridden on them, who had played on them. More, she would know intimately the men who carved them, their hopes and dreams, even, if she was lucky, get a glimpse into their lives during the period of time they worked on the chariots and horses.

She was desperate for the carousel to be authentic — one of the first ones ever made. Horses or men turned the carousel while the young nobles practiced thrusting their spears through the rings in preparation for tournaments. Then masters of sword and spear taught young men to battle using the carousel for similar practices. Later, it was rumored, the wives and children found fun on the carousel and that was how it slowly evolved into the modern-day carousel. She might even find out if that was the truth, just by touching the carvings.

Charlotte could barely contain her excitement. The "curse" of an illness sounded so like that surrounding the Egyptian pyramids that she was filled with curiosity and knew she could probably get answers about what illnesses the previous owners actually died of. Which would only add to the mystique of this ancient carousel.

"I don't want you to touch anything until I've had a chance to do it myself," Tariq decreed in a voice that said he meant business.

She frowned and rubbed at her temple, where an ache had begun that fast. "Did you just try to use a compulsion on me?" She couldn't keep the note of accusation out of her voice as she pushed down hard on the throbbing pulse point.

"If I did, it was inadvertent. And I probably did. I'm used to using a little compulsion on the children to keep them out of danger. It's also a tool I use with Liv to keep her nightmares at bay. Unfortunately, it doesn't work on Emeline. I cannot help her no matter what I try."

It was his voice that saved him. The genuine regret that he couldn't help Emeline over her nightmares. She could almost forgive him. Almost.

"What happened to Emeline?"

"We don't know exactly. She hasn't really spoken since we took her back from Fridrick's boss, Vadim. She went into the tunnels with Danny and Blaze to try to get the girls back. While she was down there, she was taken."

She was silent a moment knowing he wasn't giving her much information, but she didn't want him to overload her. She had enough to worry about with Fridrick threatening Genevieve and Lourdes. She lifted her chin and met his vibrant blue eyes. Eyes a woman could get lost in. She'd gotten lost more than once, so she knew.

"Did you use compulsion on me last night?"

The blue eyes didn't waver. Didn't blink. She watched them change. That gentle, sweet look he had disappeared, replaced by one so predatory she took a step back and one hand went to her throat defensively.

"Last night was beautiful. Every single moment. Why would you want to pick it apart?" he countered.

He didn't sound hurt or regretful. Nor did he sound guilty or innocent. He asked a question in a tone she couldn't read.

"I acted out of character last night. You had to know I've never been with another man. I never let other men touch me. Not once. The thought of it was . . . abhorrent. Yet the moment you touched me, I responded."

"Detonated."

"What?" She blinked. His tone was once again readable — smug satisfaction.

"You detonated when I touched you. That belongs to me and to no other man. Me. After searching for you for so long, believe me, *sielamet,* I loved that. I loved that every time I reached for you, you didn't hesitate. You made me feel extraordinary, and when I kissed you, after, you looked at me as if I were the only man in the world. I want to be that for you. The only man in your world."

She *had* detonated when he touched her and she knew it would happen again. Every time. "I don't want you to ever use any form of compulsion on me. Not. Ever." She stated it firmly so there would be no mistake. She would do everything in her power to care for and please this man, but she had to know he would respect her boundaries and want to care for and please her as well.

"I have taken a vow to cherish you and place your happiness above my own. It is an irrevocable vow. Once said, the words cannot be undone."

Wait. Wait. Wait. Her heart began to ham-

221

mer too hard. Too loud. Too fast. He had said *a lot* of things to her in his language. It had been sexy. But it also had been uttered in a deep, firm, committing voice. What had he said? *You are my lifemate. I claim you as my lifemate. I belong to you.* She had loved when he'd said it. She had no idea what a lifemate was, but it had sounded hot and sexy when he'd given her that title. A woman above all others to him. That was how she took it because she'd wanted to believe she was special to him. And she'd wanted desperately to belong to him.

She didn't do one-night stands. She didn't hook up. Intimacy meant something to her, as did giving the gift of her body to someone. She made no judgments on others, but she wasn't wired that way, even when she'd wished that she were. What else had he said? He just stood there, watching her like the predator again. Waiting for her to figure it out.

"Say it. In English. Whatever you said last night," she ordered softly. She wouldn't be afraid or intimidated by him no matter how big or dangerous he appeared.

"I offer my life to you. I give you my protection. I give you my allegiance. I give you my heart. I give you my soul. I give you my body."

The blue eyes never wavered. "And I did give you all of those things. I meant every word. For me, there is no taking it back. For you, there is no way to take it back, either. We're bound together."

She wanted to shake her head, to deny what he said, but she was an intelligent woman — most of the time — when her hormones weren't ruling her, and right then she felt the pull of him, the threads binding them together. She might walk away physically, but she knew she would suffer for a lifetime if she did. No one else would ever satisfy her. She would think of him day and night and need him. Crave him.

"There was more." Because she needed to know.

His gaze remained absolutely steady. "I take into my keeping the same that is yours."

He made the statement in that voice, the one that melted her. The one she couldn't resist. But this time she understood. He wasn't touching her, frying her brain. She understood. Her heart stuttered. He'd done that. Somehow in the night between his touch, his possession and his vows, he'd managed to take into his keeping her body, heart and soul. She kept her gaze on his.

"Your life will be cherished by me for all my time. Your life will be placed above my own for all time. You are my lifemate. You are bound to me for all eternity. You are always in my care."

She moistened her lips with the tip of her tongue. He took a step toward her and she stepped back, lifting one hand to ward him off. "No. Stop. I have to think."

He shook his head and walked toward her. "There is nothing to think about. This decision was made last night and again this evening." He sounded implacable. Fierce. Unafraid. Certain.

How could he be so sure when she was freaking out? She had been certain until that moment he had pushed at her mind, trying to force her to obey him. It was a small push, but she'd caught it. She had the same reaction when anyone tried to manipulate her. Her actions the night before and again this evening had been out of character for her. He hadn't exactly denied compulsion, although she hadn't felt it being used on her and she would have . . . wouldn't she?

He just kept coming until he had her back against the half wall, the hand she'd put out to ward him off smashed right against his chest. He captured that hand and held it tight against him, right over his heart.

"Do you feel that, Charlotte? Do you hear that? My heart beating? Do you feel the rhythm of your heart?" He put his other hand over her heart, fingers stroking caresses over the curve of her breast.

"It isn't fair," she whispered.

"What isn't fair?"

"Owning me with a touch." Her whisper was barely audible and her gaze slid from his blue eyes down to his hand covering hers on his chest.

"You still do not understand, *sielamet*." He lifted her chin with his thumb and forefinger. "You own me. Body and soul. I would never harm you. Not under any circumstances. Whatever you feel for me, I feel even more for you. You make my body come alive. You gave me everything. When a man has had nothing at all, when he's lived long in a dark, gray void and a woman brings with her the warmth of sunlight and laughter when he's been cold, joy and happiness when he has none, he will do anything for her. Anything at all to make her happy. You are that woman for me."

When he said things like that she couldn't resist him. She didn't want to resist him. He let her know she wasn't alone in her madness. He was in as deep as she was — if she could believe him, and she did. There had been no sweet courtship, no getting to know each other. She didn't know a single thing about him, other than what she'd learned from the occasional magazine article. Still, her instant acceptance and out-of-character reaction to him alarmed her. Even his instant reaction to her, as if he'd known her forever.

"I don't trust this," she admitted. "Why do you?"

"I have told you why. For me, I knew instantly. It is the way of my people and has been for centuries. I know it isn't the same for you, but I also know you feel the connection between us. You've been in my mind. You would know if I was lying to you."

She raised an eyebrow. "Would I?" Her gaze strayed to the carousel horses wrapped so securely. He was offering her a safe haven for Lourdes, a beautiful home not only for her niece and her, but also for Genevieve and even Grace if she would accept it. He was offering himself to her. And a job. The job she most wanted in the world.

"You would know, Charlotte," he said softly.

The way his voice got inside of her always melted her. Always. He didn't need to try to control her mind; his voice controlled her body. Maybe her brain, too, because she found it hard to think clearly around him.

"I want this, Tariq, what we have growing between us, I really do. I appreciate every single thing you're offering me. I especially appreciate that you intervened last night with Fridrick. I was really scared, and it was clear he knew where Lourdes was, even though I thought we'd hidden her carefully this time. You and your friends saved her as well."

"But?"

He tipped his head to one side and his eyes, so vibrant and pure blue, studied her with that unblinking focus he seemed to have. It reminded her of a pure predator's. A delicious shiver went down her spine, and it oc-

226

curred to her that the twinge of fear added to the temptation that was Tariq Asenguard. He stood there, looking gorgeous and sophisticated, a wealthy businessman reputed to be extremely intelligent and shrewd. He could be gentle. His touch brought paradise. And then he could look absolutely dangerous, as he did right at the moment.

He was waiting for something. Alert. Watchful. She knew if she made the wrong move he would attack, but how or why she wasn't certain. She only knew that the threat was there, lingering in the air. The shiver turned into something else, fear welling up to become panic. She found she couldn't breathe, couldn't drag enough air into her lungs. She also knew the attack would be in some form she would never be able to resist.

"Stop it." The command was a whiplash. "I would *never* hurt you. It would be impossible for me to do such a thing. Unthinkable. I won't let you go, but you aren't a prisoner. I would choose to use persuasion, and I can be very persuasive when something is important to me. You, Charlotte, are the most important person in my world."

She moistened her lower lip with the tip of her tongue, stalling for time. She wanted him, wanted everything he was offering. What she didn't trust was the terrible need inside of her, the hunger for him. It was overwhelming. *He* was overwhelming. He made her feel things she'd never imagined in her wildest dreams.

"I'm not someone who works well with dominant males." It was her way of telling him she wasn't in the least submissive. He *commanded.* He ordered. When he wanted something he got it; there was no doubt in her mind. No matter what Tariq said, he was pure alpha male.

"I am not going to tell you I don't have a dominant personality, because I do. That said, I don't want a submissive woman. I want an intelligent woman thinking for herself. I want a strong woman to help me figure out what to do with the enormous problems I have facing me. Do I make decisions fast? Yes. Absolutely. I want my woman to be able to do the same. You're that woman. Will it always be easy? We have five children to look out for. Five. Two are already teens. All of them are traumatized. We have Fridrick and his bosses with their army coming after Emeline, Genevieve and you. We also have the threat of the three men following you from Paris. I don't need a submissive woman, Charlotte; I need a warrior. A woman walking beside me. Fighting beside me. Standing in front of those children with me. A woman unafraid to listen to whatever Emeline or Liv needs to say, to hear them and not curl into a protective ball when the monstrous truth of what happened to them comes out. I know that woman is you."

She closed her eyes and took a deep breath, knowing she was going to jump off the cliff. "I hope you're real, Tariq, because once I give you everything you're asking for, I won't ever be able to get it back." Her heart. Her soul. She was already in so far over her head so fast she feared she was already lost. That last little part of her, the one he knew she held back, but was demanding, that would cost her everything if she lost.

"I've already given it to you, *sielamet*. Everything I am or will ever be. I meant every word I said to you. I gave you — me. I want the same from you. Come all the way into my world. Be my woman."

He whispered the words, yet she heard each one clearly. His voice wrapped her in strong arms. She felt protected and cherished with just his voice. He wasn't touching her and yet she felt his arms surrounding her. She would always have him. That man. The one standing in front of her, looking at her with those incredible gemlike eyes. Seeing only her.

She took a breath, knowing the truth. She was already lost. It didn't matter if she gave him that last little piece of her; she already was tied to him in a way she couldn't explain, and she knew leaving him would be nearly impossible. "I already am your woman," she whispered.

"Are you scared?"

She nodded, not looking away from that deep blue gaze. She couldn't. He still hadn't blinked. Still looked predatory. Dangerous. She was willingly giving herself to a man who would always have that edge to him.

"Don't be. You're safe with me."

She believed him. But . . . "Am I safe *from* you?"

He stared at her for an eternity, holding her captive with just his eyes and his charisma. A slow smile curved his mouth and crept into his eyes, lighting them more, turning the blue a vibrant sapphire. "No, *sielamet.* I want to eat you alive. The taste of you is forever on my tongue. The feel of you surrounding my cock, tight and hot, your skin, softer than anything I've ever felt, that wild hair, your mouth, all of you is branded into my mind, my bones, wrapped around my heart. You are not safe from me and you never will be, but you'll like the way you aren't safe. I can promise you that much."

He sounded wicked. Tempting. Sexy. Her sex clenched. Went damp. Heat rushed through her veins. She couldn't stop the slow, answering smile curving her own mouth. "Okay then. Show me what I'll be working on and tell me what you plan on paying me. I just want you to know that sleeping with the boss is never a good idea. I'll have to think long and hard about which I want most.

230

I truly love carousel horses, so you might lose out if they're what I think they are."

"If that's going to be a problem, Charlotte, I can write it into our contract that the job comes with certain other duties."

She burst out laughing. "Don't you dare. Just open the packaging for me. I'm really drawn to that one." She pointed to a wooden horse encased in Bubble Wrap and a crate. She longed to touch it, to feel the wood beneath her fingers so she could learn about everyone who had ever touched the horse. Once she got that pull, that intense draw, she knew the object was very old and had a lot to tell her. Wood was her favorite medium. It seemed to absorb so much more than man-made substances.

Tariq smiled again, taking her breath. With his easy, fluid steps he seemed to glide through the various wrapped bundles lying on the floor until he got to the one she was compelled to touch. She stood close. Holding her breath. Anticipating. Not daring to hope but hoping anyway.

Tariq was careful with the packaging, removing it one strip of wood at a time to reveal more of the Bubble Wrap. She watched him closely. His hands barely seemed to touch the wood, and he loosened the nails just by pulling. She knew he was strong, but he made dismantling the crates look easy. She was fairly certain she could open the others

231

without help.

"Tariq."

Both turned at the sound of his name being spoken, but Charlotte realized she wasn't in the least startled. She'd heard and smelled the man leaning his upper body and head into the room with one foot still on the basement stair. She recognized him from the previous night. He was tall, like Tariq, with long dark hair and cold-as-ice, black-as-night eyes. He was handsome, but in a rough, bad boy way, although, like Tariq, he wore a suit. Where Tariq looked as if he stepped off the cover of *GQ* magazine, his partner, Maksim Volkov, looked as if he'd grace the cover of a biker magazine.

"Need you for a moment. Won't take long."

Tariq frowned at him, but straightened, leaving the very corner of the horse peeking out at Charlotte. She tried not to stare at the faded wood, but it was seductive, beckoning to her, a thousand voices whispering just because she was in such close proximity.

"I'll be right back," Tariq assured. "Wait for me. If there's a curse on that thing, I'd rather it fall on me than on you."

"So sweet of you," she murmured, and stepped even closer to the carousel horse. Tariq *was* sweet, but if there truly was a curse, she would know the moment she touched the wood.

"I mean it, *sielamet,* you are not to touch

232

that thing until I have had time to examine it." He used his voice that brooked no argument, the one that said he was in charge and everyone jumped to obey him.

She nodded, a little distracted, and when Tariq went up the stairs with Maksim, she stepped closer to the antique horse. The whispers grew louder when she extended her palm and placed it carefully just above the wood peeking out of the wrap. Immediately she heard the sound of children laughing. Voices murmuring softly. Drawing her into that tunnel of time she lived to enter. To see worlds lost. People already gone. Glimpses into the past. Various languages. French. Hungarian. Italian. Romanian. A language she didn't understand but had heard recently, the one Tariq spoke.

Excitement was a dark drug in her veins. This could really be it, the find of a lifetime. A genuine horse carved hundreds of years ago for the express purpose of training young men to thrust spears, swords or arrows through rings with precision. She would be able to establish an exact timeline. She'd know when the horse had changed hands, where it had been, which families had owned it and the country they were in when they had it.

Ricard Beaudet had spent his entire career, even most of his life, searching for this very item. She stepped close enough to bump the

Bubble Wrap with her knee, her hand trembling as she slowly lowered it until the wood whispered against her hand. Beckoning. Calling to her. Accepting her. Ready to give up every secret. There was no resisting that call. She laid her palm gently on the exposed wood, her fingers unerringly finding the grooves of the carving.

Around her the walls of the basement shimmered and then disappeared. Everything went dark, but she wasn't alone — the voices were there, calling out to one another in various languages. Happy. Laughing. Sobbing. Anguish. Children. Adults. They were there with her in that dark place. She shivered in the cold, feeling as she always did when she first made contact with an ancient object. It was icy cold until she managed to connect with a time and a place. She was looking far back, trying to ignore the mesmerizing, seductive lure of the voices.

She hunted through time for the woodcarver. The closer she got to him, the more she could feel it. The more the cold receded and she felt warmth. Heat. The voices grew. Men laughing. Talking together. One man with his back to her worked with the block of wood, his knife moving in soft, gentle strokes, his hands caressing the wood with care and love.

The men spoke in Tariq's ancient language. She couldn't understand what they were saying, but she heard the teasing notes of laughter in their voices. They were giving the carver a hard time. She found them interesting. All were of the same race. Tall, wide shoulders, long black hair, stunning men with muscular physiques that would set them apart easily. Two of them practiced sword fighting, going at each other repeatedly, but they seemed evenly matched, so much so that they were involved in the conversation with the others gathered around the wood-carver.

"Which part of 'Don't touch that until I check it out' didn't you understand?" Tariq snarled the question from behind her.

Charlotte jumped, still in the past, a little disoriented. The wood-carver turned his head and looked directly at her. He had the same wide shoulders as the others. The same long black hair. The same powerful muscles rippling over his tall frame. But his eyes were vivid blue. Intense blue. Eyes she'd looked into when he'd made her come apart in his arms.

She gasped and jerked her hand away, feeling the sting of a splinter biting at her finger as she did so. It couldn't be Tariq. Maybe an ancestor. That was why he collected carousel horses. He knew someone in his family had carved these horses. She put her finger to her mouth to soothe the tiny wound, staring at the carver.

He stared back at her, his face totally

exposed under the light of a full moon. He was . . . *gorgeous.* There was no mistaking him. He looked no more than thirty or thirty-five, just exactly like Tariq. *Exactly* like Tariq because it *was* Tariq. It wasn't possible. It didn't make sense. But she knew absolutely that the man staring at her was the same man snarling at her, revealing the true predator he actually was.

9

"Oh. My. God." Charlotte whispered each word. Shocked. Knowing. Trying to tell herself it was impossible. She couldn't look away from the man from another time crouched in front of the block of wood, staring at her with his beautiful blue eyes, watching her intently, utterly focused on her as if even then he could actually sense her presence, see her.

Tariq Asenguard had been the wood-carver. *Her* Tariq. The man she had given her body, heart and soul to. She'd entrusted her niece and her best friend to him. Her brother's throat had been torn out. His blood had been taken. The three men in the bar, the ones that had driven a stake through another man's heart, they had to have believed they killed a vampire.

She touched the soft swell of her breast. His mark. His brand. Just touching with her fingers through the thin material of her blouse caused her sex to clench. Remember-

237

ing the feel of his bite. The most erotic thing she'd ever experienced. She touched her mouth, remembering it being on his chest.

"Oh. My. God." She whispered it a second time, tasting him in her mouth. On her tongue. Hot. Spicy. Wholly hers. All for her.

The walls around her curved. Went dark. She could only see those blue eyes watching her without blinking. She shivered, the cold seeping into her body. She raised her hand to her throat defensively, unable to look away. Suddenly she was back in the present, looking right into Tariq's eyes. He was only a foot or so from her, watching her carefully.

Charlotte backed away from him, taking a step to the side to try to get an angle on the stairs. "You took my blood." She blurted it out, just like an idiot in a horror film, not playing it all cool and smart.

"Is that a question?"

He didn't sound remorseful. Not in the least. She wanted to glare at him but she was too scared. "Yes." The single word was spoken so low she was surprised it came out of her mouth.

"Yes, I took your blood."

She nodded as if in agreement with him. She took another cautious step toward the stairs, making certain to keep a distance between her and Tariq. He didn't appear to move and the expression on his face never changed, yet he was blocking her escape and his blue eyes were more predatory than ever.

"Charlotte, your heart is beating too fast. Take a deep breath and hear my heart. Let yours slow to the rhythm of mine."

She'd done that before. Her heart had beat in absolute sync with his. She'd thought it was sexy; now she thought she was in real trouble. She tried another step. She deliberately didn't blink, didn't look away, watching him the whole time to see if he moved. He didn't, yet once again he was standing in front of her, blocking her escape route. If she screamed, no one would hear her.

"What are you?" Her voice was low. She couldn't keep the fear out of it.

"What I am *not* is a vampire. That is what you're thinking and it isn't true. I hunt vampires, but I am Carpathian. My soul is intact and I have never killed while feeding." His gaze didn't waver from hers.

She rubbed her cold arms, her mind racing, trying to figure out her next move without triggering aggression from him. "What are you going to do with me?"

"I already told you that. We have had this conversation, *sielamet.* You gave yourself to me, and I have made our vows."

Our vows. He had to be referring to the words he'd said in his native language. He'd made vows for both of them. A little hysterical, she tried to picture herself telling Genevieve about how she'd accidentally slept with a vampire. Or a vampire hunter. Whatever. Either way, he seemed intent on taking her blood.

"This is so like me," she muttered aloud. "I choose the one man who has been on earth for centuries. He likes mind control and taking blood from people."

"Charlotte."

"Don't." Now she was getting angry. She could feel the surge of her temper building like a volcano inside of her. "You seduced me and you took my blood. Don't bother to lie to me because I remember you doing it now."

"I cannot lie to you. It is impossible. Stop looking for a way out. There is none. You cannot outrun me. Just stay and communicate with me."

He wanted communication? She'd give him communication, although he wasn't going to like her way of talking. She reached down and pulled at one of the crate slats, then snapped back up, swinging the board at his head. He didn't try to sidestep the blow, but his hand came up to deflect and the board shattered into pieces.

Throughout the attack, he didn't change expression. His eyes darkened. Became more predatory than ever. Her heart jerked hard in her chest and she wanted desperately to run, but her feet seemed frozen to the spot.

"Sielamet." He expressed so much with one word. This was a reprimand. A gentle one,

but still a reprimand.

"I want to leave." She stuck her chin in the air, wanting him to see that she meant business. She was leaving his property, taking Lourdes and Genevieve with her whether he liked it or not.

"You cannot leave. Our vows were said. Your soul is tied to mine for all time. You will not be able to leave without harming yourself. Already you feel the pull between us. You cannot eat properly. You haven't had anything other than water this evening."

She pressed her fingers against her lips. Every single word coming out of his mouth was the absolute truth. It was also terrifying. "What did you do to me?"

"I am bringing you fully into my world."

Her heart stuttered. Her stomach did a slow, scary somersault. His voice was implacable. She knew his tone warned her not to argue. Her chin went up another fraction of an inch. "Which part of 'I'm not the submissive type' did you not understand?"

He sighed. "You can fight me, *sielamet,* but it won't do you any good. You know I can protect you from Fridrick and you know I will. I will always stand in front of you should there be a threat. Not only to you, but also to Lourdes. Everything I said to you earlier I meant. You are my woman, and your niece, Danny and the girls, they are my family. A war has started and whether you like it or not, you're involved. Fridrick and his masters targeted you. They went after Emeline, Liv, Amelia and Bella. There were other women down in those tunnels, women who didn't fare very well. We chased them out of there, but they got away. They haven't gone far, because Fridrick would never be so bold without an army behind him."

She shook her head. "I'll take Lourdes and leave. They won't find me."

"They will find you. They'll always find you. Lourdes won't be as important to them as you will be. If you don't cooperate with them they will use her for food, or give her to one of their puppets, like with Liv."

His expression still hadn't changed. He still hadn't blinked. Now she knew what a true predator was. Subconsciously trying to protect herself she wrapped her hand around her throat, covering it. "Why did you take my blood if you aren't a vampire?"

"I am Carpathian, an ancient race. We exist on blood, but we do not kill those we use to feed. We are careful. Respectful. Our prey never know we took their blood."

She winced at the word *prey*. Somehow she knew he deliberately was being stark, raw, not wrapping what he was in pretty words to mislead her.

"We seem immortal, but we can be killed. We do have longevity and sometimes that is more of a curse than a gift."

Charlotte studied his face. He hadn't taken a step toward her. He hadn't tried to touch her. She knew if he did, he would be able to convince her of anything. That would have made it so much easier. When his hands or mouth were on her, she would have flown to the moon and back with him. So why wasn't he touching her? She almost wanted him to hold her, kiss her, convince her that she didn't want to leave him.

Because she didn't. The idea of being separated from him made her physically ill. "You can't expect me to calmly decide to go along with all this."

"I can and I do. You have genuine feelings for me. I am in your mind, and to make it fair, at any time, you can be in mine." He nodded his head toward the tools neatly laid out on the table. "I suspect your psychic gift is strong, and it involves reading antiques. That was how you realized I am far older than I look."

Was there a faint note of humor in his tone? If there was, it didn't show on his face or in his eyes. His gaze was as watchful as ever. His expression very serious.

"Yes, I saw you carving the horse. You were surrounded by your friends."

His expression changed then and she realized she'd triggered a long-forgotten memory. He looked sad.

"They were giving me a hard time. The Malinov brothers, all five of them, were there that evening. They liked to discuss politics. They didn't always agree with our prince and they wanted debates going all the time. It was tiresome, but that night, they were just having fun. Fridrick was there as well. The prince's lifemate was close to having her first child. A son. He would be the reigning prince one day. It was a time of great joy."

She studied his face. "Why does the memory make you so sad?" She felt his sorrow, felt it like a weight pressing down on her. She had the unexpected urge to go to him and put her arms around him to comfort him. She forced her feet to stay where they were. This entire revelation was far too scary to even consider. She believed every word he said to her.

"That night was a fun night, but later, some years later, it all turned wrong. Terrible. I had never given the carousel to the prince for his son. I hadn't finished it. Work got in the way. I had to chase vampires, and the piece was never finished. Later, when I went back to it, that's when everything went wrong."

Charlotte could feel his anguish, although she wasn't certain he could.

"The Malinovs had a sister, Ivory. A beautiful girl. Everyone loved her, especially the brothers. Ivory was ultimately betrayed by the prince's eldest son, the one I was originally carving the horse for. At that time, there was unrest between human factions and a war broke out. We were interrupted and had to choose sides. Many of my people, including the Malinovs, didn't think we should involve ourselves in the wars of humans. They avoided them other than to feed."

"Like cattle to humans."

A little shudder went through her body at the way he'd put that. Tariq had "fed" from her. She touched the brand on the swell of her breast, and the mark pulsed and throbbed. Instantly, as if connected, her sex matched that strange, hungry beat.

"*Sielamet,* I do not 'feed' in that way from you. It is erotic and intimate with you. We are meant for each other. My people do not regard your people as cattle. At least, most do not."

She ignored that, not ready to engage him in battle again. Besides, she was curious. "Did something happen to Ivory that night?"

"That first night, when we were having fun, Ivory had not yet been born. Neither was Draven, the prince's eldest, but I think things were set in motion that night. The Malinov brothers argued with the prince, wanting to stay out of the human problems. When he didn't take their advice, they became more and more openly defiant over the years. They mellowed a little after Ivory was born, but the night Ivory was betrayed and she was thought lost to us, all five of the brothers

245

chose to turn vampire. Ruslan, the oldest, led the others, and they followed him straight into hell. And they did so with a plan in place — with a terrible purpose. We are seeing the results of that plan here, in this city, right now."

"And the carousel horse?"

"I finished carving it later. I saved the wood and worked on it over time. The night the Malinovs made their decision to become undead, I had finished it along with the chariots. I was helping train several young men and I wanted the carousel for that purpose. I thought the men I was training too young for battle, but I liked them. I'd assembled the carousel and the horses and chariots were hanging from chains when Ruslan and his brothers came to try to recruit me to their plan."

"To become a vampire?" There was a little squeak to her voice.

"They didn't even suggest that they were considering such a thing. What they did want to do was even worse. They intended to kill the prince and his entire family. It was risking every single Carpathian to do so."

This time, the pain in his voice was too much for her and she took a few steps toward him before she could stop herself. The need to comfort him was so overwhelming she felt sick when she forced herself to stay frozen in place. Taking those few steps had put her in

246

closer proximity, and now, from the anguish in his voice, she could feel the pain radiating off him as if it had been stored up for so long and now the emotional dam was gone and *everything* was pouring out of him.

"The Malinovs always came up with idiotic schemes to overthrow the prince, but it was mostly for debate. Usually they debated with the De La Cruz brothers, but it was just talk. Just that. At first I thought they weren't serious, but then I could hear the anger and resolve in their voices. I knew they meant it. I knew they planned to assassinate the entire Dubrinsky family. They believed their line was sufficient to take the place of the Dubrinsky line."

Something in the way he revealed the information, the incredulous note in his voice, the absolute shock that anyone would think that, made her realize there was far more to the story than he was telling her. Something was very special about the Dubrinsky lineage for him to have such a reaction. He didn't believe for one moment that the Malinovs could take the Dubrinskys' place; if they did so it would somehow be the downfall of his people.

"What happened?" she prompted when he fell silent.

"They left very angry and I never saw them again as my friends. As Carpathians. Ivory, the one person they lived and cared for, had disappeared and they turned vampire that night. *All* of them. Deliberately. They didn't wait until it was too late, until there was no hope of finding lifemates and the memories of love and friendship were totally gone."

Her head jerked up and shock took hold, a thousand lightning strikes hitting all at once as realization dawned. She'd heard that word from him often. *Lifemate.* "Tariq, what does that mean? No hope of finding a lifemate and memories are totally gone. What would that have to do with turning vampire?"

He sighed. "Carpathian males over time lose their ability to see in color and to feel emotion. We're the dark half of the soul and without the light to provide the way, we sink further and further into a gray world of nothing. We hunt the vampire, but it is only our honor that keeps us from joining them. When you cannot feel anything, you look for that one moment when you can. There is a rush when taking blood during a kill and the temptation of feeling at least that. The temptation whispers to you night after night. For centuries. Unrelenting."

She moistened her suddenly dry lips. He hurt and that made her hurt. She didn't know if she was feeling his pain or if it was her own, but he clearly felt the loss of his friends. If the things Tariq had told her were true, he had suffered. "How do you know she's the right one?"

His blue eyes drifted over her face. There was stark possession there. Raw emotion so deep it shook her. "There is only one, Charlotte — she holds the other half of one's soul. She could be in any century. We thought only Carpathian women could be lifemates, and our women had slowly disappeared until we had so few there were no children to bring us hope. The prince found Raven, and she was human. That gave the rest of us the will to continue when we were already long past our endurance."

"What happens when you find your lifemate? How do you know she's the right one? How can you tell?" Because he believed she was his, and she believed he belonged to her. And that was just plain crazy.

"When I heard your voice, I began to feel for the first time in centuries. Real emotions. More, I could see in color. Beautiful colors I hadn't seen in so long I'd forgotten they existed. When I told you I do not see other women, I meant that. My cock reacts only to you. Only for you. My body would never accept another woman. You are my lifemate. My only."

She held his words close, so close they sank into her heart. A little shiver crept down her spine. He lived in a world she could barely imagine.

"I saw you once," he said. "A long time ago. When I was carving the horse. I turned and saw you. Looked right at you. I knew you existed, and I searched for so long. I didn't ever want to think I couldn't find you, but time passed and eventually . . ." He trailed off.

Charlotte couldn't help the small gasp that escaped. She raised her fingers to her lips, pressing hard to keep back the shock of what he'd just revealed. He'd seen her. Far back in time, he'd seen her when she'd entered the tunnel, pulled by the memories in the wood. She put her finger in her mouth and tasted her own blood. Wincing, she removed her finger and rubbed the injured pad along her thigh.

"Do you have any idea how bizarre and scary everything you've told me is? I only know about vampires through horror films and books. They were fictional. Mythical creatures to scare us at Halloween. Not. Real."

"They are very real, *sielamet,* and something is going on here that we do not yet understand. Something that involves you, Genevieve and Emeline. We found bodies beneath the cities, women in various stages of pregnancy. We believe the Malinovs are trying to establish their own empire. If they try to turn a woman who is not psychic she will go insane. A psychic woman, however, one with strong gifts, can handle the conversion."

Charlotte really didn't like the sound of that. "Conversion?" Her voice came out high. A mousy squeak.

He nodded, his eyes on her face. "It takes three blood exchanges to bring a gifted human into our world."

She closed her eyes tight. Remembering. His mouth on her. Her mouth on him. That taste bursting in her mouth, addicting, setting up a terrible craving. His words, so gentle, so loving, his language, so sexy and intriguing. This was becoming more and more real. Her brain was finally allowing her to process everything he'd said. It was putting all the pieces together to give her the full picture. Tariq Asenguard was converting her, and eventually she would be the mother of all those children.

"I saw the film *The Lost Boys*," she warned him.

"I did not see this film." There was mild puzzlement, but the eyes didn't waver.

She took a step back again, once more retreating. "A kick-ass film. Funny and scary. A vampire trying to put together his own family."

"This is not a film, Charlotte. You are my family. My lifemate. The children are lost souls in need of help. I came to their aid because down through the centuries, that's what I've done. What I always have done. I take in the lost and I care for them. If that is not what you want to do, I will stop. But you are mine."

There was finality in those words, and studying his face, she could see there was little wiggle room around his declaration. He believed it absolutely and the scary thing was — so did she. She took another step back, shaking her head. It was too unbelievable. Fridrick murdering Genevieve's boyfriend and her grandmother. Murdering Ricard Beaudet and then Charlotte's brother. Tariq writing to Ricard — such a coincidence. The three men who followed them from Paris. Giving herself to a man she didn't know after years of not allowing anyone to touch her. What was wrong with her that she was being swept down a path there was no returning from? She wasn't that kind of woman.

She'd always been strong and confident, her own person. Independent. Too much so according to her brother. Yet one touch, one look, just Tariq's voice alone could make her want to please him. Want to give him every-thing — anything he wanted. That *so* wasn't her. She couldn't just believe every incredible word coming out of his mouth. She knew, from touching the carousel horse, that he was ancient. She saw him, felt him, even thought he'd seen her looking at him. Now she knew he had.

"I did."

Her heart jumped, stuttered and then began

to pound. He'd heard her thoughts. He was inside her mind. He could read her escape plan almost before she came up with one. Worse, he'd confirmed what she'd suspected.

"That moment was the one that allowed me hang on so long. To stay with humans. To come up with the idea of the clubs. I knew you were somewhere in the world, although I had convinced myself I made you up. I didn't actually 'see' you so much as I felt your presence. So strong. I smelled the fragrance that is so uniquely you. I smelled it in the club and knew you were close."

He inhaled, taking in her scent, drawing it deep into his lungs, his eyes watchful. She knew if she moved he'd be on her. She just didn't know what he'd do.

"I want to take Lourdes and leave." She tried to keep her voice even. It was too late to hide the fact that he'd totally freaked her out. She needed to get away from him. From the whispers of the wooden horse, now calling to her. She stuck the pad of her finger into her mouth again, sucking on the stinging splinter. It wasn't there. She thought it had penetrated the skin and broken off, but it had just ripped a small laceration, which now just stung. She was grateful she didn't have to fish out a piece of old wood from her finger — a small thing, but it gave her something else to think about.

"You hurt yourself?" Instantly he was alert.

"It's nothing." God. *God.* The concern in his voice. That shook her. His eyes had gone soft. Beautiful. He was the most gorgeous man she'd ever laid eyes on. All hers. Offering her everything. Was she really going to throw that away? She took another step back, away from temptation. "I didn't even get a splinter."

"Let me see." He held out his hand to her.

Panic set in instantly. He couldn't touch her. He just couldn't. She would go to pieces. Melt. Give him everything he wanted. Anything. She had to be careful because every step she took she could be entering deeper into a trap.

She put her hand behind her and shook her head. "No." That was decisive. "You stay there and let me think this through. I know you're capable of controlling minds. I know vampires in movies can do that, especially if they've taken blood from the victim."

"You aren't a victim. You are my lifemate, my woman, meant to be cherished and protected. Never a victim, Charlotte."

His voice. Mesmerizing. Velvet. Stroking caresses. If that wasn't mind control what was? She shook her head, trying to make a decision when she felt more like the proverbial cornered prey.

"Do I have freedom of choice?"

"Choice in what? You have all kinds of freedom. You are gifted and becoming even more so. Can you not tell the difference in your senses? Your hearing? Your eyesight? Your ability to move? Every sense you have is already heightened. You have the freedom to speak your mind, to make decisions, all the things every human values so much."

"You're leaving out my decision to remain here — with you. What about that?"

He tipped his head to one side, still studying her. "The human world is very concerned with rights and privileges. Entitlement. Carpathians are about duty and honor. Responsibility. Our lives are very simple in that regard. My duty is to my prince and my lifemate first and then to my people. Your duty is the same. In that there is no decision to be made. It. Is. A. Fact. Can you deny the truth of that?"

She couldn't. She wasn't Carpathian and she hadn't been raised in his world, but there was no denying that something powerful was between them. The connection grew stronger the more she was in his presence.

"There is no out for either of us. No divorce or separation. We are one, together yet separate. We cannot be apart. Not comfortably and not for long. You are two-thirds into my world. Already you are changing."

She shook her head. "That's not right. You don't have my permission."

"I don't need your permission. It is your duty."

She tipped up her chin, anger sweeping through her. "You don't get to dictate my life. You can't just force me to accept you."

He was there then. Right in front of her, his body crowding hers, his arm sweeping around her back to keep her from falling as he propelled her backward fast. So fast. Her back hit the wall and she was caged. Held there. "You gave yourself to me, Charlotte. There is no taking that back. I told you then what I would do couldn't be undone. The vows were made. In my world, we are man and wife. Our soul is once again back together, my dark to your light."

She had. She'd done that. She even knew she was doing something crazy at the time. Something momentous. Still. She shook her head. "Not this. Exchanging blood. I didn't agree to that."

"You agreed to be mine. To come into my world." He cupped her chin in the palm of his hand, forcing her head up. "There is no going back now. It is far too late for that. Even if I let you go, which would never happen, you would not survive and neither would I. We're tied together."

His thumb slid along her cheek, a soft caress that caught at her heart. She was terrified, yet at the same time she felt safe the moment he touched her. Safe. Protected. Belonging. He was magic. She knew she would never see another man. There was only

Tariq. It seemed as if she'd known him all her life.

"I didn't know what I was agreeing to," she whispered, because there was no way to get her voice above a whisper. "I don't want to be in a world where I have to look at human beings as prey."

"You are not a predator, *sielamet.* You are the light to my darkness. You will always be you, a sweet, courageous woman lighting the way for her man."

"You're a predator," she accused.

"Exactly. I will always be one. I was born to hunt and I will continue to do so. But I have always stayed in the world of humans, drawn to them, protecting them. That night, the night the Malinovs turned, they came back determined to wipe out the entire village where I worked to train the young men for battle. Fridrick and his brother were with them. Two others. It was a bloodbath, Charlotte. So many people killed unnecessarily because I refused to join them. They needed me dead. They wanted that. I became one of their bitterest enemies that night and I have hunted them through the centuries."

She winced at the term *centuries;* she couldn't help it. Centuries was a long, long time.

"Do not look so frightened. I will always be at your side. Always. You will be able to protect Lourdes and the others right along with me." His mouth moved over her cheek, little kisses whispering against her skin. So soft. So compelling. His tongue teased the seam of her mouth. His body was warm and hard, the hand under her chin spanning her throat so that her pulse beat into his palm.

"I'm absolutely terrified," she confessed.

"*Sielamet,* I know this is a leap of faith for you, but we can do this. You. Me. Very few people can have what we can. Together. I have so much love for you, Charlotte. So much. And it will only grow. Look into my mind and you'll see everything you need to believe. I'm asking you to take that leap and believe that I'll catch you. Let me have you in this lifetime and all the ones to come."

He made his plea, his lips against hers, so that she felt each word sliding inside of her. Going deep. Her heart beat loudly. Hard. Followed the exact rhythm of his. She . . . wanted . . . him.

"What happens if I agree?"

"I take your blood for the third exchange. You take mine and you'll go through the conversion. I've asked Maksim what happens. Blaze went through it. He said it was tough to watch, terrible on her. He also said if you embrace it, know for certain you choose it, it isn't as bad. I'll be with you and taking as much of the pain and fear away as possible, but honestly, it will be tough."

She counted five heartbeats. Took a breath.

Drew him into her lungs. "You want me to do this? To feel pain?"

His thumb slid over her cheek again, traced her high cheekbone and then moved lower to press into the small indentation in her chin. "Absolutely not, *sielamet*. The last thing any man wants for his woman is for her to feel pain. I would do it for you if I could. I will stay with you every moment and shoulder as much pain as your body allows me, and in the end when I can, I'll send you to sleep so you won't feel all of it, but unfortunately, to bring you into my world, I have to take you out of yours."

She swallowed, visions of horror films rising. "Like a vampire." One hand slid up the wall and then she circled his wrist with her fingers — or tried to. Her fingers wouldn't go around his wrist so she just dug in and tried to pull his hand off of her throat.

"*Not* like a vampire. Are you going to lie to me and tell me it wasn't erotic when I took your blood? You participated, Charlotte. You wanted what I had to offer because you recognize me. You know what I am to you."

Looking into his eyes — eyes that were twin blue flames — she knew she was lost. She was his. But what he wanted . . . What he demanded was terrifying. Giving up what and who she was to become something else. She shook her head. "I'm not that brave or strong."

His lips slowly curved into a smile. His mouth was beautiful. Tempting. When he smiled it was even more so. The smile crept up to warm the blue of his eyes, turning the flame hotter and brighter, dazzling her. "Charlotte, you were willing to face down a serial killer with a can of wasp spray you had in your purse. You stepped in front of your friend Genevieve, and you tried to protect me, a total stranger to you. Do not tell me you don't have courage. Only a woman of great courage would do the things you did."

"Or a crazy one," she muttered, unable to pull her gaze from his sinful mouth.

He brought his mouth down on hers with exquisite gentleness. A barely there brush. A whisper of a caress. Heat spiraled through her instantly, and she needed more. He gave her more, his tongue teasing along the seam of her mouth, and she opened for him, needing his kisses. Melting into his body. There was no denying he belonged to her. Not when he kissed her. Not when his arms drew her so tightly against him, nearly crushing her, yet at the same time offering his protection, his shelter. Making her feel precious and cherished. And wanted.

You will still be you, Charlotte. You are incapable of becoming a vampire. No woman of the light could possibly do so.

The words didn't matter as much as the emotion pouring into her. His emotion.

Intense. Real. *Hers.* He was hers. It didn't matter that he wasn't altogether human or that he lived in a world of violence. She lived there, too. She'd lost her brother and her mentor. Genevieve had lost a boyfriend and her beloved grandmother.

Charlotte linked her fingers behind his neck and held on, kissing him back. Giving him everything.

Yes. Her breath hitched. It was a momentous decision. One she knew she couldn't take back and it was terrifying, but being without him was even worse. *But not yet. I have to make certain I still take care of Lourdes. And I'm still very, very scared.*

I am as well, he admitted. *Stay with me through the conversion. Don't shut me out. No matter what happens, stay open to me. Give me your word, Charlotte. I need to know you'll give that to me.*

She pulled her head back and he leaned down to rest his forehead against hers, his blue gaze drawing her in. Asking her this time. Wanting her to give him that as well.

Charlotte sighed. "Will I die?"

"It will feel like death, I've heard. Your organs will change. It isn't easy, *sielamet.* That I can't take away, no matter how much I want to be able to do it for you. But if you really make this choice, in your heart, in your head, when the time comes, it will be easier.

261

Accepting it. Letting it happen and not fighting it."

She knew he was trying to reassure her, but the unknown was still frightening. "I have to go see to Lourdes. I've left her alone with Genevieve too long. And we have to sort out where Genevieve will live."

"For now, she can live in this house. That will allow her to care for Lourdes during the day should she have need. Eventually, when I know Lourdes and the other children can take it, we'll bring them into my world. They'll be much safer that way."

Charlotte shook her head and tried to step back, but the wall was right behind her. "You can't make that decision for them. They have to do it when they're adults." She wasn't even certain what "it" entailed, but it felt huge. Changing one's entire species. Living differently. She didn't even know what that was. Another terrifying thought occurred. "You don't sleep in a coffin, do you? Because I am *so* not doing that."

"No. But we do not go out in the sun. That can burn us. We can handle early morning and early evening. Every Carpathian's sensitivity is different, but as a rule, we can't take the sun. We must sleep during the day, and we're at our most vulnerable then. I'd guess your three stalkers from Paris are vampire hunters and they kill anyone they suspect, vampire, Carpathian or human. They aren't in league with Fridrick."

"How do you know?"

"I'd know. We can scan minds, and if a vampire has taken over a human and made him into his puppet . . ." He trailed off, his blue eyes going wide. "Those men with Fridrick were human. I didn't feel them, not even when I scanned their minds, yet clearly they were under Fridrick's control."

He stepped back, keeping his hands on her shoulders. "We have to find out what they were doing in the tunnels before we drove them all out. Maksim just told me that when he went back under the city to find out what they were doing with all their experiments, everything was destroyed. All the equipment. The cages. Their control room with their computers. It's all rubble. We need that information or we're only guessing at their intentions, and now it's lost to us."

"I can get it for you. If there's rubble down there, I can still 'see' what it was used for by touching what's left of it," Charlotte said. "I've been doing that kind of thing since I was a child. Of course I never actually told anyone but Genevieve and the people at the psychic testing center in France, but I figured I had plausible deniability if anyone found out. I'm really good at it."

Tariq stared down at her for a long time, his expression a mixture of awe, approval and pride. The way he looked at her made her feel warm inside. She'd give a lot to see that look on his face often.

"You would be willing to go down in the tunnels and sift through the rooms with us? It could be very ugly, *sielamet.* You saw what they did to Liv. Reliving others being tortured can mess you up in ways —"

She put her hand on his arm to stop him. "I wouldn't have said anything if I didn't think I could handle it. I touch antiques all the time. I've run across torture before. I know it can be ugly, but if this helps get rid of Fridrick and any of his friends, I'll help in any way I can."

That earned her another kiss. A long one. One she could take with her when she went into a vampire's lair.

10

Charlotte stuck the tip of her finger in her mouth. It hurt. Not bad, just a dull, irritating ache. She'd looked at it several times closely to make certain there wasn't a splinter left in from the carousel horse, but there was nothing but a tender, red spot. Sucking on it didn't help. In fact, the moment it was in her mouth, it throbbed annoyingly.

She'd spent the rest of the evening with Lourdes, well into the night. She wasn't in the least tired and neither was her niece — or any of the children. All of them had slept through the day. She'd put Lourdes to bed, had a wild dawn with Tariq and then slept in Lourdes's bed, only to wake with Tariq in his bed. Now she was being taken to an underground maze below the city where Fridrick and his boss, Vadim, had tortured men, women and children.

"This is dangerous, isn't it?" she asked, keeping her voice low.

She was surrounded by Tariq's friends.

They kept her in the center and she knew it was deliberate, although they acted casual, so much so that most of the men ignored her after they nodded to her in greeting.

She recognized his partner, Maksim, and the one called Dragomir from the night before. Dragomir was terrifying. If she hadn't been clamped to Tariq's side, she might have run. He didn't look as if he had a gentle bone in his body. If anything, he looked like a killing machine. She tried not to stare at him. He wore his hair in a long, thick braid that fell to his waist. Every inch or so a leather thong wrapped the hair so that the braid was in intriguing increments running down his back. One would think it would make him look a little feminine, but it actually added to his hard, scary look.

There were triplets Lojos, Tomas and Mataias, all with weathered features and long, streaming hair. According to Tariq, Tomas had been in a battle with vampires, had been severely injured and was still supposed to be healing but had joined them anyway, just as he had in the parking garage.

She recognized the one called Siv as well. She tried to send him a tentative smile to thank him for rescuing Lourdes, but she didn't get a response out of him.

Dragomir glanced at her. "She should not go into that place of madness. She is sensitive, Tariq, far too sensitive." He spoke as if

266

she weren't there.

"She can tell us everything they were do-ing, and we need to know," Tariq explained. "Without her, we won't know what we're up against."

"It is dangerous." Simply that.

The way he said it, without any emotion at all, yet at the same time, with an order, an expectation to be obeyed, made Charlotte cringe. She realized instantly that other than Maksim and Tariq, these men lived in a cold, gray world of nothing. She couldn't help feel-ing a little afraid of them and yet at the same time feeling compassion toward them.

Dragomir was not at all like Tariq. He wouldn't want his woman to walk beside him into danger. He wouldn't expect her to go into tunnels and use her gift in order to benefit them all. He was older than Tariq, although she couldn't tell by how much, only that whatever had happened to him had turned him into a very dangerous being. He wouldn't be asking his lifemate whether she wanted to come all the way into his world with him. He'd simply take her there. She had a feeling Siv was the same way.

"Hang on, Charlotte," Tariq said softly, wrapping his arms around her and lifting her easily to cradle her against his chest.

She had no option but to put her arms around his neck and hold on. She looked around for a car. Any kind of vehicle. They weren't anywhere near the parking lot. Gene-vieve and Lourdes had gone to bed, as had Danny and his sisters. Emeline's lamp was still on, but other than that one faint beacon of light, the night was very dark on the side of the property away from the lake. She tightened her fingers convulsively when the ground began to drop away, grateful she'd had playtime with Lourdes again before deciding to go with the men to the tunnels. The idea had seemed sound then; now she wasn't so certain, but soaring across a sky was maybe worth it after all.

"Tariq." She breathed his name, wanting to hide her eyes, but unable to do so, not when she could stare at the house and lake from above. He didn't hesitate or falter. Neither did the other men, still grouped in a tight circle around her.

"It's easier and faster to get from one place to the other this way," he explained.

That *so* wasn't an explanation. But flying through the air was totally kick-ass. She opened her mouth to speak and the wind whipped every word away from her. She chose to use their more intimate path. *Will I be able to do this by myself?*

Male amusement. *At last. Something about my world that pleases you.*

You please me. Flying *really* pleased her. Flying was possibly the coolest thing in the

268

world, once you got over the shock that someone could actually fly. She would be doing a lot of flying in the future.

Tell me why Dragomir thought it was too dangerous for me to go with you. Because, honestly, if a man like that was worried, maybe she should be as well.

Tariq was silent for so long she didn't think he'd answer her. She watched the houses and lights below her and then finally looked up at his face. Every single time she did that — looked fully at him — he took her breath away. Not just the beauty there, but the depth of feeling he had for her.

His blue eyes drifted over her face. *You are so brave, Charlotte. Many, even most, Carpathian males do not want any danger touching their lifemates. However, each lifemate is different, with different needs. For instance, Blaze, Maksim's lifemate, is a warrior through and through. She doesn't particularly want to have to fight vampires, but she certainly wants to know how to do so and to become skilled at it. She needs that. So Maksim can do no other than provide for her what she needs.*

And I need to do this. She made it a statement because it was the truth. She didn't want to fight vampires, but she certainly wanted to know how. She wanted to become the best fighter possible. She wouldn't want to actively go hunting, but she wanted to

269

know she could defend herself and her children — *all* the children — from the undead should she have to. *Blaze has the right idea.*

Yes. I spent a lifetime or two training young men for battle. I talked it over with Maksim and have no problem teaching you and Blaze and any of the other women here on the property who would like to learn.

You're very progressive. She couldn't help but bury her face between his neck and shoulder so she could kiss behind his ear and tug at his earlobe with her teeth. *I need a progressive man.*

When we go into dangerous situations, I expect instant obedience.

She flinched. There went his progressive status. *Tariq, I'm actually quite intelligent. I know enough, without you or anyone else telling me, that you're far more equipped and experienced at this type of thing than me. It's your world, not mine.*

He started to speak and she shook her head, feeling his thoughts forming in her mind. *It isn't my world yet, but even if I were fully in it, I would still expect you to take the lead and kill the monsters. I don't mind helping you in any way that I can, but all by myself I can figure out that I don't have the experience you have.*

She didn't try to keep the attitude out of

270

her voice. Did he think she was crazy? She had no problems wading into a fight. She backed up her friends, and she'd back up her man. She totally would take care of her family, but the idea that he thought she'd be silly enough to try to battle it out with the likes of Fridrick if she didn't have to do it was just plain crazy.

I told you not to touch the horses and you did.

Okay. He had a point. She'd totally done that. It was an accident of sorts, but still, she'd done just that. *When I'm around old things, I like to touch them. It's a compulsion.* As she answered, she stroked his face with the pads of her fingers, hoping he'd laugh.

I can see my woman has a lot of sass in her.

At least she could feel his amusement. *I have to keep up with your bossy tendencies. Remember the part about you giving me what I need? I need you to lose the bossy business.*

She felt more of his amusement and liked it a lot. That blossomed into full laughter, and she absolutely *loved* that.

They settled to the ground just outside a vacant building. "There's an entrance right here. The tunnels lead to a little underground city. The Malinov brothers prepared very well for this." Tariq put her gently on the cracked sidewalk. "They bought up most of these properties, and we think they're using the harbor to go out to sea on boats. They buy men and women from the trafficking rings and take them out where no one can see them all die."

A little shudder went through Charlotte. "Is that what they wanted us for? To feed on and kill?"

"No, Charlotte." He shook his head, his gaze moving broodingly over her face. "Down there, you'll find the reason hopefully just by touching the cages. We think we know what they're doing, but need to be certain. We found the bodies of several young women in various stages of pregnancy. We believe they are trying to find mothers for their children. Those women have to be capable of becoming lifemates."

Maksim led the way down into the tunnels. Tariq followed him. Charlotte stuck her hand in Tariq's back pocket in order to feel more at ease in the labyrinth with all the twists and turns.

"They're looking for their lifemates so they can have children?" she echoed faintly. Who would want the likes of Fridrick as the father to her children? That was the worst possible thing she could imagine.

"It is impossible for them to find lifemates. Even if one stood in front of them, they have chosen to give up their souls. They cannot bind her to them. No, they are looking for gifted human women strong enough to carry their children. How that is possible I don't know, but it is certain they are trying. We found . . . remains. We removed the bodies but had not gotten to the skeletons and bones. Those are still buried in the debris."

Charlotte felt a little frisson of fear creep down her spine. She couldn't imagine what someone like Fridrick would put a woman through, and according to Tariq, he was not the worst, not the man in charge. She *really* didn't want to be around to meet him.

They halted beside a door that was broken and held up by just one hinge. Beyond that, there was nothing but dirt, concrete and what looked like twisted steel. Tariq turned to her, put his hands on her waist and pushed her back two steps.

"Right there, Charlotte. I want you in sight at all times. All of us will clear out the rubble and then you can do the reading for as long as you can take it. When you tell me, I will pass every word along to the others. But stay close, don't wander off."

There wasn't going to be any wandering. This place gave her the creeps. The sconces remained high up on the walls and Dragomir waved a hand toward them to light them. She didn't think that made being in the tunnels any better. She could see splashes of blood on the curved walls here and there, as if the hallways had been deliberately and artfully decorated that way.

"Say you understand, *sielamet.*"

His tone could be a whip or a caress. This was the whip. He meant business. She nodded because already, even without her hand hovering on any object, she could hear the whispers. Agony. Waiting for death. Praying for death. She choked down the bile and did deep breathing. At the first test of true fire, she wasn't about to vomit all over the floor and prove to Tariq that Dragomir was right. She might be sensitive, but she was still a woman with a woman's power, and no way would she fold before she even got started. If there was any way to help other women Vadim and Fridrick were torturing, she would do whatever it took to save them.

"Honey, I'm not moving from this spot," she assured.

Tariq studied her face, seemed satisfied and then turned back to the door. A wave of his hand sent it floating to the ground out of his way. He pressed both palms down over the mess of concrete and dirt and slowly raised his hands. To her shock, the debris lifted away, leaving half-smashed cages and the remnants of a table and revealing another door beyond the first. The moment Tariq cleared the front room he moved to the second one, removing that door, glancing over his shoulder at her, giving a silent command not to move.

She glanced uneasily around her. It was

quiet. The Carpathians had spread out, going to other rooms in order to clear debris, and they worked in absolute silence. They communicated telepathically so there was no need for conversation. For some reason, that annoying spot on her finger throbbed painfully and without thinking she stuck the injured pad into her mouth.

Go outside and wait. Right now. Do not talk to anyone. You are not safe. Go outside and wait. Right now. Do not talk to anyone. You are not safe . . . The words were soft. Insidious. Compelling. Repeated over and over like a loop in her head she couldn't get rid of. A warning? Her own radar telling her she was in trouble? She shook her head to try to clear the sound, but it persisted, like a broken record that was stuck on those phrases only.

Twisting her fingers together, she tried to place the voice. Was it one of the other Carpathians trying to get inside her head? It didn't sound like them. The voice didn't sound like anyone she knew. *Tariq.* She defied the voice, needing to get anchored — and Tariq could do that for her.

Right here, sielamet. Step into the room but don't touch anything until I'm with you. I'm at the far wall working in the second room. I can see you.

She gave a little sigh of relief. Not only did Tariq's voice calm her, she felt a fresh breeze

275

coming from somewhere, pushing out the stale air and the odor of blood. That little bit of wind couldn't block out the whispers growing louder. Children's voices crying for their mothers or fathers. A woman weeping. Screams of many, both adults and children. She wasn't touching anything and yet already the walls in her mind were tunneling. At least the voice was gone. The hideous, sweet, compelling voice, trying to force her to leave.

Charlotte took three steps into the chamber and shuddered. Vile things had taken place in this room. A room of torture. Experiments with human beings. The cries were louder here. The anguish stronger. She could barely breathe.

You are not safe. Leave now. Get out of there. You are not safe.

The voice was back, whispering, not as loud, but no less strong. *Tariq.* She was afraid to say anything out loud. There was a feeling of danger, of doom. Her heart pounded so hard it felt like it might explode, and everything in her wanted to obey that voice, to turn and run, to get out of that unholy place.

What is it, sielamet? He must have heard something in her voice because he came back to the opening, the door that had kept ten-year-old Liv locked in with a monster feeding on her. His blue eyes searched her face and he stepped closer.

At once his warmth hit her, driving out the

cold that she hadn't even known had crept into her bones. She found herself trembling and she held out a hand to him. She needed to believe in something right then because she suddenly realized the world Tariq lived in held real monsters. Horrible deeds were done, and he lived knowing that every single moment of his existence. He hunted these creatures — beings capable of committing the kinds of torture on children that surrounded her.

Tariq instantly closed his fingers around hers and tugged until she was against his body, against all that heat and steel. He seemed invincible. Strong. For the first time she was very glad he was a predator, and she knew he had to be in order to find and destroy monsters. She inhaled him, taking his scent into her lungs, tucking herself beneath his shoulder, her front to his side so she could wrap her arms tightly around him, holding him close to her.

What is it, Charlotte? His voice was nothing less than a caress.

She loved the way he could soothe her with just that intimate voice stroking through her mind like the touch of his fingers on her bare skin. *I'm hearing someone else. I'm not touching anything, but I hear a voice telling me to get out, that it's not safe here. I don't recognize the voice, but a strong compulsion is anchored in it.*

She was very close to him so she felt the jerk of his body. The sudden coiling in him. She was anchored in his mind and knew he didn't like what she'd said at all. In fact, his first thought was total rejection. Then wariness.

Open yourself to me, sielamet. You are mine to care for. To cherish. To protect. I would never harm you. Let me into your mind all the way.

She hadn't realized she had barriers up. She didn't know how to do what he asked.

I can push through them, but it would be very uncomfortable. You have natural shields, which is why compulsion doesn't work on you. You feel it, but you don't have to act because it is nearly impossible to use mind control on you with the strength of the shields you have. That's why this is so bizarre.

He didn't say he didn't believe her, but she could tell he was shocked. She bit her lip hard and tightened her hold on him.

If you can talk to me like this, mind to mind, can't all Carpathians?

On a common path. If he were using the common pathway, all Carpathians, including me, would be able to hear. Sometimes you can direct to one individual, but in your case, we've exchanged blood. I'm in your mind. I would hear.

She moistened her lips and took another look around at the terrible torture chamber. Chains lying in the pile of dirt and concrete.

Tariq had brought the objects to the surface and in some cases, as with the cages, he'd repaired them without touching them. If she wasn't surrounded by the evidence of torture and didn't have a freakish voice in her head attempting to command her, she would think that ability Tariq had was *way* cool. Right now, she just wanted to run.

I don't like your world, Tariq. It's terrifying. Still, she rested her head against his heart, letting the steady beat calm her. *How else could this voice be speaking to me? Can he hear what we say to each other?*

Tariq didn't answer right away. She felt the push further into her mind and it was — intimate. Heat rushed through her veins. Her body went soft against his. She pressed her face into him and consciously tried opening her mind to his, knowing he would see everything. Her thoughts. Her doubts. Every fear. Every desire. It was both humiliating and exhilarating. He would know her better than anyone else ever could.

I love who you are, Charlotte. Every single thing about you. The parts of you that make you afraid of sharing with me, I'll handle with care. I do not see anyone else in your mind, but if I stay here with you and he speaks again, I will be able to hear.

How could he do this? she repeated. Anxiety shook her. She didn't want anyone else in her

279

mind. Tariq was different and she accepted his presence even though she kept admonishing herself to marshal her thoughts.

He would have to take your blood or somehow get his blood in you. You've been with me. No vampire could get into the compound. There are safeguards there. Strong ones. All the Carpathian hunters wove a shield in order to protect Emeline and the children from Vadim Malinov and his brother, Sergey. Vadim exchanged blood with Emeline and we believe he or Sergey did with Bella and Liv. But you?

Relief swept through her. *I've never been near either of those two vampires. Until you mentioned them, I'd never heard of them.* She took a deep breath and looked around her. *Maybe I conjured up the voice because the pain and suffering in this room is so horrific my mind is playing tricks in order not to fall apart.*

His hand came up to cup the back of her head, pressing her face deeper into him. *You have not conjured up anything. Dragomir was correct in saying you are very sensitive. I should have taken care of you, not allowed you to come here.*

She didn't like the word *allow.* She just didn't. The rest of it, okay, that was all fine, but . . . *Strike the word* allow *from your vocabulary.*

Instantly amusement spread throughout her mind. *I'm old-fashioned. Really old-fashioned.*

I'm a very modern woman and if you've been in my mind you know I am. I carry wasp spray in my purse just in case. That should tell you something right there.

It tells me you're strong enough to do this, and that you want to.

Maybe *want* was a little strong. She glanced around the room, took a breath and then stepped away from Tariq to lay both hands on the top of the table. Screams erupted in her mind. She winced but held on. *There were four victims before the man. The male Carpathian. They have such glee that they were able to capture him. They lost seven of their best men and it took eight others to take him, but now that they have him, they can drain him of blood and keep him weak. He would be the base for the experiments.*

She looked up at Tariq, her heart once again pounding. "I hear his voice. The same voice speaking. Did you hear it?" she whispered to him, afraid to speak telepathically now that she recognized that the man in charge of capturing a Carpathian and torturing him there on that table and in that room was the same man speaking to her.

Tariq nodded slowly, a muscle jerking along his jaw. "I recognize that voice. That was Vadim Malinov speaking. He's the one giving the orders to his men. Are you absolutely certain that's the same voice you heard warn-

281

ing you earlier?"

She nodded and moved on now that she had identified the strange voice in her mind. "Four women came before the captured Carpathian."

"When you tell me what happened, use the common path so the others can hear as well."

She'd forgotten that the others could hear her through her link with Tariq. She nodded. *The four women were on this table before the Carpathian hunter. They were used at first for food; several vampires took their blood on a regular basis and they hurt those women for their own amusement. And then . . .* She broke off. She hated this. Hated what was done to those women and what came after. *They raped them and impregnated them. Each of them. One at a time. They forced the women to consume a mixture of blood from the Carpathian and from the oldest and strongest of the vampires. The one called Vadim. He wants children so they can rise up with him to take control of the human fodder as is their right.* Her knees were shaking. She feared she might just fall down.

Tariq wrapped his arm around her to steady her. She pressed closer to him, grateful for the support. She felt each of those women's emotions. The terror. The horror. The need to fight back. Submission. Despair. And then pain. So much pain.

The babies. She whispered it in her mind. Sharing that with all of them. The screams of the unborn as they twisted in the womb, on fire, burning, the acid eating them from the inside out, in the same way it ate away at the mothers.

Enough, Tariq ordered. *Let go.*

She shook her head. *We need to know what they did to that man. What they wanted from him. The head guy . . . vampire . . . whatever . . . likes to talk. He talked to the women constantly, taunting them, making them aware they were nothing in his eyes, only vessels to carry something he wanted. He talked when he hurt them. He talked when he raped them. He would have talked when he tortured the Carpathian.*

Tariq brushed his hand down the length of her hair. *The Carpathian tortured is Val Zhestokly. He was in bad shape when Blaze found him. She set him free and Emeline gave him blood. In return, he hunted with us to get her back from Vadim. He is healing at the moment.*

Charlotte shuddered at the thought of what Vadim wanted to do to Emeline. Even to be close to the vampire would be horrible, let alone to have him touch you, or sink his teeth into you. She needed to visit Emeline immediately and offer friendship if nothing else. Emeline needed to know she had friends, people she could talk with.

She pressed her hand into the table, right over the large spot of dried blood. She knew it was Val's. The man had endured far worse torture than the women. It was as though Vadim and his friends were trying to find out just how much the hunter could endure before he died. Or cried out. He never made a sound. Not one single sound. The vampires systematically cut him almost into pieces. They tore his flesh open, and he didn't respond. Who could do that?

The torture went on for more than a year — she couldn't tell how long, but it was a very long time. Vadim or other vampires held him in their prison, keeping him so low on blood that his body nearly succumbed from that alone, but they knew how to keep him alive. They used every torture device known, modern and ancient, to break him. He seemed unbreakable.

Charlotte sifted through the history as fast as possible, gaining an entirely new admiration and awe for the Carpathian hunters. She felt a kinship with Val now that she'd shared his suffering. She didn't know him. She'd never even seen him, not alive and well, just this pale, worn image of him with the lines drawn heavily in his handsome face. His body was covered in scars, old and new. He had the same drifting tattoo she'd caught sight of on Dragomir. She knew she could find the origin of that if she went back far enough, but she had to come forward. She had to find out what Vadim's sudden surge of elation was as she neared the last few weeks.

You are not safe. Run. Run now before you die in there.

His voice, that terrible sweet sound, she recognized. Whispering to her. Commanding her. She knew he'd taken aim and thrust the compulsion at her because her head nearly exploded with pain and at the same time, her body spun around of its own accord prepared to flee. Tariq's arm was a band around her rib cage, holding her to him, his breath warm in her ear.

That is Vadim. Be careful when you answer me — stay on our path. It is different — a subtle difference only, so you must be careful. You are certain you have never been close to him?

She shook her head, keeping her eyes closed tight, afraid to look around her, afraid that Tariq might suddenly let her go and she'd be facing the threat alone. Vadim Malinov was a far worse threat than Fridrick. She'd sensed Fridrick in the background. He'd taken Carpathian blood a few times and done his share of torturing, but no one was as evil as Vadim, not even his brother, Sergey.

He has never touched me. Look into my memories. Into my mind. He's not there. I didn't know he existed until I met you. I don't know how he's doing this.

285

Köd alte hän. Tariq snarled the words, his voice a soft growl that sent a shiver through her.

What does that mean? She tipped her head up to look at him, hands still on the table, connecting both of them to Val Zhestokly and the Carpathian's suffering.

Tariq's eyes had gone to pure blue flames. "It means 'darkness curse it.' Swearing in Carpathian doesn't sound as bad as swearing in today's modern language, but believe me, Charlotte, it is."

She did believe him, mostly because of the way he said it, the tone he'd used. He didn't like that Vadim was in her head and he couldn't figure out how the vampire had gotten there. *Keep holding me while I find out exactly what Vadim wanted from Val.*

She didn't wait for Tariq to agree. She moved forward from the past to just a few weeks earlier. She had to reach for the right time she needed, and when she did, she took a deep breath and allowed the walls of the tunnel to grow around her, sealing her in with the memories solidified right there in the blood and wood.

Vadim approached Val, who was chained in a small, uncomfortable cage like an animal. Clearly the vampire was filled with mocking glee. *I have found the right one. The others will die soon. They are too weak and cannot pos-*

sibly carry my child, the one to destroy Mikhail and his entire lineage. But this one, she has tested very high, and she will soon be here in the States. I've set things in motion already, and I have discovered just how important you are to this project. Do you know what that means, Val? Do you have any idea?

Vadim waited but Val didn't deign to look at him let alone answer him. Vadim waved his hand to unlock the cage. He reached in with deliberate slowness, wanting his victim to see what was coming.

The vampire struck hard and cruelly, tearing into Val's throat, his teeth sharp and huge. Chained and weak from lack of blood, from all the torture of whips and chains and knives, Val couldn't do anything to protect himself. He continued to be silent, stoic, completely ignoring the cruelty of Vadim's assault.

Vadim drank his fill and then shoved the Carpathian away from him, smearing the blood on his lips with the back of his hand. Val made no attempt to sit up straight, remaining slumped against the bars of his cage. Vadim watched him. *It burns, doesn't it? The hunger. It eats away at you until you can't think of anything else. That need. Every waking moment it is there with you. You had your chance to join us, but you were too stupid to see the reality of what the Dubrinsky line was*

287

doing — becoming weaker and weaker. Draven should have shown you that.

Val made no acknowledgment of Vadim's declaration. The Carpathian merely looked at his tormentor with no expression whatsoever. Charlotte had never seen a man so ravaged and torn, so tortured, and yet he was stoic. She knew he felt pain because she felt it through her connection to him.

The more she touched each vignette from the past, the more she understood the players — and Tariq's world. It was violent and dangerous, just as he was. There was also something incredibly beautiful and heroic about the way the Carpathian endured his imprisonment and torture. She couldn't help but admire and respect the man. She knew he was very similar in personality to Tariq. She'd been in Tariq's mind, and now she was sharing both Val's and Vadim's minds.

Vadim. He was the most narcissistic person she'd ever met in her life. He was a megalomaniac, without a single doubt believing he was smarter than anyone else. He wanted power and believed he deserved having it. No one was greater than him.

You will always know it was you, Zhestokly, that aided me in bringing down the prince and his lineage. You and your blood. You will live a long time knowing that again and again I will use your blood to kill my enemies and raise my army. The vampire spat at Val, the spittle hitting him full in the face, but the Carpathian made no sound, no movement. He sat stoically in the cage, folded up, unable to move, his heart weak, barely able to pump. She wanted to touch him. To reassure him that he would escape. That the others had in fact come for him.

Come back to me, Charlotte, Tariq whispered softly in her mind. Again there were the small caressing strokes she was fast becoming familiar with.

Charlotte shook her head. She was so close to figuring out Vadim. They would need to know every detail in order to defeat him — because someone had to stop him. Someone had to stand up to the mastermind monster and his army of vile followers.

You've been gone too long. Come back to me.

There was a hint of steel in the voice, and her first impulse was to go back to him. This place and time were very dangerous to linger in. Tariq had noticed her presence when he was carving his carousel horse. Vadim's attention was entirely focused on Val, but at any moment he could have sensed her presence.

One more time. I haven't gotten everything yet.

She didn't wait for Tariq to answer because she knew he would demand she return. She moved to the next vignette, closer to the present timeline. She chose the day they had rescued Emeline in the hopes that it would reveal where Vadim had gone and what he was up to next.

The terrified screams of a child pierced the air. Evil laughter, a sound that rivaled nails on a chalkboard. She heard the low murmur of the Carpathian's voice for the first time, soothing the child. Talking quietly just beneath the shrieking voices of the vampires surrounding him. To Charlotte's horror, they were bleeding him dry. She recognized Fridrick and Vadim, but there were two others holding cups to the numerous wounds pouring blood from their victim.

The child — the one she recognized as Liv — sat almost on the Carpathian's lap; he had one strong arm curled around her, his hand over her eyes. His head was bent low to her ear as he whispered to her. Her screams stopped abruptly and she nodded over and over, sinking into him for protection. Charlotte knew there would be none — not for the child and certainly not for the hunter.

You grow weak, Val. So weak. If you die, there is no hope for these women. These children. Vadim turned to half face the open door leading to the other room. He gestured toward it. *They wait their turn. Your blood will feed all of them and you will be the downfall of the prince, his people, and all the humans we intend to kill or enslave.*

Charlotte turned to look and there were seven more men standing there, some grinning at the helpless child and the weakened Carpathian. The men were watching as the vampires licked obscenely at the blood. She recognized one of the faces. She'd seen him before, but where? He appeared entirely human, as did the others. They weren't pale; they didn't have sharp, bloodstained teeth.

She gasped when the memory came to her. *This* was the man Daniel and his two companions had staked. She shared her knowledge with Tariq and the others. They were all connected through Tariq.

The others were in the parking garage with Fridrick, Tariq informed her.

She hadn't gotten a good look at them. Clearly they were recruits into Vadim's army. She needed to know what he was doing. Where he'd gone. They needed answers. Charlotte tried to get closer to Vadim, to get inside his mind. What was he doing with these human men? They weren't puppets, eating the flesh of children, or begging for the Carpathian's blood, literally licking the floor to get a few precious drops. Those people had once been human, but now they seemed to be programmed by Vadim and the others to do their bidding.

Human psychics. Males. We never paid at-

291

tention to them. Vadim and Sergey must be recruiting them. Tariq informed the others.

Why is he giving them Carpathian blood? Dragomir asked.

Charlotte was aware that Tariq shook his head in frustration.

Vadim stepped close to Val, and the child shuddered and turned her face into Val's bare, bleeding chest.

Hurry, give me your answer now, before it is too late. Charlotte caught the words, Val whispering to Liv.

I want to be alive, Liv whispered, closing her eyes and turning her head to the side to present him with her neck.

Val sank his teeth into the little girl's neck and drank. Vadim stepped back, and let out a high-pitched laugh. *I knew you'd see reason. Stay alive for your little pets, Val. See how well that works out for all of you.* The nasty voice droned on, taunting the Carpathian as the man fed.

Charlotte couldn't help but be mesmerized by the way Val held the child. Carefully — almost tenderly when she knew he felt no emotion whatsoever. Still, for the child he managed to appear as if he did. Then she remembered Liv's soft entreaty. *Don't you want us?* The child could more than likely read Val as well, yet she stayed very still, her neck to one side, allowing him to take her blood.

The moment Val lifted his head, he ignored the others and used a long fingernail to open his chest. At once the child turned her face to the offering. Charlotte wanted to close her eyes. She didn't want to see the way Liv took the Carpathian's blood. It should have been sacrilegious, but instead, she found it incredibly beautiful. Val had offered her life. He tried to make her valuable to Vadim by giving the child his blood.

11

Charlotte desperately wanted to break away when she saw the expression on Vadim's face as he stepped closer to the cage Val and the child were held in. He looked . . . evil. Pure evil. His face was a mask of fury. His eyes glowed a demon red. His mouth pulled tight to reveal his teeth, stained and sharp. How could she not have noticed that before? How could she not have seen just how truly a monster he looked?

She held her breath, shoved her fist into her mouth to keep from screaming. Or maybe she should scream. She could distract him — maybe all of them — and somehow save the child from what she knew was coming.

You know you cannot. Come back to me, Charlotte. There is no need to see the rest.

She knew he meant *feel it,* because when she touched the occupants of the memory left behind in the object, she felt what they did. She wasn't ready to take on four more traumatized children — she had her hands full with Lourdes — but Liv was impossibly brave. There was no way she could abandon that wonderful, courageous child. Not ever.

She forced herself to watch in silence as Vadim sank his talons into Liv's arm and jerked her hard, dragging her away from Val. Liv started to scream. Her mouth opened and a single shrill wail rose, but the child cut it off abruptly, her gaze shifting to Val's face. He nodded to her.

Charlotte's heart jerked hard in her chest. She *felt* the warmth and courage Val sent to Liv. He'd connected with her through a blood bond and he had just assured her that he would do his best to stay with her throughout whatever ordeal she was facing.

Vadim dragged her past the other two vampires. Sergey, his brother, stabbed at the child viciously with a long sharpened nail, drawing blood. He laughed and licked at his finger, his eyes on Val. Fridrick delivered a kick to Liv as she struggled to get on her feet as Vadim continued to drag her through the seven human males toward the puppet that stood swaying and growling.

Charlotte looked at the men's faces as Vadim tossed the child to the puppet as if she were a piece of garbage. The thing resembled a human, but there was nothing left in its mind but purpose. Vadim had programmed the monster to do his bidding, but more than anything else, the craving for flesh and blood drove it. The puppet caught the child by the hair and dragged her into the next room.

None of the men made a move to help the child, but two of them frowned and stared after her, both shifting uncomfortably. They weren't altogether happy with Vadim and his new regime. She focused on them so that any of the Carpathians she was connected with would remember their faces.

I will not ask you again, Charlotte. You are ice-cold and shaking. You're too far gone. Come back to me now.

She wanted to go to him, she really did, but she also wanted to reassure Val that he made it out of there. She needed to do the same thing for Liv. The child had to know that rescue was close and that she wouldn't die at the hands of that gruesome puppet. Charlotte forced her body forward, slipping past Vadim to get to the cage where Val was held. Fridrick was at him, tearing at his flesh with horrid teeth, snarling and gobbling blood as fast as he could. Charlotte reached out to Val. She'd never thought of trying to have someone in the past know she was there. They were memories. Not real. But Tariq had known. He'd turned his head and, for one moment, she knew he was aware of her when he was carving the carousel horse. If he could be aware, so could Val and Liv.

She turned sideways and made herself as small as possible as she extended her arm, fingers settling delicately around Val's bicep. His flesh felt strange. Cold. Icy cold as if she stood in an ice cave and the cold permeated not only the atmosphere surrounding her but entered her along with every occupant.

Icy fingers crept down her spine. Very, very slowly, Val turned his head toward her, but he made no sound. His eyes, piercing cold, black as ice in a violent storm. She didn't know if he saw her, but he felt her presence. *You will survive this.* She used the common pathway she'd picked up from Tariq's mind. *So will the child.* She needed to give him that reassurance. Liv's survival was more important to him than his own. She didn't know how she knew that, only that she did.

Instantly, Vadim roared with rage, and Fridrick renewed his frenzied gulping. Sergey turned around sharply in a circle searching for an unknown presence. She let Val go abruptly, afraid she was making things worse for him. Had they heard her as well? Of course. It was a rookie mistake. The vampires had once been Carpathians. Of course they would hear anything said on that particular path. She'd whispered it. Poured truth into it. Now the monsters were alerted not only to her presence but also to the fact that Val survived. She hoped they would eventually think her whispered words had been false.

She backed away from the cage, careful not to touch any living thing. She needed to get to Liv, to assure her, to make certain the child knew she would be saved. Stepping into the next room, she saw the child on the floor, the hideous puppet tearing at her flesh in a feeding frenzy. Vadim, Fridrick and Sergey rushed past her, Fridrick nearly hitting her as he dashed through the room where a monster was feeding on a child, to the safety of the labyrinth of tunnels. The human men followed, the last two glancing down, slowing, as if they might intervene.

Vadim's voice boomed. *Quickly, they're coming. Now is our chance to get her.*

Firm hands yanked at her. She was turned into a hot embrace, a hard body radiating such heat it nearly burned her skin. A mouth crushed hers under it. The tunnel was gone and she was left freezing, shivering uncontrollably, her body icy, so cold her insides felt like shards of icicles that could shatter at any second.

It took a moment to realize Tariq held her tight against his body. His arms surrounded her and his head was down so that he could whisper in her ear, reassuring her, talking so softly she didn't think she would understand the words. It took a moment to realize she couldn't yet hear him because part of her was still in the cold, dark past.

Her legs barely held her up and she burrowed closer to the heat of Tariq's body. Clinging, when she wasn't a woman to cling.

Crying when she wasn't a woman to do that anywhere someone could see. She couldn't stop the terrible tremors or the continuous shivering any more than she could the tears.

Tariq wrapped Charlotte in his arms, holding her close, her ear over his heart, while it pounded with fear for her. He realized when he waited for her to return that somehow she actually managed to go back into the past when she touched an object. He knew astral projection was possible, but to actually go to a specific place in the past and hear and feel what was happening around her was far too dangerous. He'd never heard of astral projection taking one's spirit to the past.

Instinctively he knew she shouldn't interact with those from the memory she had accessed. The longer she remained in the memory, the more withdrawn and cold her body had become. Her skin felt like ice and she was barely breathing until it had reached the point where he felt desperately terrified for her. When he'd caught her by her arms and forced her head up, her eyes were blank, and that had been the last straw.

"I should never have put you through that." *Allowed* her to put herself in such a position. He was asking this woman, the *one* woman, his miracle, to join him in a world that would be terrifying for her. He'd spent lifetimes in it. Centuries. Taking blood to survive, sleeping in the ground, hunting the vampire, all of that was familiar to him. Not one single aspect of his world was comfortable to a woman raised in the modern world. Not. One. Single. Thing.

She didn't move, just took the shelter and comfort he offered, her hands fisting in his shirt. "You had to know. *I* had to know. The enormity of this . . ." She broke off, drew a ragged breath into her lungs and held on tighter. "It's so unreal. You've lived with this knowledge, that you could become — *that* — a monster like no other."

Tariq's heart stuttered at the sound of her voice. Soft. Distressed. In tears but trying to hide them. Her body trembled against his, shivering continuously, probably without her knowledge. Stroking a caress through her silky hair, he cupped the back of her head and held her to him.

"Coming into my world means dealing with vampires and their puppets. With their cruelty." He hated that for her. Hated that he needed her so much he knew he was going to bring her into his world no matter what. No matter that she deserved different — a good man who would worship the ground she walked on. The thought of it set his teeth on edge. He tightened his hold on her. He'd lived with honor for centuries. In his world, the male was born imprinted with the ritual binding words that tied his lifemate to him for all time. It was done. No reversing it. No going back.

"I'm sorry for that, *sielamet*. I'm not sorry that I found you, or that I claimed you, but I am sorry that you have had to see and feel the things you have."

"It made no difference to them if it was a child or a woman or a man." Charlotte continued to whisper, as if saying anything too loud, admitting vampires existed, made them all the more real to her. "Fridrick *murdered* my brother and Genevieve's grandmother."

"I know," he answered just as softly. He looked around him, up at the crumbling ceiling of the tunnel. "I'm sorry." Meaning it. Knowing that she wouldn't be able to separate him from his world. He was solidly in it, regardless of the trappings of humans. The club. His clothes. The way he deliberately lived among them.

Charlotte's body stiffened, and she tilted her head to look up at him. To meet his gaze. He was a little shocked by what he saw there. Tears still swam in her eyes, turning the color a deep emerald. Little droplets clung to her long lashes. But there was steel there. Pure strength. She didn't look at him like a woman defeated. She didn't look as if she blamed him for bringing her into the insanity that was his world.

"Fridrick murdered my brother and Genevieve's grandmother," she repeated. "I was already in your world, Tariq, only I had no idea what I was facing. I was at a huge disadvantage. Now I'm not. Now I have you and the others, and this time, I found his weaknesses. All of their weaknesses. Never tell me you're sorry for bringing me into your world. I was already there and you saved me. Fridrick would have taken both Genevieve and me in the parking garage had you and your friends not come along."

He couldn't deny the truth of that, but still, she surprised him with her acceptance of him. For him, the time was so slow. He'd searched for her for too long, and he knew the moment she gave him back the light for his soul. He knew she was his everything. It wasn't the same for her. She was human and he was moving her fast into his world.

He could tell himself — and her — that it was to keep her safe, but the truth was far different. He wanted her for himself and he wanted to ensure she was with him. He didn't want her on the surface while he was in the ground. He wanted her body pressed close to his while they slept. He wanted to wake up with her in his arms.

Now, with his fierce little warrior glaring up at him, he knew she was strong enough to accept the children he cared for, as well as Emeline and Mary and Donald Walton. His motives for bringing her into his world didn't matter to her. She had made her decision, and she trusted him with her life and the lives of the two people she held dear — Lourdes and Genevieve.

"We have to hurry and get out of here," she murmured softly. "I need to see the rest of it, but I want to go fast. I feel . . ." She broke off, looking around her, apprehension pouring off of her. *He isn't entirely gone. I feel him. Vadim. It was his voice talking to me and now I feel as if he's crouched there inside me, watching and waiting until I make a mistake.*

She communicated with him on their more intimate path, but Tariq immediately relayed the message to the others sifting through the rubble.

There is no need for her to see these dead women or feel what was done to them, Dragomir said. *There has to be a blood bond between your woman and Vadim. Find the source, Tariq, or she will become a liability we cannot afford.*

Tariq went very still, the predator in him uncoiling. Unsheathing claws. The threat was there. Dragomir was ancient. Extremely dangerous. He had been one of the ancients, so powerful and deadly that he had locked himself in the monastery with others like him. They could no longer be in the world and have those around them be safe. They were considered the most dangerous Carpathians living, which made them the most dangerous creatures on the face of the earth.

Dragomir and the others believed it was dishonorable to seek the dawn rather than give in to the never-ending whispers of temptation. When even those whispers stopped and there was only a dark void of nothing, they knew too many kills had destroyed them. They had no hope, no memories, nothing but their honor and strength to keep them from killing anything that came near them.

Dragomir was of the old school, unused to the modern ways, and he believed their women would follow where their men led. He had recently left the monastery because he'd been given renewed hope that his lifemate existed and was in the United States, specifically California. He had stopped on his way north to aid Tariq when the call went out for aid against Vadim. Tariq no longer knew if that was a good thing. Dragomir would be hard to kill, even with several experienced hunters close.

Deepest respect, Dragomir, but you do not get to say what my woman can or cannot do. Do not think to threaten her. He couldn't keep the menace from his voice. He would fight to the death for his lifemate.

As would I. She is yours; that makes her one of us. She is my sister, deserving of my protection for that alone, but with what she has done here this night and what she intends to do for

*those children, respect is part of that as well.
She should not be here to see these women
ripped apart and babies suffering every moment
of their existence within the womb. This is . . .
beyond anything I have ever seen. It is not for
the eyes of an empath.*

I agree. Because it was true. Charlotte had
no business anywhere near those bodies they
had found piled up like so much garbage in
one of the rooms. Women and stillborn
babies, stacks of bones dating back to when
the city was first built. Vadim had planned
his takeover carefully and patiently — two
traits that no vampire had ever had before.

*If Vadim is in your woman's mind, he can use
her eyes to spy. That is a fact, Tariq, and that
has to be dealt with. Once she is safe inside
the compound, he will find it much more difficult
to reach her with the safeguards in place.*

That was also the truth. Tariq glanced down
at the top of Charlotte's head. Her hair was
thick and glossy, begging him to bury his
fingers deep. He did so, gripping the mass
and tugging until she turned her face up to
his. She smiled up at him, giving him reassurance, willing to put herself out there all
over again. Absently, she brought her finger
to her mouth and sucked on it. It was sexy
and instantly his body stirred with hunger in
spite of the inappropriate setting. She did
that a lot.

Tariq went still, everything freezing with the memory of her bringing her finger to her mouth when she had accessed the memories from the carousel horse — memories of Vadim and his brothers on the night they had chosen to give up their souls. He'd been carving the carousel horse earlier and they'd been with him. They had left, found out the news of their sister and returned to recruit him to their cause. When he refused to go, they had attacked the village, going after each and every one of the humans Tariq had befriended.

Charlotte's eyebrow went up. "What?"

She returned the tip of her finger to her mouth, and this time he caught the small wince, as if it was hurting her. His breath left his lungs and he shackled her wrist and brought the hand out of her mouth, turning it up for his inspection. The finger was wet from her sucking on it. A nervous habit? Or some other reason? He turned the finger to every angle. A little red at the fleshy part of the pad, but no discernible injuries, no breaks in the skin.

"Does this finger hurt?"

She kept her eyes fixed on his. His Charlotte. Too intelligent. Already thinking. Very slowly she nodded. "I got a splinter when I jerked my hand back from the carousel horse."

He closed his eyes, the memory of her pulling her hand away from the wood fast, the moment she had connected with the past and had seen Tariq carving the horse. She'd known it was him and she'd been frightened. Of course she would be. People she loved had been murdered in a way depicted in horror films. Knowing he had lived centuries she had to have thought he was a vampire — like Fridrick.

"Did you pull the splinter out? Did you get all of it?"

She frowned and tried to pull her hand away, shaking her head. "When I looked again, the splinter was gone."

"What part of *don't touch it* did you not understand?"

He knew he had an edge to his tone, but *o köd belső* — darkness take it — he'd *told* her not to touch the *peje* thing.

She yanked her hand away from him, eyes narrowing. "What part of *I'm a grown woman and don't need anyone telling me what to do* do *you* not understand?"

His woman had a bite to her, but he'd known that all along. She couldn't be wild and passionate in bed and not have a temper. Still, his woman wasn't going to defy him when it came to her safety. That was totally unacceptable and always would be. He tightened his hold on her, pulling her up onto her toes, her face close to his. He stared down

307

into her eyes, wanting her to know he was serious.

Uh-oh. Charlotte let her breath out slowly. She'd just come up against the predator. Civilized, sophisticated Tariq Asenguard, owner of several fabulous and popular nightclubs, was gone and in his place was something altogether different. He was really upset with her. Her heart jumped and began to pound slowly. Instinctively she knew this wasn't about her defying him and touching the carousel horse when he'd told her not to — and that's what scared her much more than his terrifying demeanor. Something was very, very wrong, and it had to do with that cursed horse.

"In all matters to do with your safety you will obey me," he bit out.

It wasn't the time to laugh so she bit down very hard on her lower lip. Seriously? He'd used the word *obey*. She hadn't been very good at obeying her parents and certainly not her older brother. It wasn't the time to inform him that she definitely had a problem with anyone thinking they were her authority figure.

Tariq had lulled her into a false sense of security. He'd looked modern and come off modern, unlike his caveman friend Dragomir, who was just plain scary. She'd smash him over the head with something hard if that Carpathian belonged to her. She might kick

Tariq in the shins very soon if he continued to throw words like *obey* around, but . . . He yanked her even closer, so that she was on her toes, her body tight against his and that very handsome face inches from hers. Her heart pounded hard in her chest, but deep down she knew — she *knew* — with absolute certainty that this man would never hurt her. Never. He could posture all he wanted, but he wouldn't harm her.

So why was she so scared? Why was she terrified beyond anything she'd ever known? Charlotte flung her arms around his neck and leaned into the pillar of strength she knew him to be. He felt solid. He was solid. A rock. An anchor. The world he lived in was something she didn't understand. It seemed to be filled with nothing but danger. It shifted continually until she felt she was on a carousel that never stopped spinning. The world moved up and down like the horses and spun out of control, making her dizzy. But Tariq never seemed to be caught up in the effects of the world, or even the danger. He was solid. Real. Someone to count on.

"He's in me because of that splinter, isn't he?" she whispered. The terror that came on the heels of that reality shook her. Vadim, the vile, hideous monster who tortured men and could throw little girls to flesh-eating creatures so callously, was *inside* of her.

Instantly, Tariq's body language changed.

With his arms he enfolded her, sheltered her, comforted her, just as she knew he would. His mouth nuzzled the top of her head. "We'll get him out, *sielamet,* but it isn't safe here. We need to get you back to the compound. Dragomir was right when he said Vadim could use you to spy on us if we're not careful."

She gasped, her fingers curling into his shirt tightly, bunching the material while she hung on to him. "I can't go back there, where Lourdes and the other children are. He can't ever get his hands on Liv again. She wouldn't survive a second round with him intact, Tariq. You know that. She's barely hanging on as it is." If she were a danger to these men — the Carpathian hunters — then what would she be to the children?

"The compound is protected. Vadim compromised Emeline as well by taking her blood. She has to stay inside the fence, where we can protect her night and day. He can send an army of puppets at us during the day, and now, after seeing those human males, we know he clearly has others as well. We knew he was recruiting humans to do his bidding, but not like those men. They were different somehow. Just the fact that he gave them Carpathian blood and they *wanted* it — something is very wrong. During the hours of the day, we have to rely mostly on safeguards to keep Vadim's army out."

She took a breath. "You sleep during the day." She had to know. Maybe she had known all along. He'd told her, but she hadn't really listened. "Not because of working at the nightclub. You *have* to sleep during the day."

He nodded, his gaze holding hers captive. "Yes, we'll all sleep during the day. We can be up in the early morning hours and after the sun sets, but the effects of the sun are devastating on Carpathians." He moved, taking her with him. "We have to get you out of these tunnels and back home. I've put the call out to the others and we'll go out as a group. You'll be in the center."

It was an order, nothing less. His tone held no compromise. Was implacable. She heard that command in his voice, and she didn't give a damn. Fighting for independence was one thing when her life and sanity weren't at stake, but when she had to rely on his strengths, she wasn't about to quibble over what tone he used. Clearly he was a man used to giving orders. Right then, she was supremely grateful for his ability to take charge.

Charlotte didn't want to take a step out of the tunnels into the open. She felt extremely vulnerable, more so than she'd ever felt in her life. She had to trust these men — especially Tariq — to know what they were doing. Their grim faces told her she was in trouble. They expected an ambush. Because of her, Vadim knew exactly where they were.

311

She turned that over and over in her mind while she walked in the center of the tight-knit group through the last tunnel, the one leading out. If Vadim was inside her and could find her and talk to her, did that mean it could go both ways? Could she locate him? Track his whereabouts for the Carpathians? The idea made her feel less like a victim and more in control. She needed that, to feel in control.

One of the triplets stepped in front of the group and held up his hand.

"Lojos, Tomas and I can make a diversion, send it out first to trigger any traps they've set for us. Give us a few minutes," Mataias said.

She liked the way the leadership changed among the Carpathian hunters. No one seemed to be considered more in charge than any other, although Dragomir was the scariest man she'd ever encountered — in his way he rivaled Vadim and that was saying something. Siv was a very close second.

Immediately, as if by common consent, the rest of the pack stepped back to allow the three men to take the lead.

"The rest of you construct a safeguard around Charlotte so Vadim cannot see into her mind. Whatever he has placed in her, you have to disrupt," Lojos said.

Charlotte ducked her head, embarrassed that she was a vessel of betrayal for the monstrous psychopath vampire. Tariq pulled her snugly beneath his shoulder and wrapped an arm around her so that she felt comforted while he and the other men began chanting in their language and weaving some kind of barrier in her mind. She felt it going up, a thick shield that blocked out Vadim's possession. She knew it was temporary, that the vampire could eventually find a way through it, but for the moment, it made her feel safe.

"Mataias." Lojos pointed to a chunk of stone that had come out of the wall when the vampires had reduced everything in the underground city to rubble. "That will work for our leader."

Mataias nodded and crouched down beside the large piece of bluish rock while his brothers gathered several smaller, but solid pieces in various colors to line up behind the bluish chunk.

Tomas found a gem-filled rock and added it to the growing pile in front of Mataias. Lojos walked down the tunnel seeking something along the walls. He stopped several times to examine roots and a few plants growing rather stubbornly through cracks in the dirt or stones forming the tunnels. He seemed in no hurry and neither did the others. They remained silent and watchful.

When Lojos bent and began tugging a plant, Charlotte peeked around Tariq in order to get a good look at what Lojos was doing.

He carried the plant to the stones and placed a little segment on top of each stone. Tomas waved his hand over the rock with gems embedded in it and it broke apart. He placed gems on each of the chosen stones Lojos had put pieces of the plant on. Simultaneously, all three men stood and stepped back as if giving the rocks room. She held her breath, aware something big was about to happen, but not understanding what the men could do with a few rocks.

Their hands began to weave an intricate pattern over the stones. As they moved their wrists and arms to a rhythm only they heard, they added their voices. The tone was pitched very low. So low, Charlotte felt the earth vibrate beneath her feet. She didn't take her eyes off the rocks. The largest twitched, as if feeling the vibrations in the earth.

She felt the chanting right through her body. Shaking her up. Making her tremble. The notes were low and clean and uttered with tremendous force. The sound vibrated until the stones began to break apart. Chips at first, then larger pieces until forms began to take shape. All the while, the three men chanted, their hands never faltering as they created what were fast becoming several dragons.

Charlotte couldn't believe how detailed each creature was. The blue one was large, its body and tail growing fast. It was all stone, and its various shadings gave it a striking appearance. The gems were the eyes. The stones took on the visage of fierce dragons quickly. The commands in the voices grew as well until the tunnels vibrated with the demands. Once the dragons had taken shape, once every detail was done to the men's satisfaction, the tone of command changed, became even more demanding.

It was so fascinating to watch the rocks grow in size and take on the shape and look of dragons that she didn't notice anything else until she heard Tariq let out a low warning hiss between clenched teeth. Startled, she looked around her. Rocks in the tunnel walls as well as on the ground either shook apart or grew in size. It wasn't only the chosen rocks reacting to the notes the three men produced.

She realized the combination of their voices and hands formed the dragons, but the actual low notes shook the rocks and changed the properties in them. The ceiling could come down on them, or the earth might open if they continued much longer. As it was, there were several cracks in the ground, the walls, and the ceiling. Dirt trickled down on top of them, but Tariq waved his hand and it stopped. She noticed the other Carpathian hunters were moving their hands toward the walls as well as above and below them. Clearly they were shoring things up.

Abruptly the voices of the triplets rose in perfect harmony, no longer shaking apart the ground and the walls of the tunnel as she'd feared. Charlotte had no doubt that if they chose, the three men could have taken down the entire city beneath the one above it. They had a remarkable gift, one she wouldn't mind having. It made her wonder if all the strange shapes formed in stone throughout the world hadn't been made by them rather than what the history books proclaimed.

Fire burst through the rock, the dragons glowing orange-red through cracks. The rock itself turned molten. The chanting slid into a softer harmony and the rock bellies of the dragons began to cool, the cracks no longer glowing, finally turning dark.

The notes turned coaxing. She watched the small segments of straggly green plants shudder on each of the dragon backs. Charlotte held her breath and tightened her hold on Tariq's shirt as the green segments began to shred into fine hairs. Each individual hair floated up above the dragon the plant had been sitting on. The chant went from coaxing to pure, steely command and suddenly, as if they were spears, the separate pieces stiffened and slammed hard into the stone, so hard they buried themselves deep. Each dragon absorbed at least a hundred separate hairs of the plant.

The three men dropped their hands and

their voices went still. The tunnel was so quiet Charlotte could hear her own heartbeat. It drummed loudly, but even that couldn't distract her from watching the stone dragons intently. There was the blue leader, a large one so detailed now that she wanted to touch his scales to see if he was alive. Behind him were four smaller dragons, red, green, brown and a striking orange.

Abruptly and simultaneously, the three men clapped their hands, a single word bursting from them. The blue dragon shuddered. His great sides heaved and then moved in and out like a bellows. Very slowly his head turned first one way and then the other. His tail switched. The slightly smaller dragons began to move as well, twisting their necks and shaking their heads, breathing until the sound of the air moving in and out of their bodies filled the tunnel.

"Oh. My. God. Tariq," she whispered, pressing her forehead against his side, never taking her gaze from the five dragons. "That's incredible. An incredible gift." She'd been so fascinated she hadn't noticed the passing of time and was shocked that it had only taken a few minutes for the three hunters to make their dragons out of rock and plants.

Tariq didn't respond with words, but he tightened his arm around her so that her front was locked tight to his side.

The blue dragon took a step forward,

turned its head toward Tomas, Mataias and Lojos, eyes intelligent as it listened to the commands the three men gave it. The gem-like eyes glowed with purpose as it once again faced the entrance and began to walk slowly toward the opening. The other dragons followed, one at a time. The men moved as a group behind them.

Tariq swung around and lifted her into his arms, his brilliant blue eyes staring directly into hers. "Hold on, *sielamet*. We go out in dragon form. Keep your mind as still as possible. Vadim will try to push through the barrier. Stay strong. He'll use his voice on you to try to trick you into thinking he knows where you are. Remember, he can't get to Lourdes, no matter what he says. Believe in me through this. Trust in me."

She could drown in his eyes. Just live there forever. She nodded slowly. Who else was she going to trust? She was so far out of her element she didn't have a clue what to do. Even Genevieve, who had a vivid imagination, wouldn't believe any of this.

The last of the five stone dragons were through the opening and the others went out, Tariq and Charlotte with them. When she looked around her, as they launched into the air, there were no men, only dragon bodies in full flight. The stone dragons circled the other dragons as if they were the Carpathian hunters protecting the other dragons as they emerged. Once all of them were in the sky, the blue dragon took the lead with the others following, forming a V shape. Tariq, with Charlotte clinging to him, was on the left side, two dragons down from the blue dragon.

The formation was tight as they blasted across the sky. Suddenly, the blue dragon dove, jaws wide, fire blazing. Charlotte leaned into the black dragon's embrace, shocked that she not only saw his scales but *felt* them. Her man, Tariq Asenguard, sophisticated owner of a string of successful nightclubs, was a compact black dragon complete with wings and scales. When she looked down at her own arms, she was part of that dragon, with the same shiny black scales.

An illusion. Oh. My. God. Her dragon suddenly dove as well, mouth wide, spewing red flames. All around her the sky erupted with fire and color. Below them, an army of vampires, humans and puppets scattered, trying to protect themselves from the dragons spraying them from above with fire.

Won't the people in the city below see this?

We're protecting them. Tariq's grim response was terse.

The vampires hastily tried to concoct cover for the humans in their army. Spears whistled through the air. One hit the orange rock dragon and bounced off, the tip shattering. Even as the black dragon dove to spray his fire, she realized all the dragons continued toward the compound. They dove down, and as they came up, they were winging their way through the sky away from the failed ambush.

Stop them or your niece dies. I have her. Lourdes. She screams for you, do you not hear her?

Oh God. She could. She could hear the child's shattered cries. Everything in her responded. She *needed* to go to Lourdes.

Show me yourself. Show me which dragon you ride. Drop from it and I will ensure you live. If you do, I will spare this child. Otherwise, her death will be long and hard. She will feel every moment of pain before she dies.

He would do that. Vadim was a monster, but . . .

Sielamet. Tariq, his voice. Warm. Reassuring. He'd told her Lourdes was safe and she had to believe him.

I can find him. Follow his voice back. She wanted to close her eyes, but she couldn't. She needed to find Vadim. To see him. She searched the ground as the black dragon raced through the sky, leaving her breathless — and unable to make out a single face below her. But that voice coming at her . . . into her mind . . . was filling her with doubts.

She turned her attention to that voice wrapped in such sweetness. Sticky sweetness. False. It had a lingering aftertaste. Sweet turned to bitter. Almost like ashes. Deliberately she let herself get lost in that bitter ash. She turned her head and looked down toward the harbor. *There, Tariq. On that ship. He's there, directing all this from safety.*

The leader of the dragons made a wide circle, his followers in tight formation behind him, the circle wide enough to include the harbor. The moment the realization came to the vampires on the ground, they took to the air in defense of Vadim. Fire rained, spears of fire, great bolts that sank deep into the deck of the vessel, hit the sides and went in deep, so deep she couldn't see the spears, only the giant holes. The terrible spears penetrated the ship from every direction, a fierce, unrelenting attack as the dragons dove low, spraying the decks until the vessel erupted into a fiery ball.

She heard the shriek in her head, the scream of a madman, made more insane by the explosions of violence surrounding him. A black shadow rose, a huge one that seemed to encompass most of the sky. Immediately the dragons went after the shadow, blowing great columns of fire that tore through the shadow until it was in tatters.

Vampires rose, shrieking, throwing themselves at the dragons in a frenzy of fury, trying to protect Vadim as he raced across the sky away from the battle. Charlotte glimpsed Fridrick, not the smooth man she'd seen in the parking garage, but a vile being, with glowing red eyes and bloodstained, jagged teeth. He rose up fast and sliced at the neck of the dragon carrying her in its arms. Terrified, she closed her eyes, curling into Tariq. The body of the dragon shuddered. She felt the great wings beating in the sky, the heat of flames. She knew Fridrick had scored a hit, but the dragon continued to fly.

The battle raged for a few short minutes, but she realized the dragons were circling back in formation, protecting her. All of them. Every single male Carpathian. Protecting her. She felt tears burn. The wind tore them away, but she knew these men, regardless of their inability to feel emotion, put her before their own safety.

She heard the screams of the puppets and humans as the dragons passed overhead, but everything was a blur and the dragons stayed in formation as they headed home, Tariq and Charlotte in the very center.

12

Charlotte woke with every muscle in her body aching. The dragons might have been illusion, but riding them took a toll on one's body. She didn't open her eyes, savoring the feel of just drifting, half awake and half asleep in a warm cocoon. She'd been brutally tired the night before and could barely stand when they'd arrived at the compound.

Tariq had been wounded when Fridrick attacked them. She'd seen the blood on his shoulder and neck, but he simply shook his head and told her the others were healers and they would take care of it. He would be a few minutes and then he'd join her.

She'd expected to have nightmares, but she'd slept like the dead. She'd taken one peek at Lourdes, grateful for Genevieve, who had put her niece to bed for her. The child was sound asleep although it was early morning. She'd left a note for Genevieve to wake her if she overslept and then she remembered standing by Lourdes's bed, swaying, unable to think what to do next. Tariq had picked her up as if she were featherlight, cradling her to his chest, whispering to her to go to sleep. She'd done just that with the feel of his lips brushing her eyelids.

Now she was pressed against someone warm and solid and she found herself smiling, knowing it was Tariq. His legs were tangled with hers. One thigh was over the top of hers, and his arm was a band around her waist. His fingers moved along the underside of her breast and instantly she became aware of the fact that she wore nothing at all. She didn't want to open her eyes and face whatever new nightmare would come along; she just wanted to stay there in the bed with Tariq and shut the rest of the world out. She let herself drift in a haze of drowsiness and warmth.

Tariq's fingers stroked gently over her flesh, tracing patterns absently into her warm flesh. It felt . . . lazy. Nice. Sexy. She needed that. She needed to just lie in his arms and feel loved. Protected. Safe. His lips brushed her temple, and he shifted, sliding over the top of her, blanketing her. His hips fit snugly, perfectly in the cradle of hers. His hair was a glossy chestnut fall, drifting over her shoulder and her left breast in a sensual slide.

His eyes were warm blue, almost sapphire, like two gems staring straight into her soul. Her heart contracted. Her belly softened. Her womb fluttered and her sex clenched. His mouth moved gently over her face. Small, butterfly kisses, featherlight, yet each brush of his lips sent small tremors through her.

One hand went to her throat, circling it so her heart beat into his palm. He held her eyes as his kiss went to her chin, his teeth scraping with exquisite gentleness. His hand moved from her throat down her body, sweeping slowly over her breasts, the valley between them, to her rib cage and then her belly. His gaze never left hers and she saw it there. In his eyes. The claiming. The possession. The stark, raw love.

She didn't know how he could feel that way about her, but it was there in his eyes and his eyes didn't lie. She felt tears burning. For the first time in her life, she felt as if she belonged. As if she'd come home. She'd traveled the world extensively, looking . . . but for what she was never sure. She just knew she had never found it until this moment.

He circled his cock with his fist. "Are you ready for me, *sielamet*?"

She nodded, never looking away from his eyes. Of course she was ready. How could she be anything but ready for him? She felt as if she was made for him. Born for him. The broad crown nudged her entrance and her muscles contracted, wanting him desperately, needing to draw him inside. He was thick and hard, velvet over steel, pushing

325

through her tight muscles, making her gasp, arch her back, buck her hips to meet his invasion.

Very gently, with unhurried motion, he took first her left leg and wrapped it around him and then her right so that she hugged him with her legs, digging her heels into his thighs. He caught both of her hands, threading his fingers through hers and raising her arms to either side of her head, pinning them to the mattress.

He began to move, slowly at first, his gaze burning into hers. She knew what he was saying to her. He was making love to her. Worshiping her body with his. Making certain she heard him and that she knew exactly what he was saying to her. He wanted her looking into his eyes so she could see what he felt. He wanted her to be in his mind so she could see his thoughts, so she could know him as intimately and as thoroughly as he knew her.

With his body locked in hers, moving slowly so that the burn built and built, looking into his eyes and knowing she was going to be there forever was the most sensual, intimate thing she could ever conceive. He gave her that and it was so beautiful.

Her body followed his every movement, reaching for him. Surrounding him. As the tension in her coiled tighter and tighter, her muscles locked around him, building the wonderful friction so that each time he surged into her, streaks of fire burned through both of them. She opened her mouth in a small gasp, moving her hips to meet his, tightening her fingers through his and holding him to her with her legs.

"So close, honey," she gasped, feeling the burn building into an out of control wildfire.

"That's it, *sielamet*," he whispered. "You're so beautiful when you give that to me." He leaned forward and took her mouth. The action pressed his cock right into her most sensitive spot so that lightning streaked through her. She gasped, tightening her legs, moving with him, catching fire, letting the storm take her.

"Mine," he whispered softly, watching her, his eyes still holding hers. "Love this, woman, when I give you that, but love you so much more."

Then he was slamming into her, deep and hard, taking her with him again, so that when he emptied himself into her, she tumbled into another strong orgasm, this one off the charts, stealing her breath and sending every nerve ending into sensual awareness. She lay under him a long time, wrapped around him, surrounding him, loving being so close. He hadn't taken her blood, and a part of her had wanted that, but she knew he wanted to complete the conversion and she wasn't quite ready for that.

Tariq kissed her gently and rolled, taking

her with him so she was on top. "I need you soon, Charlotte," he said, confirming he was still in her mind and could read her thoughts.

"I know. I want that, too, but I have to make certain I have everything in place for Lourdes and Genevieve. I'm Genevieve's only family now."

He shook his head and tucked hair behind her ear. "I'll be her family as well. So will Danny, Amelia, Liv and Bella. She's already fitting in, taking care of Lourdes the way she does."

"I want to take care of Lourdes myself," Charlotte said, pressing her face into his neck. He felt strong and warm. Definitely an anchor in a chaotic world. "How am I going to do that if I'm up all night and she is up during the day? I know right now you're pushing her to sleep during daylight, but that can't go on forever."

"Lourdes can't stay a human child. None of the children can," Tariq explained, his voice gentle. "They're known psychics. The vampires are hunting psychics, even children. We've got Josef, one of our technology experts, coming to try to get information off of the smashed computers, and he's young. By young, I mean in Carpathian years. He won't be considered an adult until he's fifty, and he's nowhere near that. He'll be good for Danny to know. We haven't thought much about converting men because there are so few women. Converting males is more difficult. They have to be accepted by the ancients. Once Danny is converted, I'll have to take him to Romania, to the Carpathian Mountains and the cave of the warriors. If they don't accept him . . ." He broke off, shaking his head.

She lifted her head. "What does that mean?"

"It means there are a lot of questions I don't have the answers for. I'm consulting everyone I know who could possibly give me the odds of a child converting without too much distress. I know it can be done, but there's pain involved. I can minimize it, but I can't take it away. I've explained that to Amelia and Danny and they understand. They're both a little hesitant because they don't want Liv to suffer anymore, and of course they're afraid for Bella, just as I am." He sighed. "And now Lourdes. Before I convert the children, I have to have those answers."

She liked that it mattered to him. More and more she was discovering Tariq didn't jump into anything. He studied a problem from every angle and found solutions before he made a move.

"I don't want Lourdes or Bella to suffer. They're only three."

He nodded. "So young for this to be happening. We could try to wait, but every day that we do, Vadim could be planning something. We can't keep them prisoners here on the property forever. Sooner or later all of them will want to go places."

"If we find and kill Vadim, won't that solve the issue?"

He stroked caresses down the back of her head, his fingers threading through her hair. "I've hunted vampires for centuries, *sielamet*. There is always another one. Always. Now, with their ability to band together and use modern technology, the threat is larger than ever."

His hand moved in lazy circles down her back until his fingers found the indentations of the dimples in the cheeks of her buttocks. "There's something very enticing about your bottom, Charlie. I love when I'm behind you and watching you walk away from me."

She raised her head to look at him. His smile was all Tariq. Charm. Sweetness. All for her.

"Then again, I like the front of you very much as well. I can't say which is better. Your breasts or your butt. I've given it a lot of contemplation."

She couldn't help herself. She laughed softly and settled her face back into his shoulder. His voice was as lazy as the touch of his fingers on her skin. "You've had such a lot of time for contemplation lately."

He smacked her bottom sharply. "Watch it,

woman," he admonished.

His hand resumed its leisurely patterns as heat spread through her, and she had to press her face against his skin to muffle her laughter. Still, that heat went deep, igniting nerve endings she hadn't known existed. The intimate touch of his fingers sliding over that heat only added to the need suddenly, without warning, coiling inside of her.

"You know I have to get up and take care of Lourdes. Genevieve has been so great about it, but Lourdes is mine and she's in a new place. She needs to know this is home and I'm going to be her mom." She rubbed her chin on his chest, her hands moving over the places where wounds should have been on his shoulder and neck — but weren't. There was no sign of any laceration or burn.

Charlotte took a breath and decided to ignore the fact that a man could be healed overnight. She needed normal. "Lourdes has had enough trauma to last a lifetime, and she's only three. I can't imagine what Bella and Liv and the others are trying to deal with." Her eyes met his. "You know I have absolutely no experience dealing with children. I restore art, Tariq; I don't do counseling. I wouldn't even know where to start."

"Carpathians can read minds. You will be able to see their worst fears and you'll know what to say. We are polite and respectful and don't, as a rule, invade, not unless safety or health is at stake or we feed and have to remove the memory, but in dealing with these children — *our* children — I don't think we have a choice."

She sighed and went to roll off of him, but his arm tightened like a steel band across her back and the hand on her bottom slid down to cup her cheek, his thumb brushing strokes along the seam between her cheek and her thigh.

"Not yet, *sielamet*. I will know when the children awaken. Right now we have private moments and I need them with you. We face a long war. Vadim will not be easy to find, let alone kill."

"It worked last night. We drove him off the ship. If I can hear him, and you say he can use me to see what's happening around me . . ."

"Not here. As long as you're on this property, the safeguards we've woven together will hold. Emeline and Liv both need them."

"Still, if he can 'see' me, then I should be able to see him."

"We're removing that splinter tonight. It's too dangerous to play around with anything like that. That splinter wields power. Legend has it the carousel was cursed. The horses, the chariots. All of it. Owners and their children died and no one knew why, or they were brutally murdered with throats ripped and blood gone. We now know why. Vadim

332

did something to that carousel, and it has to be destroyed."

"No!" She pushed up with both hands. "It's a piece of history. We need to remove whatever he did. I can restore it properly."

Tariq's hand went back to rubbing her bare skin. "You have no idea how dangerous Vadim and his brother, Sergey, truly are. Fridrick presents a terrible danger, but he is nothing compared to those two. You don't ever take chances with vampires, especially master vampires. You kill them without hesitation and you keep the risk to yourself as little as possible. We have several experienced hunters here. I put the word out, and those in the area are coming here as well as watching all harbors. We know he's been moving on ships out to sea in order to keep us from tracking him."

"How in the world can he feed if he's out at sea?"

There was a small silence. Her gaze jumped to his. "Tariq?"

"Lojos and Tomas have been watching them. They discovered that they meet up with human traffickers at sea. Ships bring them to him. All bodies are disposed of before they ever return to shore."

She closed her eyes and slumped against him, wrapping her arms around his neck. "He has to be stopped, Tariq."

"I know, *sielamet,* but it will take time. He

333

has pawns like Fridrick. Fridrick isn't the only master vampire under his command. They will be sacrificed before we ever get to Vadim. He should leave this area because there are too many hunters. We think we will be able to divide and conquer that way."

Once again his fingers drew little patterns across her bottom, and it felt wonderful. She needed his intimate touch when they were discussing something as vile as Vadim Malinov. The thought of any part of a monster like Vadim being inside her was disturbing. She wanted him gone and she didn't want to chance giving him a glimpse of the children ever again. "I see what you mean about the splinter, but Tariq, I do have a way of tracking him. The carousel is in your basement. If I touch it I can find him, now that I know what I'm looking for."

Tariq frowned and the hand moving on her bottom stopped. "That might work, under the right circumstances, but Charlotte, don't you dare try on your own. I mean that. I'll know, and this time, the consequences are going to be severe enough that you won't disobey me again when it comes to matters of your safety."

She clenched her teeth and her entire body went rigid. So much for her gorgeous, perfect man. Not. So. Perfect. "Don't threaten me, Tariq. I'm not five years old, and just a little FYI, I've been in your mind and you would never hit a woman or child. I think I'm pretty safe from your consequences."

"It isn't a threat, Charlotte; I don't make threats. I am far more modern than most of my brethren, but living for centuries among humans has not made me human. I am a Carpathian male. There are things you will have to live with about me, just as there are things about you I must live with. When it comes to matters of your safety, rest assured, lifemate, I take that very seriously. When I tell you to do something, I expect it to be done. You don't have to like it, but you do have to do it."

Once again she attempted to roll off of him, but he held her in place. "Stop struggling. It is useless and rather foolish to be angry over something neither of us can change. I could word it gently and you may like the sound of it better, but it all comes down to the same thing. What is so difficult about treating your safety as sacred? Will we not treat our children's safety that way? Or Genevieve's safety? What of Emeline's? Donald and Mary's? Should we neglect them because they are older? They all need our protection."

She huffed out a sigh of resignation. She was arguing over semantics. He was right even if she didn't want to admit it. She hadn't liked him giving what sounded to her like an order. Still, she'd already touched the carousel horse without him and was enduring the consequences. It stood to reason she'd learned her lesson without him going on about it.

"All right," she conceded. "You won't have to worry. You're the expert in all matters vampire and the like, so I'll follow instructions to the letter."

His hand resumed making little lazy patterns on her skin, this time sliding up to her back and moving around to her sides so he was tracing her rib cage and the side of her breast. Her blood turned molten and liquid heat gathered between her legs. She found it amazing that he could do that to her with just his touch. Her heartbeat throbbed between her legs and pounded in her neck, where every now and then she felt the warmth of his breath.

"That's my very smart woman. Your idea just might work, although I don't like the notion of your having anything to do with Vadim, even remotely. And we'd have to make certain there was no way for another sliver to get into your skin. I'm going to remove it now. I'll be heat, a white light you'll feel within you. Be still for me."

Charlotte subsided against his chest, letting her body go soft, melting into his. She wished he was still deep inside her, but at least he surrounded her with his arms, and one leg curved around her thighs as if he knew she needed to be wrapped up while he went after

Vadim's splinter.

Tariq didn't wait. He didn't like the idea of a master vampire having put a cursed splinter inside his woman. More, if others had died because the splinter was inside of them, he had to see what it was doing. So far, she hadn't shown any signs of illness. She looked beautiful to him. A little wild. A little sexy. Just perfect. Her skin wasn't unusually warm, which might have indicated a fever — the human warning signal that something wasn't right. There was nothing at all to tell him there was something extremely dangerous in her.

He shed his body in the way of his people, becoming spirit without ego, a white, healing light that easily entered her body. He checked every organ for damage. The splinter was nowhere to be found in any vital organ. There was a subtle difference in her blood. Very subtle; at first he almost didn't notice, but the absence of the splinter worried him, so he was even more careful, determined to draw it out into the open.

He moved through her with meticulous care, sending small sound waves through her body to loosen the splinter's grip on whatever it had attached itself to. As he did so, he saw several of her white blood cells suddenly slide against a red blood cell and engulf it. He had to replay the scene in his mind several times to make certain he had seen it correctly. He watched for several more minutes but nothing else happened.

Once again Tariq sent the small sound waves crashing through her body, keeping his focus on her white blood cells. Instantly the same thing happened. A few of the white cells engulfed red cells, effectively eating them. At the same time, just to his right, along her ribs something wiggled for a moment and then settled back into the bones. His breath caught. The splinter had attached itself to the bone and had become part of her skeleton. Just the very tip remained. It was still pushing its way inside the bone.

He struck fast, using the burn of the white healing light to surround the small piece of ancient, cursed wood, to settle over it, needing to destroy it fast. The splinter didn't move. He couldn't see where her bone started and the splinter left off. Only just that little tiny piece wiggling to try to get away from the burn of white light.

He knew at once he couldn't remove it. The splinter had become part of her and would not be destroyed. Since there was no removing it, he had to forge a cell around it strong enough that the sliver couldn't penetrate it to do more damage to her body. Perhaps one of their greatest healers could perform a miracle and remove it. Unfortunately, none but Dragomir was close. Dragomir was . . . difficult. Not Carpathian. Not vampire. Somewhere in between perhaps. No one was certain whether they could trust him — including Dragomir. Siv . . . might, but again, he was very much like Dragomir. It seemed they lacked a talented healer in the area. All of them could get by, but right now, Tariq knew, he couldn't wait any longer. He had to send for a master healer, even if that meant one needed to come from the Carpathian Mountains.

He was meticulous in his work, taking his time, encasing the rib in a strong binding safeguard, weaving it with healing light the splinter winced away from. It tried to burrow deeper into the rib to escape the light and then when that failed, it curled itself around the rib, lying as flat as possible, like a fish's tail against the bone. He wove the cage stronger, thicker, layering the light through the safeguard until he was certain the splinter couldn't penetrate from any side and escape. When he was absolutely certain, he added several more layers. He wanted her safe. Only then did he move out of her body and back into his own.

He opened his eyes and she was watching him, a small frown on her face. Her hand smoothed the lines in his face, and then cupped his jaw. "You're so pale, honey. That took you forever."

He hadn't been aware of time passing, but staring into her eyes, he realized he'd been working on containing the splinter for some time. He hadn't fed, and leaving one's body and becoming pure spirit took a tremendous amount of energy.

"Tell me what you need, Tariq," she whispered, her voice dropping an octave. Husky. Seductive. A blatant temptation.

His woman had great instincts. He reached up, cupped the back of her head and pulled her face down to him so his mouth could take hers in a long, wet kiss. Hard. Meaning it. She ignited like she did for him, taking them both higher, burning hot and a little out of control. He kissed her over and over, his fist bunching her hair, controlling her head to keep her tilted just the way he wanted so he could drink his fill of her.

He kissed his way down to her chin, along her sweet jaw and down her neck to that intriguing little pulse point calling to him like a beacon. She knew, the knowledge was there in her mind, and she wanted his mouth on her. His teeth. He used them ruthlessly, scraping on her tender skin, marking her as his. He loved putting his mark on her and knew it was a trait of his kind. Possessive of their women. Needing others to know she belonged to him, was part of him — the best part.

"Keep you safe," he murmured against her throbbing pulse. "Always keep you safe." His teeth bit down, gently. He caught her skin and tugged. *"Always."* He emphasized the word, made it a command, all the while using his teeth to put an exclamation point on the end of his declaration.

Charlotte gasped, stretching her neck as if she could get away from the sharp teeth that had her trapped and held close, but she didn't pull away, instead arching her body, pressing her breasts tight against him, as streaks of lightning seemed to zigzag through her body straight to her sex. She loved when he used his teeth. She never once in her life considered that she might, but it was the most erotic sensation when he bit down. Gentle or rough, it didn't matter.

His low, husky growl stating he would keep her safe only fueled the fire in her. She wanted his teeth, even needed them. She held her breath. The moment went on for an eternity, that perfect blend of anticipation, need and the ultimate hunger. His lips moved on her neck, right over her pulse, so that her heart beat right into his mouth. Her sex clenched. Wept. Burned. His teeth sank deep and pleasure burst through pain, radiating throughout her body so that every nerve ending was alive and desperate for him. Burning for him. A wildfire out of control.

His hand slid up her back to her neck and then his fingers slid into her hair, fisting, pulling her head back even farther until there was a distinct ache. That only added to the

341

heat coursing through her veins. She felt the hard thick length of him pressed tightly against her stomach. Inches from where she needed him to be. Her core pulsed. Her sex spasmed. She shifted her body minutely. Subtly. Sliding down just that couple of inches.

Tariq didn't relax his hold on her hair, or allow her head to move at all. His mouth and teeth gripped her neck tighter. She felt that all the way to her soul. That connection. The primitive yet beautiful way they were joined together. She heard her own gasp. Her moan. She sounded . . . sensual. She felt sensual, something that had never happened in her entire life until Tariq. She wrapped her fist around the heavy length of him and guided him into her body, sinking down onto him.

His heavy erection pushed through the sensitive folds of her body, an almost excruciatingly tight fit. He took her breath. He sent waves of sheer pleasure building and building so that she felt tension coiling deep inside. His mouth moved again, his tongue sweeping over the marks on her neck to close the small wounds. Once, twice, his teeth scraped over the brand he'd left behind and each exquisite pass caused her body to bathe his shaft in liquid fire.

His hands slid down her sides, from her breasts, along her rib cage, her waist, to settle on the flare of her hips. "Move, *sielamet.* Ride me hard."

She wanted that. She sat up slowly at his urging and then leaned back when his hands pressed to her belly.

"Put your palms on my thighs."

His eyes were dark with passion. With lust. Soft with such emotion she was forced to catch her breath or her lungs would have burned raw. "You're so beautiful," she whispered, meaning it. Unable to keep her opinion inside. He was beautiful. Not just on the outside — and he was that. It was the way he felt in his mind. The way he was with the children. The way he not only wanted to protect them all, but needed to.

He watched her moving for some time, his hands on her waist at first and then as her body flushed and coiled so tightly she thought she might not live through it, they slid to her breasts. His fingers tugged and rolled her nipples, and then he was sitting up, shifting so that deep inside her, his cock burned across her most sensitive parts, creating that out-of-control wildfire. The fire overtook her, consumed her, and took him with her. She sank into him, her face in his throat, desperate for air but uncaring if she ever breathed again.

Tariq wrapped his arms around her and held her close to him. She loved the way his fingers massaged her scalp. For a long time the world stayed at bay and she could just drift in that place he sent her with his body. He held her for a long time, but eventually she felt his body tense. The moment he did, she tightened her hold on him.

"I don't want to move," she protested.

"Those three men, the ones that followed you from Paris and were in my club the other night, they are outside my gates, skulking instead of just coming up and asking to talk to me. I have to go deal with that, Charlotte."

She sighed. "I knew they weren't going to let us be. Should I go with you? Solidarity and all that?" She didn't lift her head; instead, she nuzzled his throat and pressed little kisses up his jaw. She didn't want to deal with another serial killer. Another monster. She wanted, even needed, normal. Lourdes. Genevieve. A life outside a monstrous world.

"No, *sielamet,* you stay as far from them as possible. They can't tell the difference between Carpathian and vampire and they kill indiscriminately. You, the children, Genevieve and Emeline are all in danger from them. They could pose a danger to Donald and Mary as well. I'll talk to them and see about giving them a little push to leave us alone."

"Be careful, Tariq. They were in the psychic center for testing, and my guess is, they have some kind of abilities." She pushed up with resignation and the action caused a minor quake to ripple through her body. Charlotte gasped and tightened her thighs around his

344

hips, holding him to her.

"I'm always careful, Charlotte. I've chosen to live among humans for most of my hunting years. Centuries now. I know how to fit in easily. I also know that some humans have extraordinary powers. Some are kind, the best people I've known, and others are sick and cruel, nearly as bad as the vampire. I've seen it all, and it's made me careful. You take care of the children and visit with Genevieve. Be normal. Settle in. I'm going to have to bring you fully into my world soon, *sielamet*. You will waste away if I don't. So you need to feel that your decision is the right one, the only one for you."

She already felt that way. She was more alive with him than she'd ever been in her life. She had always been seeking something — she hadn't known what, but she traveled the world to find it — only to realize now that it was here with Tariq. A family of sorts. Danger. Peace. Bliss. Everything she'd ever wanted was right here in bed with her.

"There are so many other hunters here. Can't one of them talk to these men?" She knew he was powerful, but still, she'd seen the man with the stake through his heart.

He smiled at her and stroked another caress down the back of her head, his fingers tangling in her silky hair. "The other hunters, aside from Maksim, do not have lifemates to anchor them. Can you imagine Dragomir

345

talking to those men, seeing their intentions? He would kill them immediately without thought of consequences. He doesn't live with humans, Charlotte; he never has. He has never been civilized. Just being here is probably extremely difficult for him."

"I can't imagine what he would do with a woman. He's so . . . rough."

"He is a hunter. A predator. He always has been and he always will be. Lojos, Tomas and Mataias are wild cards. Val, the hunter Vadim tortured, lies beneath the earth, healing in the soil. They feed him, and care for his wounds, which are severe. They would not like the idea of another threat to their brethren and they would also kill the three vampire hunters without thought of consequences."

"So you're saying you're the one who has to deal with them."

"Yes, *sielamet,* but I promise to be careful."

"What about the splinter?" She knew she was stalling, wanting to stay with him, but truthfully, she hated the idea of having that splinter inside her whether Vadim could see what she was doing or not.

"I'm sending for a Daratrazanoff. That lineage is incomparable when it comes to healing."

"Where are they now?" Meaning how long would it take for one of them to get there. The idea that a tiny piece of Vadim was inside of her made her feel sick, especially now that

Tariq confirmed he was even more worried about it than she was.

"In the Carpathian Mountains."

Her breath caught and held in her lungs. If Tariq was sending for a healer all the way from the Carpathian Mountains, he was very concerned about the splinter.

She didn't ask any questions. She didn't want the answers right then. She wanted normal. She wanted to visit with her friends and maybe have a cup of tea without getting sick. She wanted to hear the sound of laughter.

"You're in my mind," she whispered, bending once more to move her lips against his jaw. She loved the hard line of his jaw. He was handsome, gorgeous even, but he was all man. That jaw of his indicated his strength, his determination. He knew exactly what she wanted, what she needed, and he was giving that to her.

"Does it bother you? I try to stay just to the forefront, not intrude, but after so many centuries without you, searching for you, I find it difficult to separate entirely."

There was a hint of vulnerability in his voice. She kissed her way from his jaw to his mouth. Placing her lips right over his, she told the truth. "I love that you are in my mind. I don't like to be away from you, either."

He took her mouth the moment the last

word was uttered. One hand was at the back of her head, holding her firmly the way he did that always gave her a thrill. His mouth moved gently, though, lovingly, even leisurely, exploring and tangling his tongue with hers to stroke and caress. She loved kissing him. She could kiss him forever. He took his time and she loved that about him, too. He had somewhere to be, people to protect, but he still took his time with her as if she mattered more to him than anything else.

"This is your last night as a human, Charlotte."

It was a decree, not a question and her heart jerked hard in her chest. She was often lulled into a false sense of security because Tariq was sweet to her. He was reasonable. He was sophisticated. He was also a predator just like Dragomir, only he disguised it better. Dragomir didn't bother, while Tariq did. Tariq's thin veil of civility could shred at any moment.

Still, Charlotte knew she would choose him every single time. He was the man for her. Born for her. And she was born for him. She leaned down and kissed him again and then slowly slid off his body. He didn't have to change for her; she wanted him just the way he was.

"Okay," she agreed softly. Because for her, there wasn't any other choice. "I'll be ready." She wanted to go see Lourdes and talk with

Danny, Amelia, Liv and Bella. She wanted to visit with Genevieve and Emeline and maybe meet Blaze for the first time. Be normal in a world that wasn't hers anymore.

He reached for her as she slid off the bed, his hand cupping her face, thumb sliding gently over her lips. "I'll take care of you always, Charlotte. You'll want for nothing."

She believed him, but that wasn't what was important to her. "Just feel about me the way you do now. Always."

"It grows every single day. It will continue to grow. Your courage in taking on Danny, Amelia, Liv and Bella astounds me."

"You're taking on Lourdes and Genevieve for me."

He nodded and was up, towering over her, waving his hand to clean and clothe her. She liked her soft, vintage blue jeans and equally soft dove gray sweater. He had good taste in casual clothes. Her bra and panties were sheer lace, but the bra was supportive, and her boots were gray leather with three leather ruffles down the back. She loved them.

"You'll be able to do that yourself," he said, and bent to take her mouth. When he straightened, he was dressed in his immaculate and very sophisticated clothes. "Go have fun. Don't forget Emeline. She's ours, too."

"I won't forget. I have Vadim's splinter in me and I detest it. She hears him as well. At least we have that in common, and in Paris, we were becoming fairly good friends. Hopefully that will count for something."

She kissed him again, just a brush of her lips across his, but it was enough to claim him. To tell him that he belonged to her.

13

Lourdes and Bella were in the bathtub playing with rubber ducks when she entered the bathroom. Charlotte had never seen so many kinds of ducks. They weren't the standard yellow ones she'd had as a child. These were various characters, and the girls clearly loved them. They chattered away together, laughing like old friends — or sisters. She sent a small grateful warmth to Tariq for thinking of toys for the girls.

"They're already bonding," Genevieve whispered, sipping at her coffee. "I never thought I'd be so crazy about a couple of little girls but I love spending time with them. They make me feel . . ."

"Normal," Charlotte said, with a small laugh. "I was just telling Tariq I needed normal, and here it is."

Genevieve nodded. "I can't agree with you more. Do you want a cup of coffee? It's the best coffee I've ever had."

The thought of drinking coffee made Charlotte's stomach roll. She pressed a hand to her belly and shook her head. "I'll pass, but thank you."

"You and Tariq good?"

"Better than good. I've fallen so hard so fast. Thanks for taking care of the children while we're sorting things out. I can't tell you how much I appreciate you doing that for me."

"I wanted to. After all the things you've done for me, Charlie, this was easy." She sighed and put down the mug of coffee. "I can't stay here forever, but I have to admit I'm a little afraid to strike out on my own."

Charlotte heard the tremble in Genevieve's voice. She leaned toward her. "Do you want to leave?"

Genevieve shook her head. "Of course not. It isn't that, but I'm not about to be the fifth wheel here. This is your family and you need space to make it that way."

Charlotte shook her head. "You are my family. I don't have anyone else, Genevieve. It's the two of us. We chose each other in Paris, long before your grandmother was murdered. Way before my brother was murdered and all of this happened to us. *You're* my family. Tariq knows that. He wants you to stay. You can have your own house and eventually, when the danger is gone, live life the way you want, but for now stay here; make one of the houses yours."

352

Genevieve looked away from her, back toward the two little girls. Three-year-olds, both of whom had witnessed brutal, vile violence. They were whispering together, dunking the ducks and watching them pop back to the surface. Both would giggle when the little ducks bobbed and looked as if they were swimming.

"I want to do that, Charlie, more than anything. I want to stay. I feel safe here. I'm not afraid for the first time in months. But I don't want to rain on your parade. You deserve to be happy and to form a family with Tariq . . ."

"Stop, Vi. Seriously, just stop. Just because I found Tariq and I want to bring together these children doesn't mean I don't want you in my life in a huge way. I'll need help, a lot of help. I'm counting on you for that. I don't know the first thing about children. You already agreed to help me with Lourdes. The only thing that's changed is we have four more children, two of whom are teenagers."

Genevieve snickered. "Is that all that's changed? Four more children? A little thing like that shouldn't stop us."

Charlotte found herself laughing. Real laughter. She loved the fact that it was genuine, that she could laugh in spite of the circumstances. "Okay. Maybe it's big."

"Try *huge.* But if you're certain Tariq won't think I'm just hanging around living off him,

I'll stay and help you."

"You have your own money, Vi," Charlotte reminded with a small smile.

"I'll offer, but I can guarantee you, he won't take a cent. He's the throwback kind of man, you know, to another century. He'll want to pay."

Genevieve was *so* right. Charlotte nodded. "Whatever it takes to keep you here with us, Vi. I don't care if he wants to foot the bill. We can help out when the crisis is past. In the meantime, it's my turn to take care of the kids. You go choose a house. Make a list of everything you need to make it a home. You love lists. Wander around. See the property. I'm going to try to visit Emeline later this evening. If you see us on her porch, come by casual-like and visit with her, too, okay?"

Genevieve nodded. "I will. I'm looking forward to seeing her." She reached out a hand and pushed back Charlotte's hair to study the mark on her neck. "You're certain of what you're doing, Charlie? He doesn't have you under some spell, like in the movies? This is all unknown territory for us, and I have to confess, I'm really uneasy about it."

"I've always had some kind of shield, Vi, you know that. I don't react to mind control. That was what saved us both in Paris when Fridrick tried to make us open the door and allow him in. I want to be with Tariq of my own free will," she assured.

Genevieve nodded. "I like him. I do. It's just that, these men are very scary. They look so gorgeous that any woman might just fall hard, but underneath that beauty, seriously, Charlie, they're very dangerous, scary men. I'm not like you. I've always wanted to be, but I'm not the warrior woman." She lowered her eyes, twisting her fingers together in her lap. "I don't belong here."

Charlotte leaned into her. "Yes, you do. You're strong, Vi. Not everyone has to be a fighter. You fight when you have to. You would defend any of these children, you know you would. You would defend me, and Tariq as well. You just aren't the best at defending yourself and that's okay. We were working on that, remember?"

"It's weird, but I have this strong desire to go back to Paris, as if I've forgotten something there. Something important."

"Don't you dare. I need you here with me. I'm so out of my depth." Charlotte watched her niece and Bella play with the ducks. They splashed water and laughed together and her heart stuttered in her chest. She wanted that for Lourdes, for all the children. She wanted it for herself and Genevieve. Their lives had been turned upside down, and Tariq was trying to right them. Give them something to hold on to. A family of sorts. She planned to hang on with both hands. "Don't leave, Vi. Stay and help me with these children."

Genevieve nodded. "I'd like to say I'm staying because I know you need me, which you do. Or because these children need me, which they do. But I know I'm terrified to go off on my own. I'm not nearly as nice as I should be."

Charlotte shook her head, her smile breaking through. "You're so silly. Of course you're staying because the children and I need you. I'm terrified as well. We'd be idiots if we weren't. So we'll stick together like we've always done from the first time we wrote as pen pals in the third grade. Go look at the houses and choose one."

Genevieve flashed a wan smile. "Nothing like house hunting on someone else's property. He must have acres. Who knew?" She stood up, hugged Charlotte and went to the tub. "Auntie Vi is heading out to walk around and stretch her legs. You've had your dinner, and Auntie Charlie's here to play with you. Be good." She bent to brush a kiss on each wet head and then left the large bathroom, taking her coffee mug with her.

Charlotte watched the two girls play for some time, heating the water twice before she finally declared them both prunes and got them out to dry off and dress. She held both girls' hands as she took them out to the play yard. For the first time in a long while she felt ordinary, a regular person going about her routine. Bella on one side, Lourdes on the other, both girls chattering and laughing. She felt happy.

The outdoor carousel was the center of the play yard, the horses and chariots a riot of color beneath the overhead roof. Each steed was jeweled and ornate, carved from wood. Charlotte recognized the work as being the same as the older pieces in the house. It was beautiful, everything about it, including the platform. She knew it was a working carousel and she couldn't wait to ride one of the horses and feel what was happening to Tariq when he was carving it.

Floodlights lit the yard, casting shadows around the swings and slides. It was a child's dream, and there were new additions to it. Lourdes let out a squeal of excitement, dropped Charlotte's hand and rushed to the lead dragon sitting in the yard. There were five of them. The leader was larger and made of blue stone. Lourdes petted it and slipped her arm around one leg to hug the animal before using the tail to climb onto its back.

Bella went right past the green and orange dragons, straight to the red one. She wrapped her arms around the red stone neck and hugged the dragon tight. Like Lourdes, she climbed up the tail to the neck so she could pretend to ride it.

Charlotte watched as both girls leaned down to whisper secrets to the rock creatures, delighted with them.

"Where'd they come from?" Amelia asked, coming up behind Charlotte. She walked silently, completely at ease in the dark and blinking a little when she came into the powerful light of the floods.

"Lojos, Tomas and Mataias created them out of some stones. Aren't they beautiful?"

Amelia nodded. She moved to the orange dragon and stroked its head. "This one whispers." She smiled, a smile of pure delight. "To me. It's whispering to me."

Charlotte frowned. "I can't hear it. What's it saying?"

Amelia circled the orange dragon's neck with her arm and pressed her mouth against the ear. "It's telling me I'm safe with it. I can't hear any of the other dragons, but Bella and Lourdes are both talking to their dragons. I think they have chosen us. Or Lojos, Tomas and Mataias created them for us."

That had to be. Lojos, Tomas and Mataias were ancient hunters. They hadn't found their lifemates, yet they thought to give each of the children living on the property their own special dragon — dragons created under duress, when a battle was imminent. It was more than thoughtful, yet none of them could feel emotion for the children. What was the explanation? They were good men. It came down to that.

"Can the dragons fly?" Charlotte eyed Lourdes and Bella warily. The dragons had flown, but could they still? Certainly not with two three-year-olds on their backs.

Amelia frowned at her. "They're made of stone."

"That's true, but still, they flew before." She whispered so the two little ones couldn't hear. "The dragons defended us when we were ambushed by Fridrick and some of his vampire friends."

Amelia touched a long gash in the side of her dragon. She was silent for a moment and then she nodded. "That's what happened here. It hurt. Yes, they can fly when needed. We have only to say . . ."

"*Don't* say it aloud. Bella and Lourdes cannot be flying dragons around. Don't let them know how it's done."

To her credit, Amelia didn't laugh. "They would, too, the little demons. Bella's so smart, Charlie. Even after everything that happened, she's the most resilient of all of us. At first she was in a cage, but the monster threatened Liv with her. Indicated he would eat her alive. He actually pulled her from the cage, but she got away and from then on, she kept moving herself inside the tunnels so when a vampire or puppet tried to get her, she just simply went somewhere else. Once she knew they were bad, she played hide-and-seek with them."

"Telekinesis," Charlotte guessed.

Amelia nodded. "She wouldn't leave Liv or

me, although we both tried to make her go to Danny. We ended up making it a game, so fortunately, she wasn't as traumatized as she could have been. Liv had it the worst, and I couldn't do anything to prevent it."

The guilt and sorrow in Amelia's voice ate at Charlotte. Touched her heart. Tariq was right. The children needed guidance. Someone to love them. To help them.

"What gift do you have?"

Amelia rubbed between the ears of the dragon and then scratched the scales going down the graceful neck. "I can talk to animals."

"What did they do to you in the tunnels, Amelia?" Charlotte kept her voice low. Gentle. No one talked about Amelia or what had happened to her. They knew Vadim had given Liv to a puppet and that Emeline had been assaulted by the master vampire, but what happened to Amelia remained a mystery and she evidently hadn't talked about it to anyone.

Amelia's smile faded, and she shrugged her shoulders. "Liv had it the worst," she muttered.

Charlotte moved closer. "Whatever Liv suffered doesn't take away from what was done to you, hon," she counseled. "I hate what happened to me. It isn't as bad as what happened to Liv, but it's still mine. I have to live with it. You have to live with whatever those monsters did to you."

Amelia tightened her hold around the orange dragon as if gathering courage from the stone. She looked out over the play yard and then back at the two little girls playing on their dragons. "This is such a wonderful place for us," she whispered. "We lived on the streets after our parents died. They wouldn't keep us together in foster homes. No one would take all of us. Everyone wanted Bella, though. If we hadn't run away, we wouldn't have been able to stay together. But if we hadn't done that . . ." She trailed off, shaking her head.

"Amelia," Charlotte said softly. "Honey, it's no good to ever think that way. We make the decisions we make based on information we have at the time. You did what you thought was right. How could you possibly have known there were such monsters in the world? I didn't know. They killed Genevieve's boyfriend and her grandmother. They killed my mentor and my brother. I still didn't know, not really, not until I saw them for myself. You can't blame yourself for something that is out of your control."

Amelia searched her face for a long time, looking for reassurance. Charlotte wanted to wrap her arms around the girl, but was afraid of overstepping boundaries. She was already pressing the teen to talk to her when no one else had. Amelia had been overlooked because of the obvious damage to Liv and Emeline.

"He's going to marry you, isn't he?" Amelia said. "Or whatever is the same in their world. Tariq is."

Charlotte nodded, hoping that would buy her some credit with the girl. It was important that she connect emotionally with Amelia. Amelia needed looking after. She clearly was trying hard to be grown-up for her sisters, but she'd been traumatized as well. She needed . . . Charlotte.

"When we are married, or lifemates, as he says in the ceremony, I hope that you accept Lourdes and me into your family, as you have him. I know he plans to adopt all of you legally."

"He's talked to us about becoming like him. Fully Carpathian. I want to. Danny wants to as well, but we're worried for Liv and Bella, that they're too young and it might harm them in some way." She bit her lip hard. "I want to be Carpathian because I want to learn to be a hunter, and so does Danny. I don't care if they don't like women going after vampires. I'm going to do it, just like Blaze."

"Does Blaze actually hunt vampires?" Charlotte asked, careful to keep her tone neutral. She wasn't certain what Tariq would think of the decision. It wouldn't surprise her if Blaze did hunt vampires, given what Emeline had told her about Blaze when they were in Paris and what Tariq had said recently. Still, it would be very unusual for a human to be able to learn that quickly how to kill a vampire successfully. From what she'd seen, it would take years of experience. The vampires were old and had a lot of battle experience.

Amelia shrugged. "I'm going to learn," she repeated stubbornly.

Charlotte nodded. "I think all of us need to learn, whether or not we actively hunt them. You're young, so you'll have a lot more time than the rest of us."

For the first time Amelia seemed to relax. Charlotte hadn't told her she was being silly or stupid, and it seemed to matter to her. She flashed a tentative smile. "You're going to have to argue with Tariq for us."

"I think I'll be doing that a lot," Charlotte agreed with a small smile. "He's very . . ." She hesitated, searching for the right word. "Old-fashioned in his thinking."

Amelia nodded. "But not like some of the others." A little shiver went through her body. "They're just plain freaky."

Charlotte couldn't help noticing that Amelia continually stroked the stone dragon's neck and the touch seemed to calm her. "They can be scary," she agreed. "But Amelia, you still need to talk to someone about what happened to you. If not me, then let me find you someone else."

Amelia shook her head. "Not anyone else.

363

They'd think we were crazy. You can't go back, you know. Once you know about this other world, the monsters that live with us, there's no going back and pretending, is there?"

"Is that what you tried to do?" Charlotte kept her eyes on the little girls, but they continued talking to their dragons. Neither seemed to try to get their dragon to fly. So far neither child had thought of it.

"Yes," Amelia admitted. "I wanted to pretend all of this away." She pushed a hand through her thick hair. "Even with my imagination, I couldn't manage it."

Charlotte moved closer to the girl and laid a hand on the orange dragon's neck. The stone was warm in spite of the night. Amelia looked utterly lost and alone. She was fourteen years old and trying to be an adult for her two sisters who had suffered at the hands of monsters.

"I tried to pretend it away as well, especially when my brother was murdered so cruelly. Lourdes was there. They killed him right in front of her." Charlotte glanced over at the little girl whispering to the blue dragon. "She won't talk about it, but she has nightmares. She barely knew me when I showed up to take her home with me. We don't have relatives, so they put her in emergency care until I came for her. They wouldn't even allow her nanny to take her. I was in Europe." She hesitated and then decided to be fully honest. "Fridrick was the vampire who killed my brother. He said he spared Lourdes so I would come back to the States. They wanted Genevieve and me here."

Amelia looked over at Lourdes, compassion on her face. "I don't know what to do to help them." There was despair in her voice and etched onto her face when she turned back to Charlotte. Tears glittered in her eyes. "I can't help them any more than I can help myself."

Charlotte had been edging closer to her, and Amelia turned into her so Charlotte pulled her tightly against her and held her. Amelia burst into quiet sobs.

"I don't know how to help them, either, Amelia, but I think we're stronger together than apart. I think if you and I work together, we can eventually help each other and then the children."

There was no way she could stand there in the night, holding the weeping teenager, and not want to be a mother to her. Someone needed to help them all. She didn't think she was qualified to be a mom, but she was all they had and she was determined to be whatever they needed. "We can do this together, Amelia. Whatever Tariq decides about all of us, we can do it together. You know he won't let us down. He'll find a way for all of you to be safe outside the property, and in the meantime, we can find a way to help our little ones."

Amelia lifted her head. "Do you think so?"

Charlotte nodded solemnly because she meant every word and she wanted Amelia to see the truth. "When Tariq adopts all of you, I will as well. That would make me the mom and him the dad. He wants to make certain no one can step in and take any of you from us."

"Liv said you weren't sure about being our mother. She can read people," Amelia said carefully, clearly trying to find the right words without upsetting Charlotte.

Charlotte nodded and stroked little soothing caresses down Amelia's hair. "She's right. At the time I was just getting used to the idea of being with Tariq. I'd just taken on Lourdes, and wasn't doing such a great job with one traumatized child who barely knew me, and then he said he wanted to adopt all four of you. I didn't know if I could help you and that worried me. I didn't want to make an emotional snap decision. I want you to be healthy and happy. But after really thinking about it, I'm in the same world you're in. I've seen the monsters and what they do. I'm not a qualified counselor, but I don't need to be to be your mother. I just need to love you and find a common path so we can all connect. I'm willing to do that. I *want* to do that."

Amelia sighed and leaned in closer, wrapping her arms around Charlotte, holding on tightly — so tightly Charlotte felt the bite of that bruising grip almost to her bones.

"He touched me." Amelia whispered the horrific words, pressing her forehead against Charlotte's neck. "Inside. You know. Down there. Outside. On my skin. He put his hand on my belly and then he stripped my clothes off without touching them. One minute I had clothes and then I was naked in front of him, the one they called Vadim. He was obviously the leader. His brother Sergey was there and the one called Fridrick."

Amelia whispered the words into Charlotte's ear, clinging tightly. "It wasn't like what they did to Liv, because they only bit into my neck and my . . ." She pulled back and touched her left breast. The tears on her lashes made them spiky and wet. Heartbreaking. "Here." She laid her palm over her breast, shuddering. "And then he took his hand and pressed very hard into my belly and put his fingers in me. He said I wasn't ripe yet, but would be soon." She closed her eyes and laid her head on Charlotte's shoulder. "They were horrible. Grinning. They said someone named Addler could have me."

A little shudder went through Amelia's slim body and then she was crying again. Silently. Heart-wrenching sobs that broke Charlotte's heart. She held the girl as close as possible, whispering to her, reaching for Tariq in her mind. She wanted to be able to soothe Amelia by herself, and she knew Tariq was with Danny trying to help him understand what they all knew had to be done with the children. Conversion. Charlotte didn't want to think too much about that last step. Danny had waylaid him before he could reach the gate and insisted on talking.

Addler is Fridrick's brother. There are three of them. Fridrick is the oldest, then Georg and last Addler. He got kicked around a lot. They often travel together. All three chose to give up their souls and follow Vadim Malinov. They were there that night, tearing through the village, killing as many innocents as possible just because I'd befriended them and refused to join the Malinovs in their betrayal.

She heard the guilt in his voice. She couldn't imagine what it was like watching so many innocent people fall at the hands of monstrous vampires simply because you chose that village to live and work in.

"Is something wrong with Amelia?" Liv came up behind them, her voice trembling when she saw her older sister in Charlotte's arms.

Amelia started to pull away, hastily trying to cover up the fact that she was crying, but Charlotte didn't let her. "She's telling me about what happened to her in the tunnels. It's hard to do that, to let yourself remember and trust someone else enough to tell them, but it's also very brave. She'll be all right. We all will. We'll get through this together."

While she was talking, Liv put her hand on Charlotte's leg. Casually. Lightly. Still, Charlotte knew she was checking for the truth. Reading her. She continued to hold Amelia and stroked soothing caresses down her hair, down her back, whispering gently to her how proud she was and that they could get through this. They could help the others together. And she meant every single word.

Liv looked up at her for the first time with a fierce, possessive look, and she wrapped her arms around Charlotte's waist, holding on to her sister and locking her against Charlotte. "You'll do it then. You'll be our mother."

"I want to be," Charlotte agreed softly. "I think we all belong together, don't you?"

Liv nodded. "And Emeline. She belongs with us. She's broken, too."

Charlotte dropped her hand on top of Liv's head. "We might all be a bit broken, honey, but together we're very strong and we'll grow stronger as we get to know one another. We can help one another get through this. And we *will* get through it."

"You believe that," Liv said. "Amelia, she really believes that."

Amelia managed to stop the tears, and she just rested her forehead against Charlotte's shoulder for a moment before straightening

369

and directing a smile at her younger sister. "I know she does. And I'm beginning to believe it myself."

"What are these?" Liv asked, turning back toward the rock dragons. "They look like fun. They're all very different, aren't they? Where did they come from?" She fired off the questions rapidly.

Charlotte laughed softly, still holding Amelia. They weren't through talking but they had a good start. "Which one appeals to you?" She wondered if each individual dragon made by the three Carpathian hunters had been created with one of these children in mind. That would be . . . incredible. That would mean that in the middle of putting together a plan to leave a dangerous situation, knowing they were going into battle, they'd thought about the children and found a way to make each dragon significant and appealing to them. She loved that a Carpathian male would do such a thing.

Liv let go of Charlotte and Amelia and walked slowly around the other dragons. She put her hand on each of them. Lourdes's blue dragon. Bella's red dragon. Amelia's orange dragon. Her hand stroked down the brown one and then settled on the green one. At once her mouth broke out into a smile and she pushed her face close to the rock, whispering. Charlotte let out her breath slowly. That was exactly what Lojos, Tomas and

370

Mataias had done — created a rock dragon for each child. The children couldn't leave the property, and they were all, in their own ways, suffering from their parents' death and the events that followed, but this had been done for them. Something unusual and beautiful. She wanted to kiss each of the triplets.

There will be no kissing other men. Amusement tinged Tariq's voice.

Did you know they did this for the children? You should see their faces, Tariq; these dragons are incredible.

You don't know the half of it. We'll have to watch Bella and Lourdes to make certain they don't fly off. But they have protection as well as something fun and unique to play with.

She turned Amelia so she could see her sisters and Lourdes playing on the rock dragons, whispering to them and then laughing. "Look at their faces, honey," she whispered softly, in awe. She might not know how to help the children, but she wasn't alone in trying. All the Carpathians were willing to work toward healing them.

All children are sacred to Carpathians, Charlotte. Each child belongs to all of us. We help raise them and care for them. They are loved by all.

I thought hunters couldn't feel emotion.

She felt his hesitation as he tried to explain,

but even by touching his memories, she would never fully understand. *With children there is a softness brought only by them. Not an emotion, but a stirring, an echo maybe of what we had before we lost the ability to feel.*

She felt his sadness, his sorrow, for the hunters protecting them, the ones unable to see in color or feel the things they should even while they thought of helping children who desperately needed it. "See, Amelia, look at Liv's face," she reiterated. "She'll get through this. We all will, together. Help me help them all. Stand with Tariq and me. We can be a family. It won't be the one you had, or the one I had, but we'll be good together. All of us. Even the hunters protecting us. We'll count them as family, too."

Amelia looked back at her with a hint of laughter in her eyes. "Even the scary ones? Because there's one that . . ." She trailed off and looked around her to make certain no one else was close.

Deliberately Charlotte leaned close. "Dragomir. I know exactly who you're talking about."

"You haven't met Val yet," Amelia said. "I saw him once in the tunnels. He was as scary as Dragomir, although Liv doesn't think so. And the one Tariq calls Siv."

Charlotte nodded. "I have gotten that impression from everyone, including Tariq."

She seemed to catch a lot of thoughts even when she wasn't looking for them. She was changed already, more in Tariq's world than in her own. Food was abhorrent to her, and when she couldn't eat or drink anything, Tariq had helped her. It hadn't been easy; she had a heavy shield on her mind, something that helped when vampires wanted to control her but was a deterrent when her man wanted her to eat something she didn't want.

"Can you help Emeline?" Amelia asked. "Liv is so worried about her. She goes to see her every day, and every day she comes home saying it's worse. I feel better talking to you." Her gaze shifted to the ground. "Touching you is like holding on to an anchor. I don't know why I'm so clingy; I'm not like that naturally. You just feel so real to me. The things you say give me hope."

"I'll try to help her, Amelia," Charlotte said. "I *want* to help her. I don't know Blaze, but she's family to Emeline and she hasn't been able to do anything for her, so I don't know that I'll be able to, either, but I promise, honey, I'm going to try."

They stood together, holding each other, Amelia's hand on the orange dragon, both watching the younger children playing on the rock statues that were far more than they looked. Charlotte had an overwhelming sense of sadness. These were her children. Her family now. They were locked behind the high fences like prisoners, unable to go anywhere or have friends. Their families had been ripped apart. Tariq put them to sleep during the day, and they had an older couple watching over them in case Vadim sent humans or puppets after the children during the daylight hours when he couldn't protect them. It was a beautiful prison, but it was still a prison. She had to help Tariq find a way to get them out.

We will, Tariq whispered softly in her mind.

Charlotte was completely tuned to him. Aware of him with every cell in her body. Her mind wanted to stay in his. She needed the continual touch between them, both physical and mental. Fortunately, he seemed to need it as well. She loved that they could touch each other's mind and know the other was alive and well. She needed that reassurance as well.

What are you doing?

Sending Danny to you so I can deal with the intruders. They've set up a couple of places to spy on us. I intend to have a talk with them.

Be safe, she cautioned, unable to help herself. *We can't do without you.*

She felt the brush of his fingers along her jaw, the touch of his lips against hers. The sensation was faint, but it was there and it was enough to reassure her.

Danny strode toward her. He was a gangly young man, mostly legs and arms, but with the promise of a strong physique. He frowned a little when he observed Amelia clinging to Charlotte, her face stained with tears. "Something wrong?" he asked as he neared them.

Danny was fifteen, nearly sixteen, and he was extremely protective of his sisters. Already she could see Tariq in him. The way he walked and carried himself. Expressions. Hand gestures. The boy had serious hero worship going on. It was going to take a little more for him to accept Charlotte into their lives. He'd lived on the streets long enough to learn not to trust easily.

He reached out, snagged Amelia's arm and pulled her awkwardly to him. "What's wrong?" His voice was a replica of Tariq's. A demand. A command.

Amelia shrugged. "I needed to talk to someone, Danny. Charlotte let me. She just listened, that's all. No biggie. What were you and Tariq talking about that was so important he took you off alone? I hate that. Like it's man business and I'm not supposed to know what's going on."

Danny grinned down at his sister. "It is man business, girlie. Heap big man business." The grin faded, and he looked far older than his teen years. "In this case we were discussing what it takes for a conversion. He's worried about Liv. He has no choice with her. She can't live half in our world and half in his. It has to be soon. She isn't eating or drinking enough. And he worries that she'll . . ."

Amelia gripped his arm. "I know. I know. What did he say it was like?"

Danny hesitated. "A lot of pain. He doesn't want that for Bella or Lourdes or Liv. He can't stop it, though. If they're converted, and Liv has to be, then they'll experience a lot of pain."

"Danny, if she's converted, then all of us are. That was our agreement," Amelia said. "All of us. We stick together no matter what." She looked up at Charlotte. "He's converting you. Are you going to have him do the same for Lourdes?"

She didn't know. The thought of Lourdes in pain was more than she could bear. Lourdes was three, the same age as Bella. Even Tariq was worried about converting the children. All she could do was tell the truth. "I plan to go through it first. Then I'll have a better idea of whether Lourdes can handle it. Tariq is also consulting with a couple of expert healers or doctors. I'm not altogether certain what they are, but he wants to have all the information before any decision is made."

"If Liv has to go through it, we all do," Amelia said stubbornly. "*All* of us. If you're going to marry Tariq and be our mother, then you can't leave Lourdes behind any more than we could leave Bella."

Charlotte glanced at Danny, seeing the

knowledge in his eyes. Tariq hadn't pulled any punches, and he knew exactly how difficult it would be for a child. She shook her head slightly. What was the use of arguing with Amelia right then? She needed normal, just as they all did.

"Danny, check out the cool dragons Lojos, Tomas and Mataias made last night," she said, changing the subject, hoping he'd get the hint. "We were in the tunnels and a few of the vampires and some of their army tried to trap us inside, and the three of them made these dragons out of stone. It was the coolest thing I ever saw. The dragons actually flew. Amelia tells me she can hear the orange one whispering to her. Clearly the other girls can hear their dragons as well. I think the brown one is yours."

"Put your hand on him, Danny," Amelia encouraged.

Danny obediently stepped away from his sister and laid his hand on the brown dragon's neck. Instantly, his face lit up. The worry left him. The lines etched deep softened. Once again he appeared a teenage boy without a care. All because of three Carpathian hunters who couldn't see in color and didn't feel emotion. Still, they took the time to try to find a way to help heal children.

14

Tariq strode straight up to the heavy, ornate gate, yanked it open and went outside. He didn't hesitate as he walked down the road that led away from his estate. The two properties on either side of his also belonged to Tariq. Maksim's property bordered his, but this road led straight to the compound. One had to use a different entrance to get to Maksim's home. Tariq had ensured privacy and yet now, three humans spied on him, his woman and his children. That was totally unacceptable to him.

If these men were in any way connected to Vadim, like the other human male psychics, then they were dead men. He planned to kill them fast and dispose of their bodies. It wouldn't be that difficult. He'd been making people disappear for centuries.

He didn't hesitate or pretend he didn't know where they were hiding. He walked straight up to the blind they'd painstakingly set up across from his front entrance and stood, hands on his hips, glaring at them.

"Can I do something for you? And you might identify yourselves and which magazines you're working for." It was always better to act as if the paparazzi hounded him, which, technically, they often did. It was the best excuse of all to confront anyone spying on him.

The three men exchanged uneasy looks, and then their obvious leader stepped forward. Tariq had marked him in the club as the one to watch. Daniel Forester, tall, but not quite as tall as Tariq, and that meant he had to look up at the Carpathian. He was probably considered handsome by human standards, but his face was flushed with annoyance at being caught out.

"Daniel Forester. I don't work for a magazine." He turned to indicate the two men flanking him. "This is Vince Tidwell and Bruce Van Hues."

That much was the truth. "That tells me exactly nothing. I have family and friends and I keep my private life private. I don't like anyone spying on me . . . or them."

"We're worried about a couple of friends of ours. They were in your club a couple of nights ago and they seem to have disappeared. They were seen getting in a car with you."

Tariq remained silent. He simply stared at them. Forester wasn't telling the truth now;

rather, he was mixing lies with truth. They had powerful binoculars and they'd caught glimpses of Genevieve and Charlotte with the children on the playground.

Tariq quirked an eyebrow at them and folded his arms across his chest, waiting in silence. He didn't need to touch their minds. They didn't suspect him of being a vampire. They were chasing after Charlotte and Genevieve.

Daniel tried to hold his eyes but eventually had to look away. Tariq was a predator and he could hold a stare, fully focused, without blinking for hours. He could be absolutely still for hours when necessary. Daniel Forester was an amateur in comparison. In truth, Tariq felt a little childish playing the human male games when they had no chance of winning, but over the centuries, he'd learned the customs, and the stare down was one of them.

"Fine, we're not exactly friends," Daniel admitted, "but we were looking out for two women. Genevieve Marten, originally from Paris, and Charlotte Vintage from here. I don't know how to explain what's going on, but believe me, they're in trouble."

That, at least, was sincere. And the absolute truth. Genevieve and Charlotte were in more trouble than either woman realized. As was Emeline. And now Amelia. He hadn't thought Vadim had looked at Amelia, but after what the teen had revealed to Charlotte, it was clear the vampire was interested in her as well. Inwardly he sighed. The number of women needing protection was growing fast. He had to find a way to keep all of them safe from Malinov's master plan.

He'd sent word to the Carpathian Mountains, to the prince, letting him know what Vadim and his brother were plotting. More, he'd sent for available hunters, a healer, and with each hunter came more safeguards woven around the property, below and above it as well, in order to keep his family safe. He knew Josef was coming, a younger Carpathian male, still a child by their standards, but he was good with technology — something all Carpathians needed to catch up on.

His people were gathering, but it would take time to get his defense in a solid position, enough so he could go on the offense — actively go after Vadim and eradicate each and every one of his soldiers. They needed to find out more about the human male psychics Vadim recruited and why they couldn't be detected as vampire puppets. The men in the memories Charlotte had accessed didn't seem entirely under Vadim's control, but acted independently of him.

"Charlotte Vintage is my fiancée," he announced, using the human term rather than the Carpathian. "She is very safe. My property is guarded and has a full security system as you can see." He waved his hand toward the high fence. "Genevieve, her friend, is also staying with me. She is safe as well."

Daniel shook his head and took a step closer. "No, that's the thing. Neither of them is safe. They've been . . . targeted. I can't explain to you what that means, but I'm telling you that you can't possibly keep them safe. The men after them are ruthless. Powerful. They can get to anyone, and they'll take them. We've been following them since Paris, and someone is always watching them. Even now, someone is watching. The moment they leave your property, or maybe even before, these men will be after them."

It was an impassioned speech. Daniel Forester was afraid for Charlotte and Genevieve. There was no disguising the tremor in his voice. The genuine fear.

"I am well aware of the danger to them. We ran into these men the other night in the club's parking garage. Fortunately, I had several of my security team with me and they decided to try for the women another night."

Daniel raked agitated fingers through his hair. "You still don't understand how dangerous these men are. I don't know why they want specific women, but they kill to get them. They're vicious and cunning. They won't stop. You can't stop them."

Tariq studied the man's face. Psychic energy poured off of him. In his own way, Daniel Forester held power. This was the kind of man Vadim would have chosen to recruit for his human army. He decided to take a chance. "I've seen the way these men murder. Tearing out throats. Draining their victims of blood. You believe the ones after Charlotte and Genevieve are vampires, don't you?"

There was a small silence. Daniel glanced at his two friends, his face flushing dark as he tried to figure out whether Tariq was making fun of him.

"Vampire?" He echoed the word, stalling for time.

Tariq nodded. "That's the point you were skirting around. You believe the men after Charlotte and Genevieve are vampires."

Daniel's chin went up. His shoulders straightened. A muscle jerked in his jaw. "They *are* vampires. You can think I'm crazy, but I've seen what they do. You can't just stop them with a security fence." There was a sneer in his voice.

Daniel expected Tariq to make fun of him, but he was standing his ground. Tariq gave him points for that. "If you believe them to be vampires, then surely you must have considered that along with them, there are hunters of vampires." He spoke softly, planting the thought carefully with just the gentlest of pushes.

Tariq was well aware of "the society" — a group of humans hunting vampires. These men and women didn't or couldn't differentiate between Carpathians and vampires. They killed anyone they thought was a danger to them or to society. Often those killed were human beings, not another species. Sometimes, when on a killing spree, they managed to kill or harm Carpathians.

Daniel frowned and rubbed his temples, as if even that gentle push bothered him. "I never thought about it one way or the other. I belong to a group — and it's large, with cells in every single country around the world — that hunts vampires. Are you referring to the hunters that belong to the society?"

Tariq shook his head. "The hunters would have to be nearly immortal, just as a vampire is. They would have to follow their prey from one century to the next looking for the undead. If that was the case, those hunters, like you, belonging to the society wouldn't know the difference and would attack and kill the very men who have dedicated their lives to hunting vampires."

Daniel stared at him for a long time. He cleared his throat. "Are you saying you know there are other hunters out there?"

Tariq didn't answer the question. Instead he skirted the issue. "I'm saying that if there is one, there must be the other, and if you belong to the society, you should know that particular group, while started for a good purpose, does not discriminate before it chooses to make a kill. It has a bad reputation."

Daniel blinked several times, trying to digest what Tariq was telling him. Tariq didn't wait to see if his little chat did any good. "I can keep Charlotte and Genevieve safer than you can. You're risking your lives trying to go up against Fridrick and his playmates. They have a small army and Fridrick is by no means the worst of them. Stay out of this."

"They've killed. Brutally killed. They won't stop until someone steps in. The law can't get them. No one would believe us if we told them what Fridrick is."

"I'm saying walk away and be glad you have your lives. You don't want to be on their radar. They have spies, and they're watching my property. If I knew you were here, then they know as well. Get out of the city and stay low for a while. Fridrick won't follow you, because he wants Charlotte and Genevieve."

For some insane reason, Tariq felt a kinship with Daniel Forester. The man sincerely believed in his cause and his cause was no different from Tariq's.

"I can't just walk away when I know that *thing* is targeting two innocent women." Daniel looked around and then lowered his voice. "I think they've infiltrated our ranks as well. Some of the commands coming out of headquarters don't make any sense."

Tariq paused in the act of turning away from them. He'd intended to read their purpose and then leave them to their fate, but Forester and his friends were trying to save Charlotte's life and that earned them a warning or two.

"They have," he confirmed. "You can't trust anyone at this point. And you can't kill a vampire in the way of the movies. The heart has to be removed and incinerated. If you're staking them and not following through, they can come back again and again."

"How do you know that?" Daniel asked, suspicion creeping into his tone.

Tariq shrugged. "I like research. I spend a lot of time up at night because of the club. If I can't sleep during the day, I research anything that interests me. Legends and myths interest me." If they could lie, so could he, and his mixture of truth and fiction carried conviction. His tone was pitched perfectly for anyone hearing him to believe everything he said without a "push" to get them to listen.

"Wait," Daniel called as Tariq turned away from them and began to walk back toward the compound.

Tariq shook his head. "I'm trying to help you out, Forester. It's on you if you don't choose to listen, but Fridrick's spies will report back to him that you're here. He'll want to know why. He'll kill you the moment he realizes you can't help him acquire the women. And if he captures you and tries to use you as bait by torturing you, that won't save you, either, because Charlotte and Genevieve will never know about it. I'll see to that."

Tariq would hate it. He'd seen the torture vampires inflicted on their victims. The more fear-based adrenaline in the blood, the higher the rush the vampire got. Tariq would hate to see that happen to Forester and his friends, but he couldn't save everyone, and Charlotte, Genevieve and his children were the most important to him.

The muscle in Daniel's jaw jerked again. "I wouldn't want them to know," he agreed. "I would do the same, not let either of the women know what was happening in order to save them. But we made a pact." He swept his hand back toward the two other men. They stepped up to his side, looking every bit as determined as Daniel. "We're not going to allow those monsters to get either of those women if we can help it."

Tariq paused in the act of walking away from them. For a moment he closed his eyes. So many other human males over the centuries had been worth his respect — and they'd died hard. He didn't want to see these men go that same way. "If you really want to help me guard them, then you have to realize that either any knowledge you gain of hunters of the vampire must be removed from you or safeguards have to be put in place."

Daniel started to say something, but Tariq held up his hand. "You need to think about what that could mean. Go away from here. If you still insist that you really want to hunt vampires and destroy them, come to my club tomorrow night. We'll work something out, but your answer will be a permanent one. There will be no going back either way. Now go, before Fridrick's spies report that you were more than paparazzi trying to get a photograph of my fiancée."

"One more thing, Asenguard," Daniel said. "Charlotte Vintage has another friend, Grace. She hangs with Genevieve and Charlotte a lot. She didn't go to Paris and she's never been tested for psychic ability, but they're interested in her as well and they have been watching her. We don't trust any of the other members and we have to stick together in order to be safe. We try to look out for her, but she doesn't make it easy."

Tariq studied the man for a long moment. Grace had packed up some of Charlotte's and Genevieve's things and driven them over to the house, but she left immediately. He hadn't met her, but Maksim said she was very distracted and wanted to leave as soon as she had delivered the clothes and made certain Lourdes was safe. He nodded at the three men. "I'll look into it." This time he turned and walked away without looking back. The three men would have to decide for themselves, but he hoped they left the state and forgot all about vampire hunting.

Charlotte finally managed to introduce herself to the older couple living on Tariq's property. Donald and Mary were clearly in love. They'd been together thirty years and still held hands and exchanged secretive, loving glances. She really liked them and was happy to spend half an hour getting to know them.

Donald liked helping out with Tariq's books, and clearly it made him feel as if he had a purpose, making certain no one cheated his benefactor. Mary liked looking after the children. She had begun to develop a good friendship with them. So much so that Charlotte was fairly certain Tariq was influencing the children to accept the older couple. The children were still enthralled with their stone dragons so she left them with Donald and Mary while she paid a visit to Emeline.

She had met Emeline in Paris, where the woman had been hiding out. She had witnessed a murder, she recounted, and was lying low because she was being hunted. Blaze's father had sent her out of the country with a new identity, which she was very bad at using. She had stayed with Genevieve and Charlotte for several days, and then she'd gotten the news that Blaze's father had been murdered and she rushed back to the States to help Blaze find the men who had killed him.

Charlotte had really felt a connection with Emeline, just as Genevieve had. Emeline had lived a tough life, but she was extremely resilient and loyal. To her, Blaze was family, her sister. Blaze's father, Sean McGuire, had been the one constant in Emeline's life and she was equally loyal to him. When Blaze needed her, in spite of the danger to herself, Emeline had rushed home — right into Vadim's trap. Charlotte understood and respected loyalty and commitment.

The night was very dark with few stars and little moon. The clouds overhead boiled and seethed as if a giant cauldron had a fire roaring beneath it. Occasionally she could see lightning webbing the sky, but it was still far away, so when the thunder rolled, it was in the distance. She loved storms and hoped Emeline did as well.

The house Emeline lived in was one of the smaller ones on the vast property and it was closest to the main house. Tariq had given that house to Emeline so he could better watch over her. It was beautifully appointed, looked Victorian in design and matched with the larger home Tariq enjoyed. In particular, Charlotte loved the wraparound verandah. From the sprawling, covered deck, Emeline could watch the water and any storms that came in over it. She also had good views of the play yard so she could watch the children play and of the more forested part of the property where she might find some peace.

Charlotte went through the little gate in the small wrought-iron fence that designated Emeline's personal space. The yard was covered in masses of shrubs and flowers, seemingly growing wild yet very carefully maintained. She went up the steps and knocked on the door, all the while admiring the gingerbread detail at every window as well as the eaves.

Charlotte heard movement in the house. Slow, measured steps, as if Emeline was having trouble walking.

"I'm not feeling well," Emeline called through the door, confirming what Tariq had told her — Emeline wasn't seeing anyone.

"Emme, it's me, Charlotte, from Paris. We met in Paris. I don't care if you're not well — I want to see you. We can sit on your porch if you don't want me in the house. I know you trust Liv and you let her visit. You can trust me, too."

There was a small silence. Charlotte was certain Emeline was going to send her away just as she always did the Carpathians protecting her. Tariq said only Blaze and Liv were allowed in the house, and Emeline considered Blaze her sister. Very slowly the door cracked open and Emeline peered out at her.

Even in the night, or maybe because of it, Emeline appeared extremely pale. There were dark smudges around her eyes. She looked gaunt — in need of a doctor she was so slender. She wore a loose housecoat over her jeans and sweater. Even with the robe and sweater, she shivered continually.

"Honey." Charlotte wanted to pull her into her arms but instinctively knew Emeline would retreat from any actual contact. "Come sit with me." She waved toward the rocking chairs on the small porch.

Emeline hesitated, looking carefully around the yard. Up on the rooftops, down by the lake, she took in as much of the property as she could see. The night was dark and there seemed to be a faint red glow to Emeline's eyes, much like a cat's eyes in the dark. The shivering was continuous, and Charlotte wondered if she was in pain rather than cold.

Taking a deep, shuddering breath, Emeline stepped out of her house and slipped into the nearest rocker. "Forgive me for being so strange. I just . . ." She trailed off, all the while searching the sky with its dark, swirling clouds and the dull, almost nonexistent moon they hid.

"Tariq said the vampires couldn't come in here. They can't get to you. Blaze must have told you that." Charlotte kept her voice

392

gentle, as if she was talking to Lourdes or Bella. Emeline was exquisitely beautiful. She was probably the most drop-dead gorgeous woman Charlotte had ever seen, and that was saying something because she thought Genevieve was really beautiful. Even with her body so thin and her long hair, still thick but without its glossiness, Emeline was extraordinary — but something was clearly wrong with her. She needed a doctor.

Emeline nodded her head. "Tariq has been good to me. He did say that."

Charlotte knew Emeline didn't ever open the door to any of the male Carpathians. Danny had visited twice with Liv, and she'd allowed him inside her house both times, but he had reported that she kept furniture between them at all times.

"Honey, do you need a doctor? A counselor? Something really bad happened to you and . . ." Charlotte trailed off as Emeline clutched the robe tighter around her and shook her head.

"Don't say it. Don't say anything about what happened. I can't go there yet. I'm sorry, Charlie, but it's too soon. I just need time. I told Blaze when I could talk to her about it, I would. I just can't face it yet."

Emeline's voice shook almost as badly as her body did. She looked panicked, on the verge of flight, and Charlotte didn't have the heart to call her on it. She nodded. "It's all right, honey. I understand. Fridrick." She paused, because Emeline obviously recognized the name. When Emeline didn't say anything, she continued. "Fridrick murdered my brother and Genevieve's grandmother as well as others we knew and cared about. If it wasn't for Tariq he would have managed to kidnap both of us."

Complete horror crossed Emeline's face. She reached out with trembling fingers to touch Charlotte's arm. "You can't let them get their hands on you." She leaned closer, her voice dropping to a whisper. "You just can't. Their blood is acid. It burns and burns and never stops. He whispers to you. It will drive you insane."

Charlotte's heart jerked hard. "Can you hear him now?"

Emeline shook her head. "Only if I fall asleep."

That explained the dark circles under her eyes. "Did you tell Blaze or Tariq? They've woven safeguards to protect you. If the protections aren't working, they need to know to build stronger ones."

Emeline tightened the robe around her thin body with nervous fingers. "I don't want to be near any of them. In order for them to weave stronger safeguards, I have to let them in. Especially if he's in my mind — and he is. I just can't let another one in there as well.

Not yet. I'd rather just not go to sleep at night."

Charlotte took a deep breath, praying for wisdom. She wasn't equipped to handle such severe trauma. She had a very bad feeling about Emeline. "You know that isn't good for you, Emme. You're going to have to let them help you. Have you spoken to Blaze about hearing him in your sleep?"

Emeline shook her head. "I know I'm going to have to let them near me — the Carpathians. They're so powerful. And I can feel them, their predatory natures. They scare me almost as much as vampires terrify me." She took a deep, shuddering breath. "I can feel their natures. They're almost like the vampires. They aren't the same, but so dangerous, Charlie. So dangerous."

"But not to you. Not to the children. You should see the stone dragons the triplets made for the children. They would give their lives for you." She went silent for a moment, knowing she wasn't getting anywhere. Emeline just rocked herself back and forth, clutching at the opening of her robe with nervous fingers.

"Honey," she said softly in her most persuasive voice, "you know you have to let them help you. You can't go on this way."

"I know. I just need . . . time." Emeline's gaze jumped to the skyline again.

"At least tell me what he says to you." She

kept her tone gentle.

Emeline's hands crept up, holding the robe around her tightly against her neck as if to keep those jagged, serrated teeth from tearing at her flesh. Her gaze frantically sought out the sky, as if she was certain Vadim would swoop down and take her away. "He tells me I have to come to him."

The admission was so low that at first Charlotte didn't think she'd spoken, but then the words penetrated and she touched Tariq, needing him to hear.

"He keeps ordering me. Threatening me."

"With what?"

"Liv." Emeline swallowed with difficulty and then went into a spasm of coughing. She gasped for breath and shook her head several times, rocking her body back and forth. "He says, he'll kill Liv if I don't go to him."

She looked haunted. Terrified. Charlotte couldn't help feeling a little terrified for her, nor could she stop herself from searching the skies just as Emeline had done, or reaching for Tariq, settling into the warmth and comfort of his mind.

Both of you are safe. Vadim cannot penetrate the safeguards.

How is he getting through to her when she sleeps? She tried not to let it sound like an accusation, but it was. There was no normal, not even when she tried. There never would be in his world. It wasn't his fault, but sud-

396

denly she wanted to throw a little screaming fit where no one could hear her — except, Tariq would always hear her.

Her fingers curled around the arms of the rocker until they turned white. She *hated* what Vadim had done to Emeline, and she didn't really know the extent of what that was. She hated what he'd done to Liv, and what he was still doing to both of them. It made her feel helpless and out of control, two states she'd never been fond of.

"This sucks, Emme," she said aloud. What else could she say? Because it did. "What do you tell him?"

"That if he harms Liv, or forces her to harm herself, then I'll kill myself." Emeline turned haunted eyes on Charlotte. "I would, too. And he knows it. So far it's worked, but I can tell he's getting impatient with me. I'm worried about Liv. I want Tariq to convert her. Tell him he has to do it immediately."

The entire time, Emeline whispered, but every word pierced Charlotte's heart. She wanted to hold Emeline tight and keep her safe. She wanted to hunt down Vadim and make him suffer a long time before he died. Or maybe just kill him quickly before he fried her.

"I will, Emme, I promise. I'm going to tell him everything. You know that. You have Blaze. You know what a lifemate is." She frowned, suddenly afraid. *Can vampires have lifemates? Could Emeline be Vadim's lifemate?*

There was a small silence. She knew Tariq was listening to every word Emeline said and he was nearly as upset as she was, but in a different, more predatory, scary way. She knew he would insist on Emeline allowing the male Carpathians to aid her sleep and Emeline was going to resist.

To become a vampire, a Carpathian hunter must choose to give up his soul. In that moment, he is lost, never to be recovered. If by chance he runs across his other half, he will know and feel regret for a moment, but it is fleeting, and she will be in terrible danger. He cannot kill her himself, but he would not want that reminder alive. Emeline is not Vadim's lifemate. She would know and she would be suffering differently. Vadim took her blood and forced her to take his, just as he did with Liv. More, I think he did at least two blood exchanges with Emeline. If that is so, I don't know how she lives with the acid burning her. She refuses to allow a male to aid her.

She needs help. She's ill.

A master vampire exchanged blood with her, Charlotte.

Tariq sounded patient, as if he were explaining things to a child. That definitely gave Charlotte a target for the pent-up anger she had nowhere to put. *I know that,* she hissed back, letting him see the edge of her temper.

Sielamet, beloved. Keeper of my soul. His voice went soft and intimate, caressing her from the inside out. *I know this is difficult. To see Emeline that way and not be able to aid her is devastating, but she refuses our aid. Should we force her? Should we be as Vadim is? Taking her will? Even though it is for her own good? We are coming close to having no choice in the matter, but it was agreed we would give her time to make the choice herself. Blaze has tried with her. Amelia has. We are all counting on you. To place such a burden on your shoulders is wrong, I know it is, but we are trying to save her sanity as well as her life.*

She heard the guilt and regret in his voice. He detested her being there more than she did, but it was coming to the point where they would force Emeline to accept their aid, and all of them were afraid if they did so, they would lose her. Charlotte feared they were right.

Keep her talking. She's telling you more than she has anyone. Maksim is sending Blaze to you and after she gets there, I'll give it a few minutes and then send Genevieve. Hopefully the conversation will end on a good note, not a bad one. She'll feel surrounded by women she can trust.

She knew he was doing his best, feeling his way just as she was. "Emeline, has Liv said she can hear voices whispering?"

Charlotte knew what that felt like. Vadim's voice talking to her, commanding her to get out of the tunnels. She'd felt violated that he was in her mind and terrified that he might be able to use her as a spy. That splinter was still in her. As long as she was on Tariq's property she thought she was safe, but maybe she wasn't. She knew that voice. That horrible, sweet temptation. She studied Emeline carefully. It wasn't just the voice. She was in pain. Physical pain.

Emeline shook her head slowly. "If so, she hasn't told me. I know she doesn't sleep unless Tariq aids her." She sighed. "Maksim and Tariq have done so much for the children and me. The burden on them is almost unbearable. I can't think what it must be like for them to try to know the right thing to do. Liv can't stay in this world as she is. She's connected to Val and feels his every suffering even though he cannot and he's in the ground. I can't imagine what it will be like when he surfaces. All the children suffer, but then what do they do to alleviate that? Should they bring them into their world?" There was an edge to Emeline's voice, as if the last thing she wanted was to be in the world of Carpathians.

Charlotte took a deep breath and let it out. She wasn't entirely certain what would happen when Tariq finished the transition on her. She only knew that her senses were extremely acute and she was stronger than she'd ever been. She had no idea what it truly entailed to be Carpathian. It was possible Emeline knew far more than she did. She purposely hadn't asked Tariq for too many details, wanting to take her time to process before she made that final commitment. She had to go carefully.

"Aren't they already in that world, Emeline?" Charlotte asked gently.

Emeline pressed both hands to her stomach as a shudder of pain crossed her face. Her body shrank into itself, making her look smaller — thinner — than ever. "Yes," she whispered. "I guess we all are."

Charlotte could see her easily in the dark, although she was certain Emeline thought herself hidden. Every breath she drew was shallow. A shudder or wheeze. Lines were etched deep around her mouth. She linked her fingers, still pressing into her stomach as though it hurt, or was cramping. She twisted her fingers together until they turned white, but she kept her face as still as possible, as if they were just talking about the weather.

"Do you want to talk about it?" Charlotte asked. "I'm not Blaze, but I care about you. I have Vadim's voice in my head. I can't know what it's like to be assaulted by him, not physically, but I do know how horrible it feels to carry a piece of him inside me and know he can use that to hurt others."

Emeline shook her head slowly. "Talking about him makes me sick. I can't think about him or I want to slit my own throat." She touched her throat with trembling fingers, right over the jagged scar where Vadim had torn her open to get at her blood.

Charlotte's heart jerked hard. Emeline wasn't kidding. Clearly she'd thought about doing that very thing often. There was resolve in her voice. Steel, even.

"Honey. No." Charlotte kept her tone low. Firm. "That isn't an answer, and you know that. If you did that, you'd leave the rest of us. You'd leave Liv. She needs you more than she does any of us. We're trying with her, but she doesn't feel the connection with anyone but you."

Emeline ducked her head and didn't respond.

Charlotte felt as if she was floundering. She pressed her fingers to her temple realizing she had a headache. Instantly Tariq was there, soothing her, taking away the small pain. Reassuring her. Giving her something she knew Emeline and the children needed as well.

"Honey, you know what has to be done. I know you're afraid of them, but you have to allow one of the Carpathians to heal you enough to stop Vadim from getting to you. You have to sleep. You have to be able to eat. You can't let him win."

"What if he attacks Liv and I have no way

to communicate with him?" Emeline protested. She shook her head. "I can't take that chance. If Tariq converts Liv and stops Vadim's ability to get to her, then and only then will I consider it."

"Has Blaze explained the process to you? Tariq tells me he's trying to talk to Carpathian healers about how best to bring the children into their world."

Emeline closed her eyes tightly and then nodded. When her lashes lifted she stared out into the darkness, pain etched into her face. "She said the pain was excruciating. I don't want that for Liv, for you, for anyone, but she's not going to make it if she continues the way she is. They took so much from her, Charlie, so much. She can't wait. You have to tell Tariq that. Convince him. We're going to lose her if he waits much longer, and it won't be to Vadim."

"What about you, Emme? Are we going to lose you?" Charlotte asked quietly.

Emeline continued to stare out into the darkness. "I'm trying, Charlie. I know they don't think I am, but I have to work this all out in my head. I've never been a warrior woman like Blaze or you. I don't know how to fight him. I have to figure that out and come to terms with what he did to me. Once I can do that, I hope I can live with it."

Charlotte let silence stretch between them, hoping Emeline would continue, but she didn't. Finally, Charlotte tried prompting her. "What did he do? You need to talk about it, Emeline. If not with me, then at least with Blaze. If not with Blaze, Tariq can call in a counselor. Carpathians must have someone like our counselors."

Emeline shook her head. "I could never talk to strangers. Not about him. I can barely talk to Blaze." She sent Charlotte a faint smile, the first, but it didn't reach her eyes. "I don't know why you're the lucky one who gets to hear all this."

"Maybe because you trust me, and you know Vadim can talk to me as well. I touched a carousel horse that he put a curse of some kind on and I got a splinter from it. We can't get it out and it's horrifying to know that I've got some part of him inside me."

Emeline moistened her dry, swollen lips. "He forced his blood on me. It burned. It burned all the way down my throat and into my body. My heart and lungs. Every organ in my body. It still burns. Then he forced me to drink blood from a cup." Her voice cracked and she shook her head. Tears shimmered and several caught on her long lashes. "Drinking that blood was different, not like drinking acid, but it was still so horrible, like being caught in the worst nightmare possible."

She stroked her palm down her throat and then pressed her hand tight against her stomach as if the pain was there all over again.

Charlotte hurt for her. Again, it was all she could do not to put her arms around Emeline and hold her, but Emeline had shrunk into herself, made herself much smaller and pulled the robe tighter around her, as if that thin material could protect her somehow.

I hate this, Tariq. I hate that vampire. He's destroyed her life. Destroyed her. She's so far gone I can't reach her.

Sielamet, you've come closer than anyone else to getting her to talk. You're doing fine. You have that ability whether or not you realize it to make people comfortable and able to tell you things they wouldn't reveal to someone else.

She let him wrap her up in his warmth, wishing she could do that for Emeline. She tried, sending as much warmth and comfort as she could to the woman.

"What else did he do, Emme?" Charlotte probed gently.

Emeline shook her head, and tears spilled over, tracking down her face. "I can't think about anything else yet. I can't let it be real. I just have to take one thing at a time. One thing. Anything else will break me, Charlie. He is a monster. He touched me. He took my blood and made me take his. He whispers to me, threatens me. Threatens children. I have to hold very still and not think too much in order to survive. That's what I'm doing.

That's what you need to tell them. I'm surviving right now, and until I can process what happened to me, I can't talk about it."

"Okay, honey, I understand, but you will have to allow one of the men to help you sleep without hearing Vadim. If you don't, it will just drive you crazy. Are you afraid of them? Has Vadim made you afraid of the Carpathians?" She asked gently, feeling as if she were in a minefield.

"They make me nervous," Emeline admitted. "Blaze is lifemate to Maksim and I know I'm hurting her by not accepting him. I will. I really will. Just not yet." There was a plea for understanding in her voice. So soft. Almost faint. Her gaze never stopped seeking the night, looking for danger, looking for a threat. "Maybe when Val wakes. He knows what Vadim did to Liv, and he helped her. Maybe I can accept his aid. I don't know."

Charlotte had no idea how long it would take for the Carpathian to heal but if his wounds had been that bad, it could take a while. She wasn't certain Emeline had that kind of time. More, she was certain Emeline knew that and counted on it.

"Tariq has the most beautiful carousels on his property. Have you seen them?" Deliberately, Charlotte changed the subject, wanting to indicate to Emeline that she could relax. There would be no more talk of Vadim.

Sielamet. It was a slight reprimand.

She's done. I have to let it go. She's talked as much as she can right now. She needs normal. Just like I need normal.

Emeline turned to look at her. "I remember in Paris you talking about carousels and how much you loved them."

"I was learning restoration from a master. He was the best in the world. Tariq had contacted him asking him to come to the States to work on his carousels. He has a couple in his home that need work."

"Couldn't he just wave his hand or something?" Emeline asked.

I was so eager to restore them that I didn't think of that. Why can't you just wave your hand? You were the one to carve them.

Tariq was there in her mind. She felt him warm and gentle, caring for her, stroking her mind intimately as she tried to keep Emeline engaged in idle conversation, trying to give her normal, even if just for a few moments.

Something is lost in the restoration. I tried it with a couple of pieces and it isn't the same. I could carve them again, but then they would be made in this century and not my first works. In any case, I like working with my hands. I am looking forward to learning the restoration process.

The carousels meant something special to him. She could hear it in his voice. He didn't want to destroy the oldest carousel any more

407

than she did, maybe less so, but he would because it was dangerous to anyone who touched it. She needed to find out why. She needed to track Vadim back to wherever he was and she needed to make certain her growing family was safe.

She was claiming the children, Genevieve and now Emeline. Even the hunters protecting them — especially Lojos, Tomas and Mataias, who had been thoughtful enough to provide the stone dragons for the children and Val, a hunter she'd never met, but one who had taken the time to save Liv and give her strength in the midst of evil.

"Apparently waving one's hand doesn't restore art in the same way as the methods we use. Who knew there was something a Carpathian didn't do perfectly?"

That got the smallest of smiles out of Emeline. "I'd make you tea, but I'm not very steady on my feet."

I'll have Blaze bring tea and something easy for Emeline to get down.

Charlotte pressed a hand to her stomach. Tariq was going to have to aid her in getting down the tea. Genevieve came up the porch stairs, looking spectacular, as she always did, a bright smile on her face as she greeted Emeline warmly.

Genevieve sank down into the rocker on the other side of Emeline and instantly brought up Paris and the good times they'd

408

had there. She avoided talking all things Carpathian and vampire. She was skillful that way because she was genuine in everything she did.

Blaze joined them, bringing a little teapot and several cups along with a tray of scones. She goaded Emeline into drinking the tea, but only Genevieve had a scone.

We need a solution to this fast or we're going to lose her, Charlotte said.

Tariq was silent for a moment while Charlotte and Genevieve were introduced to Blaze. *I agree, sielamet. I'm working on it.*

The four women sat together until dawn was creeping into the night, slowly peeling back the dark to streak the early morning hours in gray. Blaze helped Emeline back to bed, and Genevieve, yawning, left. Only then did Tariq come for her, wrapping her in his arms and taking her to their bed in the huge Victorian house that was to be her home.

15

Carpathian men were beautiful; there was no doubt about it. They were also dangerous and very, very scary. Charlotte should have been thrilled at being surrounded by the tall, broad-shouldered men with their long, dark hair and faces that seemed carved from stone, and who could be models for some of the most famous sculptures. She wasn't thrilled. At. All.

She found herself looking at Tariq in an entirely different way. From the moment she'd met him, she thought of him as Tariq Asenguard, the sophisticated, civilized owner of a string of extremely successful nightclubs. He wore suits like he was born for them. He spoke numerous languages and was well educated. She didn't in any way associate him with the other hunters. Not until she saw him with them. Not until they were crowding around her with their predatory eyes and merciless expressions.

She tried to control her heart so that it

didn't sound like a runaway train, but it was difficult. She found herself studying each face. They had come to the workroom, surrounding her and the ancient carousel that Tariq had set up in the middle of the room. It was a work of art. A piece of history. She hadn't been able to take her eyes off of it, and there was something about it that made her want to go stroke her hand over one of the horses.

There were four horses and four chariots. Each was hand carved and painted in colors made from flowers, colors very difficult to duplicate unless one knew exactly what he was doing. The horses and chariots were suspended from chains and as the carousel was turned, they would swing out so the rider could thrust his spear or shoot his arrow through a small ring to practice his battle skills.

She had a mad desire to fling herself on the ancient steeds and try her luck at spearing the ring. The carousel was beautiful. It deserved to stay in existence so everyone could see it and enjoy it. There was no platform, just the horses and chariots on chains that would swing out when the carousel was pulled by men or horses in a circle. The idea that the carousel was created centuries earlier and that men and women from that time had sat on these very horses and stood on the chariots as they were turned in order to practice shooting an arrow through a ring or thrusting a spear through it was overwhelming to her. The carousel connected the present to the past.

Hard fingers shackled her wrist and she glanced up, startled. Tariq's eyes glared down at her, nearly glowing red. Her heart jumped hard in her chest. Definitely the predator. He was focused on her. Solely, completely on her. She glanced around her at the other men.

Lojos, Tomas and Mataias were extraordinarily handsome, with their tall, broad-shouldered bodies that screamed of strength. Their eyes blazed with power and they looked . . . dangerous.

She sucked in her breath when her gaze turned toward Dragomir. He was the scariest one of all, bigger than the others, and they were all *big,* with his roped muscles and flaming golden eyes, his long hair that seemed as wild as he was, the scarred tattoos that ran from his neck under his shirt — she knew those words carved into his body and inked meant something to him, something that boded ill for others, perhaps. He was clearly far different from the others. She didn't think any of them were easy in his company, and that said quite a lot. Tariq had said as much to her just the night before.

There was Maksim, Blaze's lifemate. Blaze had told Emeline, Genevieve and her very funny stories about him, talking as if he were the sweetest man alive, but looking at him now, Charlotte thought maybe she'd been exaggerating about that sweetness. There were a couple of others, men she hadn't yet been introduced to, but they looked as grim and forbidding as the others, and just as Tariq was focused on her, so were all the hunters gathered in the large room.

The room *had* been large. Now it appeared quite small and most of the air was gone. She glanced behind her, trying to see the door. It looked far away and there were two hunters between the exit and her. One was Siv, with his unusual eyes that swirled from blue to green. He looked so scary she started shaking. He also looked as if he knew she wanted to run.

Sielamet. Stop. Tariq's voice brushed intimately in her mind. It was a command, but it was also a reassurance.

Sielamet. My soul. He called her that all the time. It always made her feel special. Loved, even. It was there in his voice when he used that word, used his language. Still, what did she really know about him other than he made her body come alive when no one else ever had?

Breathe. You're holding your breath and scaring yourself. Look at me.

If she did, she would be lost. She was always lost when she looked at him, but if she didn't, they would stand here until she

413

did. Surrounded by the other hunters. They were all so much taller than she was and stronger. They formed walls around her with no way out.

Charlotte forced her gaze up Tariq's chest to his throat. She could see the faint strawberry — the mark her mouth had put on him earlier, when he'd first awakened her in the bed upstairs. It made her blush to think these men knew she'd done that — that she had been so out of control and wild she had left her brand on him. His jaw was strong, a man's jaw, and that was strangely always a trigger for her. The moment she looked at his jawline, her body came to life. Quickly, her gaze continued up to his mouth, and she nearly groaned aloud. That mouth always took her breath. So beautiful. So perfect. He knew how to use his mouth. She didn't dare stop there. Deliberately she stared at his aristocratic nose.

You are not looking at me. Give me your eyes, Charlotte. You need to take a deep breath and look at your lifemate.

If she took a breath, she would draw his scent into her lungs. She knew that. If she looked into his eyes she would drown in him. Give herself to him all over again right there surrounded by these predators, knowing he was one of them. She'd asked for this, wanted him to allow her to try to track Vadim. Even this morning, in their bed, sprawled across his body, his cock still deep inside her, both sated for a brief time, she'd assured him she could do it. She needed to free the children and Emeline. Free herself from his taint. It had seemed such a good idea then. But now . . .

I was wrong, Tariq. She refused to raise her gaze that scant bit to look into his eyes. *I don't want to be in here.*

Charlotte. Look at me now.

He wasn't asking. He'd never used that voice on her. Not ever. There was no possibility of disobeying him. A shudder went through her body, but she lifted her gaze to his. His eyes were gorgeous. Unusual. Midnight blue, glittering like gems. Giving her more, so much more. They were warm with feeling he rarely showed in front of others, feelings for her. It was impossible not to see she belonged to him. Was loved by him. Protected by him. He gave her that, and like always, just like she knew she would, she believed.

Now breathe for me, sielamet, and let's get this done if you're still willing to do it.

So intimate, his touch. The way he poured into her mind and filled every lonely spot inside of her. She'd felt so alone and different for so long, never quite fitting in anywhere until Tariq. Whatever the pull between them, that connection, she knew, even standing in this room surrounded by predators, she was willing to risk everything for him.

Charlotte took a breath. The moment she did, Tariq stepped closer to her; his arm moved around her waist and drew her front to his side beneath his wide shoulder, locking her to him. All the while, his scent went deep, comforting her like it always did.

"I'm going to put my hand on the horse and scan it before you touch it," Tariq said. "I don't want to take a chance that another sliver could enter your body. The healer has been sent for but it may be some time before he can come."

"Let me," Dragomir said.

When the Carpathian spoke, Charlotte couldn't help the little shiver that went down her spine. He spoke quietly, his voice pitched low, but that tone went straight into one's body and mind. It was as if he could get *inside* a person, into their skin and bones and just take over. It was frightening, his voice, frightening yet very, very compelling. She wasn't the only one to feel it. These men were not led. She knew that. Not a single one of them, yet they all looked at Dragomir with respect. Warily, but with respect.

"It is my duty," Tariq said, his voice equally low. Not asking. Simply stating.

Dragomir shook his head. "Your first duty is to ensure your lifemate's health and survival. Her safety. If this thing is cursed in some way by Vadim and his brothers, then

416

you cannot chance being infected."

The others nodded in agreement. Dragomir waited, and that told Charlotte he was equally respectful of Tariq. Tariq stepped away from the carousel, taking Charlotte with him. Dragomir, without hesitation, closed in on the horses and chariots. His larger body stood between her and the carousel deliberately. The other hunters pressed closer as well, forming a protective ring around her.

"The wood splinters the moment you touch it," Charlotte dared to warn him.

He didn't look at her. Not even a glance. Before, Charlotte thought the horses and chariots beautiful, artistic and historical. She had felt a compulsion to touch them, to run her hand over the flowing lines of the wild manes and stroke the smooth backs right to the long artistry of the tails. Something inside her had urged her forward, to take that step and touch. To feel. To sit on them. To be part of history.

Now, with the Carpathians standing with her, their dangerous power harnessed for her, she could look at the carousel and see its historical value, feel the pull of the beauty of such intricate carvings from hundreds of years earlier, but the need to touch them wasn't so strong.

"I think that whatever was done to this carousel called to the splinter inside of me," she admitted aloud. Instantly she wished she'd kept her mouth shut and her thoughts to herself. Every single male in the room focused on her again. She'd just been able to breathe, and now that single-minded concentration was back, their attention once more on her. "I felt it, a need to touch the wood when I was close," she continued, because really, now that she'd started, it needed to be said. To protect Dragomir and the others.

"I feel no such drawing," Dragomir assured. He ran his hand just above the horse and then the chariot next to it, shaking his head. "There is power here. Blood."

He remained totally expressionless. His tone gave nothing away. His eyes were blank and cold as if he was no longer a man. He scared the hell out of Charlotte, sadly, more than Fridrick did. She detested that she felt that way about the hunter, but unlike with Lojos, Tomas and Mataias, who were as expressionless as Dragomir, she felt there was no redemption for Dragomir. He was too far gone. Too wild. Not vampire exactly, but something else, something not human, not Carpathian, but far too powerful for his own good.

"Can you touch it without danger?" Tariq asked.

Dragomir dropped his hand to the horse, smoothed his palm over the back to the tail. "This blood shrinks from me. It gathers together deep inside the wood, where it tries to hide from me, but I feel it."

"Can you remove it?" Charlotte couldn't prevent the hope in her voice. If he could, they could save the carousel.

He shook his head, crushing her hopes. "I believe if you wish to try to track Vadim it will be safe if all of us weave safeguards and hold the blood in the center of each of these objects."

There was no doubt in her mind that Dragomir and the others could do it if he said so. He wouldn't risk her. He wouldn't risk Tariq. Whatever code of honor he lived by, and it was different from that of the others — that was certain — he believed in protecting lifemates.

"It's up to you, Charlotte," Tariq said, giving her the choice.

She loved that he left it up to her — and she detested it as well. She wanted to step right up to the carousel, to show courage, but to relive the terrible moment when Tariq realized the Malinov brothers had deliberately chosen to give up their souls and they had attacked the village where he stayed, killing the people he knew, would be terrible. Still. For Emeline. For Liv. For all of them. This had to be done.

Charlotte squared her shoulders, deliberately took a deep breath and drew Tariq deep into her lungs for courage. "We need to track him."

"I'll be with you," Tariq said in a soft, quiet voice that always stunned her. Took her somewhere else. Wrapped her up and kept her safe.

She didn't want him with her. She didn't want him to have to relive his terrible past, some of the worst moments of his life; this time, he'd be able to feel. Through him, so would the others. She would cause that. Without thinking she shook her head. "No, just let me do this alone." She stepped toward the carousel.

Tariq stepped with her, keeping her locked to his side, his grip unbreakable, his face set in stone. His eyes held hers and he slowly shook his head. Simultaneously, Dragomir, Siv, Lojos, Tomas and Mataias growled. The two others as well. *Growled.* Like wild animals. Her gaze jumped from Tariq to their faces. Maksim and the others crowded closer to the carousel, clearly not approving of her plea.

"Fine." She wanted to pretend she capitulated to appease them, but she knew she really had no choice. They weren't going to allow her to do this alone.

"Are you ready, *sielamet*?" Tariq asked, his lips against her ear, brushing so that he was kissing her even as he asked her.

She loved that about him, the little intimate gestures he made. She looked around at the men, all of them, even Dragomir, and she went from being afraid of them to feeling protected. They were predatory, but that danger was for someone else, never her.

"I'm ready. I have to focus. I need to . . ." She tried to step away from him, but his arm locked her in place, a steel band around her waist.

"Not without me."

She had to rethink how she was going to do this. If she was going to track Vadim, she had to do so delicately, without thinking about Tariq or the cost to him. Or to the others. Her touch would have to be ultralight. She closed her eyes and blocked out everything but the thought of the carousel. How old it was. The historic value. How much she loved the past and the wonderful opportunity her gift gave her to visit that past and learn about the people who had carved such beautiful horses and chariots for others.

She wanted to know about those woodcarvers. What they thought and felt. What their lives were like. The people they knew and why they did what they did in a time that was all about survival. She pushed away thoughts of all knowledge of Tariq. She wanted the surprise of what and who he was then, not imposing who he was now on that man carving the objects to be used for the carousel.

She kept her eyes closed to block out the sights of the men crowding close — and they were up against her now, touching her. One hand on her. One hand on the carousel. Each of them. That made it much more difficult to block them all out. She knew which hand belonged to which man. Dragomir smelled feral. Danger radiated off of him in waves. The others were just as bad. Even Tariq. They were a pack of wolves waiting to tear into something. Fierce, experienced fighters. She was surrounded by them, needed space, and knew they wouldn't back off.

Charlotte blew out her breath, exasperated. She had to think of a way around their protective instincts so she could do her job. She thought about the *why* of it. The *who*. Little Liv. Vadim had made her nights hell and the child was only ten. She had already suffered in a hell deep below the city, where insanity reigned. Emeline. No one but Emeline knew the horrors she'd suffered — and was still suffering.

There was Tariq. She focused on him. How did he get to be so strong? So compassionate? What would give a man such courage to face enemy after enemy for centuries? Without a family, a woman to call his own. She could understand why he wanted a woman for himself, but the children? What man would take on such a terrible burden as five traumatized children? Genevieve. Emeline. The Waltons. His family was growing, and all of them, in their own way, were broken.

She reached for a carousel horse, her palm hovering for a moment, feeling the pull of the ancient wood. Hearing the cries of children and their parents. Laughter. Sobs. Whispers. So much history. She needed to go deeper, to find the wood-carver. She caught his scent. She'd know it anywhere. Masculine. The forest. Primal. She followed that faint scent until she heard the sound of his voice.

Do you blindly follow Ruslan? What is wrong with you all? Do you know how insane this plan is? The Dubrinsky line is the vessel for our past and present. The power is what keeps our people alive. You can't replace that because you don't like the prince.

Do you blindly follow the prince? That was Fridrick's voice. A sneer. *Wiping out his family will do nothing but get rid of bad leadership. We should be the rulers of this world. Instead, we're kept like prisoners in these mountains or forced to hunt our brethren. Our women grow scarce, and yet he does nothing. He protects that son of his, Draven . . .*

The name was uttered and even Tariq winced, although she had no idea who Draven was, only that the loathing for that person was collective. She saw Tariq now. He was standing tall in the middle of several men — men he'd grown up with. Men he'd called his friends. They surrounded him, some with fists doubled. Their face flushed. Teeth clenched. A strange red glow to their eyes.

Draven should have been put down long ago. Any other with that streak of insanity, harming our women, betraying them to vampires, murdering them, would have been hunted down and sentenced to death, but he refused to do anything about him and now Ivory is gone to us. Dead. That was Vadim. She recognized his voice.

Tariq shook his head and ran one hand through his hair in agitation. *Mistakes have been made, but to plot to assassinate our prince — not only our prince but his lifemate and the other children — is lunacy. Surely you see that.*

At any other time she would have stayed and listened to history playing itself out. It was fascinating to catch a glimpse of Tariq's world. Of the man he'd been then, standing up to his friends when he was the lone dissenter. Clearly he stood up for what he believed. Still, she had to find out what Vadim had done to the carousel horses and the chariots. That required adjusting the timeline. Already the cold was seeping into her bones, a warning she'd learned to heed after traveling into the tunnel. Shivering, she moved forward to the next night. It wasn't safe staying too long.

The world was on fire. There was a terrible orange-red glow and smoke was thick, so thick she was afraid to take a breath. The sounds of weeping, of screams, rose on the wind while the smoke swirled and the flames crackled. She caught glimpses of Tariq fighting viciously, ferociously, his body in constant movement, shifting from one shape to another. He moved with blurring speed and his hand plunged into the chest of one man and ripped out the heart. It was the most gruesome thing Charlotte had ever seen.

She concentrated on the carousel. The horses lay on their sides, beautiful and colorful, but when she looked closer she could see splashes of blood on them. The chariots were scattered in the dirt, flung there by unseen hands. To her horror, she saw the leg of a child peeking out beneath one, streaks of blood on the calf and heel. Another covered a woman, facedown in the soil, her arms flung wide. There were cracks in the wood as if whoever had thrown them was in a rage.

Her breath caught in her lungs and she found herself jerking back involuntarily. She recognized Fridrick, but just barely. Just a day earlier he'd been handsome and fit. Now he appeared twisted. Evil. There was a maniacal cruelty in his eyes and his teeth appeared sharper and longer. Even his fingernails were longer. The man with him had to be Vadim. She recognized him from the earlier vignette.

Vadim threw everything in his path out of his way. Two men rushed him, both with swords. Charlotte wanted to scream a warning, but she stayed silent. This was history and it had to play out the way it had happened. Vadim laughed, the sound both evil and chilling. He slammed both arms down against the swords, blocking the blades and sending them spinning away, and then he grabbed both men by their heads.

Look away. That was Tariq. Her Tariq. Standing with her, watching all over again as the village where he lived and worked was destroyed and the people he loved were brutally murdered.

She did as he asked because he was suffering. He needed her to look away. She found him in the battle, whirling through the attackers, a lone man standing up to an army of vampires. *How did you do it? There were so many.*

They were newly made. I didn't save many of my people.

My people. That was telling. It wasn't true that he hadn't saved many; already she could see the vampires retreating, killing as they went, but falling back, unwilling to engage the hunter as he cut them down.

Vadim's movement caught her eye and she turned her attention to him once more. The two men he'd killed lay like broken dolls and he kicked their bodies out of his path. One by one his brothers joined him. Then Fridrick and two others. They cut their wrists and

426

dripped blood collectively into the wood of each horse and chariot, a black spell spewing from their vengeful mouths.

While Tariq fought off the small army of recruits, the Malinov brothers defiled his creation with their tainted blood. Then Vadim stood over each of the horses and chariots. Charlotte watched in horror as a small shadow was wrenched from him at each of the carvings. The shadows seemed alive, writhing as if in pain, wiggling like tadpoles. Vadim's blood was dripped onto the things, and then each man spit, mixing his saliva with Vadim's blood. The small, shadowy, wormlike creatures desperately tried to return to their maker, but Vadim sent the shadows deep into the wood.

One of those things was inside her. It had entered her, and even Tariq couldn't remove it. She shivered, the cold so far into her bones that now she felt frozen. There was more to do, more to understand.

She fought to stay close to Vadim, although his presence repulsed her. The battle raged in the background and yet he didn't even look at the army he'd created that Tariq was fast destroying. Vadim turned his head and muttered something to Fridrick, who grinned insanely and nodded.

First Fridrick brought a child to Vadim, a young boy no more than ten. Vadim barely looked at the boy. He simply picked up the child and tore into his throat. Blood sprayed over a horse. Vadim moved in a circle making certain the blood hit each of the horses. He murmured words while he did so. At first she could only see the dying child.

Come back now.

She couldn't. There was something more. Something she had missed. Fridrick brought another victim to Vadim. A woman this time. He did the same thing without sparing her a glance. He tore into her throat and sprayed her blood over the horses and chariots. This time, Charlotte didn't look at the woman or Vadim. She looked at the blood. The shadow rose up and swam through the blood, taking with it tiny cells she would never have seen if she'd been looking through human eyes. She was looking through eyes that were mostly Carpathian. The shadow consumed red blood cells.

That was how the curse worked. The victim of the splinter would wither and die. But how did the splinter multiply? How could there be more than one victim per horse or chariot?

Come back now or I will force you to do so.

Tariq was already doing so. She felt him yanking at her, pulling, but she barely heard his voice. Icicles formed on her skin. In her hair. She breathed them into her lungs until she had to fight for every breath she took. It was right there. Right in front of her. The wasting illness. The splinter somehow consumed the red blood cells and no amount of transfusions could save the victim once enough time had passed. Vadim would know instantly where that victim was and he could, at his leisure, should he be in the area, find and kill the man, woman or child.

But how did the splinter multiply? What had he done to make certain the cycle could repeat itself victim after victim? She tried to think about it but her brain felt mushy. Detached. She was cold. Icy even, but she couldn't think what to do about it. The splinter was wholly Vadim's, yet the same one could be used over and over. How? How had he done that?

She shivered, hearing a call, one she needed to answer, but she'd forgotten how. *The saliva,* she murmured. *Something Vadim did when the others mixed their saliva with his blood.* It hurt to think, but she had to know. They had to know, but now she wasn't positive who *they* were. She shivered uncontrollably, trying to conjure up the scene in her mind, to pay attention to Vadim, not the others, as they spat onto the wiggling parasites and mixed saliva with Vadim's blood.

His lips were moving. His hands waving. She pushed the memory into her mind so Tariq could see. So the others, whoever they were, could see. It hurt, a thousand icicles stabbing her brain, but she managed it.

Tariq ripped her back through the tunnel.

His hold was ruthless, impossible to ignore. It wasn't so much on her body; Tariq had always been locked with her, his arm a band around her chest, but this was in her mind. He had commanded and now he was forcing obedience. Her barriers were down. All of them. It was the only way to enter the time tunnels. The journey back seemed longer than ever. Colder. She didn't think she would have made it back on her own.

When Charlotte found herself in the present time, she was wrapped in Tariq's arms, but each of the other males had a hand on her. Her head. Her shoulders. Both legs. One circled her ankle. The terrible shaking of her body made her teeth chatter. She couldn't stop it. She was consumed by the cold. Every breath she took, she wheezed and struggled for air. Her lungs labored and hurt. So bad.

"You have no choice," Siv stated.

That sounded ominous. Charlotte tried to look up at Tariq to question what Siv meant. What choice? About what? But she couldn't think. She was cold. So cold. And exhausted. Her lashes drifted down, weighted, she was certain, by icicles. She meant to tell Tariq to get the ice off of her, that she couldn't get warm with it surrounding her like a blanket, but the effort was too much.

"*Sielamet,* you cannot go to sleep," Tariq said. "Stay with me. Talk to me."

She had the sensation of moving and knew

he was carrying her, taking her somewhere. She tried to turn her head into his shoulder to burrow deeper, but his usually hot body wasn't even warm. She only found more ice. Sheets of it.

"Safeguard," she whispered. "He used the word *safeguard.*" She hadn't known what that meant when Tariq had used it, but now she knew Vadim had somehow turned the tables on her. While she spied on him, she hadn't thought that he might have safeguarded his cruel work in some way.

No. No. No. Tariq felt the blow like a terrible punch to his gut. His heart stilled, stopped beating and then became frantic. His breath caught in his throat, and he couldn't control his heart as it hammered out a protest. This couldn't be happening. Not after finding her. Not after being with her. Laughing with her. Falling in love with the woman she was. Tariq crushed her frozen body against the warmth of his. She was fading too fast. Her heartbeat far too slow.

"Maksim, Dragomir, any of you, did you catch the weave he used for the safeguards he erected around the horses and chariots just before he removed all evidence of his having been there?" Tariq wanted every single man to give input. He couldn't afford to get it wrong. He had an extraordinary memory when it came to spells and weaves, but this was too important.

He found himself praying to whatever gods there were, every one he'd ever heard about in his long life. *Don't take her.* Whatever happened, he would follow. He would never allow her to travel into the unknown without him but . . .

The children. She stirred. In her mind. Sluggish. *Can't think.*

That was bad — very bad.

Sielamet. Hang on for me. Hang on to me. Stay in my mind. Stay with me. He was begging. Running so fast he was a blur, but holding her spirit in his mind. He could see that weak flickering light. Pleading with those gods he wasn't sure existed, but imploring anyway.

He knew the others followed him as he took her through the maze in the basement. They were all just as worried. Every breath Charlotte took was labored. Every puff that emerged from her mouth was coated with ice, tiny particles that were slowly freezing her lungs. Even the shivering had stopped, and that was a very bad sign. He couldn't afford to wait another minute. He glanced at Maksim and nodded his head.

Maksim took off ahead of him, moving through the basement walls until he came to what appeared to be a solid concrete wall. Palm facing the solid slab, he flicked his hand to his left and the concrete slid out of his way revealing dark, rich loam. Minerals sparkled throughout the bed of soil. It was spread completely under the basement, a rich reservoir painstakingly brought from the richest soils found in the United States. This was a place of healing. This was where Tomas had stayed for two weeks and had recovered. He had offered the same to Val, but the ancient had refused and had gone to another place in the forest to heal.

"No one could have foreseen this." Dragomir all but growled it.

The others echoed the sentiment, absolving him, but did it really matter? There was no absolution. He had allowed her to go into a situation alone and unprotected. There was no feeling better about it, no loss of guilt or anger or fear. Terror. It was there. Grabbing him by the throat and crushing him under its weight. He couldn't lose her. Not now. *Stay with me. Stay for me. I need you, Charlotte.*

Tariq waved a hand and opened the soil, giving himself plenty of room. He floated, Charlotte cradled in his arms, down into what appeared to be a double grave at least eight feet deep. The minerals sparkled when the faint lights on the ceiling overhead illuminated the dark loam. Up on the decks above the soil, the Carpathian hunters formed a circle around the opening and began to chant. Hand and arm movements were coordinated, reversing what Vadim had done centuries earlier.

Charlotte tried. For him. He felt it. The rising of her spirit just briefly. The smallest of flickers, and then her light faded.

Tariq didn't waste any time. He sank his teeth into Charlotte's neck, that pulse that should have been tripping with fear, but was barely there. He took her blood fast. She didn't feel the bite or the drawing, so he didn't try to soften the effects. He just took enough for an exchange, watching her the entire time.

Her eyelids were so fragile, almost transparent under the fog of ice, eyes moving continually behind them. Her lashes were long and thick, lying in twin crescents against her pale skin. She shuddered. Labored for breath. Wheezed. He reached for her spirit even as he drank, surrounding that small fading light so that she couldn't escape him. His blood didn't warm her body as it should have. He'd encased the splinter, making certain it couldn't break free, but it was using her bone marrow as a resource to continue to infect her.

Between the splinter and the safeguards, Charlotte was in trouble. The moment he'd taken enough blood, he swept away his clothing and used his fingernail to tear a laceration over his chest muscles. Immediately he cupped the back of her head in his hand and pressed her mouth to the ruby beads bubbling up. *Drink, sielamet. Drink for both of us.*

He pushed command into his voice, cursing that he'd allowed her to stay too long in the tunnels. She had no sense of time passing there, but he'd known she was getting close to her limit. He hadn't banked on Vadim's safeguards from centuries earlier, working to destroy her.

Her mouth barely moved. He scowled and pressed her closer, taking her mind from her, uncaring in that moment that he might have to face her later if she objected. Ruthlessly he forced compliance, even when her body was far too tired to obey. She had no other choice than to do exactly as he commanded. Her mouth began to move against him, drawing out the vital blood that would sustain her life and ensure that nothing would take her from him. Hot rich blood that would fill her organs, heat and reshape them. Change her. Transform her. Save her.

Don't let it be too late. Let me have her.

While she fed, he removed their clothes with a simple wave of his hand and encased both of them in the rich soil, burying all but their heads so that the earth could do its job and care for her, warm her. Bring back heat into her freezing body. When he was certain she'd taken enough blood for their third exchange, he held her close, using his own body heat, slipping into her body with his spirit to facilitate her body's ability to bring her temperature up.

Inside her, he found . . . ice. He'd been standing with her, his arms around her. The other Carpathian hunters had been touching her — hands on her — but they couldn't go where she led. It had happened so fast. Without warning. They could see the events unfolding in their minds, but they weren't present and couldn't know that Vadim had woven so foul a safeguard. The memories held in the wood took Charlotte with them back to wherever they were born. That journey was dangerous, and if she stayed too long, she was without the ability to stay warm. The safeguard was simple enough in that it played on the weakness of the recipient. Already cold, Charlotte became freezing. More, the woven spell compounded the effect, twisting the internal organs into icy, frozen lumps.

The chants of the Carpathian males rose and Blaze joined them, standing beside her lifemate, Maksim, her voice adding a feminine note to the deeper voices rising in an effort to save Tariq's lifemate. Val Zhestokly arrived, looking pale and even staggering a little, the signs of torture still very evident on his body. He wasn't alone. To Tariq's horror, Liv was with him, holding his hand. Standing on the very edge of what to the child had to look like a grave. Tariq closed his eyes. This was going to be bad. So bad.

16

Taking a deep breath, Tariq opened his eyes to look at the child. "*Csecsemõ* — baby — you cannot be here. This could go very, very wrong."

"I would not have brought her if the message was not important, *ekäm* — my brother," Val said, his voice rusty and without any emotion.

Tariq sighed. "You understand this is going to be bad. We could lose Charlotte."

Liv stared down at him with her haunted eyes, shaking her head. "Emeline said to do exactly what you're thinking. She does need all of us. Every single one of us. I told the others to help. Emeline said it's the only way to save her, Tariq, and we need her. We need you. None of us will survive without you."

He groaned softly, smoothing back Charlotte's hair. "Don't say that, Liv. You have Danny, your sisters and Emeline. You have Val. The connection is strong between you. He woke at your call."

A shudder ran through Charlotte's body when she'd lain as if dead. A block of ice in his arms. No longer shivering. Her spirit merely a faint, flickering light he'd surrounded and kept from moving down the tree of life. He whispered to her. In her mind. In her ear. Softly. Lovingly. Letting her know she wasn't alone.

I am with you always, sielamet. Keeper of my soul. Of my heart. Where you go I will follow.

A frown flickered over her face. Her eyes moved back and forth behind her eyelids. A small shake of her head. *Children.* They were there in her mind, a worry that they couldn't do without him.

I cannot survive your passing with honor, Charlotte. He gave her the stark truth. *I must follow or become the very thing I have hunted for centuries.* Dishonor. Forcing his fellow hunters to find and destroy him. He was ancient. Experienced in battle. They would have trouble, and he could as easily kill them as they could him. The idea . . . He shook his head. *I go where you go, sielamet. Always.*

"Tariq, we can save her," Liv reiterated. "I know we can. Emeline knows things. She sent for me. She said you know what to do. We have to band together. One mind. All of us. We can do it."

"*Csecsemő,* she must go through the conversion. It is . . . difficult. I cannot take away

438

the pain and she is very weak. It is not good for you to be here, to see this."

Liv stuck her chin out, her fingers wrapped around Val's hand so tightly they were white. "I know I'm ten. I know that, but I have gifts, and I know what is truth in someone's mind when I touch them. I know what is in Emeline's. She sees reality in dreams and she *told* me. She told me to run and get Val. She said to tell you that you were right to call everyone in even though it feels wrong. She said modesty or bravery isn't important, just easing the conversion for her. You were right all along in your thinking for the children. She said that all the Carpathians and I needed to connect our minds with yours. Charlie needs to be in the soil, just like you have her. She said, *'Hold on to her, Tariq.'* And then she said this is how to convert the others and me — all of us together — and you were the one who knew it; you were just afraid of losing any of us, but it has to be done."

He'd lost control of his woman and she was dying. Now, he'd lost control of his child. Little brave Liv. Ten years old. She could already hear everything on the telepathic common path they all used. She was old beyond her years and far too young for the terrible things that had happened to her. Things he couldn't prevent.

He had to trust Emeline to know what she was talking about. He had to believe that she

439

would never risk Liv. Never. She was trying to save the child as well as Charlotte, although he would have preferred she come herself or talk to Amelia. He glanced up at Maksim.

Maksim raised an eyebrow, but Blaze nodded several times. "Emeline would never tell Liv to be here if it wasn't important, Tariq."

He didn't understand why Liv had to be a witness, but Charlotte's body suddenly writhed in his arms and he could think only of saving her. The soil kept her from moving or thrashing, but the wave of pain was so sudden, so intense, he was certain of its own accord her body would have curled into the fetal position. He turned her on her side, his arms holding her against him, the soil packed tightly to hold her fragile body in place while the blood reshaped her organs and got rid of the toxins.

All along, Tariq had been trying to think of a way to aid the children in their conversion. He'd thought of — and discarded — several ideas, but his mind kept returning to the idea of all the Carpathians together aiding the children as the conversion took place. They were far more powerful as a whole. No one had thought to try it.

A male turned his lifemate, and it was a grueling, difficult process, and most females would find it objectionable for any other to see them so vulnerable. Naked, sick, in most cases convulsing. Stripped of all dignity. No

440

woman would want anyone to see her like that and no man would want that for her. Still, the idea, no matter how many times he'd dismissed it, kept coming back to him because it was logical. Together, they were extremely powerful.

Tariq would do anything to spare his woman pain. Even sacrifice her dignity. Now, when her life was at stake, he had no other option. He had to have the others there, and if Emeline had dreamt this was a success because the others were present, then he'd take that flicker of hope and hold on to it.

Pain slammed into Charlotte's body, nearly crushing her under its weight. He could feel it through her. Excruciating. Robbing her of breath. Of mind. Of focus. For a moment he wavered. How could she take this? How could any of them? A ten-year-old child, let alone a three-year-old.

The chanting swelled in volume and then the others poured into Charlotte through him, a lifeline like no other. Tariq was shouldering as much of the pain as possible for her and surrounding her spirit at the same time to keep her from traveling too far from them. The others took small portions of the pain, bites out of it until there was very little left for Charlotte to bear. Her body writhed and contorted under the onslaught of the conversion, but the soil gently held her along with Tariq. When her body expelled the toxins, the earth quickly absorbed them and whisked them away from her, leaving her clean.

Still, even with the power and coordinated efforts of all the Carpathians present, the healing chants and the unexpected, even shocking boost of Liv, Danny and Amelia, Charlotte continued to fade. They kept pain from her, but the toll on her body from Vadim's icy safeguard and the presence of the splinter in her body were impossible for them to counteract.

Holding her to him, Tariq realized he had no choice but to do something about that splinter. Vadim might not be able to go after her red blood cells, caged as he was, but the subtle influence was there. That influence was killing her body. She was already slipping away from him. Regardless of the danger, he had to take the chance.

Dragomir, she is still fading. Vadim's splinter remains within her. I think together we could extract it. I warn you, it will fight us.

He needed Dragomir to know they were in for the fight of their lives. As soon as the cage around the splinter was released, Vadim would do his worst. He would sense his prey was weak and would strike hard with everything he had at his disposal. To rid her body of the splinter in the middle of the conversion was madness, but Tariq had to go with his gut. Emeline had reminded him of that

442

by sending her message through Liv.

It is too dangerous. We should wait.

We have to do it now. He's attacking her. If we don't stop him he will win this battle in the end. We will successfully convert her with very little pain, but she will die. He put conviction in his voice. In his mind. He knew he spoke the truth. He was a good enough healer to get by, but not like Dragomir was reputed to be. Tariq would rather have waited for a Daratrazanoff, one of a line of legendary healers, but he had run out of time.

You hold your woman to you.

Unexpectedly it was Siv who intervened, a man much like Dragomir. He had also been in the monastery, a place where very ancient hunters retreated when all was lost to them. No memories. No emotion. No color. Not even the whisper of temptation. After centuries of hunting vampires, they believed it was cowardice to seek the dawn so they withdrew into the monastery to protect humans and Carpathians alike. Siv had left half a century before Dragomir, probably around the same time Val had left.

I will aid Dragomir while you hold her spirit in your hands.

The unexpected offer was humbling to Tariq. Like anyone else, he was uneasy in the presence of the three legendary hunters. Any male wearing the tattoo art of the monastery

443

was unpredictable and extremely dangerous. He had welcomed them as hunters, as brethren, but he watched them closely.

I will add my strength to my brothers'. That was Val.

I will safeguard them and you while Maksim's woman and the others shoulder her pain, Nicu said.

There it was. Solidarity. What it meant to be Carpathian. They were far from the mountains of their birth. Far from their prince and his power. Still, they stood together as they always had in times of trouble. Protecting their women and children.

I will hold in mind the safeguards woven around the splinter to cage it in. Take great care that he doesn't attack one of you, Tariq cautioned.

Dragomir made a sound. A single note of disgust that spoke volumes. He had known the Malinov family — not Ruslan and his brothers, but their parents. Clearly he didn't think much of them or the threat they presented, and that was what worried Tariq the most. If those from the monastery, locked away while the world had changed so drastically, while their enemies had changed, underestimated the danger, they could fall. Tariq knew they used the ancient method of sharing information to catch up on everything they had missed over the lost time. All Carpathians did so, but the intricacies of technology, of the sophisticated weapons man had developed, the monitoring systems, the dangers of cell phones and cameras, all would be difficult for an ancient to understand overnight.

All the while Tariq held Charlotte close, feeling the shudders and contortions of her body, holding her waning light to him beneath their blanket of mineral-rich soil. *I am with you, sielamet. Do not try to stray too far from me. You will feel the others enter. The light will be powerful. They are coming to aid you, to remove all trace of Vadim from you.* He didn't want her to fear the others, and he knew it was a huge thing to her to get rid of any part of Vadim. Knowing that they were removing the shadow from her might help to keep her with him.

Her light had moved inches downward, journeying away from her body, bumping into the circle he'd created to contain her. *I am with you,* he whispered again. Softly. Intimately. Into her mind. *Stay with me, Charlotte. With us. We need you. All of us.*

Dragomir was so powerful that when he entered, pure spirit, it felt like an invasion. A takeover. More, his spirit wasn't pure light as all healing spirit was. Tariq had never witnessed a spirit so ravaged. It was more streaks than solid. More ivory than white, and that ivory was stained and worn.

445

Siv entered next and like Dragomir's, his presence was an intrusion of sheer dominance. His spirit was no longer white and solid, but a mix of silver streaks and white light.

Val was last to enter. His entry was slow and there was a brief flash of pain he couldn't prevent the others from feeling as he shed his body to become spirit. Like those of the other two from the monastery, Val's spirit was a different color than expected, more an antique gold, not in the least bright, but tarnished gold, with dark streaks running through the light.

Tariq had nothing to reference such spirits by, so again, he had to go with his gut and believe that all three were there to aid Charlotte before all else. He gathered her closer to him and felt the heat as they swept through her body, paying attention first to every organ, ensuring her body was accepting the conversion, and then speeding the process along.

The three lights, ivory, silver and gold, moved toward her rib cage and the barrier Tariq had constructed around Vadim's splinter. Ivory took the center, facing the splinter fully, while gold went to the left and silver to the right. They studied the situation carefully as they began unweaving Tariq's safeguards.

The splinters attack the red cells, Tariq reminded them. Charlotte had sent them the information on the common path, but he had found out before, when he was first examining the splinter's destructive path.

He has made himself a killing worm traveling throughout the ages. I have seen this done by a mage, but no Carpathian has ever done so. Dragomir's voice was mild, a deference to Charlotte's failing body.

These vampires have mixed with mages. That was Siv. He, too, spoke softly, including Charlotte on the common path.

We grew up with Xavier's father. He knew more than his son could ever know, Val said. His voice hitched just that little bit but enough for Tariq to know the out-of-body experience was costing him.

His name was Alycrome. As he reassured Charlotte, Dragomir and the other two hunters continued to take down the safeguards around the splinter. *He had no problems teaching those of us who liked to learn. I sat at his knee when I was no more than four. I was but twenty when he showed us how to splinter off and send pieces of who we were into others.*

Siv took over the instruction, murmuring all the while they spread healing light throughout Charlotte's body and yet still kept patiently taking down the layered safeguards.

Alycrome told us no man had the right to take over another unless it was self-defense, sur-

vival, or saving the life of another. Putting a shadow of one's self into another is a form of aggression. A strike to take over that person and render them a puppet to one's will.

Tariq's arms pulled Charlotte closer as she shuddered against him. He had wondered how Vadim kept the human psychics from being complete puppets, needing flesh and blood to survive, yet still kept them under his control. Splinters. Vadim was using splinters of himself, small shadowy leeches to slip into and feed on the host. Vadim could control thoughts subtly that way. The more inclined the host was to carry out orders, the easier it was for Vadim to take control. He was smart enough to offer each human in his army whatever that man desired most. Tariq sent the information to the others so they would know what they were facing in Vadim's human army.

The thing one has got to remember about splinters, sisarke, but everyone chooses over the centuries to forget, is what they do to the kuly who is so peje ignorant as to use it, Dragomir continued.

Sisarke is little sister *and kuly is literally* a worm, *a demon devouring souls. Peje is* burn *or in your language it would be* fuck. *A very bad term. Vadim is nothing more than a worm, Charlotte, and we will rid you of him for all time.* Tariq spoke gently, holding her light in that circle he'd made to ensure she didn't slip away.

She was no longer fighting to get free; she lay very still, allowing his blood to work through her system, removing all traces of the human she had been and reshaping her as Carpathian. On some level she was aware, very aware, of the spirits of the men inside her body, helping to heal her even as they worked. She was listening, and it was helping to combat the pain and fear of conversion.

Alycrome impressed on all those who would listen that each splinter taken from the creator was a piece of him gone, diminishing him, Dragomir said. *Xavier didn't care to listen. He spent his time learning every dark spell without learning the repercussions of them.*

He thought he was above consequences. He thought himself smarter than his father. That was Siv. *Ah. Now I see it. The worm. A little fishtail causing such trouble. Do not worry, sisarke; this will be no problem for your lifemate and the three of us. Give yourself up to him while we dispose of this kuly.*

Tariq was very aware of the shadowy fish-like wiggling splinter buried deep in Charlotte's rib. He could see the tail of it writhing under the combined powerful lights of the three ancients. He had missed Alycrome's teaching by only a few short years. Xavier had risen as head mage after the death of his father, and Tariq had studied under him. Xavier certainly hadn't taught any of them that using a splinter would diminish the creator.

Siv and Val moved abruptly, joining Dragomir, so that there was only one powerful beam, the energy from all three ancients concentrated in one hot blast as they poured light over the worm. The tail began to smoke. The worm wiggled hard, surging back and forth, the bone a trap now rather than a haven.

The three ancients refused to let up, pouring white-hot energy onto the tail of the splintery shadow. Charlotte gasped and arched her back, half sitting, the soil falling around them like a shower.

Tariq covered her face and wrapped his body around hers, blanketing her, holding her in place. *She feels that.*

It is Vadim attacking, Siv said. *He feels that heat. This splinter is part of him. It burns. And where it burns is in his brain.*

The shadow thrust forward, trying to penetrate deeper into the bone. It couldn't burrow fast enough, so it tried backing out. The tail began to curl into blackened ash. Frantic, the shadowy parasite flung itself sideways, crashing into the bone over and over with hard, short bursts of power to either side.

A flash of crushing pain told Tariq and the

others forming the circle that Vadim had broken the rib, but not punched through the bone to escape as he intended.

"She can't take that," Blaze whispered aloud. "She's too far gone." She wrapped her fingers tightly around Liv and pushed the child's head against her thigh. "Tariq, stop them."

If he stopped them, it would give the splinter time to consume her red blood cells and perhaps find another place to settle where they might not find it. Charlotte detested having the thing inside her.

I'm with you, sielamet. Right here. They are destroying the splinter, and he's fighting back. Stay with me. I need you here with me. He murmured the words into her mind, but more, he pushed feeling there. Poured himself there. Filled her with him.

She moved then; her spirit moved against the circle he'd formed, but to his astonishment, it moved forward, back toward her body and away from the waiting shadows holding the tree of life.

Remove him. I don't care about the pain. Get him out of me. Each word was distinct. Faint, but distinct. Charlotte wanted Vadim gone from her and she gave her consent to the three ancients to do what was necessary.

She settled into him, her spirit sliding up against his. *Merging* with his.

"Tariq, you have to stop this," Blaze reiter-

451

ated. "She's too weak."

There was a moment of silence. A breath. An inhalation and exhalation collectively so that it was heard throughout the basement.

Your woman, your call, Dragomir said.

Against him, Charlotte's body shuddered in pain. Her eyes fluttered, lashes opening just barely. There was a plea there. More, there was absolute trust.

Get him out of her. Now. Tariq knew his woman. She was a fighter, a woman of courage. Charlotte would want this even more than he did. Vadim had no place in their world, their sanctuary.

Charlotte tried hard to rise above the pain. She could see it etched into Tariq's face, and she knew it was very, very bad, far worse than she felt, and she definitely felt it. Still, with all of them shouldering most of the pain, she knew even the children could take it and that gave her comfort. If they added more Carpathians, would that take even more pain away from Bella and Lourdes? From Liv, Amelia and Danny? Because they had to be converted. She knew that with the same certainty as every single Carpathian in the room.

First and foremost there was Liv. She was connected to all of them through Val. He'd forged that path to save her, but now all of them could see what had been done to her. The puppet tearing into her flesh with savage teeth. The noises of him gulping her blood.

452

The burn of Vadim's blood as he forced it into her — the horror and terror of taking the vampire's blood.

At night, in her sleep, if she dared to sleep, the vampire came to her and whispered demands. He wanted her to kill her sisters and brother. To kill Tariq. He told her how to kill him. He told her what he would do to her if she didn't obey him. It was no wonder the child looked so haunted. More, if he whispered those commands to Liv, what was he demanding of Emeline? The trauma had taken its toll on Liv. She planned to end her life if Tariq wouldn't convert her. She was convinced she would eventually go crazy and hurt her family.

I will never let that happen, sielamet. She is watched day and night.

You have to convert her. Like this. With everyone helping. This is why Emeline wanted her here, so she could see and feel how it is done. There was no other explanation. Emeline could see into the future through her dreams. If she wanted Liv there, it was for a singular purpose — she needed to be converted, and Emeline didn't want her to be afraid.

Tariq was such a good man. There was no ego — and that, she decided, was what made him such a good choice for a husband and father. He didn't care who was credited for what. He didn't have to be a hero, and that made him one in her eyes. He allowed three

453

ancients *inside* her, moving through her body, and more, her mind, in order to bring her peace. To remove a threat to her. She loved him all the more for that.

Through Charlotte, all those present felt Vadim's cunning hatred of all Carpathians, but in particular of the prince and his family. He cared nothing about women or children, only about what use they could be to him. She caught flashes of him ripping through several people, drinking blood, splashing it around and shoving them off a ship. She knew the others did as well. Nothing was sacred to him. Nothing at all and yet . . . his entire focus was on the Asenguard compound. There was something there he wanted and he would sacrifice every one of his soldiers, his pawns, his massive army to get it.

Charlotte felt another blast of pain as the splinter buried in her rib changed tactics. Now that her rib was broken, the thing had more wiggle room. It swayed from side to side under the terrible, relentless blast of white-hot energy. She forced herself to lie as relaxed as possible, drawing strength from Tariq's arms while the splinter attacked her. It was an attack, nothing less. Vadim wanted to force her to stop them. She was just as determined the vampire wouldn't get what he wanted.

I'm in love with you, Tariq. She needed to tell

him and now seemed a good time. Her body hurt like hell, and she knew his did as well. He felt far more pain than she did and she figured letting him know what he meant to her was a good way to tell him thank you.

Tariq's arms tightened and he buried his face in the nape of her neck. *More than life, Charlotte. The very air I breathe. You are fél ku kuuluaak sívam belső, my beloved. You are also truly and literally hän ku vigyáz sívamet és sielamet, keeper of my heart and soul.*

When he spoke in his language, in that beautiful, mesmerizing voice she loved, the one that felt like love, the splinter went very still, as if it were paralyzed. Instantly the three ancients struck hard, blasting it with energy and the white-hot light. Charlotte felt that terrible flash, the burn along her broken rib. She took a breath and let it out slowly, trying to ride on top of the wave of pain.

The splinter couldn't escape the light pouring over it, through it. Her rib felt as if someone were taking a torch to it, and she knew Tariq was shouldering most of that pain as well, shielding her as he would from every other terrible thing that came her way. Just as he would shield their children.

I don't know how to tell you in your language, which sounds sexy and beautiful when you speak to me, but you're the keeper of my heart and soul, Tariq. For as long as you want me, I'll be your woman.

She meant every word and surprisingly, her voice sounded soft and loving. No, it *felt* soft and loving. So much so that she heard Vadim shriek his anger and frustration. She felt his fear and it rocked her — rocked her that the terrible monster she thought unstoppable could know fear when the Carpathians facing him didn't feel it at all. She reached for Liv.

See, baby? He's as afraid of us as we've been of him.

He is. There was wonder in Liv's mind. Shock. Knowledge.

Charlotte was too weak to go to her. She didn't even know if she could ever stand again, and the three ancients were deep inside her, determined to rid her of the splinter. Beneath the layers of soil, Charlotte was naked. She had no idea how much of her the others had seen . . .

Sielamet. Just that. One word. But it carried so much meaning. Right now it was male amusement. A reprimand. *I would shield you always. Carpathians do not share well with others.*

She loved that in the middle of life and death, the conversion, the struggle to destroy a monster's hold on her, Tariq was always the calm eye of the storm. So steady. Her rock. He thought to keep her naked body from the others and she was grateful to him. Grateful that when her body expelled all toxins, he shielded her and the earth absorbed everything, keeping the mess from the sight of the others.

She thought it strange that she simply accepted lying in soil, using it as a blanket, packed tightly around her. The knowledge that they were packed in the dirt should have made her heart pound in trepidation, but her mind was too occupied with whether she could take more of that terrible burn in her ribs. That and the fact that the older children should be able to go through the conversion without harm or too much pain.

Relax, Charlotte, Tariq advised. His hand moved soothingly over her back as he pulled her into him, her front to his front.

She hadn't realized she had tensed up, fighting the pain, but it was growing worse, burning along her rib until she wanted to scream. She glanced up at Tariq's face. It was stoic. Without expression. She moved through his mind . . .

Don't! It was a sharp command.

She knew. He was taking most of what she felt while the three ancients attempted to destroy the splinter. Vadim fought back, attacking her, trying to force her to make them stop. Again, Tariq stood solidly between her and pain that would have been far too much for her.

She put her hands on his chest, shocked

how the soil responded to her movement, almost anticipating what she wanted. She felt warm and cocooned. Closing her eyes, she began to breathe deeply, slowly and steadily, using her meditative breathing to stay relaxed. She pushed everything out of her mind but that splinter.

You will not defeat me. I will kill those children in front of you. Your lifemate's blood will run like a river over you as I allow Fridrick to take what is rightfully his.

Tariq's body jerked once, the only sign that he heard. Blaze and Liv both made a sound of shock, of denial. They all heard Vadim's sneering voice.

Dragomir, Siv and Val poured the white-hot light on the splinter, widening their blast so that there was nowhere for the tiny parasite to go. It had smashed the bone almost beyond repair, but Tariq had stopped Charlotte from feeling the worst of that pain and she remained still, refusing to call a halt to the slow, tedious work of extracting Vadim's shadowy splinter from her body.

We will find you and destroy you, piece by piece, Tariq answered. His voice wasn't goading — his tone was matter-of-fact, as if it was a forgone conclusion that eventually Vadim would be caught and destroyed.

Charlotte couldn't stop the shudder that ran through her body as the master vampire

458

retaliated against her, the splinter jamming itself into one of the many cracks and smashing the bone. Vadim poured power into the splinter vengefully, focusing on hurting her, wanting her to scream at the ancients to stop.

Her body stiffened in spite of her commands to stay relaxed. Every muscle tightened. She was already exhausted from the journey back through the tunnel, every inch of her covered in ice; then the conversion, her organs reshaping, her body becoming that of a different species; and now the master vampire battered her, bruised her, broke not only one rib, but succeeded in smashing through two others.

Don't stop, she implored the ancients. *No matter what, don't stop.*

The three men were relentless, determined and without mercy. Their combined light followed the shadow everywhere it went, into every nook and cranny, refusing to allow it out of the bones of her rib cage and into her body, where it could do even more damage. Vadim felt every bit of pain the splinter did. Every burn. Each time more of the tiny object succumbed to ash.

In the end, Vadim realized there was no saving even the smallest piece. The head of the splinter buried itself as deeply as possible in Charlotte's rib, wanting to exact more revenge, knowing if the hunters wanted to kill it, they would have to cause excruciating pain to Charlotte.

Do it, Charlotte and Tariq hissed simultaneously.

Tariq's arms tightened around her and he cradled her close to him, trying to shelter her as the ancients took what felt like a blowtorch to her ribs. She gasped and pressed her open mouth against Tariq's chest. A solid wall. His heart beat a steady rhythm.

The Carpathians surrounding them began a chant; they repeated the same thing over and over. *Muonìak te avoisz te. Muonìak te avoisz te. Muonìak te avoisz te.*

What are they saying? Even she could hear the gasp of pain in her voice, but it didn't matter — she needed something to fill her mind and push the pain away.

They command the shadow to reveal itself. To show itself to the ancients.

She knew the exact moment when Vadim realized he couldn't save any portion of the sliver that had been pulled from his brain. The splinter went wild, slamming over and over into her ribs and then succumbing to the terrible concentrated fire. The white-hot energy consumed the last of the shadow, turning it to ash so that it crumbled and fell into tiny pieces and drifted away under the watchful eyes of the ancients.

She could feel them, the terrible toll the fight had taken on them. They were out of their bodies, pure spirit, and yet they didn't

460

retreat. They set about healing her broken ribs and moving through her body inch by inch to make certain there was no trace of Vadim and that every organ and cell in her body was healed.

The three ancients swayed with weariness when they returned to their forms. They sank into the rich soil, crouching low as if to catch their breath, although none of them made a sound.

"Val?" Liv's voice trembled, but she sounded very brave. "I can feel that you're hungry." She stepped close to him and swept back the hair from her neck. "I couldn't help Charlotte, not really, but you can have my blood."

There was silence in the basement. Dragomir and Siv both turned toward Liv and gave her small, courtly bows, although they were more like nods — but were definitely gestures of respect for the child.

Val wrapped his arm around Liv. *"Sisarke,* you are incredibly generous to offer such a precious gift to me. I am hungry; that is true. When one leaves their body it takes a toll. *Ekäm* — my brother, Lojos — has offered as well and he is much larger than you. I can take much more blood from him without harming you. I thank you, *sisarke."*

Val stood slowly as Lojos approached, keeping his body between the ancient hunter and the little girl. Extending his wrist toward Val,

Lojos nodded to the child, who wrapped her arm around Val's leg. "*Saasz hän ku andam szabadon ekäm* — take what I freely offer, my brother." With one fingernail he cut a long, deep gash in his wrist. Val took the offering and drank.

Tomas offered his wrist to Siv with the same ritual words, and without hesitation, Mataias extended his wrist to Dragomir. It was Maksim who fed Tariq. There was something pure and beautiful in the way the Carpathians took care of one another. Charlotte knew all Carpathians were uneasy in the presence of Dragomir, Siv and Val, but they stepped up without a thought to their own safety and took care of their brethren.

She didn't know what it was that set the three men so apart from the others. The triplets were scary predators, that was easy enough to see, yet the three men who had come to her aid had something else about them that defined them, something that wasn't human or civilized. They were more animal, but cunningly intelligent and so experienced in battle it was frightening.

Sielamet. You must rest now. They healed you, but you are exhausted. Blaze will see to Liv and the other children. She'll talk to Genevieve so she'll know to look after Lourdes for a couple of nights. When you wake, I'll be with you.

This was the hard part. She'd accepted the conversion and all that came with it. She'd embraced being Carpathian, but . . . There was this. Sleeping in the soil. She had to admit, it felt comforting, even soothing, but it wasn't over her face.

Reading her need for a few moments' delay so she could come to terms with sleeping in soil, Tariq changed the subject. "Emeline wanted Liv to see what she faced. She also wanted her to have confidence in the fact that the Carpathians would be there for her when she needed them."

"That's true." Charlotte snuggled closer to him. She was tired. Exhausted. She trusted him to make certain she didn't feel as if she were buried alive.

"I just wonder how Emeline can have faith in us for the others, but not for herself."

"I think she just needs time." Charlotte kissed his throat and closed her eyes. "I do need to sleep, Tariq. Just don't let me wake still under the soil."

"Of course, *sielamet.* I have you. Always."

17

Deep beneath the soil, under the basement of the huge Victorian mansion, Tariq's eyes snapped open and he willed the earth to open above him and took his first breath. Charlotte was in his arms, and as he gave a thought to be thankful she was asleep, she stirred. Her eyes opened, and he could see the panic in them.

I can't move.

It is the paralysis of our kind. The sun is still high. We cannot move during these hours. While giving her the explanation, he was already assessing the reason he'd been awakened before the sun had set.

Her heart went wild. *Seriously, Tariq, I can't move at all.*

Tariq scanned the compound. *Let your heart follow the rhythm of mine. Relax. Ordinarily we sleep during this time. I'm surprised you awakened.* He shouldn't have been surprised. He should have expected that anything to do with the children would draw her attention.

That stopped her panic. *What's wrong? Why did I wake up?*

Feel the compound above us. Let your mind expand to encompass all of it. You want to look above and below the compound as well. Always when you awaken you must do that. It allows you to feel if an enemy is near. In this case, you should find . . .

Liv. She's by herself, walking away from her house. What is she doing? Fear crept into Charlotte's voice.

Deep inside, he had to admit, he felt that same fear, but he refused to allow her to see or feel it. Liv was fragile. Too fragile. He worried she would harm herself. He should have considered converting her the same night he converted Charlotte. He'd been so concerned they'd harm the children, that the pain would be too great for them, but they'd found the way to do it. He just had lingering doubts. They were children. Still . . .

He touched Liv's mind. She was sound asleep. He wasn't in the least surprised at that; she often walked in her sleep.

I'll show you. I built a command center down here in the event this place was ever attacked during the day when I couldn't defend it as well.

But we can't move. Not a muscle.

It can be done with patience and practice. I had many years to figure out how to do this. I have lived in the human world for centuries.

I've had to adapt to modern ways and think in terms of modern warfare.

He waved his hand without moving his arm and a console appeared low, on his right side. Overhead, a bank of screens lit with an eerie glow. The entire compound, every house, the fence lines, the shore, all of it appeared on various screens. Liv walked slowly, steadily, one foot in front of the other, away from the houses and toward the gate.

Donald. Mary. Liv is up again. Tariq sent the call, certain they were already on the move, prepared for Liv's daytime escapades. The couple was always ready to intercept her when she sleepwalked and get her back to bed.

Almost as soon as he sent the alert Donald and Mary came onto the screen, strolling hand in hand as they always did when they were together. They caught up to Liv just as she entered one of the corridors Tariq had designed and made sure were always erected during the day. The corridors were a maze, and every few feet doors could drop down if necessary to trap someone inside. Not visible to the naked eye, the maze made it nearly impossible for Liv or any of the children to wander off during daylight hours. The corridors led to the front gates from several directions, but because they were unseen, they were very difficult to get through.

They watched as Donald gently put his

hand on Liv's shoulder and Mary circled her with a comforting arm as she bent to talk to the child. A few moments later, Liv cried and shook her head repeatedly as the couple firmly turned her back toward the house she shared with her brother and sisters.

I should be the one to comfort her and put her back to bed, Charlotte said, her eyes on the screen. *I hate this feeling of helplessness.*

Tariq had had centuries to learn to endure. Charlotte was new at it and aside from her initial panic when she found herself paralyzed, she had done well controlling her heart, keeping the rhythm steady and her breathing even.

You can't just rely on the screens, sielamet. Expand your mind. Encompass the compound. Be aware always of your surroundings.

Charlotte's eyes were glued to the screen and the progress the Waltons made with Liv. Liv sagged against Donald, forcing him to take most of her weight. She stumbled several times as if she still wasn't all the way awake. When the camera caught her face, tears tracked down in a steady flow.

How can you stand this, Tariq? It must have been hell when you first brought the children here.

That much was true. It was still hell. Like Charlotte, he wanted to go to Liv and comfort her. The best he could do was send

467

warmth into her mind and soothe her before helping to send her to sleep. Shockingly, he found Val in her mind, soothing her as well. Her restlessness had awakened him, too. Tariq was going to have to give that some thought: the fact that a restless child could awaken a powerful, dangerous ancient and he would take the time to try to soothe her was so extraordinary that it bothered him. He didn't like mysteries.

The first few days after they arrived were bad, he said to Charlotte. *I didn't know what to expect from them — especially Liv or Emeline. Emeline never leaves her house other than to sit on her porch, and that's rare. Liv walks in her sleep nearly every single day. Mary and Donald expect it now.*

Liv and Emeline both are afraid to sleep because Vadim can come to them while they're unaware. He demands Emeline come to him or he will force Liv to harm herself.

Tariq sighed. He was well aware that even with the safeguards woven by the combined efforts of all the Carpathians, they couldn't prevent Vadim from attacking from within the two females. The vampire had taken their blood, forced Emeline to take his. His puppets had torn into Liv with their teeth, spreading their master's blood like a virus.

It is Emeline Vadim visits in her sleep, and he gets to Liv through Emeline's dreams.

He had no way to stop that. No matter how they'd tried to weave safeguards over both houses where Liv and Emeline stayed, Vadim still managed to attack while they slept. Mary had held Vadim in check in his attacks on Liv with her extraordinary gift. She sang, and the melody and lyrics soothed and put the child to sleep and then followed her into her dreams so that Vadim hadn't been able to get through.

He'd asked Liv if Mary's songs were still helping; she'd shrugged and shaken her head and then shrugged again. He'd touched her mind to see her memories. Vadim was the biggest part of her memories; in fact he was slowly taking them over, as if she really had been infected by a virus.

I shouldn't have waited, Charlotte. I was so afraid of harming her by the conversion, by acting too fast without thinking it all the way through, that she's suffered, perhaps unnecessarily. Emeline isn't mine. I have no idea what is the right way to go about helping her.

She needs time.

Charlotte's voice soothed him, but . . . *I'm not certain she has time — if any of them have time. We have to come to a decision on Liv and act on it this next rising.* That told him he was still concerned about converting the girl and what harm could be done to her. He was a man who was thorough. He studied a problem from every angle and then attacked it with confidence, but these were children and he was responsible for them. More, he cared about them. If he lost Liv in the conversion, he would never forgive himself.

Liv was now in bed, Mary singing softly and Donald sitting on the opposite side, holding Liv's hand. Even as she drifted off, there were tears on her face.

I should be there with her, Charlotte reiterated, and her voice broke.

That little catch in her voice made his heart hurt. *Sielamet. It won't be much longer. We're building something good here. I'm going to send you back to sleep and when we next wake, we can call the others to help in converting Liv.* It was all he could give her. Her tears broke his heart, just as Liv's did. The only solution was to bring Liv fully into their world. It wouldn't change what happened to her, but it would give her other tools to deal with the trauma, and Vadim wouldn't be able to get to her.

I would like to go on record that this paralysis thing is for the birds. Seriously, Tariq, the rest of it, even the blood thing and being in the ground, I can deal with, but not being able to move sucks. Anyone claustrophobic might have a real problem with this.

Just like that, Charlotte managed to push the harsh realities of his life away to replace them with a softness and warmth inside. With

470

amusement. She was so perfect for him. For the children. For his fellow hunters, the ones she was a little afraid of, but still worried about and admired and respected.

You do realize it is impossible not to fall in love with you. He took his gaze from the screens and watched her face. The softness. The way she looked as if she might cry.

That's how I feel about you.

Mary has a beautiful gift. She can sing Liv to sleep. If I could sing, sielamet, I would sing you to sleep, but I don't have that gift.

He felt her smile, and it touched him somewhere deep inside. If it was possible to love a woman completely in such a short period of time, he was already there. He knew her intimately, inside and out, and she was everything he'd ever wanted.

Sleep now, my love. I will wake you in the soil so you can practice opening the earth and closing it over you.

I'm not certain I'm ready for that, Tariq, but I'll try.

There it was again. One of a thousand reasons. It scared her to think about the soil closing over her head — a very human reaction — but she was willing to give it a try. For him. He saw that very clearly. But not *just* for him. She wanted to be independent, and she wanted to be able to take care of her children.

471

He added that to the already thousand reasons he'd fallen hard, and he sent her to sleep. He would wait until he was certain Liv had settled and didn't need further aid. His greatest worry was that she would harm herself. He watched Donald and Mary slowly get up and slip out of Liv's room, retreating back to their small cottage. They'd lived in their car so long that anything larger than the little cottage was daunting to them. They held hands all the way back to their home, strolling rather than hurrying.

The camera system was thorough, allowing him to see every square inch of his compound. He'd designed the defense system himself, working with Josef, the young Carpathian he considered a genius. He'd never actually met Josef, but they communicated regularly via computer and cell phone. The boy had ideas, a really good grasp on modern technology and how it could help living and working right in the city the way Tariq did. He liked the kid and wished he'd relocate to San Diego and help him and the other hunters track down the women in the database for psychics.

Tired, he took one last look at Liv to assure himself she was all right and down for the day. She appeared to be sleeping soundly, and then, just as he started to shut down the system, he saw her body jerk. Hard. Like a seizure. She thrashed on the bed and then sat up, shaking her head over and over, wiping her face with her hands as if trying to remove something from her skin.

His first thought was to call on the older couple again to settle her, but when Liv got off the bed, he saw her movements were jerky. Like those of a marionette. Or as if she was fighting for freedom. He'd taken her blood. He had taken that of all the children. It allowed him to know their thoughts and whereabouts at all times. It kept them safe as well as keeping the other hunters, Emeline and Blaze safe.

Tariq touched her mind very gently, always careful to be respectful. No one liked their thoughts monitored, especially a child like Liv. The moment he touched her mind, he knew she was asleep, yet fighting an unseen demon. Chaos reigned. The need to get up and go somewhere was a compulsion. She didn't know where she was supposed to go, but she wanted away from her brother and sisters because . . . A low growl slipped out of his mouth. She had been directed to kill her brother. Her hand had even curled around a kitchen knife earlier but then she'd managed to turn the blade toward her own stomach and instantly the compulsion was gone, to be replaced by a stronger one. She wasn't to harm herself.

Vadim. That answered the question as to why Liv didn't want to sleep and whether the master vampire could reach the child as he did Emeline. They thought since she was receiving Vadim's voice through Emeline's dreams that he couldn't possibly give her commands. Liv had vague, uneasy memories of dreams of the master vampire during her waking hours. She didn't realize he was directing her to do his bidding while she slept. She just knew she didn't want to sleep.

Donald. Mary. Liv is up again and I believe she's sleepwalking under Vadim's direction. You'll need to intercept and stop her immediately.

Liv was on the move, this time leaving the house and turning away from the front gate. She looked at it several times and nodded her head, but then turned toward the main house. Was Vadim's army out there right now? Waiting for Liv to bring down the safeguards? She could invite them in, but she'd have to get through the invisible labyrinth of corridors, and he doubted she could do so. In any case, Mary and Donald would stop her if she got close.

He felt the stirring in his mind. Donald getting out of his comfortable chair. Calling to Mary, who was in the kitchen fixing them a bite to eat.

While Liv stumbled toward the main house, he saw Emeline come out of her house and stand on her porch, looking around warily as she did each time she emerged. In the light

474

of the sun, he could see how pale and gaunt she was. The trauma to her had taken its toll. She was a beautiful woman, by any standards, but there were dark circles under her eyes and she was so thin she shivered continuously as if she couldn't regulate her body temperature.

Tariq swore softly in his own language. He wasn't Emeline's lifemate, but he felt responsible for her. More, he admired and respected her as did Maksim, Blaze's lifemate. He was going to have to intervene soon. No matter that Emeline had asked for time; she was wasting away right in front of them. As with Liv, he would have no choice with Emeline, either.

Liv disappeared into his home. He had no idea what she was planning to do and it made him uneasy that she moved through the hallway unerringly, as if she had a purpose now. She didn't pause at Lourdes's or Genevieve's door, but continued on to the large kitchen.

Liv, wake up, honey. You're sleepwalking. He was gentle, not wanting to startle her, but kitchen meant knives. If necessary he could muster up the strength to remove a weapon from her hand from the distance where he was, but it wouldn't be easy.

She stumbled, but kept walking, right past the block of knives sitting on the counter, straight to the door of the basement. Now he was really uneasy. What could she possibly be up to? More importantly, what was Vadim up to?

Liv. He poured more strength into his command. *Wake up now.*

The sun was at its highest peak. He was at his weakest. He'd designed his security system to prevent intruders from harming the occupants of the compound. The safety nets he had for the children were mainly outside the houses.

Donald, she's in my house, coming down to the basement. Be prepared for a battle and protect yourself if necessary. Have Mary use her voice to counteract Vadim, but you have to wake her up fully and then keep her awake.

Like Charlotte, he detested that he was helpless, lying in the healing earth while his child was in trouble and he couldn't get to her. Already, he thought of Liv and the others as his children. His family. He needed to be the one to go to her and hold her safe in his arms when she was threatened.

He still didn't understand how Vadim could get to the child in spite of the powerful safeguards woven around the compound. It should have been impossible for the vampire to get so completely to the child, so how . . . A memory came to him. In passing, Maksim had mentioned to him that Blaze and Emeline were very, very close and Emeline saw

476

things in her dreams. She had dreamt of the tunnels running beneath the city and the vampires and monsters occupying that labyrinth. She'd shared the dreams with Blaze — literally.

Blaze didn't have that gift — Emeline did — yet night after night, Blaze dreamt the same dream, running the tunnels to save the children, over and over until the two women had perfected their abilities in their dreams. Emeline had projected her dreams into Blaze without realizing she was doing so. She was close to Liv. Very close. Liv went to see her every evening. They already knew that Emeline had projected her dreams of Vadim to Liv, but she was awake on her porch. Was it possible that once Vadim had that path to Liv, he didn't need Emeline to keep it and now he had complete access to the child?

On the monitors he saw Donald and Mary stepping out of their little yard and heading across the compound toward the house, hand in hand as usual. He pushed a sense of urgency into them, wanting them to hurry. He had a bad feeling.

Liv went down the wide, wooden steps and turned away from where Charlotte and Tariq rested toward the large workroom where the unassembled carousel horses were along with all the tools and paints. She went right to the bundles that contained the horses and chariots that Vadim had placed his blood in.

Liv! Wake up! Get out of there. Don't touch those horses. He gave the order, pushing command and compulsion into the child's mind.

Still, it was too late. He knew it the moment he saw her enter the workroom. She rushed across the room straight to the cursed horses and chariots. Even as he gave her the commands she was already bending over the nearest horse, the one Charlotte had touched most recently, the one where Vadim's blood had spewed a curse over every man, woman and child who had sat on it.

Liv gripped the horse's neck and swung up into its saddle, her legs clutching the horse's sides. The moment she was in the saddle, the thing rose into the air, coming alive, bucking and snorting, whirling around over the other horses and the chariots. Instantly, the horses sprang to life, the chariots exploding into action.

Donald, get Mary back to the house! Tell Emeline to get under cover and stay there. Tariq had his eyes on the monitor, knowing Fridrick, Vadim's general, had an army waiting outside the gates. He felt them now, a powerful force.

He pushed the red button on the console with his fingertip and instantly a voice came back to him. "Is this a drill?"

"It is not." It took a tremendous effort to use his voice, but he'd practiced for this day.

He knew exactly what to do. The small army of human men, men already trained to fight in wars, men he'd trained himself to fight vampires and puppets, as well as other monsters, were on alert and now they'd been activated. Response time was under six minutes.

A series of explosions rocked the gate and walls of the compound, but the safeguards held. Overhead a rocket tried to penetrate from above, but it bounced away and exploded harmlessly. Liv's horse spun around and around, like a madly whirling carousel out of control, the other horses following suit. The chariots joined them. Liv led them through the house, still whirling so that the child had to clutch the horse's neck to stay on its back.

Liv screamed. She clearly had come awake now, but was unable to get off the horse. She tried, struggling wildly, terror on her face. Beside him, Charlotte stirred, her eyes opening, horror already spreading through her.

Liv. Her voice was surprisingly calm. She used the pathway through Tariq's mind to get to the child. *Hold on and try to relax. Just hold on. It's moving too fast to try to jump off, honey.*

The calm in Charlotte's voice penetrated and Liv stopped screaming and bent over the neck of the horse, her arms and knees tight around the wood as the horse burst out of the house and into the open.

Tariq began to press the green buttons on the panel at his fingertip. There was a bank of them. One was for Danny's bedroom. Others were for Emeline's room, Amelia's, Bella's, Lourdes's, Genevieve's and the Waltons'.

Get in your bedroom, Emeline. It was one of the few times he'd ever used the Carpathian path to Emeline. Blaze and Maksim had ensured she had it so she could communicate with them all, but she despised anyone in her mind, so out of respect, they avoided talking to her telepathically. Emeline turned and ran back inside. He could only hope that she did as instructed.

Donald, get Mary into the bedroom. He could see the older couple running for their house. They'd been told what to expect if the compound came under attack. This was the only way he had of protecting them against humans as well as the monstrous puppets Fridrick, as general of Vadim's army, would send against them.

One of the green buttons activated the lift that sank each room into the ground, making it a sealed panic room that was inaccessible to any outside source. The floor covered the opening so that it was impossible to know the room was underground or that there was a room at all. Josef had thought the idea up and at the time, Tariq thought him a little fanciful, but it was a sound idea and one that

480

would keep the occupants of the compound from harm.

He could see on the monitors as each member of his family was dropped beneath the surface so they were safe underground and impossible to detect. The rooms were sealed with good airflow and amenities, even a bathroom, just in case the stay was longer than expected.

Danny and the girls could move from room to room; they were all connected once below the surface. At the moment, they were still peacefully sleeping and unaware. Genevieve's and Lourdes's rooms connected. Like the other children, they slept, the push Tariq had given them still holding. Donald and Mary were on their own. He saw that they were safe beneath the ground, but he couldn't see Emeline. He hadn't put cameras in her home. She'd insisted she wouldn't stay if he did. He could only hope she'd obeyed the order and that she was afraid enough of Vadim that she didn't hesitate.

His gaze went back to Liv. Charlotte's gaze had never left her. The child was calmer because both Tariq and Charlotte were in her mind, anchoring her, soothing her and more importantly, keeping Vadim and his commands at bay. There was nothing to be done about the wildly spinning horses. Already, Tariq could feel the buildup of energy as the horses and chariots spun madly.

The horses were now in the center of the compound and had formed a complete carousel, they and the chariots acting as if they were suspended from chains and whirling faster and faster so that Liv's steed was forced outward by the centrifugal force. All around them the explosions kept coming, bouncing off the safeguards so that none penetrated the fortress Tariq had created.

Liv clung to the horse as it swung out so fast and hard that it appeared to be on its side as it whirled madly. In the middle of the carousel, a dark force began to rise, a cloud, spinning just as fast. In the center and flashing through the darkness were streaks of fire, of lightning.

Tariq swore. Vadim always prepared for everything. He overprepared. It was a characteristic his brothers had often given him a bad time about, but now that preparation served him well.

What is it? Charlotte sounded scared.

There was no way to save Liv. She couldn't get off the horse, and Tariq knew an explosion was coming, one that would blow right through the safeguards from the *inside* and allow Fridrick's army of puppets and humans entry. The others would be safe, but Liv . . .

No. Beside him, Charlotte tried to struggle. To move. When she couldn't she stared in horror at the screen, her gaze glued there in spite of the bloodred tears tracking down her face. *Tariq.* She whispered his name in his mind. An intimate connection. A plea. Tariq wanted to reassure her, but he couldn't.

The cloud rose, whirling as fast as the horses. And then a figure came running across the yard, onto the screen where Tariq could see. Emeline. She wasn't safe below-ground; she was leaping, timing her leap exactly, putting her life on the line to catch Liv around the waist and yank her from the spinning horse. The force of the wooden animal sent them flying through the air. Emeline tucked Liv into her and tried to land in a protective ball. She hit the ground hard. Too hard. Emeline rolled like a rag doll, her arms outstretched, clearly unconscious. Liv rolled as well, not as far as Emeline, but she'd hit the ground hard enough to stun her.

They're alive. He breathed the knowledge into Charlotte's mind. Relief was tremendous, but he knew what was coming. His fingers inched their way to find Charlotte's hand so he could thread them together with hers. *Beloved, this will not be good. Take a breath.*

The explosion rocked the compound. It put deep cracks in the ground and several walls in the houses cracked. A tree groaned and then slowly toppled over. The chariots and horses went flying. One landed in a tree. One in the middle of the dragons. Another in the playground. Splinters of wood became arrows and spears, knifing through the air, looking for a target.

Stay on the ground, Liv, Tariq ordered the child.

She moved, a writhing of pain, but her hands had gone flat to the shaking ground to push herself up. At Tariq's command she hesitated and looked cautiously around. Emeline was absolutely still and he could see a thin trail of blood seeping out from under where her head was. Her hair was a fan around her, thick and dark, so dark it appeared almost blue. Thin red streaks matted the strands and soaked into the ground. Charlotte's fingers tightened around his as Fridrick's army poured into the compound.

The humans tossed pipe bombs at the houses. Several threw grenades. Tariq recognized some of the human men who had been in the tunnel when Charlotte had accessed the memories from when Liv had been thrown to the puppet. Puppets swarmed the compound. Liv let out a small shriek and began to cry.

Stay quiet, baby, Charlotte advised. Her eyes frantically searched the screens. Smoke was filling the air, making it difficult to see everything.

Without warning, the blue dragon in the play yard stood on his back legs, spread his wings, and fanned them so that the smoke was driven back. Charlotte caught a glimpse of a series of small boulders artfully placed in the garden. They were only a few feet from Liv.

Can you make it to those boulders, honey? Look to your left and behind you. There's just enough room for you to slip between them.

If you stay low, Liv, I can shield you, Tariq added.

Sobbing, crawling on her hands and knees, Liv hurried across the few feet to the edge of the garden where the boulders were. She squeezed between two of them and went to her tummy, pulling her knees under her in an attempt to imitate the rocks around her.

Tariq instantly began to weave a shell of protection over her. It wouldn't help if she moved, but as long as she stayed there, it was a cloak of invisibility the attackers couldn't penetrate. His security force would be arriving any minute and then chaos would really reign.

Emme hasn't moved. Charlotte filled his mind with worry.

There was nothing he could do for Emeline. She lay to the right of the play yard, her body on its side, arms flung out, blood a halo around her head. She'd saved Liv's life. Liv wouldn't have survived the explosion, but there was no telling what price Emeline paid for her courage.

Time and again explosions hit the houses, as the men and puppets marched through

485

the compound, determined to destroy everything. Tariq held the safeguards around the homes, keeping them intact. His last option was to bring water from the lake onto land. He had created a bowl effect that would allow him to flood the entire acreage, sweeping Fridrick's soldiers away, but with Liv and Emeline in harm's way, he couldn't do that.

The blue dragon took to the air with a battle cry, a roar that rent the air. Behind him the other dragons took to the sky, wings beating hard enough to clear the smoke as they circled above the men firing weapons at them. One man put a rocket launcher to his shoulder and took aim at the green dragon. The blond human beside him seemed to stumble right into him, knocking him off-balance, catching Tariq's attention. The rocket went off far to the left of the dragons. The man with the rocket launcher immediately shoved the blond human who had stumbled into him. The clumsy man lifted his hands and shrugged his shoulders as if to say he was sorry, it wasn't his fault.

Tariq took note of him. He was one of the men who had shaken his head and frowned when Vadim had thrown Liv to the puppet. He had studiously avoided looking at the master vampire, but had exchanged a long look with a dark-haired man in the group. Tariq tried to spot the other man in the crowd of soldiers. Most had their attention on the dragons circling above their heads. Not one of the dark-haired men, and not Mr. Clumsy. The two broke off from the group and hurried around the puppets toward the replica of the larger mansion — Emeline's house.

He lost sight of them as several larger men, looking less human and more puppet, took up the screen the two human men had been on. Clearly they were on a separate mission from the others. Tariq realized the soldiers were wreaking as much havoc as possible in the compound, trying to blow everything up and create a diversion. These men were the ones on the real mission. Two broke off and came toward the main house. Two went toward Emeline's house, and the last two toward the house where the children stayed.

They're after the women. Emeline. Amelia and maybe Liv. Genevieve and you, Charlotte. All of this is to get the women. The rest of it is for show to throw us off, Tariq told her.

You can't let them get to them.

They can't get to them. Only Liv and Emeline are still in harm's way. So far, no one has spotted Emeline lying so still. They aren't expecting her out in the open like that. There's smoke and chaos. But they'd find her. He knew they would. It was only a matter of time.

The dragons are attacking. He heard the worry in her voice. She was afraid they could burn Emeline or Liv in their scorching fire.

Don't move, Liv. Stay very still, even if they get close to you. The child shuddered and wept silently, her fist jammed in her mouth. Tariq knew it had to be terrifying to see and hear the beasts that had torn into her flesh and tried to eat her alive.

Just as the dragons dove down, mouths yawning wide, fire pouring from them to sweep over the puppets and men in the compound, Tariq's team of soldiers arrived. They were a small group, but elite, and they carried the right equipment to combat the macabre puppets. Tariq touched the dragons, impressing on them not to harm his security force or Emeline and Liv.

Fridrick's soldiers were forced to defend themselves, caught between the dragons and the newcomers. The puppets had been programmed by their master and they would fight to the death and beyond if possible in order to carry out their orders. The human males stood and fought as well, something that surprised Tariq when he was rarely surprised by anything. That told him that either they each carried a splinter of Vadim, or they were programed through blood. Or both. In any case, it was a hard-fought battle between the two forces.

Tariq trusted his small but very skilled unit of soldiers, so he turned his attention to the six giants. The first two had reached the children's house. They didn't bother to try the doorknob; they simply hit the door hard simultaneously. Sparks flew around their fists and both men jumped back, howling. Two fist marks were burned into the wood. Cursing, they kicked at the door over and over, but all they did was burn the soles of their boots. Finally, one dropped his hand to the doorknob and twisted. The door opened for them because Liv had left it unlocked. The two men rushed inside only to find the building empty. They knocked over furniture, angry that they'd missed their prey.

At the same time, two men rushed into Emeline's home and the other two into Tariq's home. They found the buildings empty, too. Furious, they rushed outside. The six men converged in the center of the compound. One turned his head and frowned. Every muscle in Tariq's body froze as he followed the man's gaze straight to Emeline lying so still on the ground.

Tariq sent his command to the dragons and instantly they pulled up and flew away from the heavy fighting in an attempt to intercept the six men. Fire rained down. One of the six giants rolled away from the others as five of them took the brunt of the dragon attack. Two caught on fire. One fell to the ground, rolling to try to put the flames out, while the other ran for the lake. Gunfire broke out and two of the giants went down, thrashing,

489

wounded, but not dead. The fifth man tried to follow his partner, but was cut down when Matt, the head of Tariq's security force, shot him point-blank in the heart.

Tariq turned his attention to the last giant, the one now crouching beside Emeline. He grabbed her hair in his fist and lifted her head. Clearly she was still out. There was blood on the side of her face and on the rock lying on the ground beside her. She'd hit hard enough that it was a huge concern, but now she was in the hands of Vadim's half human-half puppet.

As he rose, dragging her up with him, the two human males who had rushed to Emeline's house ran around the porch toward him. At the same time, Liv leapt up, screaming at the giant of a man, determined that he wouldn't take Emeline.

"No! You can't have her. I won't let you." She shrieked at the man as she got to him, punching and kicking his leg.

The two male psychics Vadim had recruited separated, one yanking at Emeline, dragging her out of the giant's arms while the other attacked. Snarling, the giant slammed his fist into the blond man's forehead. The blond man fell over backward as if he'd been hit with a sledgehammer.

Tariq's soldiers were converging and the dragons circled above them, readying for a pass at the giant. The blond man's partner stumbled away from the huge, monstrous half puppet, Emeline in his arms. Snarling, the giant reached down, snatched up Liv and turned and ran toward the gates, calling out as he did so. Immediately what was left of Fridrick's soldiers closed ranks behind him, racing after him, holding off Tariq's men so the giant could escape with his prize.

Charlotte screamed soundlessly, over and over, struggling to move, to overcome the terrible paralysis of the Carpathian people. *Not again. He can't have her again, Tariq.*

Be calm, sielamet. He won't kill her. He'll use her as a bargaining chip to get Emeline, Genevieve and you. We will be able to retrieve her this rising. Every hunter is well aware of what has happened and they will go with us to take her back.

But she'll never recover. The trauma. She wasn't safe. Even here, she wasn't safe. She'll always know she wasn't and she'll never feel safe again.

We will do our best with her, Charlotte. It is all we can do. Allow me to send you to sleep again. There is no point in lying here unable to move with your mind in chaos and your heart in agony. He would send her to sleep no matter what. He couldn't stand Charlotte suffering. With her mind so open to him now, she never thought to raise the barrier to protect herself even though it was so automatic with everyone else.

She took a breath and looked at him, tear tracks little red streaks down her face. She nodded and instantly he sent her back to sleep and then turned to direct his small band of men to cleaning up and seeing to Emeline. He wanted the two men who had aided Emeline held until he could examine them and find out what they knew and why they had changed sides.

18

Liv is still terrified, Val whispered to Tariq on the common path two hours before sunset. *I have promised her we will come for her, but the puppets are deliberately taunting her. I fear she will try to force them to kill her.*

Tariq and Val had taken turns staying in her mind, a task that had been daunting when both were so weak. The giant of a man Fridrick had put in charge of the attack on Tariq's home seemed to be the one who had taken Liv. He protected her from being torn apart and eaten alive by the insane puppets, but he didn't stop them from scaring the child; in fact he seemed to take great amusement in her fear. Throughout the day, he'd mocked, sneered and assured the puppets in front of her that Fridrick would give the girl to them to eat.

She says his name is Billy and that he took her to an abandoned warehouse. She can hear water. Tariq supplied the information. *I will rise in another half hour. How soon can you join me?*

I cannot follow you until the sun has set. You will only have Maksim to back you until that time, Val said with regret.

Tariq could hear the weariness in his voice. Val had taken the last shift with Liv and he was still healing from his time spent with Vadim. Torture took its toll on the body, even that of an ancient Carpathian.

Tariq had programmed himself to wake well before sunset. He needed to get a jump on Vadim and Fridrick. Vampires couldn't protect themselves, even by manipulating weather and clouds, from the sun. His lifemate, coming into his life, provided some protection for him. She'd brought light back into his soul and that would allow him to awaken in daylight and plan his battle. Unfortunately the other hunters would not be able to go with him.

Blaze will come with us and Charlotte. Tariq didn't want his lifemate anywhere near the vampires, especially Fridrick, but he knew exactly what the undead would do. *Fridrick will insist on an exchange. Liv for Emeline, Charlotte and Genevieve. They are determined to have those three women. Charlotte will know this and she'll insist on making the exchange.*

There was a stunned silence. *You cannot possibly allow your lifemate to put herself in such danger.*

Tariq sighed. Val, Dragomir, Siv and Nicu had rarely mingled with any culture or society of humans. They hunted in cities at times, but they struck fast and hard and got out without ever having to interact with humans. He had lived with humans throughout his long existence. He studied them and he studied their women. He wanted to be the best man he could possibly be for his life-mate, trying to learn as the world around him changed.

He knew modern-day women often expected a partnership, not a dictatorship. Blaze was such a woman. Charlotte as well. She wanted to make her own decisions, and as long as he felt he could control the danger to her, he was more than willing to give her what she needed. He wanted a partner, someone with ideas and opinions of her own. Now, with the children, he understood that need in him more.

Charlotte will do whatever it takes to get Liv back. Vadim will know that we don't have Emeline to give him. She's in need of medical aid. My team has been attending to her and she has a concussion. Blaze will appear to be Genevieve.

Again there was a silence. Val wasn't happy with the decision. *That is two women we cannot afford to spare. If they kill them, we will lose two of our warriors. This is a bad time, Tariq.*

495

The enemy has grown strong while we have been complacent. I never expected the Malinov brothers to amass such knowledge and to be able to bind vampires and humans alike in their war against us.

They were always intelligent, Val. Always thinking of ways to overthrow the prince. No one thought they meant the things they said. We thought they liked to debate. By the time anyone knew they meant every single word and had planned the assassination of the prince and his entire family, it was far too late. They chose to become vampires, and they put their plans into motion.

Three are destroyed.

Others, such as Fridrick and his brothers, seek to take the places of the dead, Tariq pointed out, because it was true. As fast as they killed the undead, more rose up.

Fridrick is cruel, but he lacks the intelligence and patience of the Malinovs. There is great care in their planning. Vadim has sat like a bloated spider in the middle of his web, pulling his strings together slowly, so that no one noticed until he was ready to challenge us. He's ready, Val, and he needs Emeline, Charlotte and Genevieve in order to carry out his plans. He targeted them months ago and everything he has done has been to acquire them.

Val flooded the Carpathian pathway with assent. *No vampire would stay in the vicinity*

496

with so many hunters gathered in one place unless he could not leave for some reason. He goes out to sea to regroup, but he does not leave. That is all the more reason to keep your lifemate close.

Tariq knew he would never convince Val that Charlotte should be a part of the rescue, so there was no reason to continue to try. It was getting close to the time that he needed to be up and planning his assault on the warehouse where Liv was being held.

Sleep while you can, Val. When you wake, bring the others with you. Someone will have to stay behind to guard Emeline, Genevieve and the children. I'll keep them asleep as long as I'm able. At the moment they are in their safe rooms sleeping under compulsion, all but Emeline.

It is done, Val vowed. *Kulkesz arwa-arvoval, ekäm.*

Walk with honor, my brother. Tariq repeated the sentiment back to the Carpathian in English. He meant every word. Val was a good man. A strong one. An elite hunter. He had endured torture beyond imagination and survived to help a small child through a horrific nightmare. He had forged a bond with Liv, one Tariq didn't altogether understand. Val couldn't feel, and yet that bond was strong enough to allow the ancient hunter to awaken from his sleep and attempt to soothe

497

and steady the child through the daylight while she waited for the vampires to decide her fate.

Tariq turned his head slowly to look at the woman lying tucked into his side. Very gently, using his fingertips, he pushed back the thick fall of hair from her face. This rising they faced a battle for a child's life. Possibly her soul. Liv would never survive intact without conversion. If they did that, the other children would insist they follow her into the Carpathian world. He had no choice but to chance the conversion, just as he had no choice but to allow Charlotte to risk herself when the time came. They were parents. There was no question that they would risk everything for their children. It didn't matter to him that other hunters he respected might not agree with their decision — it was theirs to make.

Wake, beloved, and come to me. See me. The earth has healed you and you are fully in my world. Wake now.

He made certain the soil was open above their heads and their bodies were clean and fresh after their resting. Charlotte's long lashes lifted and the impact of her beautiful eyes felt like a punch to his gut. Hard. In there. Dead on. For a moment she was all his, soft and loving, a ghost of a smile there for him. Then she was present, in the moment, and the daylight battle and kidnapping of their child came flooding back.

498

"Liv," she whispered, her throat closing on a lump. "Tariq, she's so frightened. I can feel her through you and she's terrified. She wants to die. She's figuring out a way to provoke them."

He had known Charlotte was strong from the moment he'd laid eyes on her. As he'd gotten to know her, had been in her mind, the conviction had grown. When she'd awakened from her slumber in the earth because Liv had been sleepwalking, that had cemented his knowledge. Now, as she woke, she automatically scanned his mind, learned every detail of what had gone on while she slept.

"We're going to get her, *sielamet.* Your first time in the sun will be vicious. It will feel as if you're burning. You can take it, Charlotte. If we don't get everything in place before Fridrick rises, we might miss our chance to get her back."

Charlotte nodded immediately and allowed him to help her into a sitting position. "Tell me what you need me to do."

There had been no hesitation, and he was proud of her for that. "We both have to feed. Our security crew is still here, guarding the property. They've been cleaning up. I told them to gather every single piece of the carousel horses and, wearing thick gloves so there was no chance of getting a splinter, put them in bags and bring them to the workroom. I will ensure all pieces are accounted for down to the smallest sliver. When I am certain, I'll feed and then you will."

She touched the tip of her tongue to her lips, looking a little apprehensive, but she didn't protest. "Reach out to her again, Tariq. Let her know we're both with her."

"She knows, beloved." He was as gentle as possible. "She's holding herself together by a thread. We can't snap that thread, nor do we want anyone to be aware we're communicating with her. They have to think we won't be on the move until sunset."

"You reassured her all day," she protested.

He nodded, gathering her into his arms and brushing his mouth gently over hers as he floated them to the surface and then closed the soil behind him. "We did. Val woke as well to aid me. But she asked for quiet to try to concentrate. She said she was afraid she'd betray the fact that I was with her. She was very close to falling apart so I told her I'd give her that, but would stay connected with her."

Charlotte bit her lip and nodded her understanding. She didn't like it, but Tariq knew she understood. It took every ounce of Liv's courage to keep from wailing and screaming for them to come for her. She could see it in the child's mind, just as he could. She could also see the small cage she was in as well as the horrifying puppets surrounding it. They were brutes with rotting flesh sloughing off. Jagged, serrated, bloodstained teeth. Fetid breath. No longer human, craving blood and flesh, they were monsters beyond anyone's imagining, let alone a ten-year-old child's.

"I need to get to her, Tariq. I *need* to. I can barely breathe."

He felt the same way. He was cool and calm, able to push emotion aside, and yet, with Liv taken, his gut was twisted into hard knots and his lungs refused to cooperate. His child. He'd promised her she would be safe and they'd taken her a second time. He had no idea what that would do to her, but he was fairly certain she would be scarred for life, no matter how good they made things for her.

"We'll get her," he reassured, letting her see the truth of his statement, his firm conviction, because there could be no other outcome. They had to get their daughter and bring her home safe.

He clothed them as he took her through the house to the front door. "You'll need to wear special sunglasses at all times, Charlotte. Don't take them off until sunset."

"What else?"

"You will follow my instructions to the letter no matter how much you want to go to Liv. If you trust me, Charlotte, and you'll have to for us to pull this off, then you need to remember, no matter how bad it seems, that I'll get Liv away from them."

She looked him straight in the eye. "Absolutely, Tariq. I won't let you down."

"It could get bad. Bloody. Your impulse will be to do whatever Fridrick tells you. If things go bad, they'll hurt her in front of you to make you compliant. You have to trust me then more than ever. Our job is distraction and getting the safeguards down. The others will take out the guards and engage the army. Val will get to Liv. Believe that. Val will get to Liv."

"Whatever it takes. I can be strong for her."

He searched her mind and saw only acceptance. She would stand with him. Do whatever it took to bring Liv home, even if it meant seeing her suffer.

"These men that came to aid us are our personal security. You'll see them around the club when we go there, and they'll be training here off and on. We need them to protect us during daylight hours. They are aware of what we are. I've taken their blood and know each of them and their hearts and souls. They're good men, Charlotte, and today they risked their lives for us." He wanted her comfortable with them. They would always need a security force to help in their protection during daylight hours.

She nodded. "What about the two men that helped Emeline? I saw them in the tunnels. You're worried about what to do with them.

They helped her." She made it a statement.

Tariq could see she was concerned about what he might do to them. "*Sielamet,* you are such a kind, compassionate woman, unlike your lifemate. If they threaten us in any way, or if Vadim or Fridrick have planted them here to try to harm us, they will be killed. There is no arguing that point. I want to give you the moon, anything you ask for, but granting them mercy if they are our enemy is not something that can be done."

She lifted her chin at him, and he found he liked that little gesture. Maybe he just was so far gone he liked everything about her, especially now, when they were both so focused on getting Liv back.

"If they are enemies, Tariq, threatening our family, what you decide to do with them is entirely up to you. Have no worries that I might protest. I've seen what these people do, and remember, I was in that tunnel when Vadim threw Liv to that disgusting, vile puppet and no one lifted a finger to help her."

He wasn't about to point out that no one could have helped her and lived. The tunnel was filled with vampires and puppets. There was no aid for a hero. He was fairly certain the two men despised what was happening and had wisely bided their time in order to maximize their chances to escape and maybe lend aid when they could. He didn't say that to Charlotte, although she caught his thought,

503

because she gave a little sniff of annoyance.

Hiding a small smile, he took a breath, shoved his sunglasses on his nose, made certain hers were on and opened the door. At once a thousand needles pierced his skin. His flesh was seared to the bone, even with his long sleeves and gloves. The pain burst through him and then he contained it, tuning his mind to Charlotte. He heard her gasp, but she cut off her admittance of pain and tried to pull her mind from his.

"No, beloved, you have to allow me to aid you through this." On her, the sun felt as if it burned through her skin, raising blisters instantly. He had made certain her clothing covered every inch of her body, but still, she was scorched right through the heavy material.

"Tariq, it is no more than when I was a young child and stayed swimming too long in the pool," she assured. "I can take it. I'm starving, though. All I can think about is putting my mouth on you."

She said it to distract him, forgetting he was entrenched in her mind, regardless of whether she tried to protect him by throwing him out. It couldn't work now that they were lifemates and she was fully Carpathian. He knew her inside and out as she did him — or would, once she got over her shyness of touching his mind.

He took her hand and allowed her the

504

untruth because she thought it would spare him and she needed that right now when her child was in a cage surrounded by monsters. He took her to Emeline's first. As they crossed the compound, he waved his hand to repair any damage done to the buildings. In spite of the rockets and grenades, there was very little damage — his defenses had held. The dragons were back on the playground, a few scratches and dings in their scales, but no real damage had been done to them.

Emeline lay in her bed, her face so pale she looked almost translucent. Maksim leaned against the wall in the corner farthest from her. One ankle was crossed over the other and he stared out the window rather than look at the gaunt woman in the bed. Emeline's head was bandaged and clearly Blaze or Maksim had cleaned her up in the way of their people because there wasn't any evidence of blood anywhere on her.

Blaze sat on the edge of the mattress and swept Emeline's hair from her face with gentle fingers. "I love you, Emme. Don't slip away from me," she murmured softly as they entered the room.

Emeline's gaze jumped to Tariq's face as he entered, and she looked frightened. Threatened. He sighed and smiled at her as gently as possible. "Thank you for saving Liv, Emeline. She would be dead if you hadn't risked everything to save her." He wanted her to know it wasn't just her life she'd risked. She knew Fridrick's army was there to take her to Vadim and still, she'd launched herself out into the open and saved Liv's life.

"She's mine, too," Emeline said and then gasped for breath. She wheezed with every breath she took.

Tariq knew she didn't want interference, but he couldn't be in the same room with her and not help. He waved his hand to calm her breathing, to ease the terrible tightness in her chest. Before Emeline could protest he leaned down to brush a kiss across Charlotte's mouth. "Excuse me, ladies, I must feed. We need to get moving as soon as possible to put our plan into action."

"You have a plan?" Emeline's gaze jumped to his face again. This time there was the beginning of hope.

"We do. We'll bring her home, Emeline," Tariq assured. He jerked his chin at Maksim and the two left the house together. "How hurt is she?"

"She didn't want Blaze to examine her, but the medic said concussion. She won't allow us to use our skills on her. She wants nothing to do with Carpathians, Tariq. Nothing at all, especially with the men. She tolerates me because of Blaze, but she's uneasy with me in the room. I thought it would get better, but it's actually gotten worse."

"It hasn't been that long since she was attacked, and it probably didn't help that Fridrick's army penetrated our defenses and managed to take Liv again. There is no way she feels safe now."

Maksim casually used his lengthening fingernail to cut a long, deep line in his wrist. He offered the blood to Tariq rather absently. They'd been partners for a long time and hunted together frequently. That meant they shared blood and saw to each other's wounds. Neither thought much about it although Maksim murmured the ritual words.

"*Saasz hän ku andam szabadon* — take what I freely offer."

"You can spare this? We have to be at full fighting strength."

Maksim nodded. "I fed twice, first for Blaze and then again for myself. Our security team was very cooperative."

Tariq bent his head to Maksim's wrist, accepting his answer. Maksim knew what was at stake. They were far from the Carpathian Mountains and had to create their own sense of family. Maksim and Blaze were part of Tariq's family just as he knew he was part of theirs. They relied on one another to guard their lifemates. Blaze was precious to them. She had represented hope for Tariq, another reason to hang on no matter how long he had to endure that gray world of nothing.

Blaze was a warrior through and through, and Tariq found it interesting that Charlotte

507

was as well. Charlotte wasn't skilled in fighting as Blaze was, but she had the spirit and courage of a fighter. He would never forget that moment in the parking garage when she'd tried to protect him.

When he'd taken enough blood to feed Charlotte, he closed the laceration on Maksim's wrist and stepped back, looking around the compound. His first order of business was to make certain they had every single splinter from the carousel. He didn't want there to be any mistakes. The children couldn't accidently stumble across one of Vadim's evil shadows. He waved his hand and sent wind swirling through the yard, a magnet for the ancient splinters of wood. His security team had handled the larger pieces but there was no way for them to get every splinter. He had to do it. He sent the debris into the basement, where the rest of the carousel was waiting.

"The two men aiding Emeline," he ventured as they continued across the compound toward the small guardhouse where the prisoners would have been taken. "They were both in the tunnel when Liv was thrown to the puppet."

"I remember," Maksim said. "Vividly. That child has endured far too much in her short life."

As they approached the house, the head of security, Matt Bennet, stepped out to greet them. He was armed and looked grim, but Tariq had always noted the man rarely smiled. "Sir, we picked up three other prisoners just a little while ago. They claim they're friends of yours and have information you need."

Tariq wanted to groan aloud. He knew *exactly* who those men were. Idiots. Had they witnessed the attack? More than likely. He knew they wouldn't leave it alone. They'd all but told him they wouldn't. He had two of Vadim's human soldiers locked up, a child missing and now the three vampire hunters.

He sighed and shook his head. "Thanks for getting here so quickly."

Matt nodded. "We tried to follow the child, but we lost her. The main force engaged with us, allowing them to slip her away."

"We'll get her back. In the meantime, I need to see the three crazies who just won't stay away from this mess."

Matt led the way inside. Maksim followed Tariq. He needed to feed again to gain strength and taking the blood of spies seemed fair, even though the security detail had no qualms about providing for them.

Daniel Forester leapt to his feet when Tariq and Maksim entered the room. Vince Tidwell and Bruce Van Hues were a little slower to get up, and both eyed Matt warily. Vince sported a bruise on his jaw, and Bruce had lumps on his forehead and temple. Daniel moved stiffly, holding his ribs.

"We drove up to talk to you," Daniel said, the words spilling out of his mouth fast, "when a man burst through your gates carrying a child. There were soldiers and disgusting-looking creatures following and then your soldiers engaged with them. We saw that the man carrying the child was slipping away while the others fought, so we followed him."

Tariq shook his head. "You have no idea what kind of fire you're playing with." He wanted to shake all three of them, but on the other hand, he couldn't help but respect their courage. They'd seen Vadim's puppets and they'd still followed the very intimidating half-human hybrid in order to find out where he was taking Liv.

"I told you, we're committed to destroying these things. They have an army that can't possibly be vampires because the sun would kill them." Daniel made it a statement, but then he frowned. "Right? Vampires can't go out in the sun?"

"No, they can't," Tariq said. "But you aren't trained to fight these creatures and eventually, when you go up against one, you're going to die."

Daniel gestured toward Matt. "He fought them."

"He's trained." Tariq was aware of time ticking away. "I have to get to Liv. You're going to stay here until I get back. Matt, keep

510

an eye on them. I want them contained where I know they're safe."

"You said if we thought about it and decided for certain, we could help. We decided. We're not without some skills. We could be assets to you."

Maksim smirked as he moved toward Daniel. "Do you really want to see what you'd be getting into? We hunt the vampire, and in order to do that, we have to live, century after century. We exist the way they do. On blood. Sleeping in the ground. We have powers you can't imagine, just as they do. If you're an asset we can count on, that means you provide blood when needed."

Daniel scowled and refused to give ground. "I'm not afraid of you."

"You should be," Maksim said, and hooked his hand around the back of Daniel's neck, yanking the man to him. Without hesitation, he sank his teeth into Daniel's neck.

Daniel didn't move, but his two friends did. Both rushed toward Maksim, who simply held up a hand. The two men bounced back as if they'd hit an invisible barrier.

"That's what you're going to be dealing with," Tariq said. "Where did they take Liv?"

Breathing far too fast and loud, Vince, his eyes on Daniel and Maksim, face pale, tried to answer, but stuttered a little. "Warehouse. Out by the harbor." He gave the address.

Tariq left them to Maksim's mercy. Maksim would take blood from each of them in order to monitor them at all times. If he deemed it necessary, he would remove their memories of all events that had transpired. If he believed the three men would be assets to them, he would turn them over to Matt for training. If that was successful, Maksim and Tariq would continue that training until they were as elite as Matt. Only then would Tariq approve them joining the fight.

Tariq needed to visit the two human males who had aided Emeline. Matt had them under guard. The two ex-soldiers guarding Vadim's recruits nodded to him when he entered the room. These two men had served countless missions for their country. They never hesitated, no matter the odds. He liked them both. He hadn't known it until Charlotte came into his life, but he remembered the two men because they were excellent at learning how to kill a vampire. Like Matt, they showed no hesitation.

Vadim's two human psychics both looked very apprehensive and tried to get to their feet, but failed, due to the shackles on their ankles.

"Your names," Tariq bit out. He was very aware of the position of the sun. He had to time everything just right.

The blond spoke first. "Ryan Jenkins."

The dark-haired man went next. "Andrew Wilson."

"Tell me why I should keep you alive." Tariq laid it on the line. He would kill them if there was the slightest hint that they had come to spy or harm his family in any way. "Make it fast — I have a child to rescue."

"You can't get into that warehouse without Fridrick bringing down the safeguards. It's a trap. They're expecting you to follow. They've got a hidden army there," Ryan said hastily. "You can't just walk in and get her."

Tariq was very aware of that fact. He simply shrugged. "So far I'm just getting impatient. Why were you working with Vadim?"

"Fridrick approached us. We had done some psychic testing at the Morrison Center here in the city. He told us he had a job for us using our particular skills," Ryan answered for both of them. "He took us to Vadim. The man was too smooth and I didn't like the whole setup, especially when he started messing with our minds. I have a kind of shield that stops most attacks, but he got through and he forced us to drink blood. Not his. Another man's blood, a prisoner's. Then he put something in us. Something that works on us day and night to do his bidding."

Tariq kept his face blank. More splinters. Vadim had no idea that he was diminishing his power by inserting the pieces of himself into others.

"He's recruited at least fifteen psychics, all male. Two work in your club. He said you couldn't detect them because they have Carpathian blood covering whatever it is he put into us. There was no way to go against him, not even when he let those monsters he created hurt that child." There was genuine disgust and repugnance in his voice. "It made me sick to stand there and watch that shit, knowing if I made one move to stop them, those monsters would kill me and I wouldn't have a chance to save her."

Andrew took over. "While Vadim sleeps, we can try to fight him, but he's too powerful when he's awake. That thing inside of us won't let up. It's hard to fight the compulsions."

Tariq nodded. "You knew they were after Emeline."

Both men nodded. "We made up our minds that when they struck here, we'd fight them and maybe have a chance to prevent them from taking the women. They wanted us to bring four back to them."

Four. Emeline. Charlotte. Genevieve. And that had to mean Amelia. She was only fourteen, but Vadim and his army of vampires wouldn't care about her age. They would have taken her as well.

"If we couldn't get the women, we were to take any of the children. Fridrick said they would bargain for the women, that he knew once they had the kids the women would do anything to get them back," Ryan continued.

"You can't let them trade themselves for that child. They're going to kill her anyway. There's no saving her." There was genuine regret in his voice.

Andrew shook his head. "Those things, that giant of a man Vadim created — they're so strong you can't fight them. Killing them is next to impossible. He gave them his blood and the Carpathian prisoner's blood. Vadim likes to experiment, and these hybrids, as he refers to them, are killing machines. They don't seem to have any feelings at all for caring. They're especially cruel. Vadim's got at least six or seven of them guarding that warehouse along with I don't know how many of those monsters. He feeds them women. Slaves he buys off the cartels or prostitutes they pick up in the streets. He promises them he'll give them immortality. That's why most of the other psychics haven't fought him. They want his power."

"They'll never get it," Tariq said. "They won't live long. Puppets die fast, but while they're alive, they wreak havoc everywhere they go."

"Can you get whatever he put in us out?" Ryan asked. He shook his head. "I just went for a job interview and ended up their prisoner. You have no idea the things they've done. The experiments. The women they've hurt and killed." He lifted his shackled hands to his eyes and pressed his fingertips to his temples. "I can't look at those things anymore. I can't stand it. I've gotten to the point that if they killed me, I wouldn't care, not if I had to keep seeing the sick things they get off on."

Andrew nodded. "So if you can't get it out of us, you might as well kill us. We aren't going back, and the moment Vadim wakes, he'll come at us."

Tariq knew that was true. Vadim would know the two men betrayed him and he would make them suffer before he killed them. He'd force them to do the very things they were trying to run away from.

Tariq made up his mind. Both men were telling the truth. He heard the honesty in their voices. He could take their blood later, but now he had a woman to feed. "I'm out of time. I have things to do, so to ensure your safety, I'm sending you both to sleep. Vadim won't be able to reach you. And when he wakes, you'll be the last things on his mind. I don't know if it will be possible to remove the splinters, but we've done it once. We'll try. I'll be back in a few minutes."

He dissolved in front of them, shifting so that he was a stream of molecules. *Charlotte. Come to me. The carousel in the yard.*

He'd dreamt of taking her on that carousel. It was magical. He'd designed it, carved the horses and added a few unique touches. He wanted to see Charlotte on the horses, wearing nothing but her long hair.

She was waiting for him, sitting in the golden chariot with its streaks of fire running jagged through its side. He could see the hunger in her eyes. Felt it beating at him as he approached. She looked beautiful and a little fragile, her gaze soft and warm, but holding a sorrow that would be ever present until they brought their child home.

"*Sielamet.*" He whispered the endearment softly as he gathered her close and pulled her to his chest.

The moment her mouth was on his bare skin his body shuddered with pleasure. Her teeth sank deep in an erotic bite, connecting them in the intimate way of his species. He wrapped his arms around her and threw his head back, savoring the feel of his woman against him. Skin to skin. Shocked, he glanced down at her and found she'd already learned how to shed clothes. At once his hand went up to cup her breast as she fed, his thumb sliding over her nipple, a whisper of breath. All the while he shielded them from any eyes.

You wanted me naked on your carousel.

I did, beloved. But I need you naked on my carousel when I have time to do something about it.

I know. I just wanted you to have a small respite before the war begins. I love you, Tariq.

Let's get our daughter back.

Just like that she licked at his chest to seal the small evidence of her teeth and clothed them both. He couldn't fault her on her attention to detail. "How did you learn how to do this so quickly?"

She smirked at him. "I spent time around Vi and she's a total fashionista, so I learned to be one as well. I like clothes. I like your clothes. I asked Blaze to show me and she did. It isn't that difficult once you get the hang of it. I even managed to make Emeline smile when I first made a few mistakes."

A small, child's voice flowed into his mind. Broken. Filled with sorrow — and resolve. *Tariq, please tell Danny, Amelia and Bella that I love them. Tell Emme I'm sorry. And Val . . .*

Liv's voice cut into him and Tariq's head snapped up. *Don't you dare!* He poured every ounce of command into his voice. *We're coming for you.*

I knew you would. I don't want anyone else to die because of me. I can't stand his voice in my head. I can't stand knowing he might make me hurt my brother or sisters. Or Emeline. Or you.

There was a stirring in their minds. Val flowed in. Power flowed with him. *You will not do this, Liv.* There was power beyond imagining, an ancient who had been born in fire and pain, tortured beyond conception, one relentless, brutal predator. *You are far too young to understand yet, but you hold my honor in your hands. You will choose life and you will endure until we get to you. Do you understand me? You will not choose death, because when you do, you choose it for me as well. That is totally unacceptable to me. Live for me.* It was a command, nothing less.

19

Small waves lapped at the harbor, the sound deceptively soothing. Bats dove through the air catching insects as the sun began to sink slowly into the choppy water. The wind rose as the sun went down, bringing ominous patches of churning gray.

That's Fridrick's work. Tariq had known all along he wouldn't be facing Vadim. Vadim would never chance risking himself against the combined power of the Carpathian hunters. He would send his pawns in his place. Not his brother, Sergey, but Fridrick and his army of newly made vampires, puppets and the hybrids. Fridrick would have one or more of his brothers with him as well.

Tariq waited. Breathing in. Breathing out. He was a hunter, and patience was everything. *How could you know?* He sent the query to Val. A Carpathian male rarely knew a female was his lifemate before she was sexually mature. Only then, when he heard her voice, would his world change. Tariq knew even at her young age, had she been mature, Vadim wouldn't have thrown her away.

Val Zhestokly had risen at last. All the Carpathian hunters had. Tariq had already fully scouted the area around the warehouse and harbor and knew exactly the count of guards outside. He had time to examine the safeguards and knew it would take several of them working in unison to bring it down and they would be under heavy attack. That wouldn't work. They had to get Fridrick to take down the safeguards. He also had the count of those inside, the majority of Fridrick's army, through Liv.

She isn't of age. She could not possibly have restored colors and emotions to you. He tried not to sound like a father, wary and protective, but he felt that way.

Liv had gone through so much, and Val was . . . well, one of those who had secluded himself in the monastery because he deemed himself not safe to be around others. He'd left it of his own accord, for his own reasons, and fallen into Vadim's hands, where he'd been tortured for an extensive length of time. He was a good man. Honorable. A warrior of amazing skills, but too hard for Tariq's Liv. Val wouldn't claim her until she was of age, but that would still be too young for him. She would be forever too young for such a hardened warrior.

She is mine. Eight years from this day I will

521

claim her as my lifemate. Until that day, I will be close to help you protect her.

There was finality in Val's voice. Tariq sighed and rubbed the bridge of his nose. It wasn't as if he didn't have enough problems. *I ask again as she is my daughter; how would you know? You cannot just claim her.*

There was silence. Val had said his piece and he wasn't going to argue. That didn't bode well for their future. Tariq sighed again. At least Liv had listened to Val and had subsided in her cage, no longer trying to get the puppets to attack her.

The wind rose on a wild shriek. Fridrick. He was testing them, seeing if there was any response to the penetrating note he'd sewn into the wind. At his right side, Maksim just looked bored. Blaze, looking exactly like Genevieve, stood close to Charlotte. The two women were tucked against the side of the building, deep in the shadows. Neither made a movement as the wind tore through the parking lot, whipping debris into a wild frenzy, whirling it and throwing it with such force paper actually penetrated a power pole a few feet from them.

The Carpathian hunters quietly stalked the hidden guardians scattered around the warehouses. On the rooftops. In the alleyways. Three roving. The triplets arrived first, Tomas, Lojos and Mataias. They killed the three roving through the complex of dirty, unkempt buildings. Nicu snapped the necks of two others on the rooftops across from the warehouse where they held Liv. Siv and Dragomir both swept through alleys and between the warehouses, killing the remaining puppets and hybrids as they went.

Charlotte held her breath, twisted her fingers together nervously. If she blew this, Liv would die. She had to believe in Tariq, in the other Carpathians, and play her part. More, she had to believe that no matter what happened around them, Val would get to Liv and bring her home safe.

She watched the whirling leaves to the right of the warehouse. They lifted and moved to the left, then the wind took them high. Her stomach dropped. *He's here.*

I see him, sielamet. You are not alone. Stick to the plan and keep Blaze close.

Tariq had carefully explained to her that if she were in mortal danger, if the hunters thought Tariq's lifemate might be killed, they would all come to her defense, not Liv's. They couldn't afford to lose one of their women. Losing Charlotte meant losing Tariq as well. But Val had dropped his bombshell and that changed things. She knew it did. Time meant little to Carpathians and knowing Liv was in the world made the waiting for her to grow up and mature fully much easier.

He cannot feel.

He has to feel something or he wouldn't know.

He wouldn't be so gentle and focused on her, she protested. She had to believe Val would save Liv no matter what. All the while she connected so intimately with Tariq, she watched those whirling leaves. The moment Fridrick materialized right by the warehouse door, she stepped into view, "Genevieve" right behind her.

Fridrick spun around, saw them and carefully looked for their escort. Charlotte shook her head. "I was able to rise before Tariq and made my way here. I knew where to come because two of your men were captured and they said you had taken Liv here. I'm asking you to allow me to trade places. Genevieve is willing as well."

"Genevieve" pressed trembling fingers to her mouth, but didn't say anything at all. She did shift just slightly, still a couple of steps behind Charlotte but also to her left. Charlotte was well aware Blaze was giving herself room to attack should she have to.

Fridrick continued to look around, scanning the area, looking for anything that would tell him the women were bait. "Why wouldn't I just take you without freeing that horrible little brat?"

"Because I'm willing to die and I have a knife in my hand. So does Genevieve. I can kill myself before you make it to me. You have to know Tariq converted me. I may be new at this, but I'm fast."

"You would kill your lifemate as well," he pointed out.

"She's a little girl."

"She's nothing." Contempt was written on Fridrick's face. "Food for the master's puppets. So many children — sometimes for fun we put them in the hold of the ship and let the puppets in with them. So amusing. I will allow you to watch the show, just for not coming to me the first time I told you to."

"We don't have much time," Charlotte said, her chin up. She couldn't think about children down in the hold of a ship screaming as the puppets were let loose on them. She just couldn't. Right now, it was all about Liv.

"Tariq will be coming after me any minute. I won't give up Amelia, and Emeline has a concussion. She can't be moved. So if you want to make the exchange, it's for Vi and me and you have to do it right now before the hunters come. They'll come in force, and once they do, you know Tariq will never negotiate. I'm his lifemate. He won't give me up."

She sounded convincing. Very convincing. Tariq was proud of her. She appeared as she had in the parking garage, a woman of courage who had no idea who she was squaring off with. She treated Fridrick as she might a human male threatening her. Blaze, in Genevieve's form, hovered behind her just as Vi had done in the garage.

Fridrick smirked at her and beckoned with one long-nailed finger. "If you want her, come to me then."

"I'm not moving until I see her," Charlotte said stubbornly. "Compulsion doesn't work on me and time is flying by."

Charlotte! What have you done? On cue, Tariq sounded the fearful and outraged life-mate, left behind because he couldn't stand the sun. *Do not give yourself to the undead. I forbid this.* He used the Carpathian common telepathic path. *I am coming for you. Get away from him.*

The corners of Fridrick's mouth widened, not so much into a smile, although it was certain he thought he was smiling, but more like an open gash where his mouth was, revealing his teeth. He wasn't bothering with his appearance and his teeth were not nearly as white as they had been in the parking garage.

"How sad for a once-great warrior that he cannot control his woman." Still smirking, Fridrick began to unweave the safeguards on the warehouse. His hands flashed with blurring speed as he removed them and flung open the door. He turned to wave Charlotte and Genevieve inside.

Tariq struck, materializing in front of Fridrick, his fist slamming into the vampire's chest, fingers grasping at the withered heart.

Fridrick screamed, blood and spittle spewing from his mouth.

"Kill her. Kill her." The vampire shrieked the command even as he bent his head to tear at Tariq's flesh, trying to get to an artery before Tariq could extract his heart.

Val and Dragomir pushed past into the warehouse, Siv and Nicu flanking them. Puppets rushed them. Two of the giants turned toward the cage where Liv huddled, making herself as small as possible. Lesser vampires appeared, one after another, rushing into the warehouse at Fridrick's bidding. Blaze leapt into action, following the vampires, Maksim materializing at her side.

The scent of brimstone filled Charlotte's lungs. It was ghastly and stung her eyes.

Hyssop oil, Charlotte. I need it now — pour it over me. Quickly.

Charlotte's breath caught in her throat. *I have no idea what that is.* She didn't. Tariq was calm, but he clearly needed the oil and fast. Fridrick writhed and fought, punching and kicking and biting, trying to keep Tariq's hand from extracting his heart. Finally, in desperation, he caught Tariq's arm with both hands and exerted all his strength to keep the hunter from withdrawing his heart.

The ground shook. Inside the warehouse Charlotte could hear screams and curses, the sound of agony and victory, but outside the air was heavy with the scent of burning

527

asphalt and all insects had gone quiet.

Suddenly a pot of oil was at her feet and she looked around to see Dragomir striding toward her, a bow and arrow in his hands. He looked grim, even for him. He tossed her a bow and arrow as well. "Pour the oil over your man and dip your arrows in the pot. If you have to, cover yourself in oil. They'll be fast. Faster than you can imagine, but you're Carpathian. That makes you fast."

She'd never shot a bow and arrow in her life, but something horrible was coming and she needed to keep Tariq safe. Even as she flung the pot of oil over him, Fridrick's brother Georg leapt from the roof onto Tariq's back. Dragomir was on him in seconds, moving so fast he was a mere blur. Instinctively she flung oil over Dragomir and turned to face whatever was coming at them.

What is it? She had to know.

Hellhounds are coming.

Hellhounds? She didn't know what they were, either, not really, but it didn't sound good. Her stomach dropped as the ground shook as if an earthquake were trying to shake the asphalt apart.

You can do this, Charlotte, Tariq said, as calm as ever, as if he weren't fighting for his life. *The pot will always be full of the oil. You'll need it. Aim ahead of them and let them run into the arrow. Go for their eyes; that's the kill*

528

shot. A throat shot will slow them down.

Dragomir added his advice. *Don't look directly into their eyes. Don't allow their blood or saliva to touch you. If you have no choice, make certain it touches only where the oil covers you.*

The ancient had Georg on the ground and was trying to extract the vampire's heart. She could see that both vampires had slammed their fists into the chests of the hunters and it was a fight to see who could take the heart first. The sight sickened her. Although she couldn't feel Tariq's pain, she knew he felt it, because he was blocking her.

Charlotte's heart stuttered as the first of the hounds came into view, pounding toward her on gigantic clawed feet. Teeth filled his open mouth and saliva hung in poisonous strings. Eyes glowed a terrible, hideous red, looking only at Tariq. Behind it, four more of the beasts broke cover and pounded toward them. One had three heads.

She stepped toward the leader and raised her bow. Her hand shook. The knowledge of how to use it was in her head, pushed there by the two ancient hunters. Taking a breath, she let the arrow fly. It missed the hound's eye and lodged in the massive neck.

Instantly she let a second arrow go, not looking at the other hounds or how close they were to her. The hound was nearly on Tariq when it suddenly screamed, slid to a halt and staggered. Her arrow had hit true. The beast shook itself and slowly turned its head toward her. Time slowed down. She could hear her heart thundering in her ears, roaring so loud it drowned out every other noise. As the hound changed direction, leaping toward her, she let the third arrow fly.

The hound pulled back his lips to reveal massive, dripping, razor-sharp teeth. She could see its canines were like those of a saber-toothed tiger of old. The beast took a shuddering step toward her and then collapsed.

Charlotte knew time had slowed down for her, but while she'd been concentrating on the leader, the other four hellhounds had almost reached them. She began shooting arrows as fast as she was able. Another hound skidded to a halt, shuddered and went down. That was two out of five.

One got past her and leapt at Dragomir, trying for his back. While the hound was in the air, she flung the entire bucket of hyssop oil over the beast. At once his fur began to smoke and fall to the ground. Giant blisters appeared all over the hound's back and sides. It dropped away from Dragomir and turned toward her. Charlotte shot it through one eye; the arrow quivered, not penetrating deep enough for the kill shot, but then she had to turn toward the one coming at her.

She managed to get off one shot before the hellhound leapt, taking her down to the ground. The hound's breath was horrible. She dodged the stream of venomous saliva and plunged the arrow deep into the beast's eye, using every bit of strength she could muster. Rolling, she got to her feet and ran toward the oil bucket, wanting to douse herself. Before she could get there, the last hound, this one three-headed, leapt at Tariq, red eyes glowing with evil intent. Clearly directed by Fridrick, it sprang on Tariq's back, tearing at his flesh with the hideous teeth of one head while the other two heads reached around to sink teeth into his arms.

She couldn't see more than one of its eyes. She ran at it, shooting the arrow into the one eye she could get to, close range, scoring true, but the hideous creature didn't even flinch. She had to get it off of Tariq.

Charlotte envisioned a sword — a long, lethal sword with the sharpest blade imaginable. The hilt fit into her hand as if made for her. She gripped it with two hands and ran to Tariq's aid. He was utterly calm, intent and focused on extracting Fridrick's heart. He didn't try to escape the savage teeth of the hound, or let on that the poison dripping in long threads from the three mouths burned through his skin straight to his bones.

She sliced through the massive neck of the head that was attacking the arm Tariq was slowly pulling from Fridrick's body. The head dropped to the ground, those vicious eyes suddenly focused on her. Taking a deep breath, she sheathed the sword and let loose two arrows, right into the eyes that stared at her from the ground.

Lightning forked through the sky and laced the clouds above. Fridrick shrieked as Tariq pulled the heart from his body and tossed it beside the severed head of the beast. The hellhound went into a frenzy, ripping at Tariq to try to kill him. Dragomir tossed Georg's withered, blackened heart down beside that of his brother. Even as Fridrick's heart rocked, and then slid toward Fridrick as the vampire slumped to the ground, lightning struck fast, incinerating both hearts and the head of the hound.

The second head of the beast chewing on Tariq's arm lifted to let out a howl. The third head didn't seem to notice, teeth still tearing into Tariq's back. Because Tariq was covered in hyssop oil, the fur on the hellhound began to smolder and slough off. Blisters covered the thick, bumpy skin. Tariq reached back with his bare hands and caught the beast's massive head and, spinning hard, broke its neck. Startled, the creature fell back to the ground. One head cocked awkwardly to one side, the other head down low, eyes focused on its intended victim. The hound scrambled to its feet and began to stalk Tariq.

Movement caught Charlotte's eye and she spun around to find a hound stalking her. One arrow protruded from one eye. It had its head cocked to one side and it stared at her malevolently. She hadn't killed this one, only made it very, very angry.

Charlotte backed up, tripped and went down hard on her bottom. She slashed at the monstrous hound with the sword, drawn a bit awkwardly from the scabbard. The blade sliced through the massive throat and black blood poured onto the ground. At once the asphalt smoked and hissed.

Everything happened so fast she didn't have time to be afraid. She had to keep moving or the thing was going to kill her. She couldn't get up. Her feet slid in the oil that was splashed on the ground and she couldn't get a good purchase on the asphalt. Then Drago-mir was there, shooting the beast in the eye with an arrow and slamming a bolt of lightning into the carcass before it even hit the ground.

He yanked her to her feet and both turned to find Tariq, torn, bloody and triumphant, the three-headed hellhound at his feet.

Val fought his way through the wall of puppets. Fridrick would sacrifice them to stop the hunters from getting to Liv before the hybrid could kill her. He kept his gaze glued to the cage, where the child lay curled in a tight ball, in the fetal position, her hands clamped over her ears and her eyes shut tight. There was blood on her clothes, up high by her shoulder. Some in her hair. A steady stream of tears tracked down her face, but she wept silently.

He slammed his fist through a puppet and shoved him off, uncaring that the blood was vampire enough that it burned like acid. A hybrid tried to stop him, to delay him, by swiping at him with a machete. Still not taking his gaze from Liv, Val hurtled the huge wall of muscle and flesh out of his way. Already the hybrid closest to the cage had yanked at the lock, breaking it and flinging it aside. The giant of a man reached in with his huge hands, caught hold of Liv and dragged her out of the cage.

Liv didn't struggle. She squeezed her eyes closed tighter and lay limp while the hybrid shook her like a rag doll. He wrapped one hand around her throat, and then Val was on him, seizing his head between his hands and wrenching hard. There was an audible crack and he caught Liv before she fell to the floor.

"Keep your eyes closed, *csecsemõ*," he ordered. *"Pesäd te engemal."* He switched to English. "You are safe with me, *kislány*." He crushed her body to his chest and began to make his way through the heavy fighting toward the door. One big hand kept her face firmly pressed to his chest while he raced through the warehouse toward the door Tariq and Dragomir had cleared. Around him the battle raged with the ferocious fury of the Carpathian ancients.

Lesser vampires snapped and postured at the Carpathian hunters, but they were out of their element and they knew it. Val didn't bother to look at them as he took the child out of that hellhole and into the night. Whips of lightning rent the air and struck the asphalt again and again as Dragomir and Tariq cleaned the parking lot of hellhounds, vampires and tainted, venomous blood.

Charlotte stood off to one side, a bow slung over her shoulder and a sword in her hand. She looked a little worse for wear, hyssop oil all over her. She glanced up as Val strode out of the warehouse with Liv in his arms. Her face lit up, relief softening her features.

"Val, you have her."

Tariq swung Charlotte into his arms as he and Dragomir closed ranks behind Val. They took to the sky, leaving the mop-up to the other hunters. Liv was in need of care immediately.

I didn't get a chance to see her, Charlotte lamented. *She's hiding her face against Val. I don't know if they hurt her physically.* They certainly had harmed her emotionally. Liv was at her limit. She'd looked so small and fragile next to the hunter with his roped muscles, scars and monastery tattoos. Still, he'd looked gentle as he held the child, as gentle as a man such as Val could look.

Val says a few scrapes, but mostly they frightened her.

Tariq could hear Val whispering reassurances to Liv in their language. He wouldn't be at all surprised if Liv understood him. She seemed able to assimilate languages fast, another gift. She didn't answer him, remaining so silent that it worried him.

Val didn't slow down even in the compound. He took Liv through the main house to the basement, where the mineral-rich soil was spread out and very deep. Tariq paused long enough to put Charlotte on her feet and make certain to bring the panic rooms of the other children, the Waltons and Genevieve back to the surface. If they woke from their slumber he didn't want them frightened. Charlotte followed Val down to the basement and through the labyrinth to their resting place.

Tariq, his intention is to feed her. I don't know how to stop him. There was panic in Charlotte's voice. *He's having her take enough blood for an exchange.*

Tariq was already on his way down and he put on a burst of speed. He entered the ring of decking overlooking the sleeping grounds. Below him, Val held Liv close to his chest, cradling her in his arms. She looked tiny and broken. Already he had opened a laceration over his heavy muscles and pressed her mouth to the drops of blood there. "Drink, *csecsemõ*. Take what I offer."

"What are you doing?" Tariq demanded. "We have to make certain no harm will come to her before we convert her."

"I keep my word, Tariq," Val said without looking up. He pushed back the tangled silk of Liv's hair. "She said she would live if I promised to convert her. I am keeping that promise. This is her second true exchange. When they get back to the compound, my brothers will gather and one of us will bring her fully into our world. You are her father and it is your call whether you do so or I do, but it will be done." It was a decree, nothing less.

Tariq swore in their language. He didn't like to be pushed into converting a child without a healer there. He knew it would take a while before one of the Daratrazanoffs arrived, so he believed he had plenty of time. The thought of harming the children kept him from bringing them fully into his world, although he knew he would have to do it. He might be her father, but a lifemate took precedence over that. It was Val's decision, not his, and they both knew it.

"Val, she's ten years old."

"She's a hundred," Val said. "I cannot feel unless it is caring for her, not yet, but it is there, just within my grasp. I knew the first time I made the exchange with her in the tunnels, but I was so far gone that I did not acknowledge it even to myself. It is rare for a Carpathian to know before his lifemate is mature."

He stroked her hair with gentle fingers as he fed her. Liv took his blood just as she had when they had been locked together in a cage.

"You realize what a complication this is." Tariq had enough complications. "Liv is a child. I'm her father, and protector."

"Now she has two protectors," Val said. Very gently he inserted his fingers between Liv's mouth and his chest. "Enough, *csecsemõ*. I must take your blood. Do you understand what that means?"

Tariq frowned down at the hunter holding the child. For the longest time she didn't move, and he found himself holding his breath. When he tried to touch her mind, Liv had shut down. She wasn't thinking beyond being converted. It was the only thing she thought about. Her entire being focused on that alone. He saw her head move, the slightest of nods and then entirely voluntarily, she turned her neck to allow Val to take her blood.

Tariq was first and foremost a Carpathian. He'd already claimed Liv as his daughter. He couldn't help but be proud of the fact that she was already embracing their way of life. She had wanted to kill herself. She'd been so close to taunting the puppets into dragging her from her cage and killing her. Val had stated that he couldn't survive without her, and even at her young age, without really knowing much about the lifemate process, she had endured those hours waiting for them to come for her. She'd trusted that they would.

Tariq knew Val didn't feel anything sexual for his lifemate, it was impossible, but he would protect her with the very last breath in his body. He wouldn't leave her for long and that meant Tariq had another elite hunter to help guard the compound and his family.

"She's ours," Charlotte murmured. "She may eventually belong to Val, but for these next few years, she's ours. Call the others to aid us. You convert her, Tariq. Between us, we can keep her safe."

Tariq nodded. He was weary from the fight and the wounds he'd sustained. He'd cleaned himself up and stopped the bleeding from all injuries, but he needed to heal them. All the Carpathians would be exhausted. Most had injuries, but if Liv needed this now, then it would be done. "I have to hunt, *sielamet*. I will tell all of them to do the same and then return here. When Val is done, you take Liv while he hunts. All of us need to make certain we're in the best of condition."

"What about Danny and Amelia? Should they be here?" Charlotte asked.

"They have the right to be. Danny kept his family together after their parents died, and they believe what happens to one happens to them all. They should be here, but I don't want them to witness the conversion should anything go wrong. The other hunters would be uneasy with them there. I'll explain it to them and how it is best if everyone is focused on Liv and not on them."

"They'll understand." Charlotte touched his lips with gentle fingers. "I think I like him, although he scares me a little." She nodded toward Val.

Tariq caught her hand and brought her fingers to his mouth. "I am so proud of you, Charlotte. I know you were scared, but you fought like a pro. Facing those hounds isn't easy for a Carpathian hunter, let alone a newly converted human."

"I didn't have time to think about it or I would have fainted," Charlotte admitted with a small laugh. "You got the worst of it killing that horrible Fridrick. You never hesitated, not even when the hound began to tear into you."

She couldn't believe him — covered in the oil, venomous teeth tearing into him, the vampire's acid blood burning through his skin, he'd just calmly kept withdrawing the heart no matter what happened to him. "Did you get all the poison out?"

He nodded. "I did the moment I got that

thing off my back. A hellhound's venom is nasty stuff." He leaned in to kiss her. His Charlotte. He hadn't really had time to tell her how much he appreciated her, how much he loved her. How scary it had been for him to know she was facing the hounds — and yet she'd done it and kept them, for the most part, off his back. Had she not been there for him, Fridrick might have won that battle.

"Go, honey," she said softly. "The faster you get back, the quicker we can help Liv."

Tariq took the time to kiss her once more. She was pale, and needed blood as well. She wasn't aware yet that when you expended that much energy you always hunted after to regain it.

It took him only half an hour to meet with Matt, feed, and then go to Danny and Amelia and explain what had happened. Genevieve took Bella and Lourdes into the play yard to be with their dragons while he took the two older children with him. He was grateful that Donald and Mary joined Genevieve with the two little girls, trying to give them as many normal experiences as possible when their lives would never be normal. Danny and Amelia waited for him in their home, afraid they wouldn't be able to pretend in front of the girls.

The Carpathians gathered once again on the deck above the mineral-rich soil, and this

541

time, the tension was tangible. Tariq felt as if he were being crushed under a weight of responsibility. If anything went wrong and Liv died, he would never get over the loss — and he would live a very long time. The memory of the anxiety, hope and trust he saw on Danny's and Amelia's faces would be forever etched into his mind. They would never get over it, either, and possibly, they'd never forgive him. Converting a child? He searched his memory. He was centuries old and he couldn't remember it ever being done. He knew it had been — but the children weren't *his*.

Charlotte threaded her fingers through his and looked up at him with eyes filled with trust and belief. With solidarity. *It's my decision, too,* she whispered into his mind, filling him with her. *We make this decision together. All of us. It has to be done, Tariq; everyone knows she won't survive otherwise. This is her one chance.*

At once a bit of the weight lifted. He wasn't alone in this decision or even the doing of it. They floated down to the center of the rich bed of soil, where Val cradled Liv in his lap. He continued to stroke her hair back, his fingers gentle as he murmured reassurances to the child.

Tariq reached for her, and Val instantly shifted Liv's slight weight to him. Her eyes had been closed but when Tariq's arms went around her, her eyelashes fluttered and then lifted. His heart stuttered. His little Liv was nearly gone. Val and Charlotte were both right: if they didn't take this chance, they would lose her.

Is this what you want, Liv? To come into our world fully? To be our daughter? When I complete the conversion, you will be ours. Charlotte's and mine.

Her nod was barely perceptible, but it was there. Her gaze shifted to Charlotte. Charlotte smiled at her. "Come here, baby," she whispered. "I'll hold you. Tariq and Val will be right here to keep you safe, and you'll feel all the others just as I did. They'll take away the pain. You'll feel a part of them all."

Liv's lips parted. She took a breath. "I'm not afraid."

"Of course you aren't," Charlotte said. "You know Emme would be here, but she has a concussion, a very bad one, and she can't get up."

Liv nodded and curled into Charlotte. Tariq bent his head to Liv's little neck and took her blood without waiting. She lived in a nightmare world and there was no getting her out of it. It was far safer for her to be where he could protect her at all times. He made the exchange and then opened the earth. Just as he had with Charlotte, he shielded Liv's body from the others as he floated Charlotte and

543

Liv into it, covering all but their heads. He stayed at her head and Val took the other side of her where he could hold her hand.

Her body was small and she was already more than halfway into their world. It didn't take long for the process to begin. For Liv, it was as if she had a bad flu. For Tariq and Charlotte it was terrifying, painful and seemed to last forever. Val shouldered as much of the pain as possible, and the other Carpathians took on the burden as well. Still, Liv felt every wave of pain, cried out when her body expelled the toxins and began to reshape her organs.

Charlotte crooned softly to her, rocking her little body beneath the blanket of soil. Val began to sing a lullaby softly to her in his language. *"Tumtesz o wäke ku pitasz belső. Hiszasz sívadet. Én olenam gæidnod. Sas csecsemõm, kuńasz. Rauho joŋe ted. Umtesz o sívdobbanás ku olen lamt3ad belső. Gondkumpadek ku kim te. Pesänak te, asti o jüti, kidüsz."*

As Val sang, Tariq translated the words for Charlotte and Liv in their minds. *Feel the strength you hold inside. Trust your heart. I will be your guide. Hush, my baby; close your eyes. Peace will come to you. Feel the rhythm deep inside. Waves of love that cover you, protect until the night you rise.*

Charlotte had tears in her eyes as Val sang

to her child. She was Tariq's lifemate, fully in his world, and this was the first of their children to follow her into it. The sweetness in Val's voice, coming from a hardened, scarred warrior, moved her, just as the love she felt pouring into Liv's mind from Tariq did. She lifted her gaze just once to Tariq's and he saw the answering love. The commitment he needed from her that she was his and she would help him with these broken children and the damaged adults he claimed as family.

"It is time. I can send her to sleep," Tariq said softly after what seemed like an eternity. Converting an adult was bad enough, but to see a child writhing in pain, her stomach cramping and the convulsing that accompanied the transition, was difficult, even shouldering the brunt of the pain among the Carpathians.

Charlotte kissed Liv's forehead and Tariq smoothed back her hair as he commanded she go into the healing sleep of their kind. Tariq wanted to crush the child to him, but he forced himself to just continue stroking her hair until the terrible fear inside him subsided. Liv was safe. She was in their world and hopefully they could find a way to ease the trauma enough that she could be a happy, healthy child again.

Val trailed his fingers over her hand. "She is very brave, but I'm grateful that this is over and she survived. She has a will of iron, this one."

"That is true. She was determined to come into our world. I don't think there's going to be any stopping Liv once she recovers." Tariq had his doubts about Liv recovering — health, yes — but from the things that happened to her, perhaps not. Still, with Charlotte, he would do everything he could to see that Liv lived a happy and healthy life.

"I am grateful it is over as well, but we're not finished," Tariq said. "We have to destroy every single splinter Vadim carelessly put into the carousel horses and chariots — that's eight of them — and the ones he put into the two male psychics we're holding prisoner."

"We need to feed after this," Nicu said. "We cannot take the chance that Vadim's splinters will escape us. Some of us have wounds that need attending." He glanced pointedly at Tariq.

Tariq nodded, wincing a little at the idea of Matt and his men being descended upon by the ancients, especially those from the monastery. He kept a discreet eye on them as they fed from the security detail as well as the two prisoners and the three society members. Only the guards were spared, as no one wanted them to be weakened.

Dragomir saw to the wounds of all those injured in the battle and then he had to take more blood. Tariq and Maksim stood silently by as he used the three vampire hunters, Daniel, Bruce and Vince, once again. Tariq noted he wasn't gentle, nor was he unkind — he simply didn't notice the three as important in his world. They were truly nothing more to him than a source for sustenance.

Tariq was grateful when Dragomir joined all the other hunters gathered together, making their way to the other side of the basement, where the workroom contained the cursed carousel.

"With each splinter destroyed, more of Vadim's power will be taken from him. This is a small victory for us. Vadim is out at sea, unaware that what we do here will begin to diminish his abilities. He will feel it when we destroy them, but I doubt he will realize we have taken a very real strike against him," Dragomir stated.

"If we can track him at sea," Tariq said, "that might be the place to destroy him. Less mess to clean up in the city."

Lojos shook his head. "Vadim has a very good detection system. He's out there on the ocean and can see and scan for miles. He's running right now, with Fridrick and Georg destroyed as well as half of his hybrids and most of his puppets. He lost seven lesser vampires, pawns to him, but still needed. It was a decisive victory for us, even though Vadim, Sergey and Fridrick's youngest brother, Addler, remain to build another army."

"Out of curiosity," Maksim said, "what are we going to do with our resident vampire hunters? Nothing seems to faze them. I took their blood and they still want in. Every hunter has taken their blood, and they haven't panicked or protested."

"Let's hand them over to Matt and his team to train. If Matt thinks they're up to it then we'll get involved. At least they can be monitored so we can keep them out of trouble," Tariq decided.

Maksim nodded. "That's a good idea. If we try to train them ourselves, some of the other hunters might decide to join in."

Tariq raised an eyebrow and the two men looked at each other with faint smiles. It was good to share a little bit of humor after such a harrowing time.

The Carpathians gathered, forming a circle around the splintered carousel. They wove safeguards around the circle between them and the carousel to keep the splinters from escaping. The safeguards were strong, the strands interwoven by each separate hunter until they blended together with a strength impossible to penetrate. They had never taken a master vampire down this way, destroying him by inches. If Dragomir was correct and the high mage had told him that splintering one's self diminished power, then the hope was that destroying Vadim's splinters would eventually damage his strength as well.

Tariq lifted his hand to move it in a circle, commanding the chariots and horses to reclaim every bit of wood as well as the blood and splinters of shadow. The horses jerked and rocked, but couldn't escape the powerful command. The dust and debris shifted, swirled and then coated the various horses and chariots until, when they settled, the carousel was completely intact.

Chains rattled, hovered over the wooden pieces and then hooked into them, lifting them so they could spin off the ground. The Carpathians began to chant, their voices rising, filling the basement with power until the entire carousel shuddered and rocked, cringing to escape the assault on it. Blood began to seep out of the sides of the wooden carvings. Droplets ran down the sides. Dark shadows appeared, several of them, scurrying like tiny parasites in an attempt to flee the attack, moving over the wooden horses and chariots, seeking grooves to hide in, but there was no way to hide from the combined power of the ancient Carpathians commanding them to show themselves.

Lightning zigzagged through the room. Thunder shook the house, booming from inside the basement. The carousel began to spin faster and faster, as it had done in the yard, but the ancients slowed it down, so that it pushed and fought against the power. Suddenly the lightning forked, slamming hard into all eight pieces, the four horses and four chariots.

A hideous shriek rose, deafening in the confines of the basement. The carousel turned dark, smoke rising and with it, Vadim's face, swirling in the smoke, eyes wide with shock, mouth open as he emitted the shriek. The face distorted, elongated, wavering in the smoke to slowly disappear. All the while his voice screeched and wailed. His teeth snapped viciously, but there was nothing he could do to stop the relentless assault by the hunters. The splinters blackened, curled up and were reduced to ash. The horses and chariots followed suit until there was only a pile of ashes and silence.

Matt rushed in, his gun cradled in his arms, his face a grim mask. "What the hell is going on? The two prisoners are screaming their heads off, on the floor with their hands over their ears. The woman, Emeline, is doing the same thing. I tried to get in there to see if I could help her, but she wouldn't allow me inside. Genevieve went to her."

Tariq sighed. "We'll take care of it, Matt." *Blaze. I need you and Charlotte to go to Emeline now.* They hadn't considered that anyone with a splinter inside her would feel the loss just as Vadim did. It made sense. The splinters were a part of Vadim, and when any were destroyed, the others felt it. If Emeline trusted them more, she would have told them. She had to have felt it when they removed Charlotte's splinter. "Charlotte and Blaze will help Genevieve with Emeline, and we'll take care of the prisoners."

He was tired. They all were. But getting rid of the splinters was essential. Vadim would retaliate. He had held off when he knew the two men had betrayed him — and he had to have known instantly — but he thought he could use them in some manner.

"The two men, Ryan, the blond one, and Andrew, the dark-haired one, had to have a shield similar to Charlotte's," Tariq explained as they followed Matt to the guardhouse. "It allowed them to resist Vadim's command somewhat, just as Charlotte was able to resist Fridrick's."

Siv sent him a cool glance from his strange, aquamarine eyes. They swirled with colors constantly, blue and green, both vibrant. "If she can resist a master vampire's commands, she will be able to resist yours."

Tariq hadn't planned on commanding Charlotte to do much of anything unless one counted in the bedroom. Playing was fun, but in real life, he wanted his woman to stand beside him. He wanted her opinions. He was counting on her advice. He wanted her to go to the club with him and become part of that world he'd created. He hoped other Carpathians would come into their world and perhaps, through his club, find lifemates.

More, he was working with Josef, the young tech, and the database the Carpathians had taken from the Morrison Center in the hopes of reaching the psychic women before Vadim did. Now he knew he would have to figure out something to do with the men as well. He still had two working for Vadim undetected in his club and that meant finding them. He hoped Andrew and Ryan could help with that, but if not, he was confident Maksim and he would ferret them out soon enough. All in all, they'd done fairly well. They killed two master vampires, several lesser ones and nearly destroyed Vadim's puppets and hybrid army without losing any of their hunters. He'd take that any day of the week.

Ryan and Andrew lay on the floor, blood trickling from their ears, but both were aware as the hunters entered the room. They looked very apprehensive.

"We're going to remove the shadow splinters from you," Tariq assured. "You've come this far. You'll have to trust us."

Both men nodded, and that added two more to his ever-growing family.

20

Charlotte left the nightclub with Blaze a little early. She wanted to check on the children before she sprang her surprise on Tariq. Nearly a week had flown by since the battle with Fridrick and Vadim's army. Vadim had disappeared. Even looking at sea, none of the hunters had been able to follow him. Still, she felt it was the calm before the storm. She meant to enjoy every moment they had before things blew up in their faces.

Tariq had explained to her that it was the Carpathian way of life. Even if had they gotten Vadim this round, another master vampire would take his place. There were always more vampires. There would always be vampires and as a hunter, Tariq would defend those humans and Carpathians alike in his territory.

Danny and Amelia had opted to wait until the healer arrived from the Carpathian Mountains before being converted. As long as Bella and Lourdes had to remain aboveground during daylight hours, they wanted to as well, just in case, and neither Charlotte nor Tariq wanted to chance converting Bella or Lourdes without a powerful healer present. Charlotte loved the two teens all the more for insisting on staying with the little ones.

Charlotte looked carefully around her, scanning for people, for enemies, for anyone in the vicinity that might witness her shifting. She'd practiced shifting often because she loved that she could do it. Loved that she could fly. Loved that she could always touch her children and know they were safe. Liv was still in the ground healing. Charlotte, Tariq and Val took turns giving her blood, but then sent her back to sleep. Charlotte wasn't quite as good at that as the other two, so she made certain Tariq reinforced the command.

"That's good, Charlotte. You've got scanning down very well," Blaze said.

Charlotte sent her a quick grin. "I *love* being Carpathian. I've been working on Emeline, telling her all the benefits. She seems interested."

Blaze exchanged a smile with her. "I'm happy that she's letting you into her life."

"It's slow. She doesn't like me in her house. She likes to sit outside on the porch with me, but she always comes out when I visit, which is every night now. Genevieve comes with me most times."

"She's still getting headaches," Blaze said, her voice expressing worry.

Charlotte understood. She knew Emeline was getting the headaches, but she had indicated that Vadim had left her in peace since the attack on the compound. No one knew if he'd given up on acquiring her, or if he was too far out at sea to reach her. Tariq didn't believe Vadim would give up, but like all of them, for Emeline's sake, they hoped so.

"I know. And the headaches are bad. When I visited her before we left for the club, she was in tears. I asked her to allow Tariq to help ease them. She hesitated but then agreed, which is so rare for her I almost fell over. I'm hoping that means she's coming to accept Tariq and Maksim into her life as brothers."

Blaze nodded. "She's definitely more comfortable with them. Thank you for being so kind and patient with her. I love her as a sister and seeing her so broken has been really hard, especially when I've been unable to do anything about it."

Charlotte sent her a conspiratorial grin. "Between you, Genevieve and me working on her, we'll get her to come over to the dark side."

The two laughed together, and then Charlotte did one of her favorite things. She put the picture of an owl in her head, paying attention to the smallest detail, just as Tariq had taught her. She couldn't wait to work with Liv on shifting. She knew the child would love it. It was getting easier the more she practiced and when Liv was awake, she planned on the two of them practicing everything together.

In moments she was spreading wings and stepping off the roof of the nightclub. Tariq, as a rule, would never have let her go by herself, not even with Blaze, but Maksim had persuaded him. Charlotte knew he would know she was up to something and he wouldn't waste any time coming home.

The two owls made their way through the night to the compound. She loved flying and she took the longer route, flying over part of the city, looking down on the lights. Cities could be beautiful, lit up as they were. Then she was over the lake and the water gleamed under the moon. It was a cold but very clear night and stars were out. Perfect. A perfect night.

Her little owl settled on the back of Liv's green dragon and she shifted right there, so she was sitting on its back. *She's fine.* She whispered the reassurance. The green color had dimmed without Liv's interaction. Although she found it strange that a rock dragon would be worried or sad without the child, she believed it was so. *She's coming to you soon. When she does, I expect you to take good care of her.* To entice her to stay in their world. She was certain when Liv rose from the soil, the terrible things that had been done to her would be with her worse than ever. She'd been taken from the safety of her home. What would it take to make her feel safe again?

Like Tariq and Val, she worried that conversion wouldn't be enough for Liv to stay with them. The child had been so traumatized and when she woke and had to face what she'd done — allowing the enemy into their compound — she would feel more guilt. She wasn't responsible, but she wouldn't see it that way. Charlotte intended to find a counselor for the children, one maybe among the Carpathian people so Tariq would give his consent without reservation.

Danny was the first to spot her. He'd come to accept her a lot faster than she'd anticipated. She was certain that was due to Amelia. He gave her a quick grin. "Bella and Lourdes are going to freak when they see you. Lourdes wants you to take them for a ride on the dragons."

She sighed. Of course the two little ones had learned the dragons could fly. They had been told in no uncertain terms by Tariq that they couldn't fly without an adult. Genevieve was not comfortable flying on the back of a stone dragon so she adamantly refused to take the two girls.

"You'll take them." Danny made it a statement, grinning at her, knowing she rarely refused the little ones. He clearly wanted to fly as well. "I'll call Amelia. She's with Genevieve over by the swings."

Charlotte could hear the delighted squeals of the two little girls as Amelia and Genevieve pushed them on the swings. She loved that sound. Normal. Tariq and Charlotte were trying to give the children as much normal as possible. They'd let them have a couple of days off from their studies and then gone right back to their normal routine.

"Have you checked on Liv?" Danny asked as he moved away from the dragons in the direction of the play yard.

"Of course. She's fine. Tariq said another couple of days. He's being overly cautious, but we're hoping it helps heal her mind as well."

"I can't wait to see her. Amelia cried when she didn't think I was looking. She's worried about her."

"I'll talk to her," Charlotte reassured him.

"Bella! Lourdes! Amelia! Charlotte's here. We're going to fly." He bellowed it across the distance.

Charlotte winced and exchanged a grin with Blaze, who was sitting on the orange dragon. "He's a boy," she explained.

Blaze nodded, her smile widening. "I got that."

The children came running, Genevieve trailing after them at a much more sedate pace.

"Want to come flying with us, Vi?" Charlotte asked, sliding off the green dragon to sit on the blue one. She leaned down to help Lourdes on as the blue dragon extended his wing to the child.

Genevieve gave an unladylike snort and shook her head.

Blaze sat behind Bella on the red dragon. Bella continually petted the neck of her dragon, talking seemingly without taking a breath. The dragon turned its head almost backward to rub along Bella's lap. She giggled and leaned down to kiss the massive wedge-shaped head.

Danny all but leapt on the brown dragon, something he'd clearly practiced because he was very good at it. Still, like the girls, he rounded the dragon's neck with his arms and leaned down to whisper in the stone animal's ear.

Amelia was graceful as her orange dragon politely extended its wing to her. She swung her leg over and then rubbed and scratched at the scales just like her dragon preferred.

Come fly with us, Charlotte said to the green dragon. When it didn't respond she played her trump card, using her firmest voice. *You*

559

are wasting away without Liv. You need to be in excellent health to carry her on your back during flight. She'll be with you in a couple of nights and I'm not about to take a chance that you might be too weak to carry her.

The green dragon raised its head and glared at her. She had to keep a smile from her face. Instead she turned away from the creature and signaled to the blue dragon that they were all ready. Immediately he extended his wings and flapped them ferociously, stepping out away from the others to give himself room to take off. Then they were airborne and Lourdes was laughing, pressing back against Charlotte. The child's eyes were bright with wonder as they flew over the lake and skimmed the water.

Behind them came the others, Blaze and Bella, Danny and Amelia. And the riderless green dragon. They spent an hour riding the dragons in the sky, careful to stay away from populated areas, but between Blaze and Charlotte they shielded the sight from any watchers.

Good practice for you, Blaze said. *You learn so fast.*

She was learning to fight as well. She didn't ever want to face a vampire, but she was certain it was inevitable, given that she was lifemate to a hunter and this would be their lives. Watching the children grow. Keeping them safe. Educating them. Teaching them how to fight vampires.

She loved spending time with the children. Tonight she wanted them worn-out. Genevieve was in on the surprise for Tariq, although she hadn't given them details. She blushed, thinking about Genevieve rolling her eyes and fanning herself. She knew. But along with Danny and Amelia, they were all willing to help her.

The children were back inside the house, and Genevieve and the two teenagers had brought out board games, pizza and snacks as well as movies. The movies were all in 3-D, something Danny particularly loved, so he was willing to watch animated children's shows with Bella and Lourdes.

Blaze left to visit with Emeline, and Charlotte walked to the main house. She knew Tariq would first visit Liv before he came looking for her, so she started at the entrance to the basement and left a trail of rose petals. Everywhere she stepped she left the soft, red petals. At the door she took off her blouse and watched the material float to the floor to land on top of the petals.

Something about seeing the way her blouse landed on the rose petals tightened her nipples in anticipation. She could feel them, so sensitive, pushing against her lacy bra with every step she took. She'd thought about this all night, prepared for it, and that had made her burn for him most of the evening.

She left more of a trail, and then her beautiful stiletto heels were off, first one and then a few steps later the other. She kept walking across the yard, out in the open air, under all those beautiful stars.

Blaze had taught her how to shield and she'd practiced over and over for this night. She wanted to give Tariq something special. He never shirked responsibility. He always saw to her in bed, never asking for much for himself. He was bossy in the bedroom, but it was all for her, for her pleasure. She wanted to give him this night.

More rose petals, and this time her jeans landed across the path. Another enticement. Now she was walking barefoot in her lacy pale peach bra and matching thong. The thong was already wet. Just the thought of Tariq following that trail made her slide her hands down her body, following the path his would take first.

I would see to your breasts first. Cup them. Hold them out to me.

He was there but she couldn't see him. She halted and looked around.

Do as I tell you, sielamet. Don't stop walking. Continue on your path. I love to see you walking and I cannot wait to see what you do next.

Behind her? In front of her? She took a deep breath and started toward her destination once more, waving her hand to continue the flow of rose petals. Her bra landed on a particularly thick pile of petals, the red showing through the lace. The night air hit her bare skin and her nipples felt as if they were on fire. Every step increased the need burning between her legs.

Cup your breasts for me.

She'd never felt sexier in her life. She loved his voice. So mesmerizing. The truth was, she'd do anything for him. She wanted to give him every single thing he wanted. She wanted to be his woman in every way possible. She slid her palms up her body to her breasts, cupping them as he'd asked. Imagining him in front of her, watching as she lifted and held them out to him.

Thumbs on your nipples, Charlotte. Brush back and forth while you continue walking.

She was very glad she'd shed her heels. She almost hadn't, because it was sexy walking in them in just her thong and bra, but she might have stumbled. Her body was on fire. In need. Weeping for him. She did as he asked and with each brush of her thumb across her sensitive, tight nipples, her sex clenched and spasmed.

She kept walking and when she was close to the carousel, the large one in the yard, the one Tariq had carved and put together on a platform, she shed her panties, letting them fall to the ground as she stepped onto the platform.

She heard a soft rustle behind her, but she didn't hesitate; she reached for the wild-looking horse and turned her finger in a circle so the platform began to rotate. Only then did she look over her shoulder as she stood on the horse's back, hand on the pole, her hair flowing as the carousel turned and the music began to play.

He stood on the platform in his dark gray suit, looking so gorgeous her heart beat triple time. Her discarded thong was in his hand and he pressed it to his nose, inhaling her scent. That was so sexy she nearly fell off the horse, her heart thudding and her pulse beating double time in her swollen clit.

She began to climb the pole, moving to the music, letting it take her, letting her body move sensuously in a promise to him. She moved with a slow, deliberate undulating motion, her hips thrusting one way and then another, her breasts swaying in invitation.

She gave herself to him. Just him. A private dance for the man she loved. Then he was with her, on the opposite side of the pole, moving in time to the music, his hands skimming her body as she danced for him. A touch. His fingers drifting over her breast. His hand cupping her mound and sliding away. A brush against the inside of her thigh.

His clothes drifted to the platform floor, and she caught the pole, shimmied to the top and turned upside down. Slowly, like a sensuous snake she began her descent. Sliding down past his chest, she flicked her tongue at his enormous cock. It strained toward her, reaching for her mouth. She took the offering and heard his moan.

Licking and sucking, she let the carousel move her up and down, sliding her mouth over him in a tight suction and then sliding almost away. His hand moved up her thigh, rested there, just at her entrance. So hot. He filled her mouth with velvet and steel. His taste was addicting. She danced her tongue and took him deeper as the horse rode high, so that she had to nearly swallow him to keep her mouth over him. Then the horse dropped and she went back up.

His hand caught her head, fingers tightening in her hair. She loved that. His silent command only made her hotter. She took him as deep as she was able, feeling him swell, feeling the heat of his essence rising. She drank him down, and then gently laved at him, not wanting this to end, but loving that she'd given it to him.

When she lifted her head, her heart stuttered in her chest. She was looking at the predator — *her* predator — and he was wholly focused on her as if he might devour her. His eyes gleamed. His thick chestnut hair flowed wildly around him. He caught her to him, one hand on the pole, the only thing anchoring them to the carousel. She was still upside down, and he pushed her head against his still-hard cock while he yanked her legs up and around his neck so that her mound was tight against his mouth. The fingers of his hand dug into her left cheek.

He nuzzled her, and she nearly came apart. She didn't have to shave because he simply removed all hair, not wanting any barriers between his mouth and his prize. He used his wicked tongue to lap at her, taking his time, treating her like his favorite dessert. He knew exactly what he was doing and everything that she liked. He was relentless, not allowing her to climax, but driving her up over and over until in desperation, she latched on to his erection again, enveloping his heavy cock with her mouth to keep from screaming and begging.

His taste always undid her, but he was so wicked she could barely keep sucking. The fire grew and grew until she thought she might simply burn up. Then his teeth raked her clit and her body dissolved. Fragmented. Threw her into the starlit sky, where she floated in a kind of bliss. So good. So perfect.

He caught her around the waist with both hands and turned her, so that she was facing him. He lifted her over his pulsing shaft, all the while balancing on the back of the horse as it rode up and down to the music, as the carousel spun in a wide, lazy circle. She felt the broad head of his cock at her entrance, and then, as the carousel horse went up, he crouched on its back and slammed her down hard as he stood, driving into her, filling her. It was brutal. It was invasive. It was perfect.

He took her to the beat of the music. Every stroke sent fire racing through her, spreading until her veins were molten lava and her core was so hot it felt volcanic. He sent her over the edge twice, but kept going until she thought she was too sensitive to continue. He didn't stop. She loved that he didn't stop. That for once he shed his control and was wild and uninhibited, taking her ruthlessly. Still . . . she was so far gone, she was afraid she might spontaneously combust.

I can't take it.

You can take it. Feel me inside you, where I belong.

How could she not feel him? He'd taken her over. Her mind. Her heart. Her soul. Her body belonged to him. His hands had gone to her bottom now, lifting and pressing down, each movement harder than the last. Still he continued and it built again, that terrible, wonderful fire that only he could give her. Her breath came in ragged sobs, hitching in time to the music, and then he leaned into her and sank his teeth into her neck.

Her core convulsed around his cock, milking and squeezing in demand. He swelled, hotter, bigger. And then jet after jet of scorching seed filled her as her body dragged his very essence from him. Their orgasms went on for what seemed an eternity, rocking them both, and they rode it out together, Charlotte holding on to him with everything she had. All the while the carousel kept spinning around.

"I love you, Charlotte," Tariq whispered in her ear. He kissed her neck, used his tongue to soothe the sting where he'd bitten her. "So much."

"I love you, too."

"I think I'll need a surprise like this every few days."

She rubbed her face against his chest and then turned it up for his kiss. "I'm very inventive," she said when he lifted his head.

"My gain."

"You're always inventive." She squirmed over his cock, remembering how he had placed her in the bed when they'd woken, her arms above her head and her legs spread wide. Once in position, she hadn't been able to move. He'd had his way with her, and she didn't think she'd ever recover from that one.

"It's good that we both are." He kissed her again.

She buried her fingers in his wealth of hair. "I love this, Tariq. Our strange life. Vampires and puppets aside, being Carpathian is wonderful and being with you is a gift without comparison. I love our children and our weird family of ancient hunters, Emeline, Gene-

568

vieve and Maksim and Blaze."

"We're good together," he agreed. "All of us. Someday I'll take you to the Carpathian Mountains to meet more of our kind, but we're building something good here. There will always be vampires in our lives, but with the family we're building, we'll have protection as well."

"I love our life," she reiterated. She would have had vampires in her life without him, and she wouldn't have fared as well. Now she had the children. She was a mother to four girls and a boy. She had women around her she cared about and hunters sworn to protect them all. Dangerous, scary men, but powerful; she found she cared about them as well. All in all, she would take her strange life over any other.

"I love you," she said again, pouring how deeply she felt into the admission.

He kissed her and that was perfection.

■ ■ ■ ■

APPENDIX 1
CARPATHIAN
HEALING CHANTS

■ ■ ■ ■

To rightly understand Carpathian healing chants, background is required in several areas:

1. The Carpathian view on healing
2. The Lesser Healing Chant of the Carpathians
3. The Great Healing Chant of the Carpathians
4. Carpathian musical aesthetics
5. Lullaby
6. Song to Heal the Earth
7. Carpathian chanting technique

1. The Carpathian View on Healing

The Carpathians are a nomadic people whose geographic origins can be traced back to at least as far as the Southern Ural Mountains (near the steppes of modern-day Kazakhstan), on the border between Europe and Asia. (For this reason, modern-day linguists call their language "proto-Uralic," without knowing that this is the language of the Carpathians.) Unlike most nomadic peoples, the wandering of the Carpathians was not due to the need to find new grazing lands as the seasons and climate shifted, or the search for better trade. Instead, the Carpathians' movements were driven by a great purpose: to find a land that would have the right earth, a soil with the kind of richness that would greatly enhance their rejuvenative powers.

Over the centuries, they migrated westward (some six thousand years ago), until they at last found their perfect homeland — their *susu* — in the Carpathian Mountains, whose long arc cradled the lush plains of the kingdom of Hungary. (The kingdom of Hungary flourished for over a millennium — making Hungarian the dominant language of the Carpathian Basin — until the kingdom's lands were split among several countries after World War I: Austria, Czechoslovakia, Romania, Yugoslavia and modern Hungary.)

Other peoples from the Southern Urals (who shared the Carpathian language, but were not Carpathians) migrated in different directions. Some ended up in Finland, which accounts for why the modern Hungarian and Finnish languages are among the contemporary descendents of the ancient Carpathian language. Even though they are tied forever to their chosen Carpathian homeland, the Carpathians continue to wander as they search the world for the answers that will enable them to bear and raise their offspring without difficulty.

Because of their geographic origins, the Carpathian views on healing share much with the larger Eurasian shamanistic tradition. Probably the closest modern representative of that tradition is based in Tuva (and is

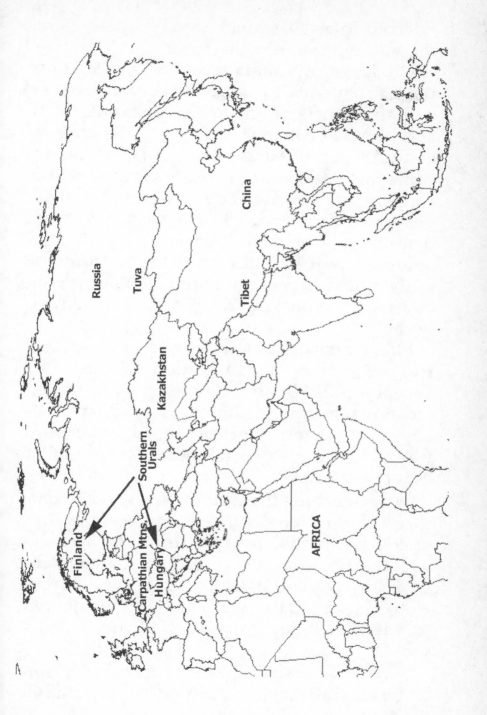

referred to as "Tuvinian Shamanism") — see the map on the previous page.

The Eurasian shamanistic tradition — from the Carpathians to the Siberian shamans — held that illness originated in the human soul, and only later manifested as various physical conditions. Therefore, shamanistic healing, while not neglecting the body, focused on the soul and its healing. The most profound illnesses were understood to be caused by "soul departure," where all or some part of the sick person's soul has wandered away from the body (into the nether realms), or has been captured or possessed by an evil spirit, or both.

The Carpathians belong to this greater Eurasian shamanistic tradition and share its viewpoints. While the Carpathians themselves did not succumb to illness, Carpathian healers understood that the most profound wounds were also accompanied by a similar "soul departure."

Upon reaching the diagnosis of "soul departure," the healer-shaman is then required to make a spiritual journey into the netherworlds to recover the soul. The shaman may have to overcome tremendous challenges along the way, particularly fighting the demon or vampire who has possessed his friend's soul.

"Soul departure" doesn't require a person to be unconscious (although that certainly can be the case as well). It was understood that a person could still appear to be conscious, even talk and interact with others, and yet be missing a part of their soul. The experienced healer or shaman would instantly see the problem nonetheless, in subtle signs that others might miss: the person's attention wandering every now and then, a lessening in their enthusiasm about life, chronic depression, a diminishment in the brightness of their "aura," and the like.

2. The Lesser Healing Chant of The Carpathians

Kepä Sarna Pus (**The Lesser Healing Chant**) is used for wounds that are merely physical in nature. The Carpathian healer leaves his body and enters the wounded Carpathian's body to heal great mortal wounds from the inside out using pure energy. He proclaims, "I offer freely my life for your life," as he gives his blood to the injured Carpathian. Because the Carpathians are of the earth and bound to the soil, they are healed by the soil of their homeland. Their saliva is also often used for its rejuvenative powers.

It is also very common for the Carpathian chants (both the Lesser and the Great) to be accompanied by the use of healing herbs, aromas from Carpathian candles and crystals.

The crystals (when combined with the Carpathians' empathic, psychic connection to the entire universe) are used to gather positive energy from their surroundings, which then is used to accelerate the healing. Caves are sometimes used as the setting for the healing.

The Lesser Healing Chant was used by Vikirnoff Von Shrieder and Colby Jansen to heal Rafael De La Cruz, whose heart had been ripped out by a vampire as described in *Dark Secret*.

Kepä Sarna Pus (The Lesser Healing Chant)
The same chant is used for all physical wounds. "Sívadaba" ["into your heart"] would be changed to refer to whatever part of the body is wounded.

Kuńasz, nélkül sivdobbanás, nélkül fesztelen löyly.
You lie as if asleep, without beat of heart, without airy breath.

Ot élidamet andam szabadon élidadért.
I offer freely my life for your life.

O jelä sielam jo˘rem ot ainamet és soŋe ot élidadet.

My spirit of light forgets my body and enters your body.

O jelä sielam pukta kinn minden szelemeket belső.
My spirit of light sends all the dark spirits within fleeing without.

Pajńak o susu hanyet és o nyelv nyálamet sívadaba.
I press the earth of our homeland and the spit of my tongue into your heart.

Vii, o verim soηe o verid andam.
At last, I give you my blood for your blood.

To hear this chant, visit: http://www .christinefeehan.com/members/.

3. The Great Healing Chant of The Carpathians

The most well-known — and most dramatic — of the Carpathian healing chants was **En Sarna Pus (The Great Healing Chant).** This chant was reserved for recovering the wounded or unconscious Carpathian's soul.

Typically a group of men would form a circle around the sick Carpathian (to "encircle him with our care and compassion") and begin the chant. The shaman or healer or leader is the prime actor in this healing

579

ceremony. It is he who will actually make the spiritual journey into the netherworld, aided by his clanspeople. Their purpose is to ecstatically dance, sing, drum and chant, all the while visualizing (through the words of the chant) the journey itself — every step of it, over and over again — to the point where the shaman, in trance, leaves his body, and makes that very journey. (Indeed, the word "ecstasy" is from the Latin *ex statis,* which literally means "out of the body.")

One advantage that the Carpathian healer has over many other shamans is his telepathic link to his lost brother. Most shamans must wander in the dark of the nether realms in search of their lost brother. But the Carpathian healer directly "hears" in his mind the voice of his lost brother calling to him, and can thus "zero in" on his soul like a homing beacon. For this reason, Carpathian healing tends to have a higher success rate than most other traditions of this sort.

Something of the geography of the "other world" is useful for us to examine, in order to fully understand the words of the Great Carpathian Healing Chant. A reference is made to the "Great Tree" (in Carpathian: *En Puwe*). Many ancient traditions, including the Carpathian tradition, understood the worlds — the heaven worlds, our world and the nether realms — to be "hung" upon a great pole, or axis, or tree. Here on earth, we are positioned halfway up this tree, on one of its branches. Hence many ancient texts often referred to the material world as "middle earth": midway between heaven and hell. Climbing the tree would lead one to the heaven worlds. Descending the tree to its roots would lead to the nether realms. The shaman was necessarily a master of movement up and down the Great Tree, sometimes moving unaided, and sometimes assisted by (or even mounted upon the back of) an animal spirit guide. In various traditions, this Great Tree was known variously as the *axis mundi* (the "axis of the worlds"), Ygddrasil (in Norse mythology), Mount Meru (the sacred world mountain of Tibetan tradition), etc. The Christian cosmos, with its heaven, purgatory/earth and hell, is also worth comparing. It is even given a similar topography in Dante's *Divine Comedy:* Dante is led on a journey first to hell, at the center of the earth; then upward to Mount Purgatory, which sits on the earth's surface directly opposite Jerusalem; then farther upward first to Eden, the earthly paradise, at the summit of Mount Purgatory; and then upward at last to heaven.

In the shamanistic tradition, it was understood that the small always reflects the large; the personal always reflects the cosmic. A movement in the greater dimensions of the cosmos also coincides with an internal movement. For example, the *axis mundi* of the cosmos corresponds with the spinal column of the individual. Journeys up and down the *axis mundi* often coincided with the movement of natural and spiritual energies (sometimes called *kundalini* or *shakti*) in the spinal column of the shaman or mystic.

En Sarna Pus (The Great Healing Chant)

In this chant, ekä ("brother") would be replaced by "sister," "father," "mother," depending on the person to be healed.

Ot ekäm ainajanak hany, jama.
My brother's body is a lump of earth, close to death.

Me, ot ekäm kuntajanak, pirädak ekäm, gond és irgalom türe.
We, the clan of my brother, encircle him with our care and compassion.

O pus wäkenkek, ot oma śarnank, és ot pus fünk, álnak ekäm ainajanak, pitänak ekäm ainajanak elävä.
Our healing energies, ancient words of magic and healing herbs bless my brother's body, keep it alive.

Ot ekäm sielanak pälä. Ot omboće päläja

juta alatt o jüti, kinta, és szelemek lamti-jaknak.

But my brother's soul is only half. His other half wanders in the netherworld.

Ot en mekem ŋamaŋ: kulkedak otti ot ekäm omboće päläjanak.

My great deed is this: I travel to find my brother's other half.

Rekatüre, saradak, tappadak, odam, kaŋa o numa waram, és avaa owe o lewl mahoz.

We dance, we chant, we dream ecstatically, to call my spirit bird, and to open the door to the other world.

Ntak o numa waram, és mozdulak, jomadak.

I mount my spirit bird and we begin to move, we are underway.

Piwtädak ot En Puwe tyvinak, ećidak alatt o jüti, kinta, és szelemek lamtijaknak.

Following the trunk of the Great Tree, we fall into the netherworld.

Fázak, fázak nó o śaro.

It is cold, very cold.

Juttadak ot ekäm o akarataban, o sívaban és o sielaban.

My brother and I are linked in mind, heart

and soul.

Ot ekäm sielanak kaŋa engem.
My brother's soul calls to me.

Kuledak és piwtädak ot ekäm.
I hear and follow his track.

Saɣedak és tuledak ot ekäm kulyanak.
Encounter I the demon who is devouring my
  brother's soul.

Nenäm ćoro, o kuly torodak.
In anger, I fight the demon.

O kuly pél engem.
He is afraid of me.

Lejkkadak o kaŋka salamaval.
I strike his throat with a lightning bolt.

Molodak ot ainaja komakamal.
I break his body with my bare hands.

Toja és molanâ.
He is bent over, and falls apart.

Hän ćaδa.
He runs away.

Manedak ot ekäm sielanak.

584

I rescue my brother's soul.

Alǝdak ot ekam sielanak o komamban.
I lift my brother's soul in the hollow of my hand.

Alǝdam ot ekam numa waramra.
I lift him onto my spirit bird.

Piwtädak ot En Puwe tyvijanak és saɣedak jälleen ot elävä ainak majaknak.
Following up the Great Tree, we return to the land of the living.

Ot ekäm elä jälleen.
My brother lives again.

Ot ekäm weńća jälleen.
He is complete again.

To hear this chant, visit: http://www.christinefeehan.com/members/.

4. Carpathian Musical Aesthetics

In the sung Carpathian pieces (such as the "Lullaby" and the "Song to Heal the Earth"), you'll hear elements that are shared by many of the musical traditions in the Uralic geographical region, some of which still exist — from Eastern European (Bulgarian, Romanian, Hungarian, Croatian, etc.) to Romany ("gypsy"). Some of these elements include:

- the rapid alternation between major and minor modalities, including a sudden switch (called a "Picardy third") from minor to major to end a piece or section (as at the end of the "Lullaby")
- the use of close (tight) harmonies
- the use of *ritardi* (slowing down the piece) and *crescendi* (swelling in volume) for brief periods
- the use of *glissandi* (slides) in the singing tradition
- the use of trills in the singing tradition (as in the final invocation of the "Song to Heal the Earth") — similar to Celtic, a singing tradition more familiar to many of us
- the use of parallel fifths (as in the final invocation of the "Song to Heal the Earth")
- controlled use of dissonance
- "call and response" chanting (typical of many of the world's chanting traditions)
- extending the length of a musical line (by adding a couple of bars) to heighten dramatic effect
- and many more

"Lullaby" and "Song to Heal the Earth" illustrate two rather different forms of Carpathian music (a quiet, intimate piece and an energetic ensemble piece) — but whatever the form, Carpathian music is full of feeling.

5. Lullaby

This song is sung by women while the child is still in the womb or when the threat of a miscarriage is apparent. The baby can hear the song while inside the mother, and the mother can connect with the child telepathically as well. The lullaby is meant to reassure the child, to encourage the baby to hold on, to stay — to reassure the child that he or she will be protected by love even from inside until birth. The last line literally means that the mother's love will protect her child until the child is born ("rise").

Musically, the Carpathian "Lullaby" is in three-quarter time ("waltz time"), as are a significant portion of the world's various traditional lullabies (perhaps the most famous of which is "Brahms' Lullaby"). The arrangement for solo voice is the original context: a mother singing to her child, unaccompanied. The arrangement for chorus and violin ensemble illustrates how musical even the simplest Carpathian pieces often are, and how easily they lend themselves to contemporary instrumental or orchestral arrangements. (A wide range of contemporary composers, including Dvořák and Smetana, have taken advantage of a similar discovery, working other traditional Eastern European music into their symphonic poems.)

Odam-Sarna Kondak (Lullaby)
Tumtesz o wäke ku pitasz belső.
Feel the strength you hold inside.

Hiszasz sívadet. Én olenam gæidnod.
Trust your heart. I'll be your guide.

Sas csecsemõm, kuńasz.
Hush my baby, close your eyes.

Rauho joŋe ted.
Peace will come to you.

**Tumtesz o sívdobbanás ku olen lamt3ad
  belső.**
Feel the rhythm deep inside.

Gond-kumpadek ku kim te.
Waves of love that cover you.

Pesänak te, asti o jüti, kidüsz.
Protect, until the night you rise.

To hear this song, visit: http://www
.christinefeehan.com/members/.

6. Song to Heal the Earth

This is the earth-healing song that is used by
the Carpathian women to heal soil filled with
various toxins. The women take a position on
four sides and call to the universe to draw on
the healing energy with love and respect. The

soil of the earth is their resting place, the place where they rejuvenate, and they must make it safe not only for themselves but for their unborn children as well as their men and living children. This is a beautiful ritual performed by the women together, raising their voices in harmony and calling on the earth's minerals and healing properties to come forth and help them save their children. They literally dance and sing to heal the earth in a ceremony as old as their species. The dance and notes of the song are adjusted according to the toxins felt through the healer's bare feet. The feet are placed in a certain pattern and the hands gracefully weave a healing spell while the dance is performed. They must be especially careful when the soil is prepared for babies. This is a ceremony of love and healing.

Musically, the ritual is divided into several sections:

- **First verse:** A "call and response" section, where the chant leader sings the "call" solo, and then some or all of the women sing the "response" in the close harmony style typical of the Carpathian musical tradition. The repeated response — *Ai Emä Maγe* — is an invocation of the source of power for the healing ritual: "Oh, Mother Nature."
- **First chorus:** This section is filled with

clapping, dancing, ancient horns and other means used to invoke and heighten the energies upon which the ritual is drawing.

- **Second verse**
- **Second chorus**
- **Closing invocation:** In this closing part, two song leaders, in close harmony, take all the energy gathered by the earlier portions of the song/ritual and focus it entirely on the healing purpose.

What you will be listening to are brief tastes of what would typically be a significantly longer ritual, in which the verse and chorus parts are developed and repeated many times, to be closed by a single rendition of the final invocation.

Sarna Pusm O Maγet (Song to Heal the Earth)

First verse
Ai Emä Maγe,
Oh, Mother Nature,

Me sívadbin lańaak.
We are your beloved daughters.

Me tappadak, me pusmak o maγet.

590

We dance to heal the earth.

Me sarnadak, me pusmak o hanyet.
We sing to heal the earth.

Sielanket jutta tedet it,
We join with you now,

Sívank és akaratank és sielank juttanak.
Our hearts and minds and spirits become one.

Second verse
Ai Emä maɣe,
Oh, Mother Nature,

Me sívadbin lańaak.
We are your beloved daughters.

Me andak arwadet emänked és me kaŋank o
We pay homage to our mother and call upon the

Põhi és Lõuna, Ida és Lääs.
North and South, East and West.

Pide és aldyn és myös belső.
Above and below and within as well.

Gondank o maɣenak pusm hän ku olen jama.
Our love of the land heals that which is in need.

Juttanak teval it,
We join with you now,

Maγe maγeval.
Earth to earth.

O pirä elidak weńća.
The circle of life is complete.

To hear this chant, visit: http://www
.christinefeehan.com/members/.

7. Carpathian Chanting Technique

As with their healing techniques, the actual
"chanting technique" of the Carpathians has
much in common with the other shamanistic
traditions of the Central Asian steppes. The
primary mode of chanting was throat chanting using overtones. Modern examples of this
manner of singing can still be found in the
Mongolian, Tuvan and Tibetan traditions. You
can find an audio example of the Gyuto
Tibetan Buddhist monks engaged in throat
chanting at: http://www.christinefeehan.com/
carpathian_chanting/.

As with Tuva, note on the map the geographical proximity of Tibet to Kazakhstan
and the Southern Urals.

The beginning part of the Tibetan chant
emphasizes synchronizing all the voices
around a single tone, aimed at healing a
particular "chakra" of the body. This is fairly

592

typical of the Gyuto throat-chanting tradition, but it is not a significant part of the Carpathian tradition. Nonetheless, it serves as an interesting contrast.

The part of the Gyuto chanting example that is most similar to the Carpathian style of chanting is the midsection, where the men are chanting the words together with great force. The purpose here is not to generate a "healing tone" that will affect a particular "chakra," but rather to generate as much power as possible for initiating the "out of body" travel, and for fighting the demonic forces that the healer/traveler must face and overcome.

The songs of the Carpathian women (illustrated by their "Lullaby" and their "Song to Heal the Earth") are part of the same ancient musical and healing tradition as the Lesser and Great Healing Chants of the warrior males. You can hear some of the same instruments in both the male warriors' healing chants and the women's "Song to Heal the Earth." Also, they share the common purpose of generating and directing power. However, the women's songs are distinctively feminine in character. One immediately noticeable difference is that, while the men speak their words in the manner of a chant, the women sing songs with melodies and harmonies, softening the overall performance.

A feminine, nurturing quality is especially evident in the "Lullaby."

■ ■ ■ ■

APPENDIX 2
THE CARPATHIAN
LANGUAGE

■ ■ ■ ■

Like all human languages, the language of the Carpathians contains the richness and nuance that can only come from a long history of use. At best we can only touch on some of the main features of the language in this brief appendix:

1. The history of the Carpathian language
2. Carpathian grammar and other characteristics of the language
3. Examples of the Carpathian language (including the Ritual Words and the Warrior's Chant)
4. A much-abridged Carpathian dictionary

1. The History of the Carpathian Language

The Carpathian language of today is essentially identical to the Carpathian language of thousands of years ago. A "dead" language like the Latin of two thousand years ago has evolved into a significantly different modern language (Italian) because of countless generations of speakers and great historical fluctuations. In contrast, many of the speakers of Carpathian from thousands of years ago are still alive. Their presence — coupled with the deliberate isolation of the Carpathians from the other major forces of change in the world — has acted (and continues to act) as a stabilizing force that has preserved the integrity of the language over the centuries. Carpathian culture has also acted as a stabilizing force. For instance, the Ritual Words, the various healing chants (see Appendix 1), and other cultural artifacts have been passed down through the centuries with great fidelity.

One small exception should be noted: the splintering of the Carpathians into separate geographic regions has led to some minor dialectization. However the telepathic link among all Carpathians (as well as each Carpathian's regular return to his or her homeland) has ensured that the differences among dialects are relatively superficial (e.g., small numbers of new words, minor differences in pronunciation, etc.), since the deeper, internal language of mind-forms has remained the same because of continuous use across space and time.

The Carpathian language was (and still is) the proto-language for the Uralic (or Finno-Ugrian) family of languages. Today, the Uralic languages are spoken in northern, eastern and central Europe and in Siberia. More than twenty-three million people in the world speak languages that can trace their ancestry to Carpathian. Magyar or Hungarian (about fourteen million speakers), Finnish (about five million speakers) and Estonian (about one million speakers) are the three major contemporary descendents of this proto-language. The only factor that unites the more than twenty languages in the Uralic family is that their ancestry can be traced back to a common proto-language — Carpathian — that split (starting some six thousand years ago) into the various languages in the Uralic family. In the same way, European languages such as English and French belong to the better-known Indo-European family and also evolved from a common proto-language ancestor (a different one from Carpathian).

The following table provides a sense for some of the similarities in the language family.

Note: The Finnic/Carpathian "k" shows up often as Hungarian "h." Similarly, the Finnic/Carpathian "p" often corresponds to the Hungarian "f."

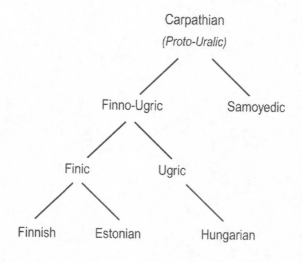

Carpathian (proto-Uralic)	Finnish (Suomi)	Hungarian (Magyar)
elä—live	elä—live	él—live
elid—life	elinikä—life	élet—life
pesä—nest	pesä—nest	fészek—nest
kola—die	kuole—die	hal—die
pälä—half, side	pieltä—tilt, tip to the side	fél, fele—fellow human, friend (half; one side of two)
		feleség—wife
and—give	anta, antaa—give	ad—give
koje—husband, man	koira—dog, the male (of animals)	here—drone, testicle
wäke—power	väki—folks, people, men; force	val/-vel—with (instrumental suffix)
	väkevä—powerful, strong	vele—with him/her/it
wete—water	vesi—water	viz—water

600

2. Carpathian Grammar and Other Characteristics of the Language

Idioms. As both an ancient language and a language of an earth people, Carpathian is more inclined toward use of idioms constructed from concrete, "earthy" terms, rather than abstractions. For instance, our modern abstraction "to cherish" is expressed more concretely in Carpathian as "to hold in one's heart"; the "netherworld" is, in Carpathian, "the land of night, fog and ghosts"; etc.

Word order. The order of words in a sentence is determined not by syntactic roles (like subject, verb and object) but rather by pragmatic, discourse-driven factors. Examples: *"Tied vagyok."* ("Yours am I."); *"Sívamet andam."* ("My heart I give you.")

Agglutination. The Carpathian language is agglutinative; that is, longer words are constructed from smaller components. An agglutinating language uses suffixes or prefixes whose meaning is generally unique, and which are concatenated one after another without overlap. In Carpathian, words typically consist of a stem that is followed by one or more suffixes. For example, *"sívambam"* derives from the stem *"sív"* ("heart") followed by *"am"* ("my," making it "my heart"), followed by *"bam"* ("in," making it "in my heart"). As you might imagine, agglutination

601

in Carpathian can sometimes produce very long words, or words that are very difficult to pronounce. Vowels often get inserted between suffixes to prevent too many consonants from appearing in a row (which can make the word unpronounceable).

Noun cases. Like all languages, Carpathian has many noun cases; the same noun will be "spelled" differently depending on its role in a sentence. Some of the noun cases include: nominative (when the noun is the subject of the sentence), accusative (when the noun is a direct object of the verb), dative (indirect object), genitive (or possessive), instrumental, final, supressive, inessive, elative, terminative and delative.

We will use the possessive (or genitive) case as an example, to illustrate how all noun cases in Carpathian involve adding standard suffixes to the noun stems. Thus expressing possession in Carpathian — "my lifemate," "your lifemate," "his lifemate," "her lifemate," etc. — involves adding a particular suffix (such as "*-am*") to the noun stem (*"päläfertiil"*), to produce the possessive (*"päläfertiilam"* — "my lifemate"). Which suffix to use depends upon which person ("my," "your," "his," etc.) and whether the noun ends in a consonant or a vowel. The table below shows the suffixes for singular nouns only (not plural), and also shows the similarity to the suffixes used in

person	Carpathian (proto-Uralic)		Contemporary Hungarian	
	noun ends in vowel	noun ends in consonant	noun ends in vowel	noun ends in consonant
1st singular (my)	-m	-am	-m	-om, -em, -öm
2nd singular (your)	-d	-ad	-d	-od, -ed, -öd
3rd singular (his, her, its)	-ja	-a	-ja/-je	-a, -e
1st plural (our)	-nk	-ank	-nk	-unk, -ünk
2nd plural (your)	-tak	-atak	-tok, -tek, -tök	-otok, -etek, -ötök
3rd plural (their)	-jak	-ak	-juk, -jük	-uk, -ük

603

contemporary Hungarian. (Hungarian is actually a little more complex, in that it also requires "vowel rhyming": which suffix to use also depends on the last vowel in the noun; hence the multiple choices in the cells below, where Carpathian only has a single choice.)

Note: As mentioned earlier, vowels often get inserted between the word and its suffix so as to prevent too many consonants from appearing in a row (which would produce unpronounceable words). For example, in the table on the previous page, all nouns that end in a consonant are followed by suffixes beginning with "a."

Verb conjugation. Like its modern descendents (such as Finnish and Hungarian), Carpathian has many verb tenses, far too many to describe here. We will just focus on the conjugation of the present tense. Again, we will place contemporary Hungarian side by side with the Carpathian, because of the marked similarity of the two.

As with the possessive case for nouns, the conjugation of verbs is done by adding a suffix onto the verb stem:

Person	Carpathian (proto-Uralic)	Contemporary Hungarian
1st (I give)	-am(andam),-ak	-ok, -ek, -ök
2nd singular (you give)	-sz (andsz)	-sz
3rd singular (he/she/it gives)	— (and)	—
1st plural (we give)	-ak (andak)	-unk, -ünk
2nd plural (you give)	-tak (andtak)	-tok, -tek, -tök
3rd plural (they give)	-nak (andnak)	-nak, -nek

As with all languages, there are many "irregular verbs" in Carpathian that don't exactly fit this pattern. But the above table is still a useful guideline for most verbs.

3. Examples of the Carpathian Language

Here are some brief examples of conversational Carpathian, used in the Dark books. We include the literal translation in square brackets. It is interestingly different from the most appropriate English translation.

Susu.
I am home.
["home/birthplace." "I am" is understood, as is often the case in Carpathian.]

Möert?
What for?

csitri
little one
["little slip of a thing," "little slip of a girl"]

ainaak enyém
forever mine

ainaak sívamet jutta
forever mine (another form)
["forever to-my-heart connected/fixed"]

sívamet
my love
["of-my-heart," "to-my-heart"]

Tet vigyázam.
I love you.
["you-love-I"]

Sarna Rituaali (The Ritual Words) is a longer example, and an example of chanted rather than conversational Carpathian. Note the recurring use of *"andam"* ("I give"), to give the chant musicality and force through repetition.

Sarna Rituaali (The Ritual Words)

Te avio päläfertiilam.
You are my lifemate.

Éntölam kuulua, avio päläfertiilam.
I claim you as my lifemate.

Ted kuuluak, kacad, kojed.
I belong to you.

Élidamet andam.
I offer my life for you.

Pesämet andam.
I give you my protection.

Uskolfertiilamet andam.
I give you my allegiance.

Sívamet andam.
I give you my heart.

Sielamet andam.
I give you my soul.

Ainamet andam.
I give you my body.

Sívamet kuuluak kaik että a ted.
I take into my keeping the same that is yours.

Ainaak olenszal sívambin.
Your life will be cherished by me for all my
   time.

Te élidet ainaak pide minan.
Your life will be placed above my own for all
   time.

Te avio päläfertiilam.
You are my lifemate.

Ainaak sívamet jutta oleny.
You are bound to me for all eternity.

608

Ainaak terád vigyázak.
You are always in my care.

To hear these words pronounced (and for more about Carpathian pronunciation altogether), please visit: http://www.christine feehan.com/members/.

Sarna Kontakawk (**The Warriors' Chant**) is another longer example of the Carpathian language. The warriors' council takes place deep beneath the earth in a chamber of crystals with magma far below it, so the steam is natural and the wisdom of their ancestors is clear and focused. This is a sacred place where they bloodswear to their prince and people and affirm their code of honor as warriors and brothers. It is also where battle strategies are born and all dissension is discussed as well as any concerns the warriors have that they wish to bring to the council and open for discussion.

Sarna Kontakawk (The Warriors' Chant)

Veri isäakank — veri ekäakank.
Blood of our fathers — blood of our brothers.

Veri olen elid.
Blood is life.

Andak veri-elidet Karpatiiakank, és wäke-sarna ku meke arwa-arvo, irgalom, hän ku agba, és wäke kutni, ku manaak verival.
We offer that life to our people with a blood-sworn vow of honor, mercy, integrity and endurance.

Verink sokta; verink kaηa terád.
Our blood mingles and calls to you.

Akasz énak ku kaηa és juttasz kuntatak it.
Heed our summons and join with us now.

To hear these words pronounced (and for more about Carpathian pronunciation altogether), please visit: http://www.christine feehan.com/members/.

See **Appendix 1** for Carpathian healing chants, including the *Kepä Sarna Pus* (The Lesser Healing Chant), the *En Sarna Pus* (The Great Healing Chant), the *Odam-Sarna Kondak* (Lullaby) and the *Sarna Pusm O Ma*γ *et* (Song to Heal the Earth).

4. A Much-Abridged Carpathian Dictionary
This very much abridged Carpathian dictionary contains most of the Carpathian words used in these Dark books. Of course, a full

Carpathian dictionary would be as large as the usual dictionary for an entire language (typically more than a hundred thousand words).

Note: The Carpathian nouns and verbs below are word stems. They generally do not appear in their isolated, "stem" form, as below. Instead, they usually appear with suffixes (e.g., *"andam"* — *"I give,"* rather than just the root, *"and"*).

a — verb negation (*prefix*).

agba — to be seemly or proper.

ai — oh.

aina — body.

ainaak — forever.

O ainaak jelä peje emnimet ŋamaŋ— Sun scorch that woman forever (*Carpathian swear words*).

ainaakfél — old friend.

ak — suffix added after a noun ending in a consonant to make it plural.

aka — to give heed; to hearken; to listen.

akarat — mind; will.

ál — to bless; to attach to.

alatt — through.

aldyn — under; underneath.

alə — to lift; to raise.

alte — to bless; to curse.

and — to give.

and sielet, arwa-arvomet, és jelämet, kuulua

huvémet ku feaj és ködet ainaak — to trade soul, honor and salvation, for momentary pleasure and endless damnation.

andasz éntölem irgalomet! — have mercy!

arvo — value; price (*noun*).

arwa — praise (*noun*).

arwa-arvo — honor (*noun*).

arwa-arvo olen gæidnod, ekäm — honor guide you, my brother (*greeting*).

arwa-arvo olen isäntä, ekäm — honor keep you, my brother (*greeting*).

arwa-arvo pile sívadet — may honor light your heart (*greeting*).

arwa-arvod mäne me ködak — may your honor hold back the dark (*greeting*).

ašša — no (*before a noun*); not (*with a verb that is not in the imperative*); not (*with an adjective*).

aššatotello — disobedient.

asti — until.

avaa — to open.

avio — wedded.

avio päläfertiil — lifemate.

avoi — uncover; show; reveal.

belső — within; inside.

bur — good; well.

bur tule ekämet kuntamak — well met brother-kin (*greeting*).

ćaδa — to flee; to run; to escape.

ćoro — to flow; to run like rain.

csecsemő — baby (*noun*).

csitri — little one (*female*).

diutal — triumph; victory.

eći — to fall.

ek — suffix added after a noun ending in a consonant to make it plural.

ekä — brother.

ekäm — my brother.

elä — to live.

eläsz arwa-arvoval — may you live with honor (*greeting*).

eläsz jeläbam ainaak — long may you live in the light (*greeting*).

elävä — alive.

elävä ainak majaknak — land of the living.

elid — life.

emä — mother (*noun*).

Emä Maγe — Mother Nature.

emäen — grandmother.

embɛ — if, when.

embɛ karmasz — please.

emni — wife; woman.

emnim — my wife; my woman.

emni hän ku köd alte — cursed woman.

emni kuŋenak ku aššatotello — disobedient lunatic.

én — I.

en — great, many, big.

én jutta félet és ekämet — I greet a friend and brother (*greeting*).

én maγenak — I am of the earth.

én oma maγeka — I am as old as time (*literally: as old as the earth*).

En Puwe — The Great Tree. Related to the legends of Ygddrasil, the axis mundi, Mount Meru, heaven and hell, etc.

engem — of me.

és — and.

ete — before; in front.

että — that.

fáz — to feel cold or chilly.

fél — fellow, friend.

fél ku kuuluaak sívam belső — beloved.

fél ku vigyázak — dear one.

feldolgaz — prepare.

fertiil — fertile one.

fesztelen — airy.

fü — herbs; grass.

gæidno — road, way.

gond — care; worry; love (*noun*).

hän — he; she; it.

hän agba — it is so.

hän ku — prefix: one who; that which.

hän ku agba — truth.

hän ku kaśwa o numamet — sky-owner.

hän ku kuulua sívamet — keeper of my heart.

hän ku lejkka wäke-sarnat — traitor.

hän ku meke pirämet — defender.

hän ku pesä — protector.

hän ku piwtä — predator; hunter; tracker.

hän ku vie elidet — vampire (*literally: thief of life*).

hän ku vigyáz sielamet — keeper of my soul.

hän ku vigyáz sívamet és sielamet — keeper of my heart and soul.

hän ku saa kuć3aket — star-reacher.

hän ku tappa — killer; violent person (*noun*). deadly; violent (*adj.*).

hän ku tuulmahl elidet — vampire (*literally: life-stealer*).

Hän sívamak — Beloved.

hany — clod; lump of earth.

hisz — to believe; to trust.

ho — how.

ida — east.

igazág — justice.

irgalom — compassion; pity; mercy.

isä — father (*noun*).

isäntä — master of the house.

it — now.

jälleen — again.

jama — to be sick, infected, wounded, or dying; to be near death.

jelä — sunlight; day, sun; light.

jelä keje terád — light sear you (*Carpathian swear words*).

o jelä peje terád — sun scorch you (*Carpathian swear words*).

o jelä peje emnimet — sun scorch the woman (*Carpathian swear words*).

o jelä peje terád, emni — sun scorch you, woman (*Carpathian swear words*).

o jelä peje kaik hänkanak — sun scorch them all (*Carpathian swear words*).

o jelä sielamak — light of my soul.

joma — to be underway; to go.

joŋe — to come; to return.

joŋesz arwa-arvoval — return with honor (*greeting*).

jörem — to forget; to lose one's way; to make a mistake.

juo — to drink.

juosz és eläsz — drink and live (*greeting*).

juosz és olen ainaak sielamet jutta — drink and become one with me (*greeting*).

juta — to go; to wander.

jüti — night; evening.

jutta — connected; fixed (*adj.*). to connect; to fix; to bind (*verb*).

k — suffix added after a noun ending in a vowel to make it plural.

kaca — male lover.

kadi — judge.

kaik — all.

kaŋa — to call; to invite; to request; to beg.

kaŋk — windpipe; adam's apple; throat.

kać3 — gift.

kaδa — to abandon; to leave; to remain.

kaδa wäkeva óv o köd — stand fast against the dark (*greeting*).

kalma — corpse; death; grave.

karma — want.

Karpatii — Carpathian.

Karpatii ku köd — liar.

käsi — hand (*noun*).

kaśwa — to own.

keje — to cook; to burn; to sear.

kepä — lesser, small, easy, few.

kessa — cat.

kessa ku toro — wildcat.

kessake — little cat.

kidü — to wake up; to arise (*intransitive verb*).

kim — to cover an entire object with some sort of covering.

kinn — out; outdoors; outside; without.

kinta — fog, mist, smoke.

kislány — little girl.

kislány kuɲenak — little lunatic.

kislány kuɲenak minan — my little lunatic.

köd — fog; mist; darkness; evil (*noun*); foggy, dark; evil (*adj.*).

köd elävä és köd nime kutni nimet — evil lives and has a name.

köd alte hän — darkness curse it (*Carpathian swear words*).

o köd belső — darkness take it (*Carpathian swear words*).

köd jutasz belső — shadow take you (*Carpathian swear words*).

koje — man; husband; drone.

kola — to die.

kolasz arwa-arvoval — may you die with honor (*greeting*).

koma — empty hand; bare hand; palm of the hand; hollow of the hand.

kond — all of a family's or clan's children.

kont — warrior.

kont o sívanak — strong heart (*literally: heart of the warrior*).

ku — who; which; that.

kuć3 — star.

kuć3ak! — stars! (*exclamation*).

kuja — day, sun.

kuŋe — moon; month.

kule — to hear.

kulke — to go or to travel (on land or water).

kulkesz arwa-arvoval, ekäm — walk with honor, my brother (*greeting*).

kulkesz arwaval — joŋesz arwa arvoval — go with glory — return with honor (*greeting*).

kuly — intestinal worm; tapeworm; demon who possesses and devours souls.

kumpa — wave (*noun*).

kuńa — to lie as if asleep; to close or cover the eyes in a game of hide-and-seek; to die.

kunta — band, clan, tribe, family.

kutenken — however.

kuras — sword; large knife.

kure — bind; tie.

kutni — to be able to bear, carry, endure, stand, or take.

kutnisz ainaak — long may you endure (*greeting*).

kuulua — to belong; to hold.

lääs — west.

lamti (*or* lamt3) — lowland; meadow; deep; depth.

lamti ból jüti, kinta, ja szelem — the netherworld (*literally: the meadow of night, mists,*

618

and ghosts).

laña — daughter.

lejkka — crack, fissure, split (*noun*). To cut; to hit; to strike forcefully (*verb*).

lewl — spirit (*noun*).

lewl ma — the other world (*literally: spirit land*). *Lewl ma* includes *lamti ból jüti, kinta, ja szelem:* the netherworld, but also includes the worlds higher up *En Puwe,* the Great Tree.

liha — flesh.

lõuna — south.

löyly — breath; steam. (*related to lewl: spirit*).

ma — land; forest.

magköszun — thank.

mana — to abuse; to curse; to ruin.

mäne — to rescue; to save.

maγe — land; earth; territory; place; nature.

me — we.

meke — deed; work (*noun*). To do; to make; to work (*verb*).

mića — beautiful.

mića emni kuŋenak minan — my beautiful lunatic.

minan — mine; my own (*endearment*).

minden — every, all (*adj.*).

möért? — what for? (*exclamation*).

molanâ — to crumble; to fall apart.

molo — to crush; to break into bits.

mozdul — to begin to move, to enter into movement.

muonì — appoint; order; prescribe; command.

muonìak te avoisz te — I command you to reveal yourself.

musta — memory.

myös — also.

nä — for.

nâbbŏ — so, then.

ŋamaŋ — this; this one here; that; that one there.

nautish — to enjoy.

nélkül — without.

nenä — anger.

ńiŋ3 — worm; maggot.

nó — like; in the same way as; as.

numa — god; sky; top; upper part; highest (*related to the English word* numinous).

numatorkuld — thunder (literally: sky struggle).

nyál — saliva; spit. (*related to nyelv: tongue*).

nyelv — tongue.

odam — to dream; to sleep.

odam-sarna kondak — lullaby (*literally: sleep-song of children*).

olen — to be.

oma — old; ancient; last; previous.

omas — stand.

omboće; — other; second (*adj.*).

o — the (*used before a noun beginning with a consonant*).

ot — the (*used before a noun beginning with a vowel*).

otti — to look; to see; to find.

óv — to protect against.

owe — door.

päämoro — aim; target.

pajna — to press.

pälä — half; side.

päläfertiil — mate or wife.

palj3 — more.

peje — to burn.

peje terád — get burned (*Carpathian swear words*).

pél — to be afraid; to be scared of.

pesä (n.) — nest (*literal*); protection (*figurative*).

pesä (v.) — nest (*literal*); protect (*figurative*).

pesäd te engemal — you are safe with me.

pesäsz jeläbam ainaak — long may you stay in the light (*greeting*).

pide — above.

pile — to ignite; to light up.

pirä — circle; ring (*noun*). to surround; to enclose (*verb*).

piros — red.

pitä — to keep; to hold; to have; to possess.

pitäam mustaakad sielpesäambam — I hold your memories safe in my soul.

pitäsz baszú, piwtäsz igazáget — no vengeance, only justice.

piwtä — to follow; to follow the track of

game; to hunt; to prey upon.

poår — bit; piece.

põhi — north.

pukta — to drive away; to persecutes; to put to flight.

pus — healthy; healing.

pusm — to be restored to health.

puwe — tree; wood.

rambsolg — slave.

rauho — peace.

reka — ecstasy; trance.

rituaali — ritual.

sa — sinew; tendon; cord.

sa4 — to call; to name.

saa — arrive, come; become; get, receive.

saasz hän ku andam szabadon — take what I freely offer.

salama — lightning; lightning bolt.

sarna — words; speech; magic incantation (*noun*). to chant; to sing; to celebrate (*verb*).

sarna kontakawk — warriors' chant.

śaro — frozen snow.

sas — shoosh (*to a child or baby*).

saγe — to arrive; to come; to reach.

siel — soul.

sieljelä isäntä — purity of soul triumphs.

sisar — sister.

sív — heart.

sív pide köd — love transcends evil.

sívad olen wäkeva, hän ku piwtä — may your heart stay strong, hunter (*greeting*).

sívamet — my heart.

sívam és sielam — my heart and soul.

sívdobbanás — heartbeat (*literal*); rhythm (*figurative*).

sokta — to mix; to stir around.

soηe — to enter; to penetrate; to compensate; to replace.

susu — home; birthplace (*noun*). at home (*adv.*).

szabadon — freely.

szelem — ghost.

taka — behind; beyond.

tappa — to dance; to stamp with the feet; to kill.

te — you.

Te kalma, te jama ńiη3kval, te apitäsz arwa-arvo — You are nothing but a walking maggot-infected corpse, without honor.

Te magköszunam nä ηamaη kać3 taka arvo — Thank you for this gift beyond price.

ted — yours.

terád keje — get scorched (*Carpathian swear words*).

tõd — to know.

Tõdak pitäsz wäke bekimet mekesz kaiket — I know you have the courage to face anything.

tõdhän — knowledge.

tõdhän lõ kuraset agbapäämoroam — knowledge flies the sword true to its aim.

toja — to bend; to bow; to break.

toro — to fight; to quarrel.

torosz wäkeval — fight fiercely (*greeting*).

623

totello — obey.

tsak — only.

tuhanos — thousand.

tuhanos löylyak türelamak saγe diutalet — a thousand patient breaths bring victory.

tule — to meet; to come.

tumte — to feel; to touch; to touch upon.

türe — full, satiated, accomplished.

türelam — patience.

türelam agba kontsalamaval — patience is the warrior's true weapon.

tyvi — stem; base; trunk.

uskol — faithful.

uskolfertiil — allegiance; loyalty.

varolind — dangerous.

veri — blood.

veri-elidet — blood-life.

veri ekäakank — blood of our brothers.

veri isäakank — blood of our fathers.

veri olen piros, ekäm — literally: blood be red, my brother; figuratively: find your life-mate (*greeting*).

veriak ot en Karpatiiak — by the blood of the Prince (*literally: by the blood of the great Carpathian; Carpathian swear words*).

veridet peje — may your blood burn (*Carpathian swear words*).

vigyáz — to love; to care for; to take care of.

vii — last; at last; finally.

wäke — power; strength.

wäke beki — strength; courage.

wäke kaδa — steadfastness.
wäke kutni — endurance.
wäke-sarna — vow; curse; blessing (*literally: power words*).
wäkeva — powerful.
wara — bird; crow.
weńća — complete; whole.
wete — water (*noun*).

ABOUT THE AUTHOR

Christine Feehan lives in the beautiful mountains of Lake County, California. She has always loved hiking, camping, rafting and being outdoors. She has also been involved in the martial arts for years — she holds a third-degree black belt, instructs in a Korean karate system and has taught self-defense. She is happily married to a romantic man who often inspires her with his thoughtfulness. They have a yours, mine and ours family, claiming eleven children as their own. She has always written books, forcing her ten sisters to read every word, and now her daughters read and help her edit her manuscripts. It is fun for her to take all the research she has done on wild animals, raptors, vampires, weather and volcanoes and put it together with romance. Please visit her website at www.christinefeehan .com.

The employees of Thorndike Press hope you have enjoyed this Large Print book. All our Thorndike, Wheeler, and Kennebec Large Print titles are designed for easy reading, and all our books are made to last. Other Thorndike Press Large Print books are available at your library, through selected bookstores, or directly from us.

For information about titles, please call:
(800) 223-1244

or visit our Web site at:
http://gale.cengage.com/thorndike

To share your comments, please write:
Publisher
Thorndike Press
10 Water St., Suite 310
Waterville, ME 04901